BAKER VAUGHAN

A NOVEL

STUART HOTCHKISS

HALSNOCH

Identifiers
Books > Literature & Fiction > Literary
Books > Literature & Fiction > Contemporary
Books > Literature & Fiction > Genre fiction > Family Saga

ISBN 9798993970028 (paperback)
ISBN 9798993970035 (ebook)

Content warning: This novel contains brief references to
sexual abuse. While not depicted in detail, this theme may
be difficult for some readers.

The author would be happy to hear from you. Please visit
his website at stuarthotchkiss.com.

First edition: May 2026

Cover design and HALSNOCH colophon by Arif Hussein.

For the storytellers who inspire,
and the story-lovers who keep the magic alive.

Prologue

JANUARY 20, 2017

Baker Vaughan's hand trembled on the unlocked doorknob, three sheets to the wind and days shy of fifty-seven. He was moments away from destroying the new life he'd built—the marriage to Libby, the respect at Trinity, everything he'd gained since Darcy Calhoun had kicked him out of her bed.

Through the gap in the door, he could see light spilling from the back of her house, the same bedroom where he'd learned the difference between sex and love when she'd made it clear he meant nothing beyond those stolen hours. Tonight, guilt and whiskey had convinced him that apologies could erase the past. He was wrong about that too.

"Is anyone home?" he called out, his Southern upbringing providing the justification he needed. *It's not trespassing if you announce yourself. It's not unlawful to check on someone who might be in danger. It's downright Christian.*

But beneath that righteous concern lived something uglier— a desperate need to prove he wasn't the man she'd dismissed, to transform years of guilt into one redemptive moment. Some men were called to serve God. Baker Vaughan was called to sabotage himself just when salvation seemed within reach.

EARLIER THAT EVENING, BITTERNESS hung over Lucky Chuck's like stale beer and fryer oil. A crowd of Trinity Episcopal parishioners crammed around one table while the forty-fifth president's inauguration replayed on every screen. Baker's own struggles—his ongoing disputes with Trinity's rector, who refused to support his ordination—compounded the collective gloom.

They'd taken forever getting seated, shuffling around to make sure the right couples sat together—a group whose tasteful scarves and Patagonia vests marked them as the kind of church group that would linger for hours over martinis and old-fashioneds, sharing plates and tipping well but occupying prime real estate on a busy evening. They'd spent the latter part of their time together on a happier note, prodding Baker about his upcoming sermon in March—a dry run at Trinity that a former bishop had arranged over the rector's objections, before Baker left for seminary in Moab that fall.

Baker wasn't ready to drive back to an empty house when the others began to leave. His new wife, Libby, was in Seattle for a symphonic festival, and he had an unused gift card from a new downtown eatery called Lucifer burning a hole in his wallet.

At fifty-six, he should have been ordained decades ago—the priest his first wife believed he'd become when she'd kissed him goodbye that November 1985 morning in New Haven, before everything fell apart.

He walked the six blocks to the restaurant with the careful deliberation of a man who'd already had too much to drink, concentrating on keeping his stride steady. He took a seat at the bar. That's where he met Russ—shiny bald head and wise eyes that seemed to see straight through him. The man insisted on buying The Devil Made Me Do It cocktails, and they went down dangerously smooth as Baker confessed his burden to someone who seemed to know exactly what he needed to hear. Later, Baker would wonder how he'd appeared at just the right moment, with just the right words, like an answer to a prayer he hadn't meant to pray.

"I probably shouldn't be telling a stranger all this, but . . ." Baker paused, recognizing the pattern even as he fell into it. The same impulse that had made him repeat the bishop's words to Darcy. The same need to unburden himself to anyone who'd listen. "I need to right a wrong."

Russ leaned in slightly. "I'm listening."

"I need to right a wrong," Baker had told him.

The story spilled out over gin and St-Germain: how he'd lived kitty-corner from Darcy Calhoun before he met Libby. How, for two brief months in 2014, this petite woman from St. Francis Lutheran Church had begged him for sex, only to kick him out of bed every time they finished their business. How his friend, a retired Episcopal bishop, had consoled and counseled him on Christmas Day, calling her a coquette, but Baker understood what he meant and didn't correct him.

"A coquette?" Russ had said, his eyes gleaming. "Your bishop called her a prick tease? That's what you're telling me?"

"Doesn't mean that," Baker answered. "A coquette is a flirt."

"Jesus Christ," Russ said, shaking his head. "I love it when church people talk dirty in French."

Baker had a history of being way too honest. When he

repeated the bishop's words to Darcy, she'd lost her shit. Being a very private person—the treasurer of secrets, the kind of woman who'd never even shared her phone number with Baker—she felt violated in the worst way. After giving Baker a tongue-lashing, she fired off an email to the bishop, intending to establish herself as a moral woman who had never meant to deceive Baker. It was a shrewd move but poorly targeted— the bishop used a shared mailbox, and her email ricocheted through the church office.

FOR OVER TWO YEARS, the guilt had been his constant companion. His attempts to contact her—Facebook messages, a Georgia O'Keeffe postcard from Santa Fe, a text reading Happy 50th Birthday—were all ignored. Baker could tell she just wanted him to evaporate.

"My wife is out of town right now," Baker had confessed to Russ. "I thought it might be a good time to stop by the neighbor's house and see if I could apologize to her in person."

Russ raised his glass and encouraged Baker's plan, looking him straight in the eye: "If you don't go now, you'll never go."

Baker remained expert at choosing precisely the wrong moment to prove he was still the man he'd once intended to become—even after five years in Idaho trying to answer the call he'd fled, even after marrying Libby, who felt like God's personal assurance that redemption was still possible, that he hadn't forfeited his last chance at grace.

The walk from Lucifer had felt amazing—cool night air sharp against his flushed cheeks, moving through clusters of late-night voices and cigarette smoke. But six blocks later, crossing the quieter residential streets with names he used to know by heart, his footsteps had begun to echo in the sudden stillness of his old neighborhood.

He'd knocked on the front door two or three times before discovering it was unlocked. Standing in her doorway, he could almost taste the absolution: Darcy's forgiveness, his own clean slate, the fantasy that receiving forgiveness could be as simple as saying "Sorry."

Now three gentle steps into Darcy's living room, Baker called out again. Still no response. Moments later, he heard a piercing scream followed by nonsensical words from his right—likely the guest bedroom. His mind raced because that wasn't her son's voice. *Was someone else living there? A woman?* He froze before his queasy stomach revolted. In a moment he would later perceive as shameful and painfully wrong, all the fettuccine and booze came spewing onto the scarred oak floor.

He was busted. Darcy had dialed 911 the minute she heard Baker calling out, and within minutes, three of Boise's finest were there. At the Ada County lockup, while an administrative officer processed his paperwork, she asked why he was at Darcy's house.

"I came with the best of intentions," Baker said. "I just wanted to apologize to her for being such a jerk when we stopped seeing each other."

"Do you want to make a phone call?" the officer asked. Baker shook his head. He certainly couldn't reach out to Libby—not from a jail cell, not after being arrested at another woman's house.

"I would have asked to call God if I thought that would do any good," he said quietly. "But this is on me; I had no business going there uninvited."

Fingerprinted, photographed, and deposited in a holding cell to sleep it off, Baker lay there in what his seminary textbooks would have called a dark night of the soul. He replayed the sex he'd had with Darcy, how close he'd come to drowning in her careful distance, and how near he'd been to choosing her seduction over his calling to the ministry.

But mostly, his mind returned to Russ—the stranger at Lucifer who had seemed to know exactly what to say, who had encouraged Baker's worst impulses with such perfect timing. As the cell's fluorescent lights hummed overhead, Baker wondered if he'd met the devil himself. And if so, whether he'd been tempted or given exactly what he'd been asking for. Six years ago, he'd come to Idaho to escape his demons. Tonight, he'd learned they'd simply been waiting for the right moment to catch up.

Chapter One

THREE HOURS INTO THE DRIVE TO BOISE, BAKER VAUGHAN'S knuckles had gone white on the steering wheel, the empty highway stretching endlessly ahead.

Light snow had started somewhere past Mackay—dry flakes that swirled across the highway like static, revealing endless wilderness pressing in from both sides. His Honda's wipers beat an unnecessary rhythm; the road was clear enough at first, just deserted. Profoundly, impossibly deserted.

Just get to the interstate. Get to Boise. Get to civilization.

He'd left Challis early that morning with something that felt like relief, trading a population of 910 for what he'd imagined would be an actual city. After three months in the remote mining town—where the nearest Starbucks was ninety miles away and the social scene peaked at Friday night high school football—Boise had taken on mythic proportions in his mind. Real restaurants. Cultural events. Bookstores.

He passed through Arco, the first community in the world to be illuminated by nuclear power, too focused on the icy road to stop and read the plaques. *There would be time for that later,* he told himself, though he knew better. The weather had turned menacing.

By the time he had reached Carey and continued on through Camas County, the snow had become treacherous. Wind howled across the exposed prairie with nothing to break its force, and ice began forming on the road. He'd gotten stuck behind a truck pulling a rickety utility trailer that swayed from shoulder to shoulder like a wooden kite, making it impossible for Baker to get around safely.

Finally, his GPS confirmed Interstate 84 was twelve miles ahead. Twelve miles to four lanes of traffic and proof that he hadn't made a catastrophic mistake leaving New York. But as he pulled into a truck stop to grab a cup of joe and a handmade donut at the Mountain Home on-ramp, he saw the highway stretched out before him—that supposed artery of American commerce and connection—and he breathed in so much air that his gut clenched.

The interstate was empty. Completely, impossibly empty. No eighteen-wheelers. No caravans of SUVs. Just gray asphalt disappearing into white nothing in both directions, as desolate as the mountain highway he'd just escaped.

He steeled himself for the final push. The trip data on the screen of his device showed that it was forty-four miles to Boise, which Baker figured to be an hour.

What the hell am I doing here?

The question came as a thunderclap—not the philosophical wondering he'd been nursing for months, but genuine panic that tasted like copper in his mouth. His ex-partner, Michelle, had left him for a Wall Street trader named Brian Cann, who wowed her with penthouse wealth and Lamborghini speed. The *New York Post* had called Baker a cuckold in print. His advertising colleagues had whispered behind his back.

Now he was a month shy of his fifty-second birthday, driving toward a city that apparently didn't exist, chasing some half-remembered calling from a life he'd abandoned twenty-six years earlier—back when he'd still believed God had a plan for him that didn't involve public humiliation and endless stretches of frozen highway.

At least the Guest House would be there—that 1895 Queen Anne Victorian he'd booked in downtown Boise, with its six artistically curated suites and spacious rooms that promised something Michelle's sterile penthouse life could never offer: history, character, warmth. The photos online had shown a beautiful historic lodge in the heart of downtown, walking distance to the capitol and the North End, with views of the foothills. Not Brian's cold platinum surfaces and floor-to-ceiling glass, but wood and craftsmanship and rooms that had sheltered travelers for over a century. Something real. Something that had endured.

Michelle was probably at Brian's place right now, warm and laughing in rooms that cost more per month than Baker had earned in a year, telling their friends how Baker had "had a breakdown" and "run off to Idaho like some kind of hermit." The image made his jaw clench so hard his molars ached.

He forced himself to breathe, kept his foot on the accelerator, and merged onto the deserted highway. The navigation still promised downtown Boise in just under an hour—impossible given the ice forming on the windshield and the way his tires slipped on black ice with every lane change.

The final forty-four miles took nearly ninety minutes, each one feeling longer than the last. By the time he finally turned onto West Jefferson Street just after one in the afternoon, his hands were shaking from more than just the cold. Inside the Guest House, he found an envelope with a welcome note and a room key instead of a desk clerk. The note promised that Christmas cookies and coffee would be available later in the afternoon. The silent lobby felt like a confirmation of every fear that had gripped him during the drive.

The heart of the city that afternoon was no different—a ghost town that made the empty interstate seem prophetic. Baker wandered through Capitol Park, where frost melted on abandoned benches and Canada geese grazed among their own droppings. No pedestrians, no cars, not even the distant click of studded tires. The silence was complete and oppressive.

"This is unreal," Baker muttered to himself, his breath visible in the crisp air. In Manhattan, he'd complained about the crowds, the noise, the constant press of humanity. Now he would have paid anything for the sound of another human voice. He pulled out his phone and dialed his friend Christian back in the city.

"Merry Christmas, you crazy bastard," Christian answered. "How's the Wild West?"

"I'm standing in downtown Boise, and it's like the apocalypse. There's literally nobody here."

"It's the holidays, dude. What did you expect?"

"Back home, half the delis would be open. People everywhere."

"Listen to yourself. You're complaining about peace and quiet. Do you know how that sounds?"

"It sounds like I'm having second thoughts about—"

"About what? About letting Michelle chase you out of town?

Jesus, Baker, one bad headline and you just…what, become a mountain man?"

The words slapped. Baker's free hand curled into a fist.

"That's not—"

"Michelle's moved on, man. She's probably laughing about how you fled to Idaho like some wounded animal. While you're out there playing pioneer, she's maxing out his credit cards at Bergdorf's."

Baker's fingers dug into the phone. "You think I should have stayed? Endured more humiliation?"

"I think you should get back to reality. You had it made, Baker—corner office, expense account, respect. And you just walked away from it all for what? So you can find yourself in a place where the biggest excitement is watching tumbleweeds?"

The line went dead.

Christian's words hit hard like Baker's best advertising—simple, catchy, and impossible to forget. *He ran away. He gave up everything he had built.*

What Christian didn't know was that Baker had started to unravel months before Michelle started packing. The sleepless nights came first, then the martinis to chase them away. His mother had been an alcoholic, so Baker knew the pattern, knew he was skating on thin ice.

That's what had sent him to a psychiatrist's office on East Seventy-Ninth Street before he left New York. He'd confessed everything to Dr. Ludwig—the implosion after twenty years with Michelle, how he was self-medicating to sleep. "Though it runs in the family, so I'm probably predisposed," Baker had added, trying to shift the blame to his DNA.

Dr. Ludwig prescribed Dalmane for the sleeplessness. What

he didn't fully grasp—or what Baker had downplayed—was how much Baker was drinking. The little blue capsules worked better than Hendrick's, helped him sleep without the morning fog. But what Baker truly needed was time to accept that Michelle's leaving might be the best thing that ever happened to him—that he'd been living someone else's life for decades.

The advertising world was his second life, the one he built after abandoning his first calling. For a quarter century, he was good at it. Better than good. He moved in with Michelle because she fit the life he constructed—successful and comfortable—yet she was uninterested in the deeper questions that still haunted him in quiet moments. Their relationship was a performance, and they were both excellent actors.

When the newspaper ran the story, the humiliation was total and public. The photos showed Michelle and Brian at some charity gala, her hand possessively on his arm, while Baker was presumably at home. His colleagues' sympathy felt worse than their mockery. The pitying looks, the careful conversations that avoided mentioning wives or relationships, the way meetings went quiet when he entered the room.

But it wasn't just the embarrassment that drove him west. It was a deeper realization. He'd spent far too much time building a life that one headline could undo. Everything he thought was solid was as carefully constructed and hollow as the advertising campaigns he created.

The silence pressed against him like a physical thing. In New York, he'd never been alone with his thoughts for more than a few minutes—there was always another meeting, another deadline, another crisis. Here, there was nothing but his own breathing and the distant honking of geese.

He walked back to the inn as the sun climbed higher, casting long shadows across the empty streets. The lobby was still deserted, but true to the promise in the welcome note, someone had left a plate of cookies and a thermos of coffee on the reception desk.

In his room, Baker sat on the edge of the bed and stared out the window at the Boise foothills. The mountains rose like a promise of something larger than himself, something that couldn't be bought or sold. For the first time in months, peace settled over him—tentative but real.

His phone buzzed with a text from Michelle: Hope you're having a good Christmas. I'm sorry about how things ended.

He stared at the message for a long time before deleting it without responding. Some conversations were finished, even when they felt unfinished. Some chapters ended whether you were ready or not.

Later that afternoon, Baker finally met the proprietor. He learned the beautiful Victorian he was staying in had been built in 1895 for a local doctor and his family, though the current owner admitted she'd never bothered to research its story. The woman spoke softly as she carried dirty sheets, her graying hair pulled back in a loose bun—someone who ran her business with quiet practicality, seemingly unconcerned with the impression she made.

"What brings you to our corner of Idaho? You don't sound local."

"New York. Moved to Challis three months ago, then decided to come here."

"New York!" she said. "That's a change. What did you do there? Wall Street?"

Baker shook his head no. "Advertising—worked for a big Manhattan agency. Spent my days convincing people they needed things they didn't."

"And now?"

"I'm trying to figure out what I need. Turns out it's much less than I thought."

"Well, speaking of advertising," she said, her gaze sparkling, "I know someone who runs an agency here."

"That's generous, but I came here to return to ministry."

"Ministry?" She looked stunned. "A charmer like you?"

Baker grinned. "After all these years of selling people things they don't need, maybe it's time to try selling them something they do need. Job security's eternal, and I hear the boss is pretty understanding about vacation requests."

She laughed and slapped her thigh. "Lord have mercy; you are something else!" Her eyebrows then rose. "So you're single?"

Baker nodded.

"I have eligible girlfriends I could set you up with."

"That's kind, but right now I just want to enjoy being single. Need to let some scars heal," Baker said with a wry smile.

"I can respect that," she said, leaning against the counter. "Just think about it."

He retreated to his room, opened his laptop, and began to write. Not advertising copy, not the clever wordplay that had made his reputation, but honest prose—the beginning of a conversation with himself that he'd been avoiding for too long.

He wrote about what had driven him from his calling years ago, about how it had felt like God's personal rejection of everything he'd thought he was meant to be. He wrote about the years of building a life on Madison Avenue, about Michelle and the careful distance they'd maintained even in their most intimate moments.

When he finally stopped, it was past midnight, and he'd filled twenty pages with words that felt more honest than anything he'd written in decades. He saved the document and closed the laptop, feeling something he hadn't experienced in years: the peace that came from honest reflection, even if only to himself.

Outside his window, Boise slept under a canopy of stars invisible in Manhattan. Baker fell asleep to absolute silence, and for the first time in months, he didn't dream about Michelle, Brian, or the *New York Post.* He dreamed about mountains and open roads and the possibility that forging a new path might not be the same thing as giving up.

THE NEXT MORNING, A Monday, Boise resumed normal operations—snow melting in steady drips from storefronts, car doors slamming, the distant hum of traffic returning to the empty streets. Baker enjoyed a hearty breakfast at Moon's Café—the kind of meal that would have cost forty dollars in Manhattan and been a quarter the size.

For the rest of that week, Baker fell into a routine of solitary exploration—learning Boise's grid of streets, its quiet corners and hidden coffee shops. Each day built toward a decision he knew he couldn't postpone indefinitely. By Sunday morning, he knew it was time to test whether his calling could withstand the rigors of actual church attendance.

He went to Trinity Episcopal, a nearby church he'd found close to the Guest House. As he sat in the back pew during the organ prelude, he picked up a visitor's pamphlet. Trinity Episcopal, built in 1892, featured Gothic Revival architecture with a nave of rare Cornish elm and Tiffany stained-glass windows. The polished wood gleamed in the morning light, releasing a subtle aroma of lemon oil and over a century of devotion. It was classically beautiful and could have been found anywhere in America.

As the congregation rose for the processional hymn, the service cast—crucifer, choir, and clergy—entered the chancel while the choir sang "Thou Whose Almighty Word," a Christian hymn based on a Swedish traditional melody. The choir first encircled and then processed through the congregation before settling into their loft.

Baker surveyed the small crowd; most were older parishioners, with hardly anyone wearing a suit or sports jacket. A spirited octogenarian with platinum hair carefully fashioned into a stylish chignon sat in the pew in front of Baker, her powerful soprano carrying above the others with joyful abandon. He would gladly return to Trinity to hear her again.

After the opening prayers, Baker focused on the rector, the Reverend James Philip "Phil" Harbaugh. Father Phil greeted the congregation, remarked on how full he was from all the Christmas meals, praised the participants in the recent Christmas pageant, and asked if there were any newcomers. Baker chose to remain anonymous. Not seeing any hands raised, the rector forced a half smile at the senior warden and began the Liturgy of the Word.

His voice and mannerisms left no doubt that he was in charge. East Coast breeding showed in everything from his Hickey Freeman suit to his careful, almost presidential bearing. He looked like Gerald Ford, but with an elaborate combover stretched across two prominent bald spots—the kind of vanity that revealed everything Baker needed to know: image conscious, insecure, and probably threatened by anyone who might outshine him.

Baker felt the familiar weight of liturgy wash over him—the scent of beeswax candles and worn prayer books, the soft rustle of pages turning in unison. The words came back unbidden: "Grant us therefore, gracious Lord, so to eat the flesh of thy dear Son Jesus Christ, and to drink his blood..." His lips moved through the syllables before he realized what was happening, glancing around to make sure no one had noticed. Just muscle memory. Anyone who grew up Episcopalian would remember.

During the rector's sermon, Baker winced as Father Phil spoke with exaggerated enunciation—every syllable overarticulated like he was performing Shakespeare for the back row: "Thuh ree-*al*-ih-tee is *found*-uh in Christ-tuh. My *broth*-uhs and *sis*-tuhs . . ." The pompous, theatrical affectation grated on Baker. Twenty minutes of this every Sunday? He'd go stark raving mad.

When the offertory hymn began, the nearby parishioner's voice rose ahead of him—clear, joyful, cutting through the lingering irritation of Phil's performance. Real devotion after all that artifice. He tapped her shoulder and asked her name.

"Margaret Thompson," she replied warmly. "You must be new here?"

"Indeed. I just moved to Boise, and this is my first time at Trinity," Baker said. "By any chance, are you related to Bishop Thompson?"

"Yes, fortunately, I am. Karl Thompson is my husband," she answered proudly. "I'm sure he would like to meet you sometime."

The warmth in Margaret's voice caught Baker off guard. After years of encountering pretentious Episcopalians who wielded their faith like a social credential, here was someone who seemed genuinely glad to meet him. No affected piety, no subtle interrogation about his occupation, his alma mater, what brought him to Trinity—just honest friendliness.

After Communion, the choir reappeared for the recessional hymn, "Songs of Thankfulness and Praise," reversing course from their earlier procession. Once again, Margaret's voice rose above the rest. Each of the other choir members seemed to fade into the background, their voices barely audible beneath her powerful projection.

Following the service and the deacon's dismissal blessing, Baker and Margaret chatted briefly, and she gave him Karl's contact information.

The congregation left the church to greet the rector at the narthex's southern door with warm pleasantries. Since Baker was at the back of the line slowly moving forward, several regulars quickly recognized that he was new and welcomed him with introductions and invitations to join everyone for coffee in the adjacent social hall.

When Baker finally reached the front of the line, Father Phil's handshake was firm and professional, his smile practiced but genuine enough. "Phil Harbaugh. Welcome to Trinity."

"Baker Vaughan. Just moved here from New York."

"New York!" Phil's enthusiasm seemed reflexive, the kind of interest that came from pastoral training. "What brings you to Boise?"

"Looking for a fresh start. Career change, actually."

"Well, you've come to the right place. What line of work?"

"I was in advertising. Madison Avenue."

Phil's expression hardened—not hostility exactly, but a noticeable recalibration. His eyes flicked down—shell cordovan shoes, tailored wool sports jacket—then back to Baker, absorbing the ease of someone who'd spent years at the top of the corporate world. "Madison Avenue," he said. "Quite a pedigree."

"It had its moments," Baker said, trying to sound modest.

Phil's posture shifted almost imperceptibly—shoulders squaring, chin lifting just a fraction. Baker had seen this reaction countless times in boardrooms: the territorial reflex of someone who'd just registered a potential threat.

"And before New York? Where did you do your undergraduate work?"

The question had a strange weight to it. "Yale."

Phil's smile tightened. "Wonderful school." He paused. "So what brings someone with your background to Trinity?"

"I'm exploring a call to ordained ministry. I was in seminary years ago, before life took me in a different direction."

"How long ago was that?" Phil asked, his tone still measured but his eyes calculating. "Seminary, I mean."

In the pause that followed, Baker watched Phil's calculation crystallize—a visible recalibration in his bearing. The rector's eyes shifted slightly—not quite looking at Baker, not quite looking away—as if weighing his options. He could be encouraging, Baker realized, could offer the kind of pastoral support that would give legitimacy to a newcomer's calling. But that would mean empowering a potential rival, someone who might eventually stand in his pulpit with better credentials and natural authority. Phil's jaw worked for a moment, then set. When he spoke again, his tone had shifted from pastoral to pragmatic—the voice of institutional gatekeeping rather than spiritual encouragement.

That fleeting warmth vanished as Phil glanced at the parishioners waiting nearby, then back at Baker. "The path to ordination typically takes years—sometimes a decade." Phil paused, choosing his words carefully. "Given where you are in life, it might not be the most practical route."

Baker felt the sting but kept his composure. "Well, I reckon that's between me, the bishop, and the good Lord. But I do appreciate your concern, Father Phil."

He extended his hand. Phil shook it, grip slightly too firm.

Behind Baker, Margaret Thompson's eyebrows rose.

BAKER WALKED BACK TO the Guest House with Phil's words replaying in his head. *Given where you are in life.* The rector's condescension shouldn't have surprised him—he'd seen enough chest-thumping behavior in boardrooms to recognize it in a church narthex. Still, being written off in front of Phil's flock stung more than he'd expected. Or maybe it was the particular cruelty of having a priest tell him his calling had an expiration date.

He spent the rest of that Sunday afternoon on a long walk through the North End, letting the cold air clear his head. By the time he returned to his room, Phil's dismissal had transformed from a wound into something more useful: confirmation that if he was going to pursue ordination, he'd need to do it on his own terms, without waiting for permission from insecure clergy who saw every new seminarian as a threat.

The next morning, Baker commenced apartment hunting and fell into the rhythm of his new Boise life with surprising ease. He secured a two-bedroom unit in the six-story Idaho Building at Eighth and Bannock, its Second Renaissance Revival facade framing the Boise foothills through expansive windows. The grandeur felt familiar—an echo of the Oaks, his childhood home in Lynchburg, where his mother, Anne, and father, Edward, had raised him and his older sister, Emma, in rooms that could have engulfed this entire apartment.

The Oaks had been filled with voices—Anne's laughter from the kitchen, Edward's discourse about inventory and customers, Emma's piano scales drifting from upstairs. This apartment held only silence and the promise of whatever Baker might choose to construct within its walls. Standing here in this Boise apartment, watching the last light fade from the foothills, Baker felt a shift. Not the certainty of his teenage years but a quieter conviction. More stubborn. The sense that walking away the first time had been the real mistake, and everything since—the awards, the campaigns, the hollow success—had just been an elaborate way of avoiding his true path.

BAKER HAD FIT LYNCHBURG and the McGraw School like they'd been designed for him—Eagle Scout at just fourteen while balancing star quarterback duties, academic honors, the works. Throughout his childhood, he learned early how to maintain appearances, how to explain away his mother's "allergy to alcohol" at family gatherings, how to pretend everything was fine even when it wasn't.

His spiritual awakening came when he was a junior, building on seeds planted years earlier. At thirteen, during his Confirmation, he'd spontaneously set up a cardboard pulpit and served Communion to bewildered classmates with cornbread and merlot from his father's cellarette—a bottle he'd had to pick the lock to access, a skill learned from watching his mother "on harder days."

His liturgy needed work, but the intent was genuine.

The light that fell across Virginia that October afternoon in 1973 possessed a golden quality that seemed to transform the present into something already past, as if the world itself were being preserved in amber even as Baker lived through it. His Schwinn carried him along Rivermont Avenue, the weight of his backpack pressing against his shoulders—algebra assignments waiting inside, along with the Salinger novel his English teacher had assigned.

Junior football practice had kept him at school well past the final bell, and then he'd lingered even longer, explaining to Tommy Morrison that similes need *like*, but metaphors don't. It had been one of those days that seemed designed to prove Baker Vaughan's effortless competence: He'd worked through polynomial equations with the kind of patient precision that made complex problems look simple, he'd launched three touchdown passes that arced perfectly through the autumn air, and he'd left everyone he encountered with the impression that he understood exactly how life worked and where he was headed.

The lie of it sat in his chest like a stone.

He shifted gears as the road began its climb toward McGraw Hills, his thighs burning with the effort. His mother would be in the kitchen by now, starting dinner with that too-careful precision she employed when she was fighting the urge to pour something stronger than sweet tea. His father would arrive home within the hour, carrying the weight of another day at the furniture store, pretending not to notice what everyone in the family worked so hard not to name.

And Baker? Baker would sit at the dinner table and tell them about practice, about his A on the calculus test, about the college recruiters who kept calling. He'd perform his role in the family tableau with the same excellence he brought to everything else.

Is this it? The question formed without permission. *Is this all there is? Perform, excel, repeat until I take over my father's business, managing inventory and pretending to be happy?*

The bike crested the hill, and Baker stopped pedaling, letting momentum carry him. The afternoon sun broke through the canopy of oaks lining the street, and something shifted. It started as warmth in his chest—not metaphorical warmth, but actual heat that spread outward like he'd swallowed something hot. His hands on the handlebars, his feet on the pedals, the October air on his face—everything became sharper, more real, like he'd been looking through a dirty window and someone had just cleaned it.

The thought that came wasn't in words exactly. More like a knowing that bypassed language entirely: *This isn't all there is. I made you for more than performance.*

Baker's eyes filled with tears. Not sad tears. Not happy tears. Something else entirely—the kind of tears that come when you suddenly understand you've been holding your breath for years and someone just told you it's OK to exhale. He coasted to a stop, one foot on the curb to steady himself, and the knowing continued: *You don't have to be golden. You don't have to fix your mother or live your uncle's dreams or throw perfect spirals. I'm calling you to something else.*

"What?" Baker whispered aloud, his voice cracking. "What are you calling me to?"

The answer settled into him like warm honey, sweet and thick and undeniable: *To lead my people. To break bread and pour wine. To stand in the gap between heaven and earth and speak truth. To be a priest.*

A car passed, the driver giving him a curious look—some teenager crying on a bicycle at the top of Rivermont Avenue—but Baker didn't care. His whole body was humming with certainty, every cell aligned in a single direction for the first time in his seventeen years. He knew this was real. Knew it the way he knew his own name, the way he knew his mother was sick, the way he knew that everything he'd built his identity around—the achievements, the accolades, the carefully maintained image—was scaffolding around an empty building.

This was the building. This calling. This *priesthood.*

Baker stood there for what might have been five minutes or twenty, letting the certainty wash through him in waves before he laid down his bike. The warmth in his chest gradually settled into something quieter but no less certain—a pilot light that had been lit and wouldn't be extinguished by doubt or fear or other people's plans for his life.

When he finally climbed back on his bike and pedaled the remaining blocks home, he was different. Not transformed in some obvious external way—he still had calculus homework and football practice tomorrow and a family that needed him to be flawless. But now he had something else too: a secret knowledge of his true purpose, burning quiet and steady beneath everything else he was supposed to be.

His mother was indeed in the kitchen when he walked in, and she turned from the stove with that careful smile she wore when she was winning her daily battle.

"Good practice?" she asked.

"Yeah," Baker said, setting down his backpack. "Mom, can I ask you something?"

"Of course, sweetheart."

"Do you believe God calls people to specific things? Like, not just general 'Be a good person' stuff, but actual vocations?"

Anne Vaughan's hands stilled on the wooden spoon. She looked at her son—really looked at him—and something in her face softened.

"Yes," she said quietly. "I do. Why do you ask?"

"I think…" Baker's voice caught. "I think I just got called to something."

His mother crossed the kitchen and pulled him into a hug that smelled like Chanel No. 5 and whatever she was cooking and something else he couldn't name—maybe hope, maybe recognition, maybe just love.

"Then you'd better answer," she whispered into his hair. "Because those kinds of calls don't come twice."

BY THE START OF senior year, the family was pressing him about college. Uncle Oscar—his mother's older brother, Yale class of '52, with the Park Avenue address and walls hung with Jasper Johns and Robert Rauschenberg—had been particularly vocal about Baker's "potential" and his own willingness to help financially. Oscar had left their native New England for Manhattan decades earlier and watched with barely concealed dismay as his sister settled into Virginia life. He'd seen what that choice had cost her, even if the family pretended otherwise. He'd do anything to prevent Baker from getting trapped in small-town Virginia the way Anne had.

When Baker finally told his uncle about his seminary plans, the conversation quickly went south. It was the first time Baker had ever heard his uncle truly lose his composure.

"Divinity school?" Oscar's voice cracked. "Where the hell did this idea come from?"

"It's something I've been called to do."

His uncle's laugh came through the phone like broken glass. "A calling? Christ, Baker, you sound like Jerry Falwell. Why don't you stay home and go to Liberty Baptist?"

Baker tried to explain the overwhelming sense of peace that washed over him during that bike ride home from school. But Oscar cut him off before he could find the words.

"People get 'spiritual experiences' from bad pizza," Oscar shot back. "You're talking about throwing away your entire future because you felt good riding a bicycle?"

Baker heard him exhale sharply.

"Yale or nothing," he continued, his voice sharpening. "I'll pay for undergrad. Period. What you do with your education after that is your business. But I'm not funding some half-baked theological adventure."

The phone clicked dead, leaving Baker staring at the receiver while his parents watched from across the room, their faces carefully neutral.

Chapter Two

WHEN HE FIRST FELT CALLED TO MINISTRY, THERE WAS Wendy. She recognized his spiritual hunger in ways his family never could—saw past all the achievements everyone else praised to something more authentic beneath. Baker could still feel the weight of her belief in him, the way she'd looked at him as though his calling were something sacred rather than strange.

He first noticed her at school during a Wednesday morning chapel service in October of their junior year. She sat three rows in front of him, head tilted slightly to the right as she listened to her father deliver a sermon about discovering grace in unexpected places.

What arrested Baker's attention wasn't merely her beauty—though the autumn light filtering through stained-glass windows set auburn highlights dancing in her dark hair. It was something in her bearing—a composure at once mature and fragile, like someone who had learned prematurely that the world could strip away everything that mattered without warning.

After chapel, Baker found himself reviewing Latin home-work with Tommy Morrison while his eyes tracked the stream of students filing past, searching for those auburn highlights. When Wendy reappeared, walking alongside Reverend George Levering as he greeted students and faculty, Baker observed how she remained close to his side—the school chaplain's daughter, protective rather than clinging.

"Wendy," Reverend Levering said as they approached Baker's group. "I'd like you to meet some of our students. This is Baker Vaughan—I believe you're both juniors?"

Baker extended his hand, and when Wendy took it, the firm-ness of her grip surprised him. Her eyes met his directly, and he saw in them a depth that had nothing to do with teenage sophistication.

"Nice to meet you, Baker," she said, her voice carrying just a trace of her New Hampshire origins. "I've heard you're quite the scholar-athlete around here."

"Guilty as charged," Baker replied, the words tumbling out before he could stop them. *Smooth as sandpaper*, he thought.

"Well," she said, "maybe you can help me figure out where I fit in around here. I'm still learning the rhythms of this place."

It was an opening Baker knew he couldn't waste. "I'd be happy to show you around. McGraw has its quirks, but once you know the secret passages and which teachers care about late as-signments, it's not so bad."

Reverend Levering watched this exchange with the careful at-tention of a father who had already buried one of the two most important people in his life. But something in Baker's demeanor—perhaps the way he spoke to Wendy as an equal rather than a con-quest—seemed to pass whatever test the chaplain was administering.

"That's very kind of you, Baker," Reverend Levering said. "Wendy could use a friend who knows his way around."

They began eating lunch together, Baker abandoning his usual table with the other academic stars to sit with Wendy in quieter corners of the dining hall where they could talk. She told him about New Hampshire, about her mother's garden and how her father used to sneak extra sugar into his coffee when he thought no one was looking. Baker found himself sharing things he'd never told anyone—lying awake wondering if he'd ever accomplish anything that mattered to him rather than everyone else, how the weight of being successful often felt like carrying other people's dreams on his shoulders.

"Sometimes I feel like I'm performing my own life," he said one afternoon as they walked between classes. "Like everyone's watching to see if I'll live up to their expectations, and I'm not sure I even know what I actually want anymore."

"That's the thing about expectations," Wendy replied, adjusting her backpack as they navigated the crowded hallway. "They're usually more about other people's fears than your actual potential."

It was precisely the kind of insight that made Baker realize Wendy saw the world the same way he did.

Their first real date came the following March. They attended a morning discussion on the Stations of the Cross at Montview, also known as the Carter Glass Estate. The house was named a National Historic Landmark in 1976 and served as a parish hall for the adjacent Saint Paul's Episcopal Church. In this beautiful space, they hung around after the discussion and realized they shared more in common than not. They had both ridden bicycles to Montview and agreed it would make sense to ride home together.

"How about stopping for some ice cream?" Baker suggested, pointing toward the shopping center where Marshall's Fair-Way Markets was located. "There's a new place called Scoopy-Doo I've been wanting to try."

Wendy's bright smile was as good as a yes. After finishing a banana split and a triple-berry milkshake, they left the ice cream parlor and saw a Rhode Island Red rooster running loose in the parking lot.

"Baker, he's so cute. Let's find where he lives," she said joyfully.

There was no apparent home for this rooster in the immediate vicinity, so the prospect of reuniting owner and fowl was unlikely. Baker asked Wendy to watch the bird while he went inside Fair-Way to make some inquiries. He made eye contact with a clerk at the front, who waved a finger.

"I'll be with you in a sec," she said.

While she helped another customer, Baker heard Wendy shouting his name from outside. The front door of the old store didn't seal properly, and her voice carried clearly through the gaps, along with the humid spring air and the distant sounds of traffic. Heads turned, conversations paused, as everyone wondered what emergency was unfolding.

"He's headed toward the old Harrison house," Wendy said.

That house had been the talk of Lynchburg for most of Baker's life since it sat alone in the downtown area like a faded Southern belle refusing to acknowledge her circumstances. The three-story Victorian loomed behind rusted wrought-iron gates, its once-grand wraparound porch now sagging under the weight of peeling white paint and decades of neglect. Baker caught up with Wendy as she brushed aside strings of ivy dangling from an outbuilding just across the property line. That spring afternoon became their pattern—explorations that often led them back to the Harrison house. Through the summer between junior and senior year, they'd meet there regularly, drawn to the property's air of abandonment.

By the fall of their senior year, as college applications loomed, the tension between Baker's future and their relationship became impossible to ignore. Wendy discovered she couldn't have both. She wanted Baker to reach for Yale, to seize the opportunities that someone with his credentials deserved. At the same time, the thought of him leaving for New Haven while she stayed in Virginia felt like another abandonment—different from her mother's death but devastating in its own way.

"You should go Ivy," she told him one afternoon as they walked through downtown Lynchburg, her voice carrying a conviction that didn't quite mask the tremor underneath. "Your uncle's right about the doors it opens. You're too talented to settle for safe choices."

"And leave you behind?" Baker asked, stopping to face her.

"I'll be fine," she said, the lie coming easily because she'd had years of practice protecting the people she loved from her own needs.

But Baker could see through her composed exterior to the young girl who'd learned at seven that people you love can disappear without warning. Her hands were shaking slightly—the only sign that she was back in that kitchen, her mother's face gray and collapsed, her father already retreating into the silence he'd never really left.

"That's the difference between us, Baker. You're afraid of disappointing people. I'm afraid there's no one left to disappoint."

It was the most honest thing anyone had ever said to him, and Baker knew then that whatever was happening between them was unlike anything he'd experienced with other girls. This wasn't the easy flirtation he was used to, the kind where charm and confidence were enough. With Wendy, he had to be real.

THE BALLROOM AT LYNCHBURG Country Club glittered with the kind of wealth that never announced itself. Crystal chandeliers cast flattering light on women wearing pearls that had been in their families for generations while men in white dinner jackets discussed market positions and summer houses with the ease of people for whom money was simply air—invisible, abundant, assumed.

Baker adjusted his bow tie—rented, like the tuxedo—and tried not to feel like an impostor. Beside him, Wendy looked radiant in a pale-blue dress her aunt had sent from New Hampshire, simple and elegant in a way that made the other girls' elaborate gowns seem like they were trying too hard.

"You look terrified," Wendy whispered, squeezing his hand.

"I'm not terrified. I'm…strategically nervous."

"That's the same thing with better vocabulary."

This was the third debutante ball Baker had attended this spring—Charlotte Preston's debut in April, Mary Catherine Whitmore's last week, and now Melissa Ashcroft's. His mother had been delighted when the invitations arrived, seeing them as confirmation that her son moved in the right circles despite the Vaughan family's merely comfortable circumstances.

"Baker Vaughan!" A voice boomed across the ballroom. Harrison Ashcroft III—Melissa's father, president of Ashcroft

Textiles, and the kind of man whose handshake could approve loans or ruin reputations—strode toward them with a tumbler of bourbon and the expansive smile Southern men use when they're sizing you up. "Good to see you, son. Heard Virginia Tech's still courting you for quarterback."

"Yes, sir, they are," Baker replied, shifting into the mode he'd perfected over years of navigating these waters. Respectful but not obsequious. Confident but not cocky. "Though I'm actually leaning toward studying theology at Yale."

"Theology?" Ashcroft's eyebrows rose. "Well, that's certainly…unconventional. What does your Uncle Oscar think about that?"

There it was—the casual mention that revealed Ashcroft knew exactly who Baker was and wasn't. The Vaughans were invited to these events not because Edward was a civic leader or Anne volunteered at the hospital, but because Oscar's name carried weight even in Lynchburg. Everyone knew he had money. Everyone assumed some of it flowed south to his sister's family.

"Uncle Oscar has strong opinions about everything," Baker said carefully. "But he raised a valid point about keeping my options open."

"Smart man, your uncle. I met him once at a fundraiser in New York. Impressive art collection." Ashcroft's gaze moved past Baker to assess the room, already done with this conversation. "Enjoy the evening, you two. Wendy, you look lovely."

As Ashcroft moved away to greet more important guests, Wendy's hand tightened on Baker's arm.

"I hate this," she said quietly.

"The ball?"

"The performance. The way everyone measures everyone else. Did you see how his whole face changed when you said *theology* instead of *business?*"

Baker had seen. He'd been seeing it his whole life—the subtle recalibration people made when they realized the Vaughans were comfortable but not wealthy, connected but not powerful, present at these events but always slightly peripheral.

The orchestra began playing, and couples moved onto the dance floor. Baker led Wendy out among them, grateful for the excuse to move, to have a purpose beyond standing and being assessed.

"My father would hate this," Wendy said as they turned in slow circles among the other dancers. Around them, girls in white gowns twirled gracefully, their dates navigating the choreography of privilege with practiced ease.

"Reverend Levering at a debutante ball? That would be something to see."

"He used to say that Jesus spent his time with prostitutes and tax collectors, not the self-satisfied rich. Then he'd feel guilty for being judgmental and make me pray with him for a more charitable heart." Her voice softened. "He's different now. Quieter. Church politics have worn him down."

Baker pulled her slightly closer, aware of the eyes watching them, cataloging this moment for future reference. Baker Vaughan with the chaplain's daughter. Pretty enough, poised enough, but clearly not one of them.

"What will he think about me?" Baker asked. "Going to seminary?"

"He will be proud when you tell him. He will also warn you that it's lonely, speaking truth to people who prefer comfortable lies."

She looked up at him, her eyes bright. "These people? They'd smile and nod through your sermons and then go back to exactly the lives they were living before. He sees it every day at McGraw."

Across the dance floor, Baker caught sight of Caroline Morrison—Tommy's sister—wearing a diamond necklace that probably cost more than his father's car. She'd asked Baker to be her escort tonight, and he'd politely declined, saying he'd already invited Wendy. Caroline had looked at him like he'd chosen a ham sandwich over filet mignon.

"Can I tell you something?" Baker said, guiding Wendy through a turn. "Sometimes I feel like I'm living in two completely different worlds. There's this world"—he gestured subtly at the ballroom—"where everyone expects me to want what they want. Money, status, the right connections. And then there's the world I actually care about. The one where I'm supposed to be doing something that matters."

"Those worlds don't have to be separate," Wendy said. "You could minister to people like this. They need God too, even if they think their bank accounts make them invincible."

"Maybe. Or maybe I'd just become like them. Comfortable. Safe. Forgetting why I felt called in the first place."

The song ended, and scattered applause rippled through the room. Baker and Wendy moved to the edge of the dance floor as the orchestra launched into something more upbeat. Groups of young men in rented tuxedos gathered near the bar, while girls in white clustered like swans, whispering and laughing.

"Baker! There you are!" Charlotte Preston materialized beside them, her blonde hair elaborately styled, her dress a confection of silk and tulle that probably required its own zip code.

"You simply must dance with Melissa. It's her night, and she was just saying how she hoped you'd ask."

It wasn't really a request. At these events, certain obligations existed—unspoken but absolute. You danced with the debutante. You made small talk with her parents. You performed your role in the elaborate theater of Southern social life.

"Of course," Baker said, glancing apologetically at Wendy, who nodded with the patience of someone who understood these rules even if she didn't like them.

He found Melissa near the champagne fountain, surrounded by admirers but somehow still managing to look isolated. Up close, he could see the strain around her eyes—the exhaustion of being on display, of having to be perfect and grateful and charming for hours on end.

"May I have this dance?" Baker asked, extending his hand.

"Finally, someone who doesn't want to talk about my dress or my plans for Hollins College," Melissa said, taking his hand with visible relief. "Do you know how many times I've heard 'You look just like your mother' tonight?"

"I'm guessing more than zero, less than infinity?"

She laughed—a real laugh, not the practiced tinkle she'd been deploying all evening. "Somewhere in that range, yes."

They moved onto the dance floor, and Baker found himself studying her face. Melissa Ashcroft had everything these occasions were designed to celebrate—beauty, breeding, the kind of effortless grace that came from never having to worry about money. She should have been radiantly happy. Instead, she looked like someone enduring an ordeal.

"Can I ask you something?" Melissa said as they turned. "Is it true you're going to study theology instead of business?"

"That's the plan."

"My father thinks you're insane. He told my mother that you're throwing away a perfectly good future on 'unproven nonsense.'" She paused. "I think it sounds wonderful."

Baker looked at her with surprise. "You do?"

"My father has my entire life planned. Hollins for two years, then marry someone appropriate—probably Stuart Whitmore, since our families have been friends forever and a merger would be 'advantageous.' Children by twenty-five. Junior League by thirty. Die having never once made a decision that wasn't preapproved by someone else." Her smile was brittle. "So yes, the idea of someone choosing their own path instead of the expected one sounds absolutely wonderful."

The song ended. Melissa squeezed his hand briefly before releasing it.

"Thank you for the dance," she said, her public smile sliding back into place. "And Baker? Whatever you decide to do—don't let them make you small. People like us, we're very good at making people small."

Baker returned to Wendy's side feeling unsettled. Around them, the ball continued its elaborate choreography—the music, the laughter, the careful negotiations of status and connection that would shape these people's lives for decades to come.

"Ready to get out of here?" Wendy asked.

"God, yes."

They slipped out through the French doors onto the terrace, leaving behind the glittering ballroom for the quieter darkness of the club's gardens. The music followed them, muffled now, as they walked past perfectly manicured hedges and flower beds.

"You know what's strange?" Baker said, stopping to lean against a stone balustrade. Below them, Lynchburg spread out in pools of light and shadow. "I can move through that world. I know how to talk to those people, how to make them think I'm one of them. But I don't want to be."

"Then don't be," Wendy said simply.

"It's not that easy. My mother wants me to be. Uncle Oscar definitely wants me to be. And part of me wonders if throwing it all away for seminary is brave or just stupid."

"Those aren't your only choices." Wendy moved to stand beside him, her shoulder touching his. "You could be exactly who you are—someone who understands that world but chooses a different path. Someone who can speak their language but says something true."

From inside, the orchestra launched into a waltz.

Through the French doors, Baker could see the debutantes spinning in their white dresses, their partners guiding them through steps they'd learned in childhood, everyone playing their assigned roles in a pageant as old as the South itself.

He thought about Melissa Ashcroft's brittle smile. About Harrison Ashcroft's casual assessment and dismissal. About all the people in that ballroom who would live comfortable, prosperous lives without ever asking whether comfort and prosperity were enough.

And he thought about the warmth that had filled his chest on that October afternoon, the certainty that had settled into him like a benediction: *I'm calling you to something else.*

"You're right," Baker said quietly. "I don't have to choose between understanding that world and rejecting it. I just have to remember which one is real."

Wendy smiled and took his hand. "Then let's go be real somewhere else. I heard there's a diner on Fifth Street that stays open late."

They walked back through the gardens toward the parking lot, leaving the music and the light and the glittering performance behind. Tomorrow, people would talk about who danced with whom, who said what to whom, the endless social calculus that governed their world.

In that moment, Baker Vaughan was just a boy who'd been called to something larger than any ballroom could contain, walking hand in hand with a girl who understood that some things mattered more than being invited to the right parties.

But the clarity he'd felt that night would soon be tested by forces far more relentless than any debutante ball.

THE PRESSURE FROM HIS family intensified as application deadlines approached. Baker remembered the Sunday dinner at the Oaks in mid-October when Oscar visited from New York and the conversation inevitably turned to his college plans. His father was characteristically diplomatic, gently probing about his applications while Anne nursed a simple tonic and lime. But his uncle had his own agenda.

"The boy's got the credentials for New Haven, Edward," Oscar had declared, cutting into his roast beef with the same precision he used to dissect his nephew's future. "Yale shaped me into who I am today. Best investment I ever made—better than any stock portfolio. The connections alone are worth their weight in gold."

Edward deliberately set down his fork. "Oscar, Baker needs to make his own choices—"

"Choices?" He laughed, gesturing with his wineglass. "This isn't a choice; it's destiny. The Vaughan name belongs there. I've already spoken to admissions—they remember the family well." He turned to Baker. "Son, you don't understand what you'd be throwing away. Yale opens doors that stay closed forever otherwise."

But then Oscar, never one for subtlety, turned to what he really wanted to say. "And Baker, you know what they say about women—they're like streetcars. Miss one, and another will come along in fifteen minutes. Don't tie yourself down to the first pretty face that smiles at you. Not when Yale is waiting."

The silence that followed was excruciating. Baker waited for his father's response. "Oscar, that's enough," Edward said quietly, then turned to Baker: "You're young, Baker. If it's meant to be with Wendy, it'll still be there after you've gotten your degree."

Even now, Baker appreciated how his father had defended him while still expressing his concerns—a diplomatic skill born from years of managing family tensions.

Over the following weeks in late October and early November of his senior year, Oscar's involvement only intensified. The phone rang during dinner on a Tuesday evening. Baker recognized the New York area code and hesitated before answering.

"Baker, I've been talking to my contacts at Yale." Oscar's voice came through the line. "The application deadline is approaching, and I can still make some calls. But we need to move on this."

Baker glanced across the dining room at his parents, who had both paused their conversation to listen. His father's expression was carefully neutral, but his mother wore that tight smile she reserved for family politics.

"Uncle Oscar, I appreciate what you're trying to do, but—"

"This isn't about what I'm trying to do, Baker. This is about what's best for your future. I had lunch with a trustee last week—mentioned your name, your academic record. He was impressed."

"I haven't even applied."

"That's exactly my point. Time is running out, and opportunities like this don't wait for indecision."

Baker could hear the impatience creeping into his uncle's voice, that tone that suggested anyone who didn't immediately see the wisdom of Oscar's plan was being deliberately obtuse.

"I'll think about it. I have to go."

"Baker, don't let this slip away. Call me this weekend."

The line went dead. Baker set the phone down and returned to his place at the table, where his parents were making a studied effort to resume their conversation about anything other than Yale.

By Thanksgiving, Oscar had returned to New York, but his presence lingered over the Oaks like smoke. Emma came home from Sweet Briar for the holiday, and the four of them—Edward, Anne, Emma, and Baker—sat down to dinner in the formal dining room.

Anne passed the sweet potatoes to Emma. "Your brother has some important decisions to make this year."

"We all want what's best for him," Edward added, reaching for the rolls. "These opportunities don't come around twice."

"You mean what Oscar wants is best for him," Emma said, setting down her fork.

"Emma," Anne said sharply.

"No, I'm serious. Even if Oscar has connections at Yale, that doesn't mean Baker should be pressured into something he doesn't want. He's a person with his own dreams, not a commodity you're trading."

Edward's voice was measured. "We're simply trying to help him see all his options."

"He knows his options, Dad. What he doesn't know is whether anyone in this family cares what he actually wants, instead of just what Oscar expects." Emma turned to Baker, her eyes blazing. "What do you want? Not what Oscar wants for his reputation, not what Dad thinks is practical. What do you want?"

The question hung in the air, unanswered, like incense—sacred and unavoidable.

Rather than answer Emma, Baker excused himself and went upstairs to call Wendy. "I know I want to go to seminary," he said without preamble.

The silence stretched long enough for him to wonder if the connection had failed. Then Wendy's voice, soft but certain: "I know you do. I've been waiting for you to say it out loud."

She paused, and he could hear her breathing on the other end of the line.

"Your uncle's approval isn't worth your soul," she told him. "Your father loves you enough to want you to be happy, even if it takes him a while to understand. And as for us . . . if what we have is real, geography is just a problem to solve, not a reason to give up."

Chapter Three

URING THE SPRING OF HIS SENIOR YEAR AT McGRAW, someone—no one knew who—donated a stunning piece of property to the school, land that stretched along the James River in the foothills of the Blue Ridge Mountains. It was all the talk of Lynchburg. The anonymous donor sparked a town-wide guessing game: Who had that kind of money? And what exactly did they expect the school to do with such prime real estate? When the school announced the gift, the only information revealed was that the donor wanted it used to help kids grow physically, intellectually, and spiritually while also generating income for the school.

Baker's curiosity about the mysterious donation was satisfied on a warm May afternoon when his mother cornered him in the kitchen moments before Wendy was due to arrive for dinner.

"There's something I have to tell you about the gift to the school," Anne said, her voice carrying the tone she used when she was about to reveal a family secret.

"You know who gave it?" Baker asked.

"Right after I graduated from Sweet Briar and decided to stay in Virginia to marry your dad, my father gifted me this land—all one hundred and nineteen acres of it, stretching along the James River as far north as Coleman Falls. One of his customers used it as barter during the Depression to stay afloat. Granddad saw no use for it himself, but he thought I, rather than your Uncle Oscar, would make the best steward until the time came to either sell it or gift it to a worthy cause when the moment was right."

His mind raced with follow-up questions, but just then Wendy knocked on the front door of the Oaks. She was welcomed with the usual Southern hospitality—gracious but exhaustive—and after the requisite chitchat about her father's health and her plans for the summer, the conversation naturally turned to the mysterious land gift.

What happened next was pure serendipity. Wendy's eyes lit up as she leaned forward in her chair. "Wait—did I overhear you talking about spare land? I have to tell you, I practically grew up at a summer camp! Paradise Retreat in New Hampshire—my father's former church ran it. I was a camper there for years, then worked as a junior counselor."

She painted a vivid picture of camp life: the pristine lake perfect for swimming and canoeing, after-dinner drum circles under star-filled skies, and outdoor Sunday services that felt more sacred than any cathedral. Her enthusiasm was infectious, and she could have continued indefinitely if the Vaughans hadn't politely interrupted to ask about the camp's origins.

Then something shifted in Wendy's expression—a sudden clarity that made her pause mid-sentence. She looked from one Vaughan to the other, her eyes widening with the dawning realization.

"Wait a minute," she said slowly, sitting up straighter. "You have land that you're trying to figure out what to do with, and I'm sitting here going on about how transformative camp was for me . . ." She pressed her palms together, almost prayerfully, and drew in a deep breath. "What if—and I know this might sound crazy—but what if McGraw School partnered with you on this? They have the institutional knowledge; you have the land. A place like Paradise Retreat, but here. For kids who might never otherwise get that experience." The words tumbled out faster now, her voice rising with excitement. "I mean, the land is just sitting there, and you're looking for something meaningful to do with it."

The Vaughans exchanged glances—the kind of wordless communication that comes from decades of marriage. Edward leaned back in his chair, stroking his chin thoughtfully, while Anne tilted her head with genuine curiosity.

"Tell us more about this Paradise Retreat," Anne said, her voice warm with interest. "You speak about it with such passion."

Wendy's face brightened even more, if that were possible. She took a breath, gathering her thoughts, clearly eager to share what had shaped so much of her youth. "It started back in the 1930s, and families have been coming generation after generation," Wendy explained, looking around the room for affirmation and seeing nothing but encouraging smiles.

"How long does the camp run?" Edward asked.

"Five months now—it started as just a summer program, but it's grown. We get everyone from kids to grandparents, church folks, and complete skeptics too."

"And it actually supports itself?" Anne wondered.

"More than that. Last year, the camp brought in half of what the church collected in donations. But that's not really the point—it's about what Dad always called 'faith, fellowship, and fun.'"

After this impressive display of knowledge and passion, the Vaughan family looked at Wendy with new admiration. Edward and Anne had already been warming to the idea of Baker taking a gap year before college—something most of their friends' children were doing in Israel or Europe, expensive programs that felt more like extended vacations than real preparation for adulthood.

But listening to her compelling vision of a summer camp ministry, they began to see an opportunity that would serve multiple purposes: giving Baker time to mature before college, allowing him to explore his apparent affinity for working with young people, and creating a lasting legacy for both the school and the community of Lynchburg. They were tired of hearing people like Oscar mockingly refer to their city as just the home of a conservative religious college. Here was a chance to give Lynchburg another identity.

At the end of the evening, Baker caught Wendy's eye across the table and saw his own excitement reflected there. Edward cleared his throat and looked at Anne, who nodded.

"Well, then," Edward said, "it seems we have a plan. You'll defer your acceptances, spend the summer getting the property ready, and if it works . . ." He smiled. "We'll have ourselves a camp."

Baker reached for Wendy's hand under the table. A year together, building something meaningful—it felt like the most natural decision in the world.

From June 1978 through the camp's official opening a year later, the project consumed Baker with an intensity that surprised everyone, including himself. He'd stand in the morning dew with blueprints spread across the hood of his car, arguing with contractors about cabin placement while pointing toward the river. He studied camp management, researched youth-development programs, and spent hours walking the property, envisioning cabins nestled among the trees and an outdoor chapel overlooking the James River.

The seed money came from an unexpected coalition. Anne had quietly written the first check—five thousand dollars from her own inheritance, presented to Baker over breakfast one morning with the simple statement, "Your grandfather would have wanted this." McGraw School matched her donation with another five thousand, approved by the board of trustees—a vote of confidence that gave the project legitimacy. With ten thousand dollars already committed, Edward spent two months working his Lynchburg connections, starting with Ashcroft over bourbon at the country club. He listened to Edward's pitch about giving local kids a chance at something better, then pulled out his checkbook on the spot. Within weeks, he'd assembled a small group of local businessmen—the furniture store owner, the bank president, another textile manufacturer—each contributing what they could. By the time Baker broke ground, he had thirty thousand dollars in commitments and a board of advisors who remembered him as the epitome of a McGraw student and trusted that Edward Vaughan's son would make good on his word.

Wendy proved invaluable as a partner, drawing detailed diagrams of Paradise Retreat's layout and sharing insights about everything from kitchen operations to counselor training. But it was Baker who instinctively understood what would make this camp different. Where Wendy saw programs and activities, Baker saw sanctuary—a place where kids who didn't fit anywhere else might finally feel at home.

That gap year changed him in ways he was only beginning to understand. What started as a way to spend time with Wendy before college became the foundation for his sense of purpose— not just his calling to ministry, but his confidence that he could serve it well. Working alongside her to build the camp from the ground up—clearing trails, hammering together wooden platform bases and stretching canvas over frames to create army-style tent cabins, developing programs—showed him what partnership could look like when two people shared the same vision.

The physical intimacy between them developed naturally during those nine months of construction, growing from the emotional connection they'd forged through shared purpose. There were stolen hours in the late afternoons when the work crew had gone home—moments when they'd find themselves alone in the old maintenance cabin, where weathered camping mattresses provided a refuge from the world beyond the property. They'd lie together fully clothed, learning the geography of each other's bodies through fabric, whispering plans for their future between kisses that left them both breathless and wanting more.

By spring, they'd progressed beyond innocent touching, though they maintained the boundaries that felt right for both of them. There were evenings when they'd walk the trails together and find places by the river where pine needles cushioned the ground and the water whispered over stones. The privacy of the construction period allowed their relationship to deepen in ways that would have been impossible once the campers arrived.

The inaugural summer was modest but chaotic: twenty-four campers, mostly local boys and girls whose parents were willing to take a chance on an untested program. A few came from across Virginia and beyond—youth sentenced by the courts, kids sent by desperate parents—supported by eager volunteers willing to trade summer ease for something that mattered. Baker and Wendy maintained professional boundaries during camp sessions, their relationship shifting to accommodate the constant presence of kids who needed their full attention.

What Baker discovered that summer surprised him. He possessed an instinct for reading the ones who needed more than activities and fellowship—the silent ones, the angry ones, the kids who reminded him of himself when he'd felt trapped by everyone else's expectations. This gift allowed him to spot the kid sitting alone at meals, sense when someone was homesick beyond the normal adjustment period, and know exactly what to say when a fourteen-year-old showed up with bruises that clearly didn't come from hiking.

He didn't realize how closely Wendy was watching him until the evening she found him on the porch steps with Milo, a sullen fifteen-year-old who wouldn't speak to anyone for three days. Baker wasn't lecturing or coaxing—just whittling a piece of wood while Milo sat beside him in silence. When the boy finally started talking about his father leaving, Baker glanced up to find Wendy standing in the doorway, something unreadable in her expression. Later, she would tell him what she'd seen: complete presence, infinite patience. Their relationship had deepened during the construction months, but it was moments like these—watching each other become exactly who they were meant to be—that showed them what their partnership could truly mean.

"I love you," Wendy had whispered one night as they lay tangled together on the narrow mattress, Baker's hand resting on her hip, her fingers tracing patterns on his chest through his T-shirt.

"I love you too," he'd replied, the words feeling both inevitable and miraculous. His heart hammered against his ribs as he forced himself to say what he'd been thinking for weeks: "I want to marry you someday."

"Someday," she'd agreed, then kissed him with a passion that made the wait seem both impossible and sacred.

They understood instinctively that what they were building together—the emotional intimacy, the shared calling, the physical desire that grew stronger each day—was worth protecting. One night in the maintenance cabin, as Baker's hands found the hem of her shirt and Wendy felt her heart stutter, she gently grabbed his wrists. "Not yet," she whispered against his ear, and though every nerve in his body protested, Baker nodded. Some gifts, they both knew, were meant to be unwrapped slowly.

The camp officially ended in late August, but its impact on Baker's calling was permanent. On the final morning, as parents picked up their children, Milo offered an awkward hug around Baker's waist and whispered, "Thank you for not giving up on me." Across the clearing, Wendy caught Baker's eye and smiled, and he knew with absolute certainty that he'd found his purpose—what ministry could look like when it focused on love rather than doctrine. More than that, he'd found the person he wanted to share that calling with.

As they prepared to leave for college—Baker to Yale, Wendy to UVA with plans to transfer north after her first semester—they carried with them the certainty that they'd discovered something rare and valuable. They'd learned to work together, to love together, to envision a future that honored both their individual gifts and their shared commitment to serving others.

By now, Baker knew two things with absolute certainty: He wanted to marry Wendy, and he was called to work with people who needed hope more than they needed anything else. The camp had become proof that ministry could happen anywhere, that sometimes the most sacred moments occurred around a campfire rather than behind a pulpit.

BAKER'S FIRST SEMESTER IN New Haven felt like cultural whiplash. After a year of working with kids who measured success by making it through another day without being ignored or getting arrested, the former camp counselor found himself surrounded by classmates who casually mentioned that their trust funds would mature when they were twenty-five.

The freshman dormitory was populated by the sons of senators, Supreme Court justices, and Fortune 500 CEOs—boys who'd never questioned whether they belonged anywhere, who spoke casually about "the family foundation" and "our place in the Hamptons." His roommate, a kid named Trent from Greenwich, Connecticut, had arrived with enough electronic equipment to stock a Radio Shack and a framed photo of himself shaking hands with Ronald Reagan.

"What does your dad do?" Trent asked the question during their first week, as automatic as breathing among their peers.

"He runs a mercantile in Lynchburg," Baker replied.

"A mercantile?"

"Yeah. Small-town stuff. But it's significant to the community."

Trent nodded politely, but Baker could see him mentally

filing this information under "scholarship kid" or "regional admission." The gap between his summer camp stories and his classmates' tales of European backpacking trips left him feeling like he was treading water in the deep end, watching everyone else swim effortlessly to shore.

"So, have you decided on a major?"

"Religious studies, probably. I'm thinking about seminary afterward."

"Good luck with that. Church is a dying business."

The academic work itself wasn't the challenge—he'd always been able to handle intellectual rigor. It was conversations like the one he overheard in the dining hall: "Goldman's recruiting early this year," one junior was telling another. "If you're not networking by sophomore year, you're already behind." The assumption that academic success automatically translated into worldly ambition wore on him like water on stone.

When the aspiring seminarian told his American history professor he was considering seminary after graduation, the man's eyebrows shot up, and he let out a sharp bark of laughter.

"Bright kid like you? Don't waste it on the ministry. There's no intellectual challenge there anymore, not to mention much of a paycheck."

Heat rose in Baker's cheeks, but he kept his voice steady. "I think you might be surprised."

He sat through the rest of the lecture in a fog, barely hearing Beckwith's analysis of postwar economic trends. His pen moved absently across the margins of his notebook, sketching the outline of mountains, then a small campfire with stick figures gathered around it. That evening, he found himself writing to

Wendy: "Sometimes I feel like I'm speaking a language no one here understands—or wants to learn."

"Look, Vaughan," Beckwith had continued, leaning back in his leather chair after class, "I get the appeal of wanting to help people. But you could do that as a social worker, a therapist, even a politician. Why lock yourself into a dying institution? When's the last time you met someone under thirty who took church seriously?"

Baker managed a thin smile. He thought of Milo clinging to him at camp, of Wendy's quiet faith, of the Sunday morning conversations that had shaped his entire worldview.

"Last week," he said quietly. "I met dozens of them."

The kids at camp came to mind—teenagers who found hope in something larger than themselves, who discovered that their lives meant more than their circumstances. But he couldn't explain that to someone who thought numbers mattered more than faces.

Beckwith's dismissiveness wasn't unique. Baker heard it again the following week in the common room when his hallmate mentioned a campus Bible study. "Oh right," someone snorted, "the God squad meets on Thursday nights." Eyes rolled. Conversations shifted with practiced efficiency, as if faith were a minor embarrassment best ignored.

It was the same response he'd gotten when he'd quoted German Lutheran pastor Dietrich Bonhoeffer in his ethics seminar—that particular passage about costly grace versus cheap grace that had struck him so powerfully during lectures. Professor Beckwith had offered a tight smile, the kind reserved for well-meaning students who hadn't yet learned to distinguish between philosophy and sentiment. "Interesting perspective,

Mr. Vaughan," he'd said, his tone pleasant and final. "Though of course Bonhoeffer's work is more devotional than philosophical in the rigorous sense." The seminar had moved on to the American John Rawls, a philosopher whose ideas didn't carry the taint of the pulpit.

These differing perspectives made Baker question everything about his calling. Late at night in his dorm room, he'd find himself pulling out Wendy's letters, reading her updates about the kids they'd worked with, remembering Milo's transformation. His heart remained convinced that serving God was precisely what he was meant to do—but Yale was making it harder to believe anyone else would understand why.

He called Wendy religiously every Sunday evening, standing in the hallway payphone while his hallmates stumbled back from weekend parties.

"How are you holding up?" she'd ask, and somehow, she always knew when he needed to hear her say, "You're still the same person who changed those kids' lives, Baker. Yale can't take that away from you."

"What about you? How are things going down there?"

"Honestly? I spend most of my time in the library. The social scene is all about football weekends and finding the right fraternity boyfriend. I thought college would feel less . . . small." She hesitated. "I miss having people who think like we do."

"I keep thinking about the kids from camp," he'd tell her. "About Maria, who couldn't sleep without checking the locks three times. About Jimmy, who'd never had an adult tell him he was proud of him. These people here...they've never met anyone like that."

"That doesn't make them bad people, Baker."

"No, but it makes me feel like I'm speaking a different language."

"You are," Wendy had said gently. "But maybe that's exactly why you're there."

WHEN JANUARY ARRIVED, BAKER waited at Union Station in New Haven like a man expecting salvation. He'd earned his place at Yale on his own—the grades, the test scores, the other credentials. But when Wendy missed the transfer deadline, Oscar had stepped in, pulling strings to get her admitted on scholarship for the spring semester.

Just the night before, he'd found himself rereading her latest letter for the third time, tracing the loops of her handwriting with his finger. Four months of twice-weekly letters and Sunday phone calls had sustained him, but nothing could substitute for her physical presence, her laugh echoing across a room, her hand in his as they walked between classes.

The train pulled into the station with a mechanical sigh, and he scanned each car as passengers disembarked. Then he saw her emerging from the third car carrying a single suitcase and a canvas bag slung over her shoulder, wearing the same confident smile that had gotten her through their first conversation at McGraw. But there was something different about her now, a steely quality around her eyes that spoke to inner conflict resolved, the look of someone who had chosen love over safety.

"How do I look?" she asked, spinning once on the platform with a theatrical flair that didn't quite mask her nervousness. "Ivy League enough?"

"You look like Wendy," he said, kissing her with an intensity that drew smiles from passing travelers. "Thank God."

The relief he felt seeing her was physical—like he'd been holding his breath for four months and could finally exhale. But as they walked toward the taxi stand, he noticed how her eyes swept across the grand architecture of Union Station, taking in the soaring ceilings and marble columns with the careful assessment of someone who'd learned to scan rooms, to understand immediately what was expected of her.

"So," she said as their taxi wound through New Haven streets lined with snow, "catch me up. What do I need to know about surviving this place?"

He'd prepared for this question during the long months of separation but now struggled to find words that would convey both the opportunity and the challenge that awaited her. "The academics are rigorous but manageable. The social stuff is . . . more complicated."

Wendy nodded, watching Gothic Revival buildings pass by the window. "I figured as much. Private school kids from Virginia are one thing. This is a different world entirely."

Her first week at Yale was a master class in adaptation. Baker watched with admiration as she navigated the complex social hierarchies of their residential college, making friends with the same intelligence and genuine interest she brought to everything else. She had an uncanny ability to find common ground with anyone—the daughter of a Supreme Court justice who was homesick for her mother's cooking, the son of a famous novelist who felt trapped by his family's literary legacy, the international students who understood what it meant to constantly translate between worlds.

But he also saw the effort it required. While his classmates had arrived at Yale with the easy confidence of those who'd never questioned their place in elite spaces, Wendy had to work harder to decode the unwritten rules, to understand references to prep schools she'd never heard of, to navigate conversations about family vacations to places that sounded like movie sets.

"It's like learning a new language," she confided to him one evening as they studied together in Sterling Memorial Library. "Not just the academics—that part's fine. But all the social cues, the assumptions about what everyone knows, the way people talk about money without talking about money."

She gestured toward a nearby table where several of their classmates were debating the merits of various summerhouses. "Listen to them. They're not trying to be exclusionary—they genuinely don't realize that not everyone has multiple family homes to choose from. It's not malicious. It's just . . . foreign."

He'd been at Yale long enough to recognize the truth in her observation. "Does it bother you?"

"Not bother, exactly," Wendy said, twirling a pencil between her fingers as she thought. "It's fascinating, actually. Like being an anthropologist studying a culture I'm now part of. But it does make me appreciate home more. The camp, your family, the way people in Lynchburg don't assume anything about anyone."

What impressed him most was how Wendy refused to let the adjustment period diminish her own sense of self. While some students from less privileged backgrounds tried to reinvent themselves at Yale, adopting the mannerisms and attitudes of their wealthier classmates, Wendy remained authentically herself. She talked openly about her father, an ordained minister who'd become a school chaplain, about growing up without much money, about the camp work that had shaped both her and Baker's understanding of their calling.

Her authenticity became magnetic. Within weeks, she'd become the person classmates sought out for genuine conversation, the one who could bridge different social groups because she treated everyone as equally worthy of attention and respect. Baker watched her navigate a dinner party thrown by some of their most prominent classmates, effortlessly moving between conversations about art collections and favorite books, making each person feel heard without ever compromising her own values.

"How do you do it?" he asked her afterward as they walked back to her dormitory.

"Do what?"

"Make it look so easy. The social stuff that is second nature to me—you just…navigate it naturally."

Wendy stopped walking and turned to face him, her breath visible in the cold January air.

"It's not easy. It's just necessary. And besides . . ." She smiled, reaching up to straighten his scarf. "I learned from watching you work with the kids at camp. You meet people where they are, without judgment, and you find something real to connect with. These Yale students aren't that different from troubled teenagers—they're just better dressed, and their problems are more subtle."

The comparison made Baker laugh, but he recognized its wisdom. Wendy had applied the same empathetic intelligence that made her effective with campers to the challenge of fitting in at Yale. She saw past the privileged exteriors to the genuine human needs underneath—the homesickness, the impostor syndrome, the pressure to live up to family expectations.

Her adjustment to the academic demands was smoother. Having switched her focus from premed to education and English literature, Wendy threw herself into her coursework with characteristic determination. She particularly excelled in her education classes, where her camp experience provided real-world context for theoretical discussions about child development and learning styles.

"I keep thinking about the kids we worked with," she told him after a particularly engaging seminar on adolescent psychology. "All these theories we're studying—I can put faces to them. I know what trauma looks like, what resilience looks like, what happens when an adult finally believes in a kid who's never been believed in before."

Her professors quickly recognized that Wendy brought a different perspective to classroom discussions. When the class debated Piaget's stages of cognitive development, she raised her hand: "That's all fine in theory, but I've watched a supposedly 'concrete operational' kid grasp abstract concepts about forgiveness that some adults never understand."

The professor paused, pen hovering over his notes. "Tell us more about that," he said, and the theoretical discussion suddenly became very real.

For the next twenty minutes, Wendy shared stories from camp—examples that challenged neat academic categories and reminded everyone that children were more than textbook case studies. Her classmates leaned forward, engaged in a way they rarely were during theory lectures. Baker watched from across the room, recognizing the same gift she'd shown with troubled teenagers: the ability to make people see what they'd been missing.

BY MARCH, WENDY HAD found her academic rhythm. Late-night study sessions in the common room had turned into genuine friendships—friends who appreciated her authenticity and wisdom, who'd crack up when she compared their philosophy professor to "a camp counselor who takes himself way too seriously." She excelled academically while maintaining her focus on education as a ministry and grew even closer to Baker as they navigated this new world together.

"I'm glad I missed the first semester," she told him one evening as they sat in the common room of her residential college, surrounded by friends engaged in animated discussions about everything from philosophy to politics. "I needed you to go first, to figure out how to stay yourself in this place. Watching you do it gave me permission to do the same."

Looking around the room—at their friends arguing philosophy over Darjeeling tea, at the warm light spilling across worn leather chairs and centuries-old wood paneling—Baker felt a quiet certainty. Whatever came next—seminary, marriage, a life devoted to ministry—Wendy would be beside him. Not because they'd promised it at seventeen, but because Yale had tested that promise and proved it real.

He knew now what he wanted—not because anyone had told him, but because the knowing had crystallized into something unshakeable. While his classmates chased Wall Street internships and his uncle's voice still echoed with expectations of corporate success, Baker had already chosen a different path. Seminary. The Episcopal priesthood. A calling that was entirely, irrevocably his own.

Wendy understood this about him in a way that mattered. She didn't try to convince him or validate what he'd already decided; instead, she asked what passage of scripture he'd been wrestling with that week, as if his conviction were the most natural thing in the world. She was intelligent and grounded, capable of holding her own in any conversation, but more than that—she was his anchor in a world that constantly tried to pull him toward paths he didn't want to follow. She didn't make him believe in his calling. She simply stood beside someone who already did.

She found her own calling too. What started as tutoring fellow students evolved into a passion for education that consumed her with the same intensity Baker felt toward ministry. They claimed their favorite corner table in Sterling Library, where her lesson plans and pedagogy textbooks mixed with his theology volumes, two vocations developing side by side—his to shepherd souls, hers to shape minds.

Summer breaks returned them to Lynchburg to help administer the camp that had united them. At Yale, they frequently remained the sole couple at faculty dinners who'd been raised outside major metropolitan areas—a distinction that bonded them as profoundly as their academic pursuits.

By graduation's approach, Baker's path was inevitable. His professors—the ones who took his seminary plans seriously—encouraged him to apply to Berkeley Divinity School, the Episcopal seminary affiliated with Yale, where he could continue his theological education without leaving New Haven. Oscar had kept his word about not funding seminary, but Baker was certain he could cobble together financial aid and work-study programs to make it possible.

The night before graduation, as they walked through the quad where they'd spent their college journey becoming the people they were meant to be, Wendy stopped beneath the elm trees that had sheltered countless other couples facing uncertain futures.

"So," she said, "we're really doing this. You're going to serve the Lord, I'm going to be a teacher, and somehow, we're going to figure out how to build a life together."

"Are you having second thoughts?"

She reached up to straighten his collar, a gesture so familiar and tender that Baker felt his defenses crumble.

"About you? Never. About whether the world is ready for us? That's a different question."

They graduated from Yale together in May and moved to Hartford that summer, settling into a small rented house. Baker took a job with an insurance company, while Wendy taught elementary school. It was their first taste of building a life together outside the structure of school—modest dinners cooked in their tiny kitchen, evenings spent grading papers and reviewing insurance claims side by side at their small dining table.

Weekends had their own rhythm: grocery shopping Saturday mornings, museum afternoons at the Wadsworth Atheneum, Sunday bike rides along the Connecticut River followed by pancakes. Both were preparing for Baker's return to seminary the following fall—the transition back to academic life, the deepening of his theological formation.

Seven months into their Hartford life, Baker knew it was time. He'd been carrying the ring for weeks, waiting for the perfect moment. Both families would be gathering at the Oaks for their traditional Christmas celebration, but Baker had discreetly arranged something more meaningful. There was no place more fitting than the family home where he'd first fallen in love and no better witnesses than the people who'd watched their relationship bloom.

Baker's heart hammered as he dropped to one knee, his

hands trembling slightly as he produced the small box housing the diamond ring he'd purchased from a stall in Manhattan's Diamond District. The room fell silent. Wendy's eyes widened, her breath catching as he opened the box to reveal a round, brilliant-cut diamond, modest in size but flawless in clarity, afternoon sunlight catching the facets and sending tiny rainbows dancing across her face.

"Wendy," he said, his voice steadier than he'd expected, "I've been practicing this speech for weeks, and I had this whole thing about vocation and partnership and God's plan. But honestly?" He squeezed her hand. "I just really don't want to do any of this without you. So—would this be extraordinary enough? Will you marry me?"

For a heartbeat that felt like forever, she stared at him, her hand flying to her mouth as tears sprang to her eyes. Then she nodded emphatically. "Yes, yes, of course yes!"

George dabbed at his eyes with a handkerchief as Baker slipped the ring onto her finger. Oscar clapped him on the back, and Anne embraced Wendy with maternal warmth, the kind she had lost when she was only eight and still believed would come back. Edward squeezed Baker's shoulder firmly, his jaw tight with emotion, and simply nodded—the kind of wordless approval that said everything a man like him needed to say. Emma broke the emotional tension by grinning at her parents and saying, "Well, Mother, looks like you finally get the daughter you always wanted," causing the whole room to erupt in laughter.

With the engagement official, they set the wedding for the following June. When George confided that marrying them at Christ Church Cathedral would be "a dream come true," their wedding venue was settled, but the timeline would be tight.

Anne hired a highly recommended wedding planner—the Miracle Worker, as she became affectionately known—from New London. Within days, the Vaughan kitchen table disappeared under fabric swatches and florist catalogs, while Wendy wandered through it all with a dazed smile, overwhelmed but grateful as Anne orchestrated everything. Baker and Wendy hardly lifted a finger. Their only task was finding a dance instructor—strictly for Baker's benefit. Wendy was a natural while he moved with the stiff confidence of someone who believes enthusiasm compensates for rhythm.

The ceremony took place in June 1984 at Christ Church Cathedral as George had hoped, unfolding with the stately beauty of Episcopal liturgy performed in a space that had witnessed such moments for over two centuries. The church was filled with the soft murmur of conversation as guests found their seats— a beautiful mixing of their worlds, from McGraw classmates to Wendy's New Hampshire friends, Yale companions alongside Baker's insurance colleagues, and extended family who'd made the journey from Virginia and beyond.

At the start of the rehearsal the evening before, George had made a bet with Oscar: He could walk Wendy down the aisle in his street clothes, circle back through the transept, change into his vestments, and return to the altar to officiate, all in under two minutes. The loser would pay for that night's dinner at the historic Lighthouse Inn in New London. George pulled it off with fifteen seconds to spare.

When the organ began the processional, the congregation rose as one. Emma walked down the aisle first, radiant in dusty-rose silk, followed by Wendy on her father's arm. George looked distinguished in his dark-gray suit, but those who knew him well could see the emotion in his eyes as he prepared to give away his daughter and then officiate at her wedding.

The sight of Wendy walking toward him took Baker's breath away—not just her beauty, though she was luminous in the afternoon light streaming through stained glass, but the certainty in her step, the smile that was meant only for him. This was the girl who'd kissed him in a parking lot while a rooster crowed, who'd supported his calling even when it meant separation, who'd built a life alongside him that honored both their individual gifts and their shared commitment.

When they reached the altar, George performed his quick change with theatrical flair, disappearing behind the carved wooden screen while Emma helped Wendy arrange her train. When he reappeared in his celebrant's vestments, the congregation applauded, delighted by the novelty of seeing the bride's father transform himself into the officiant.

The service proceeded with traditional vows, modified slightly to reflect their shared commitment to ministry. When Baker promised to support Wendy's calling to teach and serve as his partner in faith, his voice carried clearly through the stone nave. When Wendy pledged to stand beside him in whatever parish or ministry God might provide, she spoke with the quiet conviction that had first attracted him during those chapel services at McGraw.

The kiss was appropriately modest for a church ceremony, but Baker held Wendy's face in his hands for just a moment longer than custom required, whispering, "I love you" against her lips before they turned to face their gathered family and friends as husband and wife.

The reception on the church grounds was a masterpiece of Anne's planning and the Miracle Worker's execution. Long tables covered in white linens were arranged under a striped tent that somehow looked like it belonged in the English countryside. Centerpieces of white hydrangeas and roses were interspersed with hurricane lamps that would provide soft light as the evening progressed.

Oscar's date proved to be entertainment in herself—an aspiring actress from Manhattan whose dress might have been appropriate for a nightclub but seemed wildly out of place at a church wedding. She spent much of the cocktail hour posing for photos with anyone who had a camera, apparently under the impression that this was some sort of audition.

"Is she famous?" one of Wendy's Yale friends asked Emma during the receiving line.

"Only in her own mind," Emma replied diplomatically.

The first dance remained exactly as Baker had practiced it—mechanical precision that bore no resemblance to actual dancing but somehow worked because Wendy followed his lead with such grace that they looked almost elegant together. Anne's commentary—"He's never learned to dance, has he?"—became part of the wedding lore, repeated with fondness for years afterward.

The toasts were memorable for their variety and affection. Edward spoke with lawyerly precision about the qualities that made a marriage successful while also being genuinely moved by watching his son find his calling and his partner. Emma's maid-of-honor speech was witty and warm, full of stories about Baker's teenage years and Wendy's transformation from the new girl at McGraw to the woman who'd helped her brother discover who he was meant to be.

Oscar's toast was predictably focused on Yale connections and future opportunities. Still, he surprised everyone by concluding with genuine warmth, "I may not understand your career choices, but I understand love when I see it. And what you two have is the real thing." Then, with uncharacteristic emotion, he drew forth an envelope that would change everything—a check covering Baker's complete theological education. "Perhaps," he said quietly, "this calling of yours deserves the same investment I'd make in any Vaughan's future."

George's father-of-the-bride speech was the evening's emotional highlight. "When Janet died," he said, his voice steady but soft, "I thought I'd lost the chance to see her dreams live on. But watching my daughter choose a life of service, watching her find a partner who shares her deepest calling to help others—I know Janet would be so proud." By the time he finished, there wasn't a dry eye in the tent.

The evening concluded with sparklers as Baker and Wendy made their way to their vehicle—a borrowed Honda festooned with ribbons and trailing cans courtesy of Baker's college roommates. They would spend their wedding night at the Lighthouse Inn before heading to Cape Cod for a modest honeymoon commensurate with their means.

"How do you feel, Mrs. Vaughan?" Baker asked as they drove away from the church, waving to their guests who'd gathered on the steps to see them off.

"Perfect," Wendy said, settling her hand over his on the gear shift. "Absolutely perfect."

They returned to Hartford after the honeymoon, settling back into married life in their small rental house. Money was tight on their combined salaries, but they were happy in ways that surprised them both, sharing weekend mornings in bed reading different sections of the newspaper aloud to each other.

"Do you ever regret not pursuing something more lucrative?" Baker asked her one Sunday morning as they lay in their narrow bed, sunlight streaming through windows that faced east.

"No," Wendy said without hesitation. "Teaching feels right. And besides, this way we'll both be in the business of helping people—just different kinds of wounds."

The hardest part was watching their college classmates scatter to prestigious positions while they prepared for a different kind of future. Baker's insurance company colleagues were pleasant enough, but their conversations rarely ventured beyond mortgage rates and weekend plans. When former classmates visited, Baker would catch glimpses of lives that might have been—law firm-associate positions, consulting opportunities, the fast track to financial success that Oscar had always envisioned for him.

"Do you think we're making a mistake?" he asked Wendy one evening as they walked home from dinner with a college friend who'd just been promoted to associate at a Manhattan law firm.

"No," she said. "We're making our choice. There's a difference."

Chapter Four

IN SEPTEMBER 1984, THEY MOVED back TO NEW HAVEN, AND BAKER BEGAN his studies at Berkeley Divinity School. Wendy secured a teaching position at a local elementary school, and their lives found a new rhythm in married-student housing near campus. Baker immersed himself in systematic theology and pastoral care courses while Wendy shaped young minds with the same patience and insight she'd once used tutoring fellow undergraduates. Their evenings were spent in their small apartment—Baker studying for ordination exams while Wendy graded papers and planned lessons.

It wasn't the life Oscar had imagined for his nephew, but it was precisely the life Baker and Wendy had chosen together. They talked about the future constantly—his eventual ordination, perhaps a parish in New England where she could continue teaching, having children of their own someday. Baker could picture it clearly: Wendy organizing youth programs while he preached from the pulpit, their own children growing up in the warmth of church fellowship, decades of baptisms and Confirmations and steady pastoral care that would outlast them both.

"You know what Professor Wilson tells us?" Baker said one evening as they walked through campus, his arm around Wendy's shoulders. "He says the best sermons come from pastors who understand that preaching isn't performance—it's conversation. You're not trying to impress people with your theology. You're trying to help them hear what God might be saying in the middle of their actual lives."

Wendy smiled up at him. "That's what I love about you. You don't just want the collar. You want the calling."

By spring of Baker's first year, Wendy was pregnant. When the ultrasound revealed a son, they settled on the name Jack—after John Davenport, the founder of New Haven—and bought a used crib from another seminary couple whose kids had outgrown it. Baker would put his hand on Wendy's growing belly, feel the baby kick, and think, *This is what grace looks like.* A wife he loved, a calling that made sense, a son on the way. Everything he'd worked for, everything he'd hoped for, finally coming together.

The pregnancy had been uneventful until the final weeks. Halfway through Baker's second year at Berkeley Divinity School— with the finish line in sight, the nursery painted, the name chosen, their future as parents and partners in ministry within reach— everything changed. She woke him at three in the morning, two weeks before her due date. Her hand on his shoulder was gentle but insistent. "Baker. My head hurts. Really hurts. And I'm seeing spots."

He was fully awake in seconds, helping her dress, grabbing the bag they'd packed weeks ago. By the time they reached Yale-New Haven Hospital, her blood pressure was climbing past numbers Baker didn't know were possible. The nurses moved with a practiced urgency that felt both reassuring and terrifying. He held her hand in the antepartum unit while a doctor explained terms like *preeclampsia* and *progression to eclampsia* and *emergency cesarean,* and Wendy squeezed his fingers and said, "It's going to be fine. We're going to meet Jack." He believed her because the alternative was unthinkable. The surgery began within the hour. Neither she nor their son survived it.

God became a word that meant nothing.

BAKER WITHDREW FROM SEMINARY that fall. The idea of standing in a pulpit and speaking about God's plan when Wendy was dead seemed impossible. He needed distance from everything that reminded him of the calling he could no longer trust.

The house still smelled like her lotion—something with lavender that she'd rubbed on her swollen belly every night. Baker stood in the doorway that first evening, his hand on the knob, unable to step inside. When he finally did, he moved through the rooms like a trespasser. The nursery door was closed. He'd painted it himself three weeks ago, a soft gray-blue that Wendy said looked like early morning. He didn't open it.

He slept on the couch. The bedroom was impossible—her pillow, the maternity clothes folded on the chair, the stack of baby-name books on her nightstand with sticky notes marking the pages. He'd wake at two, at four, at five thirty, his neck cramped, and for three or four seconds he wouldn't remember. Then it would come back, not like a wave but like a weight, something that pressed down on his chest until he had to sit up just to breathe. The answering machine on the coffee table blinked with twenty-three messages, then thirty-one, then forty-six. He didn't listen to any of them. Students from Yale. People from church. His advisor. Wendy's hospital care providers.

He ate when his body insisted—crackers straight from the box, peanut butter scraped onto a spoon. He showered when he couldn't stand his own smell anymore. On the fifth day, or maybe the seventh, he walked past the nursery and found the door standing open. He didn't remember opening it. The crib was assembled, the mobile hanging above it with its felt elephants and moons. On the changing table, a stack of newborn diapers. Impossibly small. He'd bought them on sale, pleased with himself for thinking ahead. He closed the door and sat on the floor in the hallway until the light changed, and he realized hours had passed.

OSCAR PHONED A FRIEND and got Baker an interview at McCann Erickson in New York. Oscar had always been good at that—moving through the city's creative circles with an ease Baker envied, maintaining friendships that seemed unburdened by the complications Baker associated with intimacy. Everything transpired in a hurry. Within two weeks, Baker found himself on a train to New York, watching his reflection in the window and wondering who this person was who'd said yes without the slightest hesitation.

He found a studio apartment in Brooklyn Heights—far enough from Midtown that the commute felt like penance, close enough that he could blame traffic when he stayed late at the office. The neighborhood's tree-lined streets and brownstones reminded him uncomfortably of the life he'd abandoned, so he spent as little time there as possible.

The first year at McCann was a blur of fluorescent-lit nights and coffee gone cold in Styrofoam cups. Baker discovered that grief, if sufficiently ignored, could be converted into something the agency valued: relentless productivity. He arrived before dawn, when the streets still smelled of yesterday's rain and truck exhaust, and left long after the cleaning crews had emptied the wastebaskets and dimmed the lights. Eighteen-hour days became his anesthetic, each campaign brief a small salvation, each deadline a reason not to think about the empty apartment.

There was an irony he recognized but refused to examine: He had once tried to save souls, and now he sold desire. Yet both required the same fundamental skill—the ability to make people believe. At Yale, he had crafted sermons to transform hearts; at McCann, he crafted copy to transform purchasing decisions. The mechanics were identical: identify the need, speak to the longing, offer redemption. A bar of Ivory soap promised purity. A Coca-Cola promised belonging. He had traded one gospel for another, and if the new one rang hollow, at least it demanded nothing of his devastated faith.

His colleagues noticed his talent before they noticed his emptiness. Baker had an instinct for the emotional architecture of desire, could sense exactly which words would lodge in a consumer's mind like a hymn half remembered. He won accounts. He impressed clients. He became, within two years, someone the senior partners watched with interest. But the competence was a shell, and he knew it. Late at night, alone in his office with the Manhattan skyline reduced to a geometry of lit windows, he sometimes felt like a man performing an elaborate magic trick— making everyone believe he was present when he had actually disappeared the night Wendy died.

The work gave him what faith no longer could: problems with solutions, effort that produced results. He'd once believed his calling was unshakeable—the kind of faith that survives doubt, the kind of commitment forged through years of discernment and practice. But that faith hadn't survived watching Wendy's breath grow shallow, hadn't survived holding his stillborn son, hadn't survived the crushing silence when he'd begged God for answers and heard nothing. And if he was hardening into someone he wouldn't have recognized three years earlier, someone who could discuss market penetration without flinching at the language of invasion—well, that person was at least functional. The man he'd been before, the one who'd believed in divine purpose and redemptive suffering, had been utterly useless when it mattered most.

These early years had the quality of a long commute—necessary, forgettable, measured in increments too small to notice until suddenly you'd arrived somewhere distant from where you'd begun. He dated occasionally, brief encounters that felt like performing a role he'd forgotten the lines to, and he always ended them before they could ask why he kept his wedding ring in his desk drawer. When his boss suggested he use some of his accumulated vacation days, Baker found himself researching places Wendy had never mentioned wanting to visit, destinations that held no ghosts of her preferences.

In the outside world, Wendy existed as a carefully guarded silence—a narrative void that colleagues instinctively respected. Those who discovered fragments of her story through whispered background checks or Oscar's occasional oblique references never dared broach the subject, creating an unspoken professional boundary that Baker both cultivated and appreciated. His reticence was so complete, so meticulously maintained, that her memory became less a wound and more a sealed archive, filed away in the same methodical manner he approached his advertising campaigns—compartmentalized, controlled, utterly inaccessible.

OVER THE NEXT TWENTY-FIVE years, he built a life of polished surfaces: great pitches, successful campaigns, the cynical art of selling desire while feeling none himself. The boy who'd once helped troubled teenagers find hope became a master at manipulating desires, crafting messages that made luxury sedans seem essential and breakfast cereals feel like pathways to happiness. There was bitter poetry in it: using the same empathy that had once served broken kids to exploit the insecurities of suburban families.

Clios and Caples decorated his office walls, showcasing his talent for selling everything from fast food to financial services. Industry publications featured his campaigns, and headhunters frequently called with offers from competing agencies. Baker had found his niche in the machinery of American consumption, and he was very, very good at it.

Three years after Wendy died, he took a vacation to Puerto Escondido in Mexico and met Michelle—a refugee from a failed marriage. What began as a holiday fling became a shared life spanning two decades. They moved in together without discussion of marriage or God, a quiet compromise that Baker told himself he could live with. He'd abandoned his calling; living in sin seemed like a minor transgression by comparison. She never asked about the priesthood he'd left behind, and he never mentioned that he still sometimes felt the weight of that broken vow.

There were moments over the years—a Christmas Eve when they passed a church and he felt the pull, a conversation at a dinner party about meaning and purpose that left him sleepless—when he'd tested the edges of that old wound. Once, maybe six years in, he'd slipped into the back of an Episcopal church during a Sunday service. He'd lasted ten minutes before the liturgy felt like accusation rather than invitation, and he never went back. Michelle noticed his mood that evening but didn't ask, and he was grateful for her incuriosity.

By his late forties, he'd become the creative director that young Turks wanted to impress and account executives fought to work with. The Brunswick Pharmaceuticals campaign remained one of his most successful—and most haunting. Their new antidepressant was struggling against established competitors despite clinical trials showing comparable efficacy. The brief was simple: make people believe they needed this particular salvation.

He and his colleagues spent weeks with prospective consumers, listening to middle-aged women describe their silent desperation—the weight of unfulfilled dreams, the exhaustion of holding families together, the way happiness felt like something that happened to other people. He heard their voices crack as they talked about feeling invisible, forgotten, inadequate.

Something in those breaking voices haunted him. The same vulnerability he'd once recognized in troubled teenagers at camp, the same rawness he'd learned to meet with patience rather than solutions. Before everything fell apart.

The campaign he created was incredibly effective. Instead of using clinical language about serotonin uptake, he developed "The Life You're Missing"—a series of spots featuring women just like the ones he'd focus-grouped but transformed. Not suddenly joyful, which would have appeared fake, but steadily confident. Able to laugh at their children's jokes again. Present for their own lives.

The tagline was classic Baker: "Don't let your life happen without you."

Brunswick's new antidepressant quickly became the fastest-growing launch in pharmaceutical history. The campaign received multiple awards and led to his promotion to senior creative director. But late at night, alone in his corner office, he sometimes wondered about those women from the studies—whether those who couldn't afford the medication were still waiting for their lives to start, still believing the problem was inside them rather than the world that had taught them they weren't enough.

It was a ministry inverted with surgical precision. He'd taken their pain, repackaged it as a product solution, and sold it back to them at a premium. The success should have felt like vindication, but instead, it gnawed at him—a persistent guilt he couldn't shake. He found himself working later, drinking more, avoiding the mirror in his bathroom every morning. The promotion came with a substantial raise and stock options in parent company IPG, but also with the growing suspicion that he'd become very good at something that was slowly eating him alive.

For more than a decade, they'd made the annual pilgrimage to Lynchburg. He'd warned Michelle before they drove down—his parents were dedicated Episcopalians, both lay ministers who'd served on the vestry for years, and the last thing he needed was them probing about his abandoned calling. He'd asked them in advance to keep things light, to avoid religion entirely. They honored his request, focusing instead on Michelle's career, her family background, even some nosy inquiries about where she shopped. They particularly enjoyed hearing about her latest project, New York City's High Line Park.

He'd noticed she could entertain herself at the homestead by examining his family's antique furniture collection, running her manicured fingers along the grain of the George I walnut tallboy, casually asking about its provenance. She'd linger by the flame-veneered and Morado-banded bureau cabinet, opening drawers with theatrical care as if testing their smoothness, then mentioning how perfectly such a piece would anchor a formal dining room. At the antique Basque fleur-de-lis marquetry armoire, she'd step back with her arms crossed, head tilted like a curator, murmuring about "museum quality" and "what Sotheby's would say." He sensed she was cataloging them for some future purpose, perhaps imagining them in a larger home she expected him to provide eventually. If it doesn't happen, her expression seemed to say, I'm doomed to mediocrity.

During dinner conversations, she would steer the talk toward estate planning with practiced elegance. "It's so important to preserve family heritage," she'd say, eyes drifting meaningfully toward the sideboard. "Some pieces are just too significant to leave to chance." He ignored her obsession with his parents' belongings because he knew they'd go to Emma, and no amount of lobbying or obsessing would ever change that. She knew that too, but year after year, she kept trying, dropping hints and making her case, hoping to break through his wall of unwavering loyalty to family. The pattern only reinforced her fixation on tangible security, on things that couldn't abandon you.

AROUND BAKER'S FIFTEENTH YEAR at McCann, Oscar called from his home office a block from Gracie Mansion in Manhattan. They'd fallen into a pattern of quarterly check-ins—brief, cordial phone calls, carefully avoiding anything too personal. Despite living in the same city, they rarely saw each other face-to-face. So when

Oscar said, "Lunch at the Four Seasons. My treat. One o'clock," Baker knew something was different.

A day later—or was it two?—Baker arrived to find his uncle already seated in the Grill Room, a bottle of Château Margaux breathing on the table—the kind of wine Oscar reserved for major victories or successful portfolio exits.

"There he is," Oscar said, standing to embrace him. "The creative genius himself. I've been hearing about your pharmaceutical campaign from everyone. It's the talk of my investor circles. Clio-worthy work, Baker. Truly exceptional."

They settled into their seats, and Oscar poured the wine with ceremonial care. "You know what I love about this? You took everything I tried to teach you about business—understanding what people want, delivering what they need—and applied it brilliantly. That's not manipulation; that's value creation."

Baker took a long sip of wine, letting the Margaux's complexity distract him from the tightness in his chest.

"I have to ask," Oscar continued, leaning forward with genuine curiosity. "Do you ever think about what would have happened if you'd listened to me from the start? If you'd skipped the whole seminary detour?"

"Sometimes," Baker said quietly.

"You'd be running your own agency by now. SVP at minimum." Oscar raised his glass. "But better late than never, right? You found your way here eventually. That's what matters."

Baker clinked glasses with his uncle, watching the wine catch the light. Oscar saw a nephew who'd finally embraced his proper calling. He had no idea he was toasting a man who lay awake at night wondering if he'd sold his soul for a Clio and a corner office.

"To finding your true calling," Oscar said.

Baker drank deeply and said nothing.

The guilt followed him home to his Upper East Side apartment, where Michelle would find him staring out windows, distracted during conversations, present but not really there. After twenty years together, she'd grown accustomed to his work consuming him, but this was different—a restlessness that no amount of success seemed to satisfy. He suggested couples therapy, recognizing that his emotional distance was affecting them both; she waved it off and suggested a bigger apartment. He wanted to talk about what was wrong; she wanted to renovate the kitchen.

The unraveling began when he felt God's gravitational pull again. It wasn't dramatic in the conventional sense, but it was transformative—a persistent sense that he'd built his life around a hollow center that had expanded into a crater. All the awards and promotions were elaborate ways of drowning out the voice he'd been trying not to hear. Michelle seemed to have no framework for this kind of spiritual crisis. He knew she saw him turning moody and philosophical, qualities that didn't fit the polished image he'd spent years crafting.

That's when they started living separate lives under the same roof. He took his golf clubs to Pawleys Island with three college buddies. He played lights-out golf and came home unchanged. She took her single girlfriends on a Bahamas getaway where they gently reminded her she'd invested twenty-three years in this relationship. "You deserve someone who won't suddenly decide to throw everything away," one friend said over cocktails. "All this searching—where does it leave you?" They talked about the life she and Baker had built, the security, the comfort of knowing what tomorrow looked like. Michelle found herself wondering if she had to choose:

the tangible life they'd created or Baker's restless journey toward something she couldn't see or touch. Designer handbags don't wake up one day and decide they need to find themselves. The pattern repeated itself through Labor Day weekends and winter getaways: two people running from the same problem in opposite directions.

Baker came back unchanged. Michelle came back as someone else—silk instead of pima cotton, cashmere instead of merino, carrying a purse with logo hardware visible from outer space, and suddenly obsessed with price tags. She began quietly looking for what came next, though she never told Baker she was already planning her exit.

When their relationship became Manhattan gossip in 2011, he finally understood that running away from your calling doesn't make it disappear. It just makes you a costly kind of lost, and all those years of building other peoples' dreams had left him with nothing he actually wanted to keep.

Chapter Five

THE APARTMENT WAS STILL MOSTLY EMPTY—JUST THE LEATHER armchair he'd splurged on at a consignment shop and a walnut coffee table one of the Trinity parishioners had insisted he take after her husband passed. Minor concessions to the possibility of staying. Baker's mind kept circling back to his old life, trying to pinpoint the rare moments that had actually felt real amid all the performance.

He walked to the window and studied the Boise Front, where Shafer Butte and neighboring peaks like Mores Mountain and Deer Point caught the last light of evening. Unlike his previous New York view of stacked-glass lives, these mountains offered something profound—a patient, ancient silence that transformed urgent questions into quiet contemplations. They had witnessed countless human struggles, standing resolute and unchanged, suggesting that his current crisis was but a momentary ripple against their timeless landscape.

Every morning, he grounded himself in the natural world: hawks circling on invisible thermals, Canada geese honking their way south, magpies chattering along elm-lined streets. Some evenings, he'd drive into the foothills, watching the city spread beneath him—small enough to comprehend, large enough to hold infinite possibilities. From this elevated perspective, his apartment seemed tiny, his problems manageable, his future unwritten. In these moments of solitude, a familiar voice whispered at the edges of consciousness, asking if he was finally ready to listen again.

He'd heard that voice before—most clearly in the months after leaving Yale as an undergrad, when Oscar had hoped Baker would follow him into business, but Baker had chosen seminary instead. At twenty-three, starting seminary had felt like trusting what he'd sensed since he was thirteen, like choosing faithfulness over the comfortable future his family had mapped out for him. He never expected it to be hard. Nothing had ever been hard for Baker.

But he couldn't finish. Wendy died halfway through seminary. She never complained about the rigors of Yale, but her death broke something in him that couldn't be fixed. He abandoned his quest for the priesthood, fleeing to Madison Avenue, where he'd spent so many years he'd lost count, building the very life he'd once rejected.

Now, at fifty-two, he wondered if this quiet voice in the Idaho foothills was offering him something he didn't deserve: a second chance to complete what he'd started. The calling hadn't died when Wendy did—he had simply stopped listening, let Oscar's vision win by default, spent twenty-five years proving he could succeed in that world even as it hollowed him out. Perhaps learning to hear that voice again, to trust it despite the years he'd wasted ignoring it, was exactly the kind of redemption God specialized in: taking what seemed irretrievably broken and asking if he was finally ready to let it be made whole. But the letting—that was the choice only Baker could make.

AFTER HIS FIRST SUNDAY service, Margaret Thompson had approached him and offered genuine spiritual guidance through her husband, Karl. A week had passed. Now these reflections just grew, and Baker felt, for the first time since arriving in Boise, like he'd found a bridge between his past and whatever future lay ahead.

But tonight, he had a phone call to make. He pulled out the piece of paper Margaret had given him with her husband's contact information. After tonight's flood of memories, Baker knew he needed to talk to someone—and Margaret had seemed to sense that.

He dialed the number. After three rings, a warm voice answered. "Thompson residence."

"Bishop Thompson? This is Baker Vaughan. Your wife, Margaret, suggested I call you."

"Ah Baker. Yes, Margaret mentioned she'd met you at Trinity. She was quite impressed. She said you had the look of someone wrestling with angels. Please call me Karl. How can I help you?"

"I'm not sure where to begin," Baker said, settling into his desk chair. "I think I need to talk to someone about finding my way back to ministry. It's been…complicated."

"Yes, complicated," Karl replied with what sounded like a knowing chuckle. "In my experience, the Lord seems to prefer the long way around with most of us. Why don't we meet tomorrow afternoon? We can talk properly then."

A feeling he hadn't experienced in years washed over him. Hope. Tentative but real.

"Thank you. I'd like that very much."

Karl and Baker met for coffee at Dawson Taylor downtown. The shop drew a wider cross section of Boise than its rival across the street, which catered more to attorneys and legislators during the short January-to-April session. Baker had become a regular at Dawson. The staff knew him by name.

Karl stood out when he entered. He dressed like an unpretentious Western cleric: blue Wranglers paired with a clerical shirt and blazer—the most arresting figure in the room. He ordered decaf lattes for both of them, explaining with a wry smile that the church administrator had put her foot down about his caffeine intake. Baker warmed to the man before they'd even sat down.

Beyond their age difference, Karl was Father Phil's opposite in every way. He radiated genuine joy in his work and life. Though slightly below average height, he carried himself with such confidence that he seemed larger than he was. For a man approaching eighty, he moved with surprising energy. His ruddy cheeks, neatly trimmed soul patch, and bright blue eyes sparkled with mischief. Where Phil intimidated, Karl welcomed. Within minutes, Baker felt as though he was conversing with someone who had known him for years. After extolling Margaret and her vocal prowess, he articulated his aspiration to assume holy orders. Karl exhibited no discernible surprise because he'd been tipped off by his wife.

"Tell me about when you first felt called," Karl said, leaning back in his chair with the attentiveness of someone who took such matters seriously.

He described the bike ride in Lynchburg, the warmth in his chest, the certainty that had never quite left him even after all those years in advertising. Karl listened without interrupting, occasionally nodding as if recognizing something familiar in Baker's story.

"And you walked away from it," Karl said when Baker finished—not a question or a judgment, just an observation.

"I did." Baker's voice was quiet. "Oscar eventually paid for seminary—as a special gift when I married my high school sweetheart, Wendy. I actually went. Started the program."

"So what happened?" Karl asked. "Why didn't you finish?"

Baker looked down at his coffee. "Things changed. Life happened." He shifted in his seat. "I just . . . couldn't continue."

Karl studied him for a moment. "That's a pretty significant decision to make without a really good reason."

"There was a reason." Baker's jaw tightened slightly. "I just wasn't ready anymore. The timing wasn't right."

"The timing wasn't right," Karl repeated, his tone gentle but probing. "You had a calling strong enough to pursue it, family support, a wife beside you. And then suddenly the timing wasn't right?"

Baker met his eyes briefly, then looked away. "Sometimes things don't work out the way you plan."

"Baker." Karl leaned forward slightly. "I've been a pastor for nearly forty years. I know what evasion sounds like."

The silence stretched between them. Baker's hands tightened around his coffee cup, his knuckles whitening. "I appreciate your concern, Karl. But some things are . . . difficult to talk about."

Karl nodded slowly, not pushing further but clearly understanding that something painful lay beneath Baker's careful words. "Fair enough," he said quietly. "But whatever happened back then—it's still with you. That much is clear."

Baker didn't respond, just stared into his coffee as if it might offer some escape from the conversation. He exhaled slowly, his shoulders dropping an inch. He set the cup down carefully, as if releasing something he'd been gripping too tightly, and the small gesture seemed to settle something in him—a quiet acknowledgment that Karl had chosen mercy over interrogation.

"I'm not trying to discourage you. I'm trying to make sure you understand what you're asking for." Karl's expression softened. "But I'll tell you this: Someone who's lived another life first, who's tasted success and found it hollow—that person often makes a better pastor than the young seminarian who's never questioned anything."

Baker felt tension release in his chest. "So you think it's possible? At fifty-two?"

"Possible? Yes. The diocese has processes for discernment, for testing vocations. You'd need to meet with the Commission on Ministry, go through psychological evaluations, complete seminary if you haven't already." Karl paused, studying Baker's face. "But before any of that, you need to answer one question: Are you running toward the collar or away from advertising?"

The question landed like a stone in still water.

"Both, maybe," Baker admitted. "Is that disqualifying?"

"Not necessarily. Just means you need to be honest about your motives. This calling isn't a refuge from failure, Baker. It's a calling to service. If you're here because you couldn't hack it in New York, you'll discover pretty quickly that ministry will chew you up and spit you out." Karl's smile returned, warmer now. "But if you're here because you finally stopped running from what you were always meant to do—well, that's a different story entirely."

Karl paused, a hint of mischief in his smile.

"And aside from seminary, there's another consideration," Karl said, leaning forward slightly. "Finding a new wife. I know that might sound old fashioned, but in my experience, a married clergyman has certain advantages. The congregation relates to you differently when you have a partner. They see you as someone who understands their struggles with relationships, family, the everyday challenges of building a life with another person.

"Plus," he chuckled, "the church matrons will stop trying to set you up with their nieces."

Baker nearly choked on his coffee. "A wife? I . . . I hadn't thought about dating again."

"I'm not saying you need to rush into anything," Karl said gently. "But you're still a young man with a lot to offer. And if God is calling you back to ministry, he might also be preparing someone to walk that path with you. Just something to pray about."

Baker didn't know if Karl was right about any of it—the calling, the path, the possibility of someone to share them with. But he knew he was tired of theorizing. So he took Karl's advice: stop trying to figure everything out, and just start doing the work.

In the weeks that followed, he made the parish office his second home. The scent of burnt coffee that had been sitting on the burner for hours mingled with the musty fragrance of antiquated hymnals and threadbare carpet. The cramped space hummed with subdued activity. Filing cabinets lined one wall, their metal drawers slightly ajar and stuffed with documents. A vintage photocopier clunked softly in the corner. Sunlight permeated the tall windows, casting geometric patterns across a desk laden with bulletins, volunteer schedules, and a ceramic mug proclaiming I'M NOT A MIRACLE WORKER, BUT I CAN GET YOU A FREE COFFEE.

Dorothy Henley, a woman in her fifties, had already heard about Baker through Margaret Thompson and others—the man who'd appeared at Sunday service like an answer to prayer. When he asked about volunteer opportunities, she practically leaped from her swivel chair, her eyes lighting up behind wire-rimmed spectacles.

"If you're willing to help, I'd be delighted to put you to work immediately!"

She made him a volunteer receptionist, a role that proved far more important than it initially appeared. Baker wasn't just answering phones and greeting visitors—he was the trusted gatekeeper maintaining order amid chaos. His daily stream of well-meaning visitors ranged from the chronically homeless to Herman the postman, who expressed his theological disapproval through theatrical sighs and pointed glances whenever he delivered mail addressed to Trinity's only female priest. The look Herman would give Baker— eyebrows raised, mouth slightly open—seemed to say *You've got to be kidding me* before he folded the letter back into the rubber-banded bundle and dropped it on Baker's desk. Then there were the geographically confused Catholics whose own cathedral sat just three blocks north, separated only by low-rise office buildings and a few homes that owners hadn't turned over to developers.

One day, a man with the unforgettable name of Freddy Cappuccino—a stucco contractor from neighboring Nampa whom Baker could spot as Catholic from several rosary lengths away—arrived at the office and refused to believe he was at the wrong church. Baker escorted him into the nave to have a look around. Finding no saints in picture or statue form, Freddy pressed his hands together in prayer, bowed to Baker, crossed himself, and espressoed out through the east transept door.

Immersing himself in Boise's church life gave Baker more time to consider what he was gaining out West and less time to dwell on what he'd left behind back East. Once a week, between receptionist duties, he prepared hundreds of sack lunches— applesauce cups, Ritz peanut butter crackers, granola bars, and bottled drinks purchased at the local Costco. He offered lunch to anyone who asked, making no judgments about their need.

He became quite friendly with the regulars, including Glenn, a middle-aged sanitation worker who kept Baker updated on his progress with his sit-ups. First two hundred, then three hundred, then four hundred. By six months, Glenn had reached eight hundred—an impressive milestone. Curious about the record, Baker discovered that Mark Pfeltz of Baltimore had gutted out forty-five thousand and five sit-ups in fifty-eight and a half hours back in 1985, setting a Guinness World Record. When Baker shared this with Glenn, his response was priceless: "Just give me some time, bro."

Baker was well positioned to keep track of the pulse of Trinity's daily life. Callers couldn't directly reach a staff member unless they had that person's cell number. When they contacted the switchboard, Baker would assess the inquiry and, if he couldn't handle it himself, refer them to the church administrator or, if it was a pastoral care issue, to one of the clergy members.

One morning, the phone rang with a call from the 906 area code. A young woman with a slight accent introduced herself as a performance artist and student at Finlandia University in Hancock, Michigan, somewhere on the Upper Peninsula. *Finnish?* Baker wondered, remembering how hard it was to detect specific languages—he'd once mistaken Portuguese for Dutch on an Air Portugal flight. Better keep that guess to himself. Though he itched to handle the call personally, Canon Priest Leonard Moore was in his office, so Baker transferred the call to him. The extension light showed Leonard was on the line for thirty solid minutes. When the call ended, Leonard walked briskly toward Baker with news that only a recently transplanted New Yorker like Baker could fully appreciate.

The caller was indeed Finnish, working on her master's thesis about what motivates Americans to marry, considering that Finland had the world's lowest marriage rate. Her solution? Marry fifty different people, animals, and objects across all fifty states. Fifteen months in, she'd already wed a lobster fisherman, an Elvis impersonator, a female bartender, two cowboys, an oil rig, a cow, and forty others.

Idaho, Wyoming, and Montana remained. Calling from Salt Lake City, she had somehow found Trinity despite Episcopal churches not ranking highly in Google's "churches in Boise" results. How she discovered them remained a mystery.

The conversation about the Finnish student sparked Leonard to share his own spiritual journey. Over coffee, he filled Baker in. Born in Lambeth to teacher parents, he'd had an "idyllic" childhood—good stock, good education, raised Catholic. He left that church in his twenties: the guilt, the stance on LGBT rights, the belief that animals lacked souls, the rigid certainty, the prohibition against questions.

Leonard sought approval to participate from his supervisor, Phil, and Bishop Nicholas Gallagher, the current bishop of Idaho, before responding to Ulla, now known in most states as the "Finnish bride." Episcopalians are known to be progressive, of course: the denomination had spent decades cultivating a reputation for theological flexibility, social justice commitments, and a general willingness to let a thousand flowers bloom within the garden of faith.

The bishop enthusiastically agreed. Phil, not so much.

Gallagher, whose opinion was the only one that mattered, was precisely the sort of ecclesiastical leader who saw a Finnish performance artist's unconventional marriage project not as a threat to doctrine but as an opportunity for the church to demonstrate its embrace of human creativity and connection. For Leonard, who had fled the Catholic Church's suffocating certainties and prohibitions, the bishop's enthusiastic approval felt almost inevitable—here was institutional religion that didn't flinch at boundary-pushing, that trusted its priests to exercise judgment and imagination rather than merely enforce rules from on high.

The theatrical wedding, in the bishop's view, was exactly the kind of quirky, inclusive, boundary-expanding work that modern Episcopalianism aspired to: faith in service of human flourishing rather than faith as an instrument of control. In this sense, Leonard's path from Lambeth Catholic guilt to Idaho Episcopal openness had led him to precisely the right denomination, at precisely the right moment, to say yes to something wonderfully strange.

Baker asked Leonard if she had found her Idaho "groom." She hadn't. His pulse quickened. He practically begged Leonard to volunteer his services, framing it as theater, as quirky creativity, as exactly the kind of imaginative project that fell into his wheelhouse and the church needed. Leonard, who'd worked in theater in North Yorkshire at fifteen, needed little convincing. But Baker's insistence had an edge to it, a need that went beyond curiosity.

A real wedding was the last thing Baker wanted now. A theatrical one, though—one where everyone knew it was performance—felt like a free pass. A chance to see if ritual could move him, even without faith behind it.

Over the next few days, Baker threw himself into the planning with unusual intensity. When Ulla called about venues, she confessed she'd tried eight Boise churches before searching "the holy trinity in Boise" and striking gold. Baker cold-called Boise State's sports information director about using the football stadium and its iconic blue turf. The SID reluctantly agreed, on the condition that it be the following Sunday afternoon. There was nothing he could do about the intersquad scrimmage happening simultaneously.

The field was busy—players scrimmaging while Baker met his bride for the first time. The late afternoon sun cast long shadows across the artificial surface, and the distant mountains provided a dramatic backdrop that would make any filmmaker jealous. She was already in character: a tall, striking woman in her thirties with platinum-blonde hair braided with wildflowers, a long white dress embroidered with Celtic fertility symbols—spirals, wheat sheaves, and intertwined serpents that caught the light as she moved. Her expression remained stoically unchanged, even when Baker tried to strike up a conversation "offstage," her pale-blue eyes fixed on some distant point as if channeling an ancient Norse goddess.

Baker watched her, fascinated and slightly unnerved. She'd committed completely to the artifice, made no apology for the performance. It was, in its way, more honest than anything he'd done in his life.

Leonard moved between them in full vestments—white alb, green stole—adjusting Ulla's veil with one hand while keeping a wary eye on the scrimmaging players behind him. "Magnificent," he murmured, repositioning Baker's borrowed medieval tunic. He was playing this completely straight, treating the blue turf as if it were the nave of a cathedral, sidestepping the occasional errant football with practiced dignity.

The football players didn't mind the ceremony—in fact, several had gathered along the sidelines, sweaty and grinning, shouting encouragement and the occasional bawdy suggestion. The bride's videographer, a serious young man with an expensive camera and paint-splattered jeans, captured compelling action shots with the scrimmaging players in the background, the juxtaposition yielding the caliber of visual poetry that would render her installation thesis worthy.

Leonard had crafted the liturgy, including nearly all the traditional verses. As the familiar words flowed, Baker's curiosity intensified. They'd agreed on the russet potato and Boise State football as wedding rings—Baker's suggestion, absurd but somehow perfect. Leonard lifted them now with ceremonial gravity. "Let these items be a sign of the vows by which this man and this woman have bound themselves to each other."

Why is he doing this? The cameras rolled. Leonard blessed the potato and football with the same gravitas Baker had seen priests use for actual sacraments, and something about the strangeness felt more honest than anything he'd witnessed at the satirical *Tony n' Tina's Wedding* on Broadway. At least there, the paid guests knew it was performance. Ulla wasn't pretending this was real—she was exploring what "real" even meant. But Baker was getting nervous.

He'd volunteered for this role, but now he began to question why. As he stood on the artificial blue turf, the answer crystallized: He was testing whether words still held power when you stripped away everything official. Whether a marriage meant something because the people chose it, not because an institution sanctioned it. Whether the promise mattered more than the paperwork.

And maybe—though this thought made him uncomfortable—he needed to participate in a wedding that couldn't hurt him. A marriage that existed only for art and documentation. Safe. Contained. Controllable in a way real love never was.

The punch line approached.

"In the name of the Sawtooth Mountains and the Frank Church River of No Return Wilderness, I now pronounce you man and wife," Leonard concluded with authority and a slight chuckle.

The declaration of nonmarriage had been made, the Father, the Son, and the Holy Spirit—conspicuously omitted. The absence struck him like a missing stair in darkness. He'd expected it—they'd planned it together—but experiencing it in real time felt hollow. Was that what faith felt like when it left? Not dramatic or painful, just . . . absent? The familiar words replaced with mountains and wilderness, as if geography could substitute for divinity?

AT THE RECEPTION IN the backyard of a hospitable Boise resident—someone a Finn from the town of McCall had recommended, knowing their love for hosting parties—everything appeared authentic: white tablecloths, a three-tiered cake adorned with plastic figurines, and champagne flutes filled with sparkling cider. Ulla maintained her bridal persona, graciously accepting congratulations from the invited guests.

Baker shook hands with a succession of Ulla's art-world contacts and local friends who'd been briefed on the project. "Congratulations," they said, complicit in the fiction. Some played it deadpan, others with a wink. But several, particularly an older woman who worked at the Boise Art Museum, seemed genuinely moved, as if the performance had somehow become real in the doing of it. Baker found himself saying "thank you" over and over, the words feeling stranger each time. He was being congratulated for a marriage that didn't exist, and somehow the congratulations still landed with weight. The videographer kept filming until the camera battery died. Everyone quietly dispersed, leaving wilted strawberries and cake crumbs—debris of a marriage that had never truly begun.

Baker expected Karl to summon him for a conversation about the wedding—perhaps a gentle reprimand about the boundaries of ecclesiastical authority or, at a minimum, some concern about Leonard blessing potatoes in borrowed vestments. Indeed, two days later, Karl invited him for morning coffee at Dawson Taylor, his blue eyes twinkling with what looked suspiciously like amusement.

"So," Karl said, settling into his chair with his decaf latte, "I heard you were married last weekend."

Baker winced. "You heard about that?"

"Baker, everyone heard about it. Leonard's been showing the video to anyone who'll sit still long enough." Karl's smile was warm, not reproachful. "Tell me—why'd you do it?"

The question hung in the air between them. Baker traced the rim of his coffee cup, trying to find words for something he barely understood himself.

"It seemed like a fascinating project. Performance art exploring the meaning of marriage. Everyone knew what it was."

"But you felt something during it," Karl said. It wasn't a question.

Baker looked up sharply. "How did you—?"

"Because you're sitting here looking like a man who's discovered something uncomfortable about himself." Karl leaned forward. "What was it?"

"The omission," Baker said. "Leonard deliberately left out the Trinity. We'd planned it that way, invoking the mountains instead. And when he said it, when he pronounced us married in the name of the wilderness . . ." He paused. "It felt both completely wrong and somehow more honest than half the ceremonies I've witnessed."

Karl was quiet for a long moment, his scholarly face thoughtful. "Do you know what bothered me most about hearing this story? Not that you did it—Leonard's always been theatrical, and God knows the church needs more imagination, not less. What bothered me was learning you insisted on participating in something close to sacrilege."

"I know. It was—"

"No, let me finish." Karl's voice remained gentle but firm. "You begged to participate in a deliberate emptying of a sacrament you're supposedly preparing to administer. You wanted to perform the ritual in the most controlled environment possible—where everyone knew it was theater, where nothing was at stake—to see if anything sacred would show up anyway. Or more likely, to prove it wouldn't. That's not curiosity, Baker. That's a crisis of faith dressed up as performance art."

Baker felt exposed, as if Karl had read him completely and named a truth he'd barely admitted to himself. He looked down at his coffee, unable to meet Karl's eyes.

"You're right," he said quietly. "I wanted to see if it would collapse. If I could strip away everything—the sincerity, the divine authority, the actual commitment—and the ritual would just . . . disintegrate into nothing. Prove it was always just theater." He paused. "Ulla gave me permission to do what I'd been wanting to do anyway. She was honest about the performance. So I could be honest too, in a way. Test it without pretending I believed in it."

"And did it collapse?" Karl asked.

Baker hesitated. "No. That's what scares me."

Karl was quiet for a long moment, studying Baker with those penetrating blue eyes that had seen decades of seminarians wrestle with doubt.

"So you conducted your experiment," Karl said finally. "You tried to profane a sacrament, strip it of sincerity, divine authority, actual commitment, everything that should make it real, and it didn't collapse. Something persisted even when you tried to empty it out." He leaned forward. "Baker, that's not a failure of your test. That's your answer. You wanted to prove it was all theater, and instead you discovered that even when you treat it as theater, even when you bless potatoes on artificial turf with football players tackling each other in the background, something sacred shows up anyway. Whether you call it God or grace or the human need for ritual, it was there. You felt it."

Baker felt the truth of it settle in his chest like a stone. "I tried to prove it was empty," he said quietly, "and now I don't know what to do with the fact that it wasn't."

"Good," Karl said, surprising him. "The ones who know they're not ready are the ones who might actually learn something." He took a sip of his latte. "Now, about your next project—I hear Dorothy wants you to organize the parish directory. Less theology, more telephone numbers. Probably safer territory for now."

Baker laughed despite himself. As he walked back to his apartment that evening, Karl's words stayed with him. *The ones who know they're not ready are the ones who might actually learn something.* For years, he'd approached every challenge with confidence bordering on arrogance. Perhaps unpreparedness for priesthood formed the requisite foundation. But ready to serve in smaller ways? That felt honest. That felt like something he could do.

He didn't have answers yet—not about God, not about vocation, not about what had actually happened on that football field. But he kept showing up at Trinity anyway, answering phones and organizing files and learning the names of parishioners who'd been coming to the same pews for forty years. The work was humble, almost embarrassingly so for someone who'd once imagined himself delivering profound homilies. Yet there was something clarifying about it, about being useful without needing to be brilliant. He stopped trying to figure everything out and started paying attention instead.

Over the following weeks, the Finnish wedding story became just one more example of Baker's growing reputation at Trinity. His involvement had expanded far beyond his receptionist duties, and nowhere was this more evident than at the monthly Second Saturday Lunch, held in honor of Trinity's senior population. He usually wore a freshly ironed Sea Island cotton dress shirt, paired with a freestyle bow tie featuring daffodil, orchid, or martini prints. All the women wanted Baker to be their waiter, but none more than Grace Hamilton, a lady in her nineties of Chinese descent who had spent her formative years in Trinidad and Tobago. She regarded Baker as both a gentleman and a once-in-a-lifetime gift to Trinity.

At these lunches, she greeted Baker and invited him to join her at the table as soon as she arrived. Baker soon realized it was always the same table—truly, her table.

"Baker, my dear, I have a favor to ask of you."

She leaned in slightly to receive his kiss properly, offering her right cheek first and then her left. "But first, would you bring me a fresh cup of coffee?" As Baker left to get it, he could over-hear her telling everyone at the table about her new friend from New York.

When Baker returned with the steaming cup, Grace patted the seat beside her. "Now, about that favor," she said, her eyes twin-kling. "Next month is my great-nephew's wedding in Portland. Would you be my escort? I cannot bear the thought of going alone, and you would make such a distinguished companion."

Baker's expression was kind but apologetic. "Grace, that's so thoughtful of you to ask, but I'm afraid I can't get away right now." He squeezed her shoulder affectionately. "You'll have to tell me all about it when you get back."

Baker didn't play favorites and tried to treat everyone the same way he did Grace, and for the most part, he succeeded. His fellow volunteers couldn't keep pace with him, no matter how hard they tried. But his patience often wore thin with Chef Louise, an Iowa transplant and longtime Boise resident, who had a habit of telling the group the entire menu once—and only once—often with her back to them. If someone dared to ask her again, the capricious Louise, whose empathy filter needed a deep scrubbing, would assume the demeanor of a fractious matriarch.

"Pay attention! I don't have time to repeat myself!"

Baker had first tried to calm her down with charm, but she remained unmoved by Easterners in general and Baker in particular. After three weeks of watching volunteers scatter like startled birds whenever Louise barked instructions, Baker changed tactics.

He found her alone in the kitchen on a Wednesday afternoon, prepping for that week's evening meal. She was chopping onions with the efficiency of someone who'd done it ten thousand times.

"Louise." He waited until she looked up. "I need to apologize."

Her knife paused mid-chop. "For what?"

"Well, I realize I'm a newcomer here, and I feel like we got off on the wrong foot. I just want you to know that my intentions were never meant to undermine your authority—after all, it's your kitchen." He gestured at the industrial stove, the prep stations, the walk-in cooler. "You've been running this operation for—how long?"

"Eleven years." Her tone was wary.

"Eleven years. And I waltz in here acting like I know better."

Louise set down her knife. She studied him with the suspicious attention of someone who'd been patronized before and knew the difference between bullshit and sincerity.

"You really want to know?"

"I do."

"Then stop trying to make me nicer." Her voice was flat. "I'm not nice. I'm efficient. And if people would listen the first time, I wouldn't have to repeat myself."

Baker nodded slowly. "Fair enough. I may have a solution. What if I made sure the other volunteers were actually paying attention before you addressed us?"

Something shifted in Louise's expression—not warmth exactly, but a grudging acceptance. "That might work."

"And if someone misses something, they ask *me*. Then I'll ask *you*. That way you're not repeating yourself."

She didn't seem entirely convinced. "If you say so."

Baker shrugged. "It's your kitchen, Louise. I'm just here to help."

She picked up her knife again, but her shoulders had dropped half an inch. "Alright then. Next week, we're doing chicken and rice. I'll need you on vegetable prep at four-thirty. Sharp."

"Four-thirty sharp," Baker confirmed.

By the following week, the kitchen had a different rhythm. Baker positioned himself as Louise's lieutenant, translating her terse instructions into actionable tasks, making sure volunteers were ready before she spoke. Louise still barked orders, but the edge of frustration had dulled. She even smiled once when Baker correctly anticipated which pot she'd need next.

Father Phil watched Baker's transformation with the careful attention of a territorial animal sensing encroachment. The Finnish wedding had been strange enough, but Phil could dismiss theatrics as harmless eccentricity. What he couldn't dismiss was the way parishioners' faces lit up when Baker entered a room or how conversations naturally gravitated toward him during coffee hour. And now Louise—Louise, who'd made three vestry members cry over the years—was actually listening to him. More than listening: deferring to him.

Phil caught Baker after the Sunday service, while Baker was stacking folding chairs in the parish hall. "Baker. Got a minute?" He didn't wait for an answer. "I've invited some friends to dinner Thursday at the Gem Club. Nothing fancy—hamburger night, actually—but good conversation. You should join us."

"The Gem Club," Baker repeated, clearly surprised by the invitation. "Yes, I'd like that."

"Don't let the name fool you. It's mostly lawyers and businessmen pretending the food justifies the membership fees." Phil smiled in a way that forced a smirk.

The invitation sounded casual enough, but something in Phil's tone made Baker wonder. There was a studied quality to it, as if Phil had been rehearsing. Baker couldn't quite read whether this was an olive branch or something else entirely—some test he didn't know he was taking.

Baker noticed Phil glance at his watch, then at the church calendar on the wall. Whatever Phil's motivation, it clearly wasn't just about breaking bread together.

"Thursday at seven," Phil said, already moving past him. "I'll put your name on the list."

THE GEM CLUB'S DINING room was exactly as Baker had imagined it: sleek chrome fixtures, geometric light installations, tables draped in white polyester linen, chairs upholstered in forgettable burgundy fabric, and white wall-to-wall carpet, full of men who carried themselves like they ran the city. Women were conspicuously absent.

Baker took his seat at the ten-top, nodding as Phil made introductions around the table. Mostly businessmen, a few professionals, someone from the city planning commission. The kind of men who spoke with insider knowledge and easy confidence. The conversation flowed innocuously at first—the new development on the Boise Bench, added parking meters downtown, someone's son getting into law school.

Then the burgers arrived, and so did the real talk. President Obama had ruined everything, apparently. The economy, the country, the very fabric of American life. The men spoke casually, as if this were simply fact, passing the ketchup between declarations of what had been lost. Baker kept his thoughts to himself. All he could focus on was the contrast: these men spouting their toxic rhetoric while casually chewing their food, as if hatred were just another course on the menu.

"Obama's handling of the economy is a moral failure of tragic proportions," said the office supply store owner, opening his mouth in a pronounced manner to inhale a pickle spear.

"You'd think money grows on trees the way this Obamacare thing is going to increase welfare," added the lawn-and-garden store owner, smiling broadly with green garnish between his teeth.

The burly veterinarian seated to his right elevated matters to a new level of hatred. "I'm going to buy myself an 'Obama tag,'" he declared with a grin that made Baker's stomach turn.

Is this what Emma deals with? Baker wondered. His sister had left their mother's alma mater, Sweet Briar, after two years, calling it "an elaborate finishing school for future wives," and transferred to UC Davis for veterinary medicine. She'd dated a guy named Kenneth Cherry, but after graduation, Ken returned to rural Idaho to run his family's feed business. Emma had followed within two years—not for Ken, but to work as a country vet with the horses she'd always loved. She'd been so proud when her professors compared her to Dr. Elinor McGrath, America's first female veterinarian: Black, brilliant, and brave enough to graduate from Chicago Veterinary College in 1910, a full decade before women could even vote. "If she could handle the bullying and harassment," Emma had told him, "I can handle a few backward Idaho ranchers."

Baker shot a desperate look at Phil, hoping for some reprimand. Instead, Phil whispered, "Better for business if we let him talk. One of these fat cats joins Trinity, and that's ten grand in pledges."

Baker excused himself to his sister. Her voicemail began with the bleating of an animal, then her voice: "Hi, this is Emma. I'm not home right now, but I can take a message. Hang on a second while I get a pencil." The sound of a drawer opening followed. "OK, what would you like to tell me?"

Baker closed his eyes. *Not now, Emma.*

"Call me, please."

Standing in the marble-tiled men's room, he found himself remembering the phone call that had changed his life. The split with Michelle had left him hollow but free. Selling their Manhattan coop in the worst real estate market since the Depression felt like cosmic justice. She'd called from Challis—a dot on the map of central Idaho—offering sanctuary. "Nobody here knows the first thing about you," she'd said. "No baggage, no expectations. Just you and a lot of wide-open space to figure things out."

In the summer of 2011, he'd flown to Salt Lake City, rented a car, and driven 325 miles through stunning mountain country to reach her. His strategically timed visit coincided with Choral Rendezvous, an ecumenical gathering of the Episcopal diocese at nearby Living Waters Ranch. For three days, he sang alongside choir directors from across the West, learning fourteen new songs until his voice was hoarse, and his heart felt lighter than it had in years. At the farewell party, locals Bob and Loretta Baldwin welcomed him like family, insisting he stay for their famous sourdough pancakes the next morning.

The experience—the music echoing off granite peaks, the crystalline night sky unmarred by city lights, the sense of belonging he hadn't felt since childhood—convinced him to return for three months once he settled his affairs in New York. Emma had driven him back to Salt Lake through the Sawtooth Mountains, both quiet as they wound through valleys where elk grazed and hawks circled overhead.

"This is what peace looks like," she'd said as they crested Galena Summit. "Remember that when you're back in the city, drowning in other people's expectations."

That had been almost two years ago. Now, listening to these men spew hatred while Phil calculated donations, Baker understood what Emma had been offering—not just geographical distance from his failures but moral distance from the kind of person he'd been becoming.

When Baker returned to the table, Phil glanced up from his conversation and caught sight of his face. The rigid set of his shoulders, the forced neutrality—he knew he hadn't concealed his distress well. For just a moment, Phil's eyes registered something that looked almost like satisfaction before he turned his attention to a concrete magnate, nodding along to whatever point was being made.

Baker's phone buzzed twenty minutes later. Emma. He let it go to voicemail—he couldn't explain this dinner from the table. But knowing she had called back was reassuring. When he got home, when he could actually breathe, he'd call to tell her this was one crazy place and she'd been right about everything.

The conversation had moved on to complaints about "those people" abusing the welfare system. Baker needed an escape hatch. He turned to the man on his right—someone had mentioned he was the Boise State football team's head physi-cian—and seized on the safest topic he could find: Kellen Moore, the star quarterback and Heisman finalist.

"Do you think Kellen really has a shot, even against guys from the bigger schools?" he asked.

"Me and my buddy think he's a shoo-in," the magnate cut in. As he continued his prognosis, the table fell silent like an E.F. Hutton commercial. The wheels of greed were turning.

An awkward moment came when entrepreneur Johnny Bemus pitched his scattering urn business to Baker—the only guest who hadn't heard it before and, as Phil noted, was "loaded." Baker watched a demo of the device, which blew ashes into an inelegant cloud, accompanied by a sound like a leaf blower.

"Why would you shoot a demo while someone is doing yard work?" he asked genuinely.

Johnny's face turned florid. "That's the small motor in the urn. During an actual scattering, we play music to cover the noise. You don't hear it at all."

Everyone else began cracking up. They'd heard the same comment from other newbies.

Baker drove home from the Gem Club in silence, the taste of hypocrisy more bitter than the overpriced hamburger. Phil's whis-pered comment about five-figure pledges echoed in his mind. He sat in his car outside his apartment building for twenty minutes, watching the Boise Front silhouetted against the evening sky, think-ing of Challis and the moral clarity that distance had once provided.

Was this what ministry looked like in the real world?

Wendy would have walked out, he thought. Stared the vet-erinarian in the eye and told him exactly what she thought, then dragged Baker by the ear for staying quiet.

The memory of Wendy stung. He'd told himself that Boise would be different, that returning to ministry would mean returning to authenticity. But Phil's approach to church leadership felt disturbingly familiar—the same calculated compromises, the same worship of wealth and influence, just wrapped in clerical collars rather than expensive suits.

His phone buzzed with a text from Karl: How was dinner at the Gem Club? Hope Phil's dinner companions weren't too insufferable.

Baker stared at the message. He rubbed his face, still smelling thick burger grease on his hands. He typed back: Educational. Not sure it's the kind of education I was looking for.

Karl's response came quickly: Phil means well, but he's forgotten that the church's real treasure isn't in its bank account. Don't let tonight discourage you from your calling.

Baker considered reaching out to his friend Tim at the Washington National Cathedral. As a canon priest, Tim had seen his share of ecclesiastical politics and might offer perspective on the Phil situation that Karl, for all his wisdom, couldn't provide. Tim had always been good at cutting through the nonsense to get to the heart of things, a skill Baker could use right about now.

My calling. Baker turned the phrase over in his mind as he finally made his way upstairs. *What exactly is my calling now?* He'd thought it was ministry, but if ministry looked like tonight's dinner party, maybe he needed to reconsider.

In his apartment, he poured himself a glass of water and opened his laptop, intending to check email. Instead, he found himself scrolling through dating apps again—the same profiles he'd looked at a few times before, each one feeling more exhausting than the last. The whole enterprise felt mechanical. Swipe, match, small talk, repeat.

A sudden wave of guilt washed over him. Emma. He'd promised himself he would call her back after the dinner to tell her about his struggles with Phil and, by extension, Trinity. But it was past midnight. The conversation Emma deserved—honest, unfiltered—would have to wait. He could almost hear the disappointment in her voice, the patient understanding that would hurt far more than any direct criticism.

The next morning, Baker kept his promise. He called Emma while making coffee, needing to hear her voice before the day could pull him back into its compromises.

"So you survived Phil's networking circus," she said after he'd described the dinner. No judgment in her tone, just that steady Emma clarity he'd been craving.

"The veterinarian made a joke about buying an 'Obama tag,'" Baker said. "Phil's response was to calculate the potential donation if the guy joined Trinity."

Emma was quiet for a moment. "And you're calling me because you want me to tell you what to do about it."

"I'm calling because you were right. About all of it."

"I'm usually right," she said, and he could hear the small smile in her voice. "But that doesn't answer the question of what you're going to do now that you know I'm right."

Baker had no answer for that. After they hung up, her question stayed with him, more pointed than any accusation.

FOR TWO WEEKS, HE did nothing. Emma's comment hung in the air unanswered.

That night, he sat staring at his computer screen, Karl's words churning in his gut—something about needing to demonstrate genuine commitment, about how this was all part of the discernment process. As if finding a wife were another box to check on his path to ordination, like completing his canonical exams or securing letters of recommendation.

He started googling "matchmaking services Boise" like a seminarian completing an assignment. The whole exercise felt absurd—institutional demands dressed up as romantic pursuit. But if this was what it took to get Karl off his back, fine. He'd check the damn box. A sponsored result appeared at the top for an old-fashioned matchmaking service in neighboring Meridian that offered a free consultation. Baker clicked on it and scrolled through the website. Both Karl and Grace had articulated truths—Karl's pragmatic counsel about married clergy cultivating rapport with congregations, and Grace's more intimate suggestion that a man in his position shouldn't be spending every night alone.

It was hard to imagine another Wendy in his life. And he'd never settle for another placeholder like Michelle. But what if?

He hovered over the "Schedule an Appointment" button for a moment, then clicked it before he could talk himself out of it.

The next day, Baker arrived at the Stokely Business Plaza and was taken aback by the size. A forty-something man in business-meets-casino casual dress emerged from the back. Spiky red hair, cologne thick enough to taste. "Hi, Baker? My name is Rusty. Please, take a seat." Rusty's pitch was polished. "Let me tell you about Treasure Valley Singles," he began, explaining their personalized approach, their dedication to finding the perfect match, their track record of success. It sounded too good to be true. That should have been Baker's cue to run.

When Rusty asked if he was ready to develop a personality

profile—just to get started, no cost or commitment—Baker agreed. It seemed harmless enough. What followed: answering questions about his core values, completing multiple personality questionnaires, writing a detailed "Meet Your Match" novella outlining his relationship goals, and agreeing to a background check. Nearly two hours later, exhausted and questioning every life choice that had led him to this strip mall office, he sat for his profile photo. The picture showed dark suitcases under his eyes and a furrowed brow with deep vertical lines that looked like a Roman numeral III.

Technically, Baker wasn't yet an official member. Rusty reminded him that they only accepted the best candidates—not everyone made the cut. While Baker sat there, dazed and exhausted, Rusty stepped out briefly, then returned with paperwork. "I consulted with my partner," he said, smiling. "We think you'd make a fantastic addition to our community." The two haggled a bit over pricing, and in the end, Baker felt he'd gotten a steal of a deal by forking over $4,500. Idaho's best version of a shadchan had gotten him.

The service now had the impossible task of finding the perfect woman, perhaps even as perfect as Wendy: attractive, intelligent, adventurous, independent, in her mid-to-late forties who drank martinis, held a master's degree, owned a passport, and for fun, could name the 2012 MLB World Series MVP.

In exchange for Baker's ransom, the company promised up to eighteen dates with different women from the club until he found his match. He was assigned a personal matchmaker named Kylie, who was based in Santa Barbara, California. Baker wondered how a California woman could know what an Idaho man wanted. *Did she even know how to pronounce Boy-see?* Still, he placed his trust in her and agreed to go on a date with the first nominee. More than anything else, Baker insisted on dating someone who lived in Boise, preferably east of Thirty-Sixth Street, a generally more progressive part of town.

Kylie's first pick didn't live east of Thirty-Sixth Street—actually not even in Boise, but apparently she was perfect enough for Baker to expand his parameters. He wasn't convinced but agreed to meet her at the Cottonwood Grill downtown. Baker arrived first and watched through the window as a white F-150 pulled into the parking lot. She stepped out wearing Western boots and a turquoise midi dress, an outfit that said she knew exactly who she was and didn't apologize for it. She was warm and funny, sharing stories about working as a hairdresser in Greenleaf. Just before the meal, she turned in her chair to discreetly dispose of her gum in a napkin, then continued her story without missing a beat before Baker could get a word in edgewise.

"So where exactly is Greenleaf?" Baker asked. "About thirty-five miles west on Highway 19. Small town—less than a thousand people," she said. "Quakers settled it back in the 1900s, and it's a great place to raise a family." Baker nodded, calculating. Seventy miles round trip. He'd purposefully explained to Kylie that he wanted someone who lived in Boise. This woman seemed perfectly nice, but he could already feel himself pulling back, tallying the reasons it wouldn't work—in addition to her living so far away. Wendy would have encouraged a friend to drive to Greenleaf without a second thought if the person was worth it. She'd had that quality—genuine curiosity about people, about their stories, about possibility.

"By any chance, did your matchmaker mention that I was only looking to date someone in Boise?" Baker said. The woman appeared startled. "Yes, but you struck her as a very adaptable guy." *Adaptable.* The word hung there. Apparently, Kylie had told her something about Baker that was a stretch. The mismatch wasn't her fault—it was his, sitting across from someone and already measuring her against a ghost. "I appreciate you driving all this way," he said carefully. "But I need to be honest. The distance is a real issue for me." She took it gracefully, more gracefully than he deserved.

As her truck pulled out of the parking lot, Baker sat in his car and called Kylie. "She was perfectly nice," he admitted. "But she lives in Greenleaf. I told you—Boise only." Even as he said it, he could hear how rigid he sounded. How small. Wendy would have laughed at him for this—for being so careful about proximity when what really mattered was the person.

Kylie's second recommendation was a single mom from Boise. They met at a downtown bar crowded with what looked to be male and female Boise State basketball players. She pulled him onto the dance floor immediately, moving with uninhibited joy. Baker tried to follow but lost sight of her in the crowd. She had to shout to get his attention. When he suggested sitting down to talk, she laughed and kept dancing.

Watching her—this woman having a better time without him—he thought of Wendy. She'd understood that some moments demanded you let go, but she could also sit still. She could toggle between both. This woman had one speed. He handed her twenty dollars for a cab home.

"You left her at the bar?" Kylie's voice was sharp when he called the next day.

"She just wanted to dance. I wanted to talk. Not a good match," Baker said.

"You need to give people a chance. You're being too—"

"Too what? Too specific about what I'm looking for?" He could hear the edge in his own voice. "I paid $4,500 for this service. The least you can do is send me someone who meets the criteria I gave you." He realized what he'd just said. Money getting in the way. *God, I'm turning into Phil.* There was a long pause.

"Let me set up another date," Kylie said. "But you need to be more flexible." *Flexible.* Another ding—like *adaptable.* Baker agreed to one more attempt, and two days later, date number three called him to arrange the details. Her voice was professional, busy. "I'm pretty slammed right now, but if you really want to meet, I could do an hour on Thursday." There was a certain New York tone in her voice. "Thursday works," Baker said.

The morning of their date, she texted: Sorry, this week has been insane. Need to reschedule. Baker stared at the message. *Is this truly God's plan for me?* he thought. *This parade of mismatches and letdowns?* He didn't respond, but Kylie called him the next day. "She feels terrible about canceling. Can you give her another chance? She really is interested."

Baker called her as requested, and they scheduled Sunday brunch at a nice restaurant overlooking North Capitol. He dressed carefully—Paul Stuart blazer, Alden handsewn loafers, the kind of outfit that made him feel like himself again. He arrived early, picked a table by the window, and told the waitress it was a first date.

Twenty minutes later, she arrived in tennis whites—a polo and skort—looking like she'd just come from the court.

"Sorry I'm late," she said as she slid into her chair. "I've got a match in about thirty minutes, so I can't stay long."

Baker felt a void open up inside him. He'd gotten himself duded up. He'd given her a second chance after she canceled.

"Thirty minutes?"

"I run my own travel agency, and business has just exploded." She smiled brightly. "By the way, I like your tie."

He looked down at the tie he'd spent ten minutes choosing. What bothered him wasn't a lack of decorum—she wasn't being rude. It was the realization that she was doing exactly what he'd done for decades: filling every minute so nothing could catch up with her. He'd stopped. She hadn't.

Even when busy, Wendy knew the right time to pump the brakes. She'd had that quality of presence—the ability to make you feel like you were the most interesting thing in the room. And it struck him: he'd been measuring every woman against a ghost, conducting auditions for a role no living person could play.

"I appreciate you making time," he said carefully. "But I think we're in different places right now. You should get to your match."

He left cash on the table and walked out, his untouched mimosa catching the morning light.

He wandered to another restaurant where he could sit alone and enjoy a proper drink. Later, when calling Kylie to try and cancel his membership, he realized the problem wasn't the women. It was him—showing up with a mental checklist, tallying deficits, looking for reasons to leave before he'd even arrived. *Why am I spending a lot of money simply to appease Karl? Why am I trying to resurrect something that died twenty-five years ago, expecting the living to compete with a memory?*

Within a week, he was back online, creating his own profile, determined this time to be more honest about who he was and what he wanted. Yet such transparency forced him to confront an unsettling question: was this really a search for companionship, or merely a series of auditions for someone he doubted he could ever love?

He sat back from the screen, and this time a sudden sense of peace and calm washed over him. It was either an epiphany or a magic trick. That didn't matter. Ordination or not, he genuinely wanted another relationship, even a wife.

Chapter Six

Despite this setback with Treasure Valley Singles, he moved through life at Trinity with growing confidence—advising parishioners, discussing theology with Karl, even preparing to preach his first sermon. People sought his counsel, respected his insights, and saw in him the makings of a true spiritual leader. But put him across from a woman at dinner, and he became someone else entirely: awkward, calculating, desperately trying to fit square pegs into round holes. Two years alone after more than two decades with Michelle had left him unable to simply be present with a woman—no agenda, no expectation. Hope kept him trying, but it was a demanding companion: the same force that had brought him from Madison Avenue to these mountains sometimes woke him with a name on his lips, one he could barely say aloud.

The truth was messier, more uncertain, and ultimately more honest than any parable about divine providence. Baker had told people he'd felt "called" to leave New York, as if God had whispered directions in his ear one morning over coffee. The decision had been equal parts spiritual hunger and wounded pride, with a generous helping of practical desperation thrown in for good measure.

The logistics of leaving had been more chaotic than he liked to admit—a fire sale on the co-op, his belongings shipped west to a storage unit before he'd even chosen a destination. He purchased wheels at a Honda dealership in Jersey City across the Hudson River: a standard, unadorned Accord in alabaster silver metallic. The salesperson tried to sell him something with more flash—a bright yellow that would have announced his midlife crisis to every tollbooth operator between Manhattan and wherever he was headed. But Baker knew what he liked and didn't want to arrive in Challis looking like a cautionary tale.

Driving out of the city, Baker felt the rhythms of obligation evaporate. He had no one to answer to. For the first time in years, he could simply exist.

His first stop had to be Lynchburg: his parents, and the old campsite where his and Wendy's carefully crafted plan had somehow failed after only seven seasons. Thirty-two years since they first staked out the cabins, and he still didn't understand how something so promising had collapsed.

Baker asked his parents if they still had a copy of the camp business plan, since he had lost his own years ago. They didn't, but his mother certainly had copies of all the canceled checks made out to the McGraw Summer Camp Fund. That first night, they sat around the dinner table reminiscing about those days, and Anne's voice grew soft when she said how glad they were that Baker and Wendy had experienced such a magical gap year together. She reached across the table to touch Baker's hand.

Baker set down his fork and leaned back in his chair. "You know, she used to say the camp would be just the beginning for us." He looked down at his plate, then took a breath. "Actually, let's drive out to the site tomorrow. I'd love to see it again. Wouldn't you?"

His parents exchanged a quick glance across the table—the kind of wordless communication that comes from decades of marriage. Baker caught it, felt the slight shift in the room's temperature. Anne set down her coffee cup carefully.

"Of course, honey. It's been…well, it's been a long time since any of us have been out there."

"The new owners have kept it nice," Edward said, rubbing the back of his neck, the tell that he was uncomfortable. "They built a house where the main lodge was going to be. But the trails you two cleared are still there. The rope swings over the creek."

Baker looked up sharply. "New owners? I thought McGraw just closed the camp. That's what you told me."

His father looked away. "Let's talk about this tomorrow," Edward said quietly. "When we're out there."

Anne carefully folded her napkin and placed it beside her plate. "I think about her every time I drive past the turnoff," she said softly, her voice catching. "About both of you out there, so full of plans. About everything you were going to build together."

Edward was eager to join Baker for the visit, and Anne decided to let father and son go alone. "You two need this together," she said, already moving toward the kitchen cabinet where she kept the cooking wine. Baker's stomach tightened as he watched her reach for the familiar bottle. The whole family had walked on eggshells during those years after her recovery, and seeing her hand pause on that cabinet door brought it all flooding back— the fear, the careful monitoring, the relief when she'd gotten help. That summer when Baker was away hammering cabins into place with Wendy, Anne had thrown herself into gardening and church committees, anything to keep her hands busy and her mind occupied.

"Don't rush back on my account," she added, the words coming a little too quickly. "I have some things to catch up on around here myself."

BAKER REMEMBERED THE SEVEN-MILE drive to the main entrance almost by heart. Once he headed north on Upper Ferry Road, he felt a surge of emotion. He reflected on the long days under the summer sun, the breezy fall afternoons, even the light snow of early winter. The spiritual sweat equity he and Wendy had poured into that place ran deep.

As they reached the final turn, Baker expected to see the sign he and Wendy had designed together—trees, a river, and a cross woven together in the symbol of the Trinity, with McGraw Summer Camp painted in forest green. Instead, the painting of a black bear emerged from the weathered wood of the sign and stared back at him above the words Camp Monacan.

Baker hit the brakes harder than he meant to. The Honda lurched to a stop in the middle of the road.

"What happened here?" His voice came out tight, controlled.

Edward and Anne had rehearsed this moment for years. It had been far easier when they'd told Baker that the school had to close the camp—a half-truth that had shielded him through his darkest period. The realization hit Baker like cold water—not just that the camp was gone, but that his parents had been protecting him from this truth all along. He felt something between gratitude and betrayal, a hollowness where his assumptions about the past had been.

"Your mother and I didn't want to tell you that after the land sat dormant for two years, the people involved with this current camp offered enough to let it go finally." Edward's words came out measured, as if he'd practiced them. "McGraw sold it, Baker. They sold everything."

Baker stared at the new sign, trying to process what he was seeing. The hand-drawn face mocked him, replacing everything he and Wendy had planned with something foreign and makeshift. He could sense his father waiting for a response, but the words died before they could escape. "Why didn't you want to tell me?"

"Because you were going through a challenging period." Edward's voice was gentle but firm. "The breakup with Michelle. Leaving New York. Trying to figure out your next chapter."

"Does Emma know?"

"Yes. We needed someone to talk to about our disappointment with the school, about the guilt we felt for letting your dream slip away. We couldn't burden you with that."

Baker stayed quiet, choosing his words carefully. He closed his eyes, counted to ten, then turned to look at his father. For a moment, anger flared—at the secrecy, at the loss, at how easily dreams could be sold and replaced. But then something shifted, a weight lifting he hadn't realized he'd been carrying. Maybe the camp had always been more about Wendy than about him. Maybe holding onto it had been another way of not letting her go. A smile began to form.

"Thanks for all your effort, Dad. Let's just go explore."

It was late August, and camp was clearly in session. Baker looked for the director's office, but all he could see were girls moving about. To his left were what appeared to be the overnight facilities, including a lodge with loft sleeping, bunkhouses, and platform-tent units.

"Wow, Dad, this place has gotten so big," he said. He quickly estimated that Monacan had three times as many campers as McGraw, and all girls.

A voice called from behind. "Hi, there."

Baker turned and saw a fit, attractive woman in her late thirties to early forties, wearing a khaki shirt and trousers, approach.

"Greetings. I'm Baker, and this is my dad, Edward."

"How can I help?" she asked.

"Well, believe it or not, my girlfriend and I started a coed camp for the McGraw School, which existed here in the late seventies and early eighties," Baker said. "I'm wondering if you'd mind if my dad and I take a look around."

"You're Baker Vaughan?" she asked with much excitement. "Oh my gosh, you are truly a legend around here. It's amazing what you and, um, I can't seem to recall her name, did to prepare the camp for that first opening."

"Thank you. Wendy and I had a wonderful time doing it."

"Well then, yes, absolutely, please help yourselves," she replied. "My name is Roberta, and I'm—well, for lack of a better term, the director emerita here. Seems like I've been hiring a new director about every two years for a while now."

She led them on a tour of the grounds—the renovated cabins, the new activity center, the garden where campers grew vegetables. Roberta talked about the kids who came through, many from difficult situations, and how the land seemed to work a kind of magic on them. After an hour, Baker felt something unexpected—a sense of completion rather than loss. The land was serving its purpose, nurturing young lives in ways he and Wendy had only imagined.

As they drove back through the familiar Virginia countryside, he and his dad shared a comfortable silence, both processing what they'd witnessed. Back at the house, Anne was waiting with a thermos of coffee and a bag of homemade cookies for the road, knowing that Baker had a long drive ahead. "I know you'll find what you're looking for out there," she said, holding him close. "Just don't forget to call your old mother once in a while."

"I won't," Baker promised. For the first time in years, leaving didn't feel like running away. It felt like moving toward something.

AFTER LEAVING LYNCHBURG, BAKER traveled south and west, and his cross-country journey became a blur of small revelations and roadside encounters that would have made perfect advertising copy. The Barter Theatre in Abingdon, Virginia, where Depression-era audiences had traded vegetables for Shakespeare. Then there was Loretta Lynn's ranch in Tennessee, where he spent two hours exploring the antebellum-style architecture from the late 1800s that had housed Loretta, Mooney, and their children throughout a significant portion of her music career. Nestled in the hills alongside Hurricane Creek, the property opened to a rather mundane RV park that made him wonder, *Is this what Challis is going to be like?* When he reached the exit, instead of the usual red octagonal STOP sign, this one appropriately read WHOA!—and Baker worried he was fleeing one form of kitsch for another.

At that moment, he was not far from Memphis and called the Peabody Hotel to check on availability for that evening. Baker had researched the establishment and knew he would enjoy staying there—after days of budget motels and emotional excavation, he needed somewhere that felt like civilization. The Peabody, with its elegant rooms and ornate, hand-painted beamed ceilings, had been compared to the Paris Ritz, the Cairo Shepheard's, the London Savoy, and other distinguished hotels worldwide. Indeed, a room was available, so Baker reserved it for two nights.

He arose early the next morning, and out of curiosity, he went to visit the Duck Palace on the hotel roof. There, he spotted a man in rather plain clothes doing some heavy cleaning.

"Excuse me, sir, do you know where I can find the Peabody Duckmaster?" Baker asked.

"That is I," the man replied. "I'm a bit hurried at the moment, but how may I assist you?"

Since he was technically on duty, he acted very much in character for a man with such a distinguished title, despite having duck poop on parts of his clothing and skin.

"I hope I'm not being rude, but do you actually do this full-time?"

"Indeed, I do. Each day at nine-thirty a.m., I feed the ducks romaine lettuce, which they love. Then, I take them downstairs in the elevator, change into my official uniform, grab my gilded cane, and lead them to march down a red carpet to the fountain. Yes, my good man, it's a day's work!"

"Then I shall see you again in an hour or so," Baker said.

Baker was there in the lobby awaiting the parade, along with dozens of other guests. The spectacle of five mallards waddling down a red carpet while a uniformed man with a brass cane orchestrated their every move struck him as both absurd and oddly dignified.

Baker spent a restless night in Memphis, unable to shake his worry about his father's subdued reaction at the campsite. Over hardwood-smoked pork ribs at Corky's, he found himself wondering if his dad was hiding a health issue, or worried that he hadn't prevented Baker from pursuing the priesthood, contributing in some roundabout way to Wendy's death.

In the parking garage the next day, Baker tossed his leather satchel into the trunk and pulled out into the Memphis sauna. Anxiety filled him as the city's river bluffs receded in his rearview mirror and he advanced onto the interstate, heading west and northwest toward Salt Lake City, toward Challis, toward whatever future Emma had hinted at on their last phone call.

Outside Oklahoma City, his phone rang—the first inbound call in days.

"How the heck are you, brother?" Emma asked.

When he finished recapping his last three days, the only thing she wanted to know was: "Loretta Lynn? Seriously?" They shared a good laugh before she got to the point.

"Listen, I'm calling about your visit out here to Challis. You made quite the impression. Yes, sir, you certainly did. Drive safe. Get here soon"

THE OKLAHOMA CITY NATIONAL Memorial was outdoors—open to the sky where the federal building had once stood, reclaiming the space that violence had tried to destroy. He arrived after dusk and had the place to himself. At first, it felt like a miniature Arlington Cemetery with neat rows of what looked like headstones under dramatic lighting. Only on his second walk through the grounds did he realize these weren't headstones but chairs—168 empty chairs, each engraved with a victim's name. He dropped to his knees and closed his eyes, counting in sequence from 1 to 168. Although he didn't know a single victim's name, as the numbers mounted, he could feel the enormity of the loss and understand why grief had turned to fury.

Next was Amarillo and there he saw a sign for the Cadillac Ranch, a roadside art installation that stopped him cold. Ten Cadillacs, their front ends buried deep in the Texas panhandle dirt like chrome tombstones, their tail fins jutting skyward at identical angles. They were painted in garish colors—some covered in graffiti, others faded by sun and wind—and they seemed to defy every law of sense and gravity.

Baker parked and walked toward them slowly, his shoes crunching on the hard-packed earth. Up close, the cars were even more surreal: a 1949 Club Coupe, a 1954 Sedan de Ville, a 1963 Cadillac Eldorado—each one a monument to American excess, now half-swallowed by the prairie. He ran his hand along the rusted chrome of the nearest one, feeling the heat of the afternoon sun radiating from the metal. Then he grabbed a Krylon can from the dirt, shook it, and sprayed WENDY in red letters across the driver's side door before stepping back to snap a photo and text it to his father. No response.

By Salt Lake City, anxiety and exhaustion had merged into a familiar cocktail. He'd spent decades chasing the next opportunity, the next relationship, the next version of himself that might finally feel authentic. Now he was running toward something that might be permanent, in a place he'd never seen, answering a calling that had been interrupted nearly thirty years ago by tragedy.

Once he left the urban sprawl behind, he was awestruck by the geological transition from the desert to the rugged beauty of the Sawtooth Mountains and the Salmon River. He made so many detours to take in the scenery that the trip took nearly four hours longer than expected. By the time he reached Challis, he understood why Emma had moved there and stayed—and after a few days amid the genuine warmth of small-town Idaho, he was glad he'd returned.

Downtown Challis turned out to be a double-wide Main Street with a saloon and a beer joint facing each other in front of the Wells Fargo Bank. Baker had an on-again, off-again relationship with booze, but saloon beer or whiskey was out of the question. He was looking for something more stimulating.

Emma greeted him with the same easy warmth he remembered. She put him up in her guest room, and over the next few days introduced him to Challis properly—the river, the trails, the neighbors who waved from their porches, even the ones set well off the road on farms and ranches. On the third night, she told him about the town's Episcopalians. Eight of them, she said, part of what the diocese called Saint Philip—too few to have a church of their own, but once a month they brought in a supply priest and borrowed the Catholic church for Sunday worship. Baker knew them the moment he met them: potluck casseroles with actual spices, dog-eared copies of Mary Oliver, and enough self-deprecating humor to fill the Salmon River. They became his wine and bread, his medicine for a soul that had been starving.

He also became acquainted with Oletta Robinson, a ninety-five-year-old woman who'd lived in Challis for forty years. It seemed improbable that a woman of color with roots in Philadelphia's Chestnut Hill neighborhood had made her way to this remote mining town, but as Baker learned her story, the pieces fell into place. After losing her young husband to testicular cancer, she'd worked as a nanny for a family whose patriarch, Edward Ford, was a high-ranking executive at Hecla Mining. When Ford's frequent travels to Idaho eventually led to his transfer to Challis, he'd brought Oletta and her children with him—a journey that must have felt like crossing into another world entirely.

After weeks of hesitating to address such a sensitive subject—*Would it be rude? Wasn't it obvious?*—Baker finally spoke up.

"I hope you don't mind me asking, but are you the only Black person in Challis?"

She chuckled but acknowledged his naivete. "If you find another, please let me know."

Oletta came to adore him. "The most handsome man I've ever met," she'd say. Baker offered to drive her around town to run errands, and they always ended up at the soft-serve stand for a junior cup of vanilla swirl to brighten her day.

"You sure you don't want anything else today?" Baker would ask as they sat in his car outside the stand, and he watched her savor each spoonful.

"Honey, at my age, vanilla swirl is all the nutrition I need," she'd reply with a grin. "Besides, I know I'm going to die soon, so why not die happy?"

Often, she skipped any other food for the rest of the day, deflecting Baker's concerns about eating something healthier before nighttime. He tried bringing her other treats—huckleberry pie, bread pudding, banana cream pie—but she'd never accept anything but ice cream. This left Baker eating the desserts himself, and his waistline began to expand.

"You're not going to attract a fine-looking woman if you let yourself go," the short splinter of a woman told her middle-aged friend.

"Frankly, Oletta, kissing my sister is the most romantic feeling I have now," Baker said.

"Then follow thy Lord," she responded. "Become a priest."

It was the second time in three years he'd received such unsolicited advice. During his final months in New York, Father John Thorkelson had made the same suggestion. They'd become acquainted after a chance encounter in the church thrift shop at All Saints Episcopal, and in a short period of time, Father John had become both friend and spiritual mentor—drawing Baker back to faith through his liberating approach to priesthood and the genuine friendship that developed between them.

"Reinvent yourself as a disciple of Christ," the priest had told him. "You'd be great at it. You'd make the world a better place." He'd also said, "Faith isn't about perfection. It's about showing up, even when you're not sure why. And don't worry, celibacy isn't required!

Baker carried those words with him to Idaho. Once could be dismissed as a coincidence. Twice felt divine.

AS FALL TRANSITIONED TO winter, Emma and Baker seized every opportunity to explore the Salmon-Challis Forest before snow made the back roads impassable. They rented ATVs to explore the Lombard Trail, where aspen leaves crunched like cornflakes beneath their tires. They visited the preserved ghost town at Bayhorse, its weathered wooden buildings creaking in the mountain wind like old bones settling. And they toured the massive Yankee Fork Gold Dredge with Emma's friend Tom Reed, who served as president of the association trying to preserve the area's mining heritage, the clang of metal still echoing faintly in the dredge's cavernous belly, as though the ghosts of miners hadn't left.

One November afternoon, while delivering a difficult calf at the Garrett Ranch, Baker found himself elbow-deep in a bovine birth canal, following Emma's shouted instructions to tie twine around the calf's legs and pull steadily when she pushed. The moment felt both absurd and profound—a former Madison Avenue executive helping bring new life into the world in the middle of nowhere, Idaho.

"Well done, my apprentice," Emma said as the calf lay peacefully beside its mother.

Baker wiped his arms and hands on a cotton Huck towel, grinning despite himself. He couldn't remember ever earning praise in New York that felt half as genuine as this. They celebrated with a picnic along the Main Salmon River, known as the River of No Return from the early days when boats could navigate downstream but couldn't fight their way back up through the rapids. As they shared sandwiches, she poured wine generously into two glasses.

"Emma, I don't want to spoil the moment, but can I ask you something about what Mom did with the camp land?"

"What do you want to know?"

"Did you know she was going to give it away? Before she did it?"

"I knew," she said. "And she didn't ask me to keep it secret, but considering everything you were dealing with at the time, I thought it wise not to mention it."

"I believe intent makes up most of the moral law," Baker said. "If you were genuinely trying to help me, then I forgive you. With all my heart."

It wasn't until they visited Challis Hot Springs with Tom that Emma dropped her own bombshell. As they soaked in the waterfall-fed pools, Tom mentioned that Challis would miss them both when they left.

"Both of whom?" Baker said.

Emma hadn't told him. She was retiring. She was moving back to Lynchburg.

Baker jerked up from the hot water and moved to sit on the pool's edge. "What?"

"Well, aside from turning sixty-two next month, it's become too cold for me in winter. Too isolating."

Baker knew she'd lost her dear friend Ken two years earlier. They'd spent considerable time together, and his absence had left a hole in her daily life that Challis couldn't fill. That had to be a factor as well.

Then she shared what she'd been thinking about: "Baker, it's time for me to go home. I'd like to be closer to the folks. They're getting older, and I want to be there for them."

The revelation hit him harder than expected. Emma had been his anchor. His connection to family. His safety net if this whole reinvention experiment failed. Now she was leaving too.

To make their final weeks together memorable, she began hosting dinner parties and preparing Baker's favorite meat loaf made with local bison. There was always wine with each meal and port after desserts like huckleberry crumble and ice cream potatoes. Guests quizzed Baker about his plans as if attending a last supper.

Baker's departure for Boise was set for Christmas morning. The capital city had the energy and population that a small town simply couldn't match. His sister had seen this with her own eyes;

Challis could have been good medicine for an incurably broken Baker who wanted to retreat. But now that he was put back together, he needed more. He needed boardrooms and sanctuaries, needed a place where his calling could be tested against something larger than small-town kindness.

Two days before Christmas, standing in Oletta's driveway, Baker realized that the three months in Challis had been exactly what he needed, but it had never been the destination. It was the pause before the real journey began. Oletta had been right about following his Lord. Now he had to find out if he was brave enough to do it in a place that would demand everything he had to give.

"You take care of yourself, handsome," Oletta said, pulling him into a brief, fierce hug.

Baker climbed back into the Honda, carrying with him the blessing of a ninety-five-year-old woman who'd seen enough of life to recognize a calling when she heard one. Soon, the mountains ahead would promise nothing except the chance to begin again. This time, Baker thought, he might just be ready for whatever came next.

On Christmas morning, Baker embraced Emma in a fierce bear hug and thanked her for the wonderful experiences they had shared over the past three months. Challis would always hold a special place in his heart; it just wasn't the right place for him to relaunch his path to the ministry. He buckled up and took out a folded Idaho road map he had found in her study. Thank God she never threw anything away. As he unfolded it once, twice, three and four times, when he finally located Challis on the map, the only markings nearby appeared to be logging roads colored brown and streams and creeks that wound through the land with names older than memory.

It was six-thirty and pitch-black. The temperature stood at nine degrees. Baker had some cobwebs in his head from the two bottles of Malbec they had polished off the night before, and the map had him all kerfuffled. He really didn't have a clue where to begin.

"Baker, wait a sec," his sister yelled, jogging toward his car in her bathrobe. She had forgotten to give him a simple, hand-drawn map with yellow highlights just between Challis and Boise. Baker could see it clearly wasn't the shortest route—the highlighted path curved and meandered as opposed to the direct lines on his road atlas—but he trusted her local knowledge about winter driving conditions.

"You're a godsend," he said.

She handed him the map along with a small wrapped package, with instructions not to open it until he had found his own place in Boise.

"It's not another casserole, is it?"

"No, but you'll see soon enough. I've got to go back inside."

He took a quick look at her map and thought maybe she wasn't sending him on the fastest route, but mind you, no route through the mountains of Idaho was going to be fast. He rolled down his window and thanked her for saving him a lot of hassle. She might not have heard him because she didn't turn around. All he saw was the backside of God.

He began the journey by playing some music he hoped would blend in nicely with his meditations on God and the beauty of His creation. He started by listening to Josh Ritter's "A Girl in the War"—a song about faith, doubt, and loss that someone at Choral Rendezvous had recommended, enthusing about the Idaho-born singer-songwriter's poetic lyrics. He reflected deeply

on a day many treated as nothing more than an excuse for feast-
ing and football.

HE COULD HARDLY BELIEVE how quickly time had passed since that
harrowing Christmas Day drive from Challis. What had begun
as a desperate search for purpose in an empty downtown had
evolved into an unexpected gift: a sense of belonging. The Trinity
community had embraced him not as a refugee from Manhattan
failure, but as a person with gifts worth nurturing. He'd traveled
with Bishop Gallagher to remote parishes, spoken at diocesan
conventions, and somehow become indispensable to the spiritual lives of Idaho Episcopalians.

His relationship with Karl had deepened far beyond anything
he had experienced with anyone back in New York. He regularly
dropped into his office unannounced, and Karl welcomed these
impromptu conversations. The Trinity community saw him as
Karl's protégé, a recognition Baker tried not to flaunt. He kept
his head down and his ears open, letting his work speak for itself.

When Karl offered Baker advice, Baker perceived it as a gift.
Just because it could be painful didn't mean it wasn't beneficial.
On the day Karl thoughtfully suggested that the missing ingredient for Baker to minister effectively was a wife, Baker felt as anxious as he did on the day he took a midterm exam in calculus as
an undergraduate. He was simply overwhelmed. But his anxiety
eventually eased, and he assured Karl he would keep an open
mind about dating again.

"Good. I think it's the right move here," Karl said.

Chapter Seven

BAKER FOUND IT HARD TO BELIEVE THAT TWO YEARS HAD PASSED since he joined Trinity. He'd gained recognition not just within his parish but also across several of the twenty-six churches in the Episcopal Diocese of Idaho, traveling with Bishop Gallagher during scheduled visits to remote areas where the prelate led worship services for small congregations that couldn't afford their own priests. Baker further distinguished himself at annual diocesan conventions, drawing people into his sophisticated and deeply spiritual perspective on faith and contemporary life.

However, Baker's path to ordination remained uncertain. The diocese didn't need an additional full-time priest, and some of the older clergy questioned whether a man of fifty-three should be starting a vocation typically begun in one's twenties. Even Bishop Gallagher, who valued Baker's contributions, had expressed concerns about creating expectations he couldn't sustain.

While Baker thrived at Trinity and had become Karl's de facto protégé, troubling news from Virginia weighed heavily on his mind. During one of Emma's regular calls, her voice had lost its usual lightness.

"There's something I need to tell you," she said. "Dad had what Dr. Cummins called a 'ministroke' not long after you arrived in Boise."

Baker's stomach tightened. "Did he go to the hospital?"

"Dr. Cummins didn't think that was necessary initially. But when Dad had a second one a month later, he sent him straight to the emergency room."

The news about his father's strokes haunted Baker. Every phone call from Virginia made his stomach clench, and every silence between calls felt ominous. The situation had become too much for his mother to handle alone.

Thank God Baker could lean on Karl Thompson. He was Baker's biggest fan and spiritual advisor. The way Karl saw it, both Trinity and the diocese would grow richer with Baker serving as one of its priests. Using Baker's age against him was one of the stupidest things he'd ever heard.

Seeking his mentor's advice, Baker was delighted when Karl and Margaret invited him to visit their farm in Medford, Oregon. It was a ten-hour drive, and when he finally arrived, Karl proposed they stretch their legs and wander around their "Eden." Baker followed Karl through their orchard of apple, pear, and Elberta peach trees, past chickens and goats, admiring the pastoral life Karl had built.

When they had settled in the living room that evening, Baker opened up about his growing anxiety over his family's health and his own sense of isolation.

"I've been thinking about your advice," Baker said, "about finding someone to share this journey with."

Karl leaned forward with interest.

"I've actually been browsing the internet, looking at some interesting candidates," Baker admitted. "There are some promising profiles, but I haven't taken the plunge yet. I keep thinking about timing, about whether I'm ready for that kind of commitment while pursuing ordination."

"The two aren't mutually exclusive," Karl said gently. "In fact, having a partner who understands your calling might strengthen both your ministry and your personal life."

As they lingered over Margaret's substantial breakfast the next morning—Belgian waffles, bacon from their neighbor's pigs, eggs from their own chickens—Karl mentioned wanting to drive to Ashland to pick up the latest David McCullough book.

"I'm particularly drawn to his chapter on Elizabeth Blackwell," he said. "The first female doctor in America. She was originally a schoolteacher, you know, supporting her family." His voice caught slightly. "Whatever else she accomplished later—and it was considerable—I knew her through those early sacrifices, just like my own mother."

Baker watched this man, who could hunt and skin a rabbit, tear up at the thought of young women struggling in the world. It was a precious moment to witness. On the drive back to Boise, Baker reflected on Karl's authenticity: an enlightened change agent, an innovator, and a mentor. When he'd retired as bishop in 2004, he was practically canonized. This was the kind of priest Baker wanted to be.

Back in Boise, he continued his informal role at Trinity—assisting at Sunday services, helping Bishop Gallagher prepare for diocesan visits, occasionally leading adult education classes when asked. People sought him out after services, pulling him aside in the narthex to talk through personal struggles or career decisions or questions about faith. He'd listen carefully and offer what wisdom he could, always conscious that he was doing this without any official authority. Just a man who'd learned to be present with other people's pain.

But increasingly, his mind wandered. Someone would be in midsentence about an estrangement from their children, and he'd be thinking about his father shuffling around the Lynchburg house, one hand steadying himself against walls. Emma's voice on their weekly calls had taken on a caretaker's exhaustion that she tried, unsuccessfully, to hide.

"How's Dad doing this week?" he'd ask, and she'd pause just long enough for him to know the answer wouldn't be good.

The leaves turned gold, then fell, and Boise's North End transformed into a tunnel of bare branches. Baker walked past Trinity most mornings, his breath visible in the cold air, thinking about Karl's words: *The two aren't mutually exclusive.* Finding a partner. Strengthening his ministry. Building a life here rather than merely occupying space in it.

He hadn't made a formal declaration of intent to pursue ordination. How could he, when Bishop Gallagher had made it clear the diocese had concerns—about his age, about the lack of full-time positions, about whether he had the stability needed for long-term ministry? And then there was Karl's gentle but persistent suggestion: *The missing ingredient for you to minister effectively is a wife.*

Some evenings, after returning to his rented apartment, he'd open his laptop and log into Match.com. The profiles glowed on the screen—attractive, accomplished women who seemed to have their lives together in ways he wasn't sure he did. He'd read through their carefully curated descriptions, hover his cursor over the message button, then close the browser without typing a word.

What would he even say? *Hello. I'm a fifty-three-year-old former advertising executive exploring a calling to priesthood, still grieving a wife who died thirty years ago and another relationship that ended in humiliation. Interested?*

BY THANKSGIVING, LEONARD HAD mentioned wanting to sell his house and leave Boise to lead his own Episcopal church in Ouray, Colorado. By Christmas, Baker had started doing the math on what he could afford. By January, he realized that buying the house might be the commitment he needed to make—not to a person, not yet, but to this place, this calling, this version of himself that was still becoming. Leonard thought that, as a priest "moving up the ladder," it was impractical for Baker to own a large home that might keep him rooted for a long time. Baker saw the situation differently—he wanted roots, wanted commitment to this community. Leonard's need to leave created Baker's opportunity to stay. They agreed on a price and finalized the sale privately. Instead of divvying up the saved sales commission, they made a joint contribution to Trinity.

On February 28, 2014—his birthday—Baker awoke for the first time in his newly purchased craftsman home in Boise's North End, a house with classic character situated just twelve blocks from Trinity. He had enjoyed a wonderful sleep on his new latex mattress, and when he arose, he was able to splash handfuls of water on his face without overflowing the sink basin. He strode across the living room in his bare feet on a beautiful hand-knotted wool Oushak rug—a memento from his trip to Istanbul with Michelle, where they'd spent hours shopping while merchants plied them with apple tea. The rug's subtle mix of blue, brown, and beige brought warmth to his new home, a stark contrast to the run-down apartment he'd left behind.

Now he was fifty-four. Perhaps the older clergy had a point about his age—though their persistent refrain suggested insecurity more than wisdom. Such questions could wait.

Today, of all days, he could allow himself the simpler pleasure of being free from his apartment. It had become a real jalopy of a place, even more run down than when he arrived and not up to building code. One day, he had found himself trapped in the stairwell of the building. He never used the elevator unless he had elderly company, and he had never experienced a problem using the push bar to exit the building on the first floor until this incident. It was a harrowing two hours of yelling, banging on the door, and throwing the loose screws he found lying on the floor at the small rectangular exterior window until a passerby heard his plea to call 911 and have the fire department come and crowbar the door open.

As he sat down in the living room to enjoy his coffee, trying not to glance at the waiting to be unpacked, he thought about how nice it might be to have a woman there to share this morning ritual, among other things, after his period of solitude following his breakup with Michelle. All that time had been spent cooking for one, talking to himself, sitting in random corners, eating pies and cakes without slicing them, walking around naked, living out of a laundry basket, and not closing the door while going number two.

Baker tried unsuccessfully for weeks to have his dating-club membership fee refunded. His two conversations with the swankmeister and another with the purported owner of the business led to a dead end. He was left with legal action if he dared to risk thousands more in the event the business had deep pockets. Since neither the dates nor Scotty's cologne had injured him, he ate the loss and equated it with being on an expensive vacation on Kauai when it rained the whole time.

Leonard had been a dedicated composter, filling about fifty square feet of backyard space with organic matter that was already breaking down into rich soil. There it waited for someone like Baker to utilize it. He planted numerous Better Boy, Black Krim, and beefsteak tomatoes, along with some bell peppers and cucumbers. He watered and pruned them diligently, and by the end of summer, Baker had everyone convinced he was a master gardener.

Especially the petite female neighbor across the street. Baker thought, *I'm going to work up the courage to go over there and introduce myself to her one day soon.* That day got put off for two months. He'd taken all that time to rehearse a dozen potential introductions, discarding each as too forward, too awkward, or too transparent. What if she had a partner who worked long hours? What if she wasn't interested in making neighborhood connections? The questions multiplied with each passing week.

But one day, she handed him the opportunity on a silver platter. While Baker tended to his front yard, she was cutting the grass with a manual reel lawn mower and seemed to be expending a lot of energy. In fact, her body was bent over as if she were pushing the mower up a steep hill, even though the surface looked flat to him.

Baker went to his refrigerator and pulled out two bottles of Gatorade. He walked across the street to offer them to his neighbor, who was working in her yard. When she noticed him approaching, Baker saw her glance down at her sweat-soaked clothes, her face flushing slightly with embarrassment. Before he could say anything to put her at ease, the blades of her lawn mower suddenly jammed with a grinding sound, cutting short her work.

Baker had no idea that his seemingly smooth maneuver would eventually spiral into a calculated catastrophe. He couldn't possibly foresee that one hazy winter night two years and three months later, he would be lying in his own sick in this woman's living room, disoriented, humiliated, and facing imminent arrest. The desires and pleasures, the disgrace and fury, the exquisite disappointments and remorse that would arise from this brief journey across the street to meet an attractive woman on a sweet-scented July afternoon all remained hidden from him. In the years to come, however, Baker Vaughan would frequently revisit this moment, two cold Gatorades clutched in his hands, a brave smile spreading across his face, warmth blooming in his chest, with a future mound of trouble waiting for him just ten steps away.

"I've been meaning to introduce myself for weeks." Baker could have said *months*, but that would have sounded pathetic. "Sorry it's taken so long. My name is Baker."

"Hi, Baker. I'm Darcy. I'm sorry I look this way."

"Not at all. It's amazing how hard you're working, and you look like you could use a drink." He held up the Gatorades. "Also, I'd be plenty happy to finish cutting your grass."

Darcy politely declined—she was determined to gut it out—but told him he was such a gentleman. That word immediately resonated with Baker. He laughed to himself. *You can take the boy out of the South, but you can't take the South out of the boy.* Baker bade

Darcy adieu without committing to seeing her again, but he felt there was chemistry between them.

He was still in the midst of joining Match.com, perfecting his profile while browsing potential dates who teasingly popped up as he was on the site. He never took a deep dive to wink at anyone or send a message. With a one-month membership, he wasn't rushed. *And why feel rushed?* he thought. He was still unpacking his house and, it appeared, a possible dating option across the street that certainly didn't require an account or a computer.

About a week later, Baker saw Darcy backing her red Camry out of her detached garage. He walked toward the driver's side of the car, trying not to startle her, but he did anyway. He waited for her to regain her composure. "Hey, Darcy, I was wondering if you'd like to grab a cup of coffee sometime."

She replied in a soft voice, words slipping slightly on the *s* sounds, that she would like to do so and suggested the two meet at Earl's Java, a downtown coffee shop Baker had not yet visited. She was available that Thursday afternoon. "That works perfectly," Baker said, perhaps a bit too quickly. They agreed to meet at four o'clock—an early quitting time if she was a working woman. He was intrigued.

The two arrived at Earl's almost simultaneously. This was her place, and she led Baker to a corner table away from the windows—somewhere private for conversation. After the usual pleasantries, Baker asked her what she would like to drink.

"My usual is rather complicated, so I'll just go to the counter and place my order. What will you have?" she asked.

"Let me accompany you," Baker said.

As they waited in line, he noticed her outfit—a simple blouse paired with khaki trousers, the kind of casual, presentable clothing one might find at J. Crew or the Gap. Nothing about it suggested whether she worked traditional hours or had adjusted her schedule for this meeting.

When she began ordering, he again heard that soft quality in her voice, the way her words slipped on certain sounds. There was something appealing about it—unhurried, careful. Baker positioned himself ahead of her to pay. He ordered a drip coffee for himself, though he was well past his usual caffeine cutoff of eleven o'clock in the morning.

Back at the table, Baker began asking questions. He discovered she held an important lay position at St. Francis Lutheran Church, and he was impressed by the effortless way she described her work, even though he didn't fully understand some of the buzzwords she used. He didn't ask her for clarification because he simply wanted to hear her talk.

He told her about Freddy Cappuccino's visit to Trinity, and they both shared a good laugh when Baker recounted the visit. Darcy, being a Lutheran, told Baker, "I've never had a Catholic mistakenly come to our church." Baker studied the way she smiled, which struck him as a mix of demure and wistful—and decided that she must be a complex person. He liked that.

They went on to share basic background information. Darcy wasn't her real given name; it was Dariana. She explained that the name had origins in Persian and Greek, loosely translating to English as "upholder of the good" or "guardian of virtue."

Baker certainly had no reason to find such a name unusual. He'd grown up around people with the most distinctive names like Witcher Dudley, Fergus Goodridge, Morton Northen, and Pierce Walmsley—real Southern WASP-y folk who took great pride in their names since they were descended from families who were early arrivals in Jamestown, or so they claimed.

Darcy was born just outside Albuquerque and, at a young age, moved with her family to Kuna, Idaho, an agricultural community twenty-seven miles south and west of Boise. Her parents were spiritual bohemians, she explained, who followed many Christian rituals but completely disagreed with churches that banned abortions. The family of seven—Darcy had four older brothers—lived off the land for most of her early adolescence, and the children were homeschooled until the eighth grade.

"What was it like growing up in Kuna?" Baker asked, never having been there himself.

"Very rural," she said. "We only had one high school."

That would have been thirty years ago, as best as he could guess about Darcy's age. Yet it sounded just like modern-day Challis to Baker. He realized how bored he would have been there.

They continued their conversation to discover how they both ended up living in the same Boise neighborhood. Darcy, a recent divorcée, had just purchased her house and was living there with her teenage son, Sean. Baker could tell from some of her remarks that she was very protective of her only child. Baker shared his side of the story, focusing mainly on his time in New York with Michelle and admitting he hadn't dated anyone since.

Eventually, the topic turned to religion. Baker, of course, took the lead and told Darcy he intended to become a priest. This was certainly not meant as a test to impress her or scare her away. However, when she heard the news, her eyes widened, and Baker noticed that she had one blue eye, while the other was blue/hazel, which he felt added to her personality.

"How long does the process take?" she asked.

"Well, it's impossible to say at the moment, because the rector seems to be a bit of a roadblock."

She told him that she knew several Lutheran pastors in the area and, if he thought they could be of any help, she would be happy to make introductions. His genuine smile communicated both "thank you" and "your turn" simultaneously. Darcy then described her complicated relationship with the Lutheran church. Yes, she valued her faith and appreciated the community it provided, but as a divorced woman, she'd grown weary of the whispered judgments and the assumption that her marriage's failure reflected some spiritual deficiency. The progressive wing of Lutheranism embraced her; the traditional wing made her feel like a cautionary tale.

Furthermore, she told him she'd withdrawn her son from St. Mark's Lutheran Academy last year. She cited their refusal to teach evolution alongside creation theology, saying she didn't want her child growing up afraid of science. That revelation surprised Baker—he'd assumed religious school parents wanted exactly that kind of doctrinal purity. He found himself respecting her even more.

Time flew by; they talked and talked for nearly two hours. Baker asked if she drove to Earl's, which she did; naturally, he offered to walk with her to the car. Within a few yards of it, Baker noticed a parking ticket on the windshield and promptly removed it. She blushed, and Baker offered to pay the fifteen-dollar fine. He told her to forget about it.

Baker walked home and started looking across the street at Darcy's house. He wondered if she might appear in the kitchen window, if she was thinking about him the way he was thinking about her. He wanted to reach out, but he certainly didn't want to come across as too eager. He decided it would be best to wait a while before initiating further contact.

The day after the coffee date, a letter arrived in his mailbox. Darcy had written him a thank-you note for the coffee and, especially, for paying the fine for the parking citation. She described him as a gentleman and made it clear that she would enjoy seeing him again. Baker was thrilled and considered his next step. Since he hadn't asked her for a phone number or email address while at Earl's, his best bet was to wait for her arrival from work that afternoon and try to wave her down before she drove her car into the garage.

Somehow, he missed her arrival, but before dark, Darcy appeared in her yard, apparently looking for something. She crouched to peer under the porch, then moved to check behind the row of shrubs along the fence. She called out a name— "Muffin? Muffin!"—pausing to listen before moving on to another hiding spot. Baker walked across the street following her and asking if he could be of assistance.

"I can't find one of my cats," she said. "This happens all the time." The look on her face suggested she might have the Idaho Humane Society on speed dial. "I have four of them—all strays I've taken in."

An ailurophile, Baker realized. He was allergic to cats, but he didn't dare bring that up, not after just one date, and he certainly wasn't going to throw away his chance with her.

Baker managed to get in a "thank you" for the note and asked if she'd like to take a walk with him the following morning. He'd fallen into the habit of rising at sunrise and heading north to the Boise foothills for an hour's walk. It was exhilarating and kept him fit.

"I'd like that; I really would," she said, exasperation evident in her voice. "I just can't commit right now. I'll let you know later if I can."

LATER CAME SOON ENOUGH, and Darcy laced up her Merrells to meet Baker for what would be one of the most demanding walks she had ever taken. They navigated two-and-a-half miles of Lower Hulls Gulch, a classic Boise trail with over eight hundred feet of elevation gain. Although Darcy seemed to have a leg-length discrepancy that affected her gait, it certainly did not affect her stamina or spirit. She matched Baker stride for stride and gave him a calm and confident high five when they finished.

As they descended, he appraised her more carefully. She was squarely in his spiritual wheelhouse—a woman who apparently hadn't taken expensive vacations, who drove a ten-year-old Honda, and whose practical wardrobe seemed designed for function rather than fashion. Everything about her screamed simplicity and authenticity, the very values Baker had spent years trying to embody.

"Do you ever feel like you're missing out on the broader life?" Baker asked as they picked their way down a rocky section. "Travel, nice dinners out—that sort of thing."

Darcy shrugged. "I don't think about it much. I have what I need."

It was the kind of answer Baker had hoped for, yet something in her tone suggested layers he hadn't yet reached. Over the following weeks, as they fell into a pattern of morning walks and evening conversations, he began to notice the contradictions. She was a woman of faith who didn't seem to possess a materialistic bone in her body, yet beneath this simple exterior, Baker occasionally glimpsed flashes of a more complex woman—moments of conflict that suggested her relationship with faith was as complicated as his own.

One evening, as they sat on her porch after another hike, the conversation turned to the church. Darcy mentioned something about the whispers that followed her divorce, and her voice took on an edge he hadn't heard before. "The church has its positions," she said, looking out at the street rather than at him. "Sometimes those positions don't account for real life. For real pain." When she spoke of being treated as though her failed marriage meant a failed faith, her eyes revealed wounds that hadn't fully healed—perhaps explaining the unpredictable rhythm of intimacy and distance that would come to define their relationship.

Baker was breaking new ground. He'd taken Karl's advice about looking for a partner to heart, and he'd found a far better candidate on his own—a woman whose brand of religion had its quirks but who, most importantly, worshipped the same God.

He found it easy to talk with her about light and heavy stuff alike. He let her know that he believed in Martin Luther's doctrine of *sola fide*, or "faith alone"—meaning that God saves people not because of who they are or what they do, but because of the work of Christ. He hoped they could openly discuss their differences and find enough common ground on which to pursue a spiritual relationship. If not, seeking a romantic one seemed rather fruitless.

Baker invited her to see *The Life of Pi* at the cavernous yet nearly empty City Plex Twelve. He sensed they both knew this would be their first real test of chemistry—outside the bedroom.

The movie ran more than two hours, and for most of that time, the pair sat side by side without physically touching. They exchanged brief, flirty glances throughout, but when they inadvertently tried to use the chair armrest at the same time and made contact, Baker reached out to hold her hand.

They continued to hold hands until the end of the movie, but when they left the cinema, Darcy let go as if to imply that someone might be watching. She clearly seemed uncomfortable about something. Baker tried to extract it from her during the car ride back to the North End, but she avoided the subject.

Her son, Sean, was with his dad that evening, so she invited Baker into her house through the back door to join her for a glass of wine. They sat discussing the movie until the alcohol loosened them both. Baker asked if he could kiss her. There was no verbal answer, but their lips found each other easily. They kissed with an intensity Baker hadn't felt in years. Then Darcy grabbed his arm and pulled him toward her bedroom.

What followed was urgent and uninhibited, lasting well into the early morning hours.

By two a.m., Baker was exhausted. He suggested they get some sleep, and Darcy got up to use the bathroom. Baker remained in bed, naked, and had already drifted off by the time she returned in pajamas. She let him sleep for a few minutes, then gently nudged his shoulder.

"Hey," she said softly.

Baker opened his eyes, confused. "What's wrong?"

"I'm just not ready to sleep with you yet," Darcy said.

Baker blinked at her. "You just did."

"I meant overnight."

Baker got dressed, barely said goodbye, and then did the walk of shame across Fifth Street. For the rest of that day, the tension between them was thick. It took until the next day for things to thaw. Darcy came by to visit Baker and asked if they could talk. She was insistent in pointing out that she didn't sleep around. In fact, she told Baker he was only the third man with whom she had ever had sex. The first was her ex-husband, and the second was a guy she'd met at a wedding expo where he was working a booth for a discount marriage license service. Something about that should have given Baker pause, but he was too amused by her confession to think it through.

But that still didn't explain why Baker got kicked out of bed. He was hoping she might reconsider her decision, and perhaps his house would be a safer space than hers. The conversation that ensued was pleasant, and both felt as though it provided a fresh start. Baker offered to cook dinner for her the following evening, and she thought that was a marvelous idea. Sean would be with his dad again, and better yet, the two of them were out of town. The possibility of his stopping by the house to retrieve schoolwork or such was nil.

Baker enjoyed dry martinis made with olives stuffed with blue cheese, which he bought at the local Basque market. His shaker was large enough to prepare two martinis at once, so without much persuasion, Darcy agreed to join Baker in, as she made it very clear, "just one."

Baker had prepared most of the dinner in advance, just in case he ran short on time. All he needed to do was place the food in the oven and heat it for ten to fifteen minutes. The dining room table had been set, and his iPod playlist was filled with

Anita Baker, Teddy Pendergrass, Regina Belle, and Deniece Williams.

Before the martinis kicked in, Baker needed to say something that was already overdue.

"Look, the other night was . . . incredible. But I realize I should have said this before we ended up in bed. I'm no prude, but I'm a monogamist. I don't do casual. If we're going to keep doing this, I need to know we're building toward something real."

Darcy studied him, trying to read whether this was a commitment or a retreat. "Are you saying you regret what happened?"

"Not for a second. I'm saying I want it to mean something."

"I think that's quite honorable," she said. Then she took a massive swig of her martini.

The two were seated together on a plaid-silk couch Baker had purchased at a local furniture consignment store. The down-filled cushions allowed them to sink in closer together, and the fabric felt like a second skin.

Baker finished his first martini ahead of Darcy, so he excused himself to make another. He also offered her a second one, but she put her hand over her glass and politely declined. Baker freshened his drink, his back was turned to her, and the music may have distracted him from hearing her speak. He just assumed she was contentedly awaiting his return.

Indeed, she was. When Baker got back to the couch, Darcy was naked from the waist up.

Shit! Baker thought. *Talk about being caught between a rock and a hard place.*

"Excuse me, I have to go to the bathroom," was the best stall tactic he could devise. He sat in the bathroom for several minutes agonizing over his next move. Three weeks had passed since their first night together—three weeks of careful phone calls, tentative dinner dates, and the growing weight of expectation. What had felt natural and urgent that first time now seemed fraught with complications. He felt sinful and horny at the same time, caught between desire and the nagging voice that reminded him he was supposed to be a man of God. He reached for a sample of Cialis his urologist had given him and popped it in his mouth. *Doesn't commit me to anything,* he rationalized, though even that felt like a lie. He returned to the couch and found her sitting in a different spot. She had shifted slightly, her body angled toward him in a way that seemed deliberate.

Baker entertained her with energetic élan, and he could tell she found him refreshingly different—more sophisticated than other men she'd met, he sensed, though she'd also picked up on something intense about him, that New York edge he'd never quite managed to shed. The compliments kept coming: handsome, well dressed, well read, well traveled, a man who loved God. His heart lifted with each one, warmth spreading through his chest, his spirit blooming in response to words he didn't know he'd been hungry to hear.

When it came time for Darcy to call it a night, she stood but didn't move toward the door. Baker stood too, closing the distance between them. He reached out, his lips finding hers, but first he breathed gently onto her neck. When he started licking and biting playfully, she responded immediately—both of them moaning, caught up in the moment. He planted a little love bite on her neck, and she pulled him toward the bedroom, all pretense of leaving abandoned.

But even with Baker having the home-court advantage, history repeated itself: He found himself waking up alone again.

Two days later, Darcy texted Baker to ask if he'd like to meet for coffee at the Grind the following morning. They would arrive separately, as she was dropping Sean at school. Baker tried not to read anything into the offer, and he said that he would.

He was the first to arrive, and he ordered two drinks, even though she hadn't told him what she wanted. The Grind had one really nice place for a couple to sit—the leather sofa—so he spread himself out to save her a seat. He waited and he waited, but there was no sign of Darcy. He finally decided to text her. She replied right away, stating she wouldn't be able to make it to the Grind, and asked Baker to come to her house.

He arrived minutes later and handed her the coffee. She thanked him and invited him to sit. She appeared nervous but not rattled. He had the sense she was preparing to give him the boot.

"Baker, I need to be honest with you," she said. "I think you're wonderful, but I'm not ready to move as fast as you seem to want to. I need to take things more slowly."

Baker felt the initial sting of disappointment, but he recognized the wisdom in what she was saying. He'd been moving fast, hadn't he? "I appreciate you being straight with me," he said. "You're right. We can take our time."

They continued talking, and something shifted—the pressure lifted. They complimented each other more freely now, without the weight of unmet expectations hanging between them. When they finally said goodbye, both had genuine smiles on their faces. Sometimes slowing down was exactly what was needed.

The two neighbors saw each other nearly every day and flirted with each other through hand waves and smiles. Baker would be in his yard when Darcy pulled her car in and out of the garage. He would catch a glimpse of her standing at the kitchen sink, looking directly at him in his bedroom. Their paths would cross while shopping at the Coop or having coffee at Earl's.

This little game of cat and mouse went on for weeks, and it seemed to Baker that there would be no logical end to it unless one of them either resumed dating or blinked first. Baker had yet to confide in Karl about his frustration with Darcy, but he intended to discuss it candidly with two unmarried friends visiting from back East within the week.

Ivan and Edith had been Baker's closest friends during his advertising days in Manhattan, an unlikely pair who'd met at a dinner party Baker and Michelle had hosted years ago. Though they'd never married, they'd been inseparable ever since that night, and they had been urging Baker to reenter the romantic landscape with exceptional skill in matchmaking. Baker knew of at least three pairings they had facilitated—all enduring. When they'd heard about his move to Idaho and his tentative steps back into dating, they'd booked flights to Boise without hesitation, insisting they needed to "inspect the situation" in person. He was eager to get their read on Darcy.

His guests arrived late one evening—too late for dinner— so they stayed up at Baker's house planning the next day. Over nightcaps, Ivan scrolled through restaurant options on his phone while Edith peered over his shoulder, shaking her head at each suggestion.

"We just prefer not to go someplace cheesy," Edith said, meaning chain restaurants.

Baker suggested Gil's K-9, one of his favorites.

"Gil's K-9?" Ivan raised an eyebrow. "Do they serve dog?"

"It's not that bad—"

"No dive bars," Edith said firmly.

They settled on the Melting Pot, the local fondue restaurant—ironic given Edith's original request. "You should invite Darcy," Ivan said as they were heading to bed. "We'd like to actually meet this woman and help you figure out if there's something real here."

Baker hesitated. "She may not come. She thinks we're moving too fast."

"All the more reason," Edith said. "If she can't handle dinner with your oldest friends, that tells you something."

She had a point. Ivan and Edith were leaving for Yellowstone the next evening—it was now or never. The next morning, Baker sent Darcy a text, not expecting much. But by three that afternoon, she replied that she would join them. Perhaps the buffer of other people would actually make her feel more at ease. Baker made reservations at seven, giving him time to show Ivan and Edith some of Boise first. They toured the State Capitol Building and the Old Idaho Penitentiary—attractions that always surprised Baker with their popularity among visitors. But he saved his favorite for last: the Egyptian Theatre, Boise's oldest, with its pyramid facade and lotus-bud pillars modeled after Karnak. Josh Ritter had played to a sold-out crowd there just months earlier.

Even though the theater was closed, someone in the ticket office let them look around anyway. Part of the "Boise Kind" culture, Baker explained to his friends.

That kindness was extended further atop the Hoff Building, an art deco building originally built as a hotel and now an office space for Idaho lobbyists and political groups. The eleventh floor was occupied entirely by a law firm, whose receptionist didn't seem the least bit fazed when Baker asked if they could walk around the perimeter to see the sights of the city. The view was a stunning panorama of the entire Treasure Valley, including the cityscape and surrounding mountains. Baker pointed out specific nearby sites such as Trinity, his old apartment building, and the Boise State football stadium, and much farther away, the Bogus Basin ski area. It wasn't the Empire State Building, and it didn't need to be.

Baker texted Darcy again around five p.m. to let her know they were heading to Red Feather for a cocktail before dinner and would meet her at the restaurant. You'll have such a good time getting to know my friends. They're both really smart and very accessible, he promised.

Baker and his friends arrived at the restaurant on schedule and found her waiting. They had a head start in terms of alcohol, but Darcy caught up quickly. The meal was quite good, and the wine was even better. The mood at the table was extremely amiable, and everyone had a chance to talk about their favorite subjects—travel stories, books they'd recently read, childhood memories from different parts of the country. Notably absent was any discussion of religion, yet they all got on as new friends. They enjoyed a glass of tawny port before the evening concluded.

When they got up from the table to leave, she asked Baker if he would walk with her to her car. "Why don't you guys go ahead, and I'll meet you at home?" Baker said. During the walk, she complimented his friends and thanked him profusely for including her. Baker hardly recognized this outgoing and non-amorous version of Darcy.

"I had a great time tonight. Your friends are so interesting and thoughtful and have done so many things that I'd like to experience," she gushed.

As Baker opened the car door, she stood in place waiting for a kiss. He obliged in European style, the way he always kissed Grace at Trinity. After turning to sit in her car and starting the engine, Darcy rolled down the window to make a parting comment. "I'm going to take *you* to dinner soon," she promised.

Baker's friends thought that Darcy was rather friendly—a little bit "small town," but a promising prospect nonetheless. They encouraged Baker to give her another chance. "Maybe being her third scared her a bit, but now that a few weeks have gone by, you guys can start over."

For the next five weeks, Baker and Darcy never made it to dinner, but they did resume their romance. She shrewdly scheduled every dalliance around Sean being at home so that the overnight issue could be avoided. Baker laid on some heavy hickeys in late November, and Darcy's neck had turned fifty shades of gray, which she had to hide not only from her family on Thanksgiving day, but also, two days later, from hundreds of worshippers at a multifaith service held at her cathedral. To cover up the damage, she wore a long-sleeve turtleneck. When she went to the service, she added a gray peacoat with a popped collar and a scarf for extra protection.

Baker invited Karl and Margaret to the service, making it the first and only time they would meet Darcy. The three sat at one end of an aisle on the east side of the cathedral, and as expected, Darcy swept by. She stopped for maybe twelve seconds to be introduced to the Thompsons, touched Baker on the shoulder, and sent him an air-kiss. Then she was gone.

After the service, Karl and Baker walked back into town together while Margaret headed home to attend to something else. The walk gave Baker a chance to open up about his complicated relationship with Darcy. He'd been disappointed that Karl hadn't had a proper chance to assess her during their brief introduction, but he used that moment as a segue into everything that had been going on.

"What was your impression of her?" Baker asked. "Anything you noticed?"

"It strikes me that she has a little crush on you," Karl offered.

Once Baker got going, he inadvertently shared far more romantic detail about the past two months than Karl probably needed to hear. Baker regretted spilling such dirt, especially when Karl snickered once or twice, and quickly changed the subject.

"She's into short stories and has shared some of her work with me," Baker added.

"She writes her own?" Karl asked.

"Yes, she does, although it took a while for her to gather the courage to let me read them," Baker said.

"What do you think of them?"

"To be honest, I don't understand them," Baker said. He considered himself functionally illiterate regarding short fiction. He didn't perform well in school when studying classic American short story writers, and his teacher, Mr. Heartfield, pushed him hard to understand the essential elements of narrative structure and character development. He managed to grasp basic plot mechanics, but that was about it.

Baker persuaded Darcy to give him a physical copy of a story she had mentioned to him many times about the one and only Dietrich Bonhoeffer. Despite her attempts to explain it in a Lutheran theological context, he still didn't fully grasp its deeper meaning. Baker shared it with Karl, a published writer himself, hoping it would give him insight into Darcy. After reading, Karl explained to Baker that it had nothing to do with the church and everything to do with the feelings of emptiness and emotional pain she experienced in her failed marriage.

"Have you read the work of confessional writers, like Raymond Carver or Alice Munro?" Karl asked.

Baker answered, "No," and recounted his struggles in Mr. Heartfield's class. Karl encouraged him not to give up, and for good measure, he informed Baker that the celebrated short story writer Mavis Gallant had died six months earlier.

"Do some research on Mavis and then ask Darcy some questions about her work you might want answered," Karl advised. "See where that takes you."

Baker shared Karl's interpretation of the Bonhoeffer story with Darcy, careful to credit his friend. He watched her face for signs of displeasure, half-expecting her to resent the intrusion. Instead, she simply nodded, a faint smile crossing her lips.

"Your friend understands suffering," she said quietly, turning away to gaze out the window. The remark hung between them—ambiguous, neither quite approval nor dismissal—leaving Baker uncertain whether he'd gained ground or lost it.

CHRISTMAS WAS FAST APPROACHING, and Baker dearly wanted to be included in any plans Darcy had with her family. However, she wasn't ready for that. She wasn't prepared for sleepovers. Darcy still had reservations about indulging in PDA with Baker. Yet she asked Baker not to give up on her; perhaps in time, she would change.

Baker was losing patience. He told Darcy flatly: sex was off the table. That was non-negotiable. There were some close calls, but Baker stood his ground. Even on Christmas morning, after she had dispatched her family and come to Baker's house, she literally begged him to have sex. He declined.

The two had made plans to attend a comedy show at a downtown venue on Boxing Day evening. At least, that was Baker's belief. A few hours before the performance, he received the following text from Darcy: An old friend of mine is coming to town tonight and needs a place to stay. I'm really sorry, but I won't be able to join you tonight. Further down the text, she clarified it was a man.

Baker was furious. How dare she let another man sleep overnight in her house, even if it was, he guessed, just on the sofa? He didn't want details. He didn't need to know if they were planning to get it on or not. It simply didn't matter. He felt betrayed, even violated.

As soon as he could, Baker dialed Karl to seek his counsel. There was no answer. Baker left a message saying it was urgent and for Karl to call him back, regardless of the time. An hour before midnight, and two hours beyond Karl's usual bedtime, he did. After Baker explained his dilemma, Karl wasn't the least bit tongue tied.

"Get out of this relationship, Baker. She's nothing but a coquette."

Karl followed with other words that were cruder, but he had Baker at *coquette*. Plenty of preppy young Southern girls had given Baker blue balls as a teenager, so he was pretty familiar with the term. He knew that was not what Darcy was—in fact, she was just the opposite—just plain horny, but he didn't try to correct Karl because he understood the bishop's polemic. He thanked him, and after ending the call, Baker immediately shot off the most ungentlemanly email to Darcy: Stay the fuck away from me. You are nothing but a coquette—that's Karl's term, not mine! Surely your colleagues in the classics know of Pythia, the high priestess of the Temple of Apollo at Delphi. Let them know that henceforth you will be known to Karl and me as Pythia, the High Priestess of casual sex, the Orifice of Delhi.

The next morning, Darcy burst into Baker's house, acting like a lunatic. She paced the living room and around the couch that had endured a lot of heavy wear and tear. With each loop, she berated Baker for being such a backstabber. Her parting gesture was to throw the spare set of house keys Baker had loaned her at his face.

"You're going to pay for this," Darcy said. Then she went back to her house, muttering something about fucking never dating anyone ever again.

To redeem herself in Karl Thompson's eyes, Darcy visited the Trinity website and discovered Karl's email address. She then composed an emotionally restrained statement in defense of her recent actions. She asserted that she was not a loose woman and never intended to mislead Baker. She concluded by including the sign-off "With every good wish," before hitting the send button.

What Baker didn't know—and what Darcy couldn't have known—was that Karl had never accessed the email address she'd found. As Baker would later discover when the office administrator called, it was merely a general mailbox, much like the others they used that began with "office" or "admin." Everyone in the Trinity office would see her email except Karl himself.

Baker spoke with the office administrator, for whom he had worked so hard as a volunteer, asking him what to do with the email. What he felt like saying was, "Please print a copy and send it to the *Idaho Statesman*." But Baker knew better. He was the guilty one, and digging a deeper hole now would only serve to hurt Karl's reputation as well as his own.

As Baker set down the phone, he recognized the cruel joke of it: here he was, a man supposedly devoted to spiritual integrity, but instead entangled in a web of lust, anger, and pettiness—far from the example of grace he aspired to embody. The Darcy affair had been a detour, perhaps even a test. As he eyed his reflection in the window overlooking her house, Baker wondered if this messy human stumble might ultimately strengthen his empathy for the flawed parishioners he hoped to serve or fuck it up for the long haul. The weight of "You're going to pay for this" from an angry woman who knew about his seminary aspirations meant this wasn't about spiritual growth anymore—it was about survival. His calling, once so clear, now felt dangerously compromised.

Chapter Eight

FORGIVENESS MEANS GIVING UP ALL HOPE FOR A BETTER PAST, and Baker needed time to work on that. He understood this all too well. He kept his curtains closed most of the time to avoid simulating the scene in the movie *Atlantic City:* Burt Lancaster's admiring eyes watching Susan Sarandon stand in her kitchen, slicing a lemon, squeezing the juice into her hands, and rubbing it all over her body. He couldn't help but remember the feelings he had for Darcy, and then how it all unraveled, leaving him ashamed of how he had treated her in the end. The memory of that failure hung over him like a storm cloud, making him doubt whether he deserved another chance at love. It took nearly a month for him to forgive himself and summon the courage to try again. By New Year's Eve, Baker had done enough inner work to feel ready and proudly found his first person of interest on Match.com and sent her a message.

He had created a profile that accurately described him and uploaded a recent picture. He identified himself as spiritual, athletic, college educated, politically progressive, well-traveled, and "no children, please." He wanted to find someone in Boise who was alive with energy and open to trying new things. He also preferred someone in the age range of thirty-eight to forty-five, which Baker would admit—especially to Emma and Grace—was playing things a bit fast and loose. In his defense, he had been advised that women in their fifties would present themselves to him as being in their mid-forties without thinking twice about it.

He received a welcome email from Match.com with an initial set of women who were purportedly looking for someone like Baker and vice versa. They came with thumbnail pictures and a mix of real and made-up usernames: LonelyMe from Boise, Laurel from Eagle, TwoCutePersians from Nampa, Crystal from Meridian, Rhonda from Star, and ten other so-called best matches. Five of them were well over forty-five, and only four lived in Boise.

Baker scrolled through the dating site without enthusiasm, dismissing profile after profile. Then he saw her: RunsWithASmile, a Boise woman in her late forties with long, curly brunette hair and tight jeans. Exactly his age range. Her profile was sparse and cautious—the kind of safe, pleasant writing that revealed nothing—but it ended with a Krakauer quote: "Faith is the antithesis of Reason."

He paused on that. It suggested something beneath the surface, some friction between what she believed and what she thought. He hit the heart icon and waited. When nothing came back, he typed out a message anyway.

Days passed without a response. When he hadn't heard from her in another two days, and since no one else looked approachable, he sent a Hail Mary message asking her out for coffee. This time, she replied but remained noncommittal. He tucked his tail between his legs, thanked her for responding, and wished her the very best in the New Year and much success in finding true love. She dutifully acknowledged his sincerity with an obligatory "thank you" and said that to kick off 2015, she would be joining her polar bear group for their traditional New Year's Day swim in the Boise River, followed by a pancake breakfast prepared and served tailgate-style.

He moved on to "like" and message others and went on two or three dates. One of those dates led to sex in the back seat of his car. This time, it was Baker who initiated the "go home" command when they were finished. The woman, Katherine, was too nuts and needy. He wondered if that was what Darcy had thought of him, which left him feeling uncertain, even a bit ashamed, about his own character. But there was a positive in all this: He had a new point of comparison, and a user who called herself Smiley seemed even more desirable. When he tried to find her again, she had already left the site. So Baker threw in the towel and let his Match membership lapse.

But Match was tenacious and sent Baker a "come back for two free months" offer that he couldn't turn down. He went back on and tweaked his profile. When he saw that Smiley was back on Match too, his reaction was one of excitement, and he sent her another message. Since he had now excluded tricenarians from his target age range and added more specific details about his interests in hiking, literature, and spiritual growth, Smiley became more attentive to his message. He now painted a picture of someone genuinely seeking a meaningful connection with a woman in his demographic rather than casting a wide net. The changes suggested a maturity and intentionality that had been missing from his original, more generic approach. And she had adjusted her profile as well, adding: "Don't post pictures wearing a wifebeater, don't show me your guns or your kill, and tattoos are a deal-breaker." Baker now sensed that his competition was limited, and his confidence grew.

After a few more encouraging exchanges through Match's messaging system, Baker suggested they move their conversation to the phone. She agreed, and they began talking in the evenings. Their first call lasted nearly two hours, covering everything from favorite books to travel experiences, their thoughts on living in Boise, and stories from their respective childhoods. The conversations felt natural and unforced, neither of them rushing to fill silences or trying too hard to impress.

During their next call, Baker learned that Smiley was having a rough time on Match. He offered to listen to some of her stories. Her first prospect, KenSledder, a snowmobiler and avid beer drinker, had exchanged two or three messages with her before making what Baker considered an appalling proposal: "How about I put a harness on you and hook you up to a sled and you can run and pull me to pubs so I can get my beers? That way it would be a win-win." Baker wasn't surprised when she told him she'd been horrified and never replied.

Then there was SwissRich, who described himself as a real estate developer living in Montana. His profile pictures featured beautiful European landscapes and cityscapes, and he claimed to spend a good portion of the year in a small Swiss town near Lake Geneva, where he had been raised. Baker could see why she'd been intrigued—actually, wowed. He understood her impulse to research the guy online to verify his claims. *Why would a wealthy guy like this be on Match?* Baker had wondered the same thing when she'd told him about it. It turned out that one of his pictures, his so-called villa in the mountains, was merely a stock photo of the villa La Paisible, once owned by Audrey Hepburn. Baker was relieved when that was the end of him.

PowderHound was a building contractor who lived two and a half hours north of Boise in the town of Ketchum, adjacent to Sun Valley. From what Baker could gather, he seemed like a nice enough guy from the get-go, but not someone to whom she was physically attracted. The man traveled to Boise often on business, and on one of these visits, he called and, rather spontaneously, convinced her to join him for lunch. They'd had a good time and discovered that they had enough in common to stay in touch.

A week or so later, as she was preparing to buy a new sofa, PowderHound had called to see if she might be up for a drive. Baker learned she'd tried to explain her unavailability, but the contractor wouldn't take no for an answer. He'd offered to take her shopping instead. In the blink of an eye, he'd pulled up to her house in a Porsche Cayenne, offered to take some measure-ments of her living room, and driven her to the RC Willey store in Meridian. She'd shown him a sectional sofa that she liked, and he'd given her a no-doubt-about-it second opinion. Based on his calculations, "There could not be a better piece of furniture to fit the space."

After shopping, PowderHound persuaded her to join him for dinner in Boise's BoDo district. They had a great meal, but she had the presence of mind—and was sufficiently sober—to keep things platonic. He dropped her off at her house and asked for a kiss. She hesitated and suddenly found herself conflicted. Yes, he'd been helpful and kind, but she just wasn't ready to rev his engine and send the wrong message. So she leaned in to him, pursed her lips, closed her eyes, and gave him a tiny peck on the cheek.

"Seriously, that's it?" he had said. Smiley continued her story in her email. "I tried to tell him politely that I wasn't ready for a new relationship, but you could see him deflate right there in the driver's seat. Never heard from him again." Baker found himself both entertained by her stories and grateful that he'd eventually broken through her defenses.

He would learn later, in subsequent conversations, about the loneliness that had driven her back to the site—how she'd spent Valentine's Day alone at a neighborhood bar, surrounded by couples, thinking about the importance of sharing her life with someone. But in that moment, all he knew was that somehow, against all odds, they'd both found their way back to Match, and back to each other, on the same day.

Within days, they had confessed to each other that they were ready to meet in person. Smiley revealed herself to be Lilibeth Bradshaw, an unmarried, childless middle school math teacher and orchestra leader at the prestigious Andrus School. By the time Baker got around to asking her out on a date, she didn't bat an eye. She requested to be called by her nickname, Libby, which relieved Baker. He thought Lilibeth sounded too royal and too posh. They discussed various options for a first date and eventually decided on lunch at Bardenay, a former warehouse on Boise's Basque Block. Baker knew that most astute couples avoided alcohol on a first date, but he found a comfortable way to explore the subject.

"I have to usher at the Morrison Center after our date, so if we were to have a drink, it would have to be a good one, like a martini," he said in his usual understated way when it came to alcohol. Bardenay distilled their own gin and vodka and offered three Manzanilla olives stuffed with blue cheese as a garnish with their martinis, so Baker was really hoping Libby would agree to have at least one.

BAKER HAD A NAGGING suspicion that Libby might have done some research on him before their date. *Most people google their dates these days,* he thought, *and I'm not exactly invisible online.* He wondered if she'd stumbled across the Finnish bride video—that would undoubtedly require some explaining.

When he arrived at Bardenay around one p.m., he was surprised by the boisterous atmosphere at lunchtime. There was a fanny in every armchair, high back, and barstool—140 in total—plus dozens more patrons lined up at the long bar and approaching the hostess stand. The restaurant's architecture featured an open-beam rafter ceiling that kept the noise from the crowd manageable, but Baker still hoped for a quiet corner table.

With his romantic history weighing on his mind, he found himself unconsciously scanning for familiar faces from that very past he was worried about discussing with Libby.

After circling the restaurant's perimeter once, he returned to the hostess stand. The first person he spotted—or thought he spotted—was his ex, Michelle, with that unmistakable look: a one-piece dress, pin-straight brunette hair, and fashion sunglasses perched atop her head like a headband, that casual way stylish women wore them when they wanted the accessory visible, but the sun wasn't. His stomach dropped momentarily before he took a closer look and realized his eyes were playing tricks on him.

Then he spotted a woman who *had* to be Libby. Those warm brown eyes and that naturally curly hair resembled her profile picture perfectly, and he was not only attracted to her, but he was also a bit smitten. She radiated an air of indescribable sweetness that only authentically beautiful people possess.

The waitress seated them at the only available table—a high-top positioned directly in the center of the dining room's chaos. Baker had hoped for something tucked away by a window where they could ease into conversation without competing with the clatter of dishes and animated discussions from neighboring tables. Instead, they found themselves on display, surrounded by the lunch rush. Baker caught Libby's gaze and shrugged apologetically, but she just smiled and leaned forward, ready for the challenge of getting to know each other despite the less than romantic setting.

Soft light cast a gentle glow across Libby's face. The aromas of garlic, olive oil, and roasted herbs drifted from the kitchen, punctuated by the rhythmic clink of glasses and the low murmur of conversations. They ordered martinis before looking at the menu—cold, crisp, and perfectly balanced. The first sip burned pleasantly down Baker's throat as he watched Libby smile over the rim of her glass.

"How about the marriage to the Finn?" Libby began boldly, with a mischievous glint in her eye. "Was that for real?"

Baker nearly choked on his martini. "You saw that?"

"I may have done a little research," she said, trying to suppress a grin. "Found a video of you enjoying . . . what was it? Rye bread and salted licorice? At some reception with Finnish dolls and glassware everywhere?"

Baker laughed, both embarrassed and impressed. "And you still showed up to this date?"

"I was curious," Libby admitted. "Though I have to say, I was hoping it wasn't some kind of mail-order bride situation."

"Well, I'm flattered you googled me—and relieved the Finnish wedding was all you found," Baker said with a grin.

"So . . . was it real?"

Baker considered playing a practical joke, maybe claiming the Episcopal Church had actively supported it. "As real as that wedding may have appeared, it was just a theatrical performance."

"Well, that's a relief," Libby said, visibly relaxing. "Though I have to admit, you looked pretty convincing eating that rye bread."

Their conversation continued, and Libby shared that she was born and raised in Marin County, California, to Caucasian parents who both grew up on the East Coast. She spent most of her youth in a stylish home in Mill Valley and, beginning in the sixth grade, attended the historic Branson School in San Rafael.

"My dad—everyone called him Buddy—was this wild character," Libby said, stirring her drink. "He rode a motorcycle from Maine to California in the fifties, got into real estate in Hawaii early, and made a fortune. But before all that, he got sidetracked in Idaho after meeting some guy who told him Marilyn Monroe had worn a potato-sack dress there as a publicity stunt."

Baker raised an eyebrow.

"I know, right? So Dad ends up in Sun Valley, teaching horseback riding to celebrities—Monroe, Hemingway, the whole crowd. He learned to ski and fly planes with this daredevil friend named Dick Buek. They were both speed junkies." Her expression darkened slightly. "Dick died in a plane crash eventually. Carburetor iced up over Donner Lake." She took a sip. "Dad always said that could've been him."

Baker interrupted Libby first to comment favorably on her dad's success, but more importantly, to ask her to talk about herself. Baker wasn't interested in dating Buddy.

"I'm sorry, I've completely dominated the conversation," Libby said apologetically.

"Not at all," Baker replied. "I've been enjoying learning about your dad. My father was a very predictable conformist and never took any risks. He couldn't understand why anyone would choose uncertainty when security was available."

"You said *was*. Is he still alive?" Libby inquired.

"Well, yes, he is alive but not in great shape. He's had a couple of ministrokes, and my guess is that it's only a matter of time before the big one happens. My sister, Emma, is living in Lynchburg and keeping an eye on him, but the future is certainly not looking good."

Baker wanted to change the subject and finally got Libby to talk about herself.

"Well, it's hard for me to avoid the topic of skiing," she admitted. "I was a 'chalet girl' growing up during winter breaks. I worked at Chamonix, Sankt Anton, and Courchevel and was a bit younger than the British girls who had already graduated from boarding school."

"Did you ski for free?" Baker leaned forward, his elbows resting on the small café table between them.

"Yes. Wages were low, the hours were long, and the drinks in the local bars were cheap." Libby wrapped her hands around her martini glass, the chill seeping into her fingers. "But it was crazy to ski in some of the world's most exclusive resorts and get paid to do it." Her eyes lit up with the memory, a genuine smile breaking across her face.

The afternoon sun filtered through the café's large windows, casting gilded ribbons across their table. Baker studied her expression, noting how animated she became when talking about skiing.

"So tell me, Libby, why do you seem so normal and down-to-earth, having been raised the way you were and experienced such expensive pleasures?"

Her smile faltered slightly, and she set down her glass with a soft clink against a plate. "There was an event in my life while I was skiing in Courchevel that shook me to my core. I never thought I'd recover from it." She looked out the window, watching pedestrians hurry past on the busy street.

"Is it something you'd be comfortable talking about?"

Libby's fingers found the stem of her glass again, turning it slowly. "I'm sorry, not now. But I assure you, everything is fine. Therapy is a wonderful thing." She offered a quick smile, but her shoulders had tensed.

Baker nodded, respecting her boundary. The silence between them felt comfortable rather than awkward as he took a sip of his drink, the olives settling against the bottom of the glass.

"You know," he said, setting his glass down and running a hand through his hair, "my dad would say therapy is an unnecessary expense. 'Why pay someone to listen to your problems when you can just keep them to yourself for free?'" He straightened his posture and furrowed his brow, mimicking his father's stern tone before his face relaxed into a smile. "One of his many pearls of wisdom."

Libby laughed, her shoulders dropping as the tension melted away. She tucked a strand of hair behind her ear. "And what do you think?"

"I think..." Baker hesitated, choosing his words carefully.

"I think there's courage in confronting your demons instead of pretending they don't exist. That takes more guts than most people realize."

She studied him for a moment. "You're not what I expected, Baker."

"Is that good or bad?"

"Good," she said, tucking a strand of hair behind her ear. "Definitely good."

Baker realized that Libby might have just as much baggage as he did, and as much as he thought Buddy might be the reason for hers, who was to say that Buddy was any different from his alcoholic mother in many ways? But he didn't dwell on it too much because he was deeply engrossed in looking at this laid-back, curly-haired, sun-and-snow-worshipping goddess, enjoying what was now his second martini and learning that a flatlander like him had much to learn about living in the West.

He guessed that the subject of prior marriages would come up sooner or later, especially since neither person had mentioned it in their Match profile. Libby, of course, was itching to get to the subject of Ulla. Baker, on the other hand, was uncomfortable with the idea of volunteering the fact that he had been married once before.

"Do you have any children?" Libby asked before segueing into the question of marriage.

My mother would know how to answer this properly, Baker thought.

"No, I don't," Baker answered. Technically, he was correct, but he wasn't prepared to say more. "How about you?" he asked.

"Nope," Libby answered. "Never been married either."

"How did you avoid that?"

Libby swirled the last olive in her glass, taking a moment to gather her thoughts. "You know, people always ask that like it's some great mystery," she said with a wry smile. "The truth is less dramatic than they want it to be."

She looked beyond Baker and out the window briefly before continuing. "I've had relationships, sure. Two almost made it to marriage. But I've always been…particular. My father calls it 'impossibly picky,' but I call it knowing my worth." Her fingers traced a pattern on the tablecloth. "After my second engagement fell apart over the issue of children—I can't have them—I threw myself into teaching and built a life I genuinely loved. I traveled during summers, made friendships that matter to me, and found joy in my independence."

Baker nodded, captivated by her candor.

"There were years I didn't date at all," she continued. "Not because I couldn't, but because I was content. And yes, sometimes it was scary thinking I might grow old alone, but it was scarier imagining being with someone just for the sake of not being alone." She caught his gaze directly. "I'd rather be single at fifty than spend twenty years with the wrong person. Besides, my students keep me young—or drive me crazy, depending on the day." Her laugh was bright and genuine, with no hint of regret.

"What about you?" she asked, turning the question around. "You're quite the catch yourself."

Baker felt seen in a way that made him both uncomfortable and exhilarated. This woman didn't need him—she chose him. And somehow, that made all the difference.

"You've been married before, right?" Libby asked.

"Yes, I was married once. After that, I was in a long-term relationship," Baker admitted, then quickly added before she could ask more, "and since we're getting it all out on the table, I also have a tattoo."

"Nuh-uh."

"Yeah-uh." At this point he rolled up his pant leg far enough to show it.

"I could never get one," Libby confessed. But she didn't mention it was a deal-breaker. Not for now, anyway.

By first-date standards, the pair were venturing into taboo topics, but nothing caused any anxiety. They were curious about each other, and they kept asking each other deep and thought-provoking questions, and neither had that compulsive need to be right. They were compatible above the neck, and they had plenty of time to address their physical needs.

However, after an indeterminate number of martinis, lunch lasted three hours. Baker paid the bill and offered to walk Libby to her car. Naturally, he was curious about the vehicle she drove, hoping it wasn't a gas-guzzling SUV or something similar. It was a quirky litmus test for Baker, but he was still feeling the sting of the hairdresser from Greenleaf driving a pickup. Along the way, he casually mentioned the possibility of a date the next day, perhaps walking through the foothills, to which Libby replied, "That sounds like fun, but let's first touch base in the morning. I have a lot to prepare for school on Monday."

When they arrived at her car, Baker realized Libby drove an old Toyota Camry, and he glowed. Sure, he'd lived in the fast lane and owned plenty of expensive things throughout his life, but he didn't want any of it anymore, nor did he want to share a life with someone who did. He'd learned that lesson the hard way.

The next morning, Baker was ready when Libby arrived. He'd slept well and felt clear-headed. They drove to Camel's

Back Reserve, and he led her toward the easier trails that wound past native grasses and bird refuges—good trails, honest trails. He wasn't trying to prove anything.

When Libby mentioned she'd experienced these paths many times and suggested tackling the steep climbs, even running them, Baker considered it without hesitation. He knew his current fitness level. He knew what made sense.

"Let's stick with this route," he said evenly. "I'm not where I used to be, but what the hell. These trails are worth the time."

Libby nodded, and they set off together.

They resumed where they had left off at Bardenay. Baker needed to confess something to Libby that he considered a potential deal-breaker. As soon as the small talk ended and the hiking leveled out, he asked Libby to pause where a rocky outcropping gave her a foot of elevation. This way, he could look her in the eye.

"I'm considering a new vocation," he said.

"A new vocation?" Libby tilted her head. "But I thought you were enjoying being semiretired. The volunteer work and everything."

"I've always wanted to be a priest," he said.

Libby assumed that he meant a Catholic priest. "You mean you plan to become celibate?" she asked, rather alarmed.

Baker chuckled at her obvious concern. He drew out a long "Weelll . . . ," enjoying the moment of suspense before putting her mind at ease about his denominational flavor. "I'm an Episcopalian," he stated. "We believe in scripture, tradition, and reason. I can assure you that *anybody* can become a priest in our church."

"Including women?" Libby asked.

"Of course," Baker declared. "Even lesbians."

Baker watched as her shoulders relaxed. "Wow, I am so relieved," she admitted. "My family has always had this thing about 'the Catholics,' calling them mackerel snappers and bead rattlers. So when they see priests wearing vestments, they assume that they are papists."

He could see the tension leave her shoulders entirely. For a moment, she looked like she might lean in to kiss him right there, but something held her back. Baker found himself both grateful for her restraint and oddly disappointed by it.

By the time they concluded their walk, Baker had learned that Libby's spiritual journey included short stints at an Episcopal kindergarten in Mill Valley and a year or two of dipping her toe into Quaker water in Boise. Neither parent had provided her with a religious upbringing. Many years later, however, her dad was baptized in the Jordan River—it cost him a fortune—and became a deathbed Christian. Libby was disgusted by it, thinking he was trying to buy a place in heaven. But she was willing to explore what was giving Baker so much fulfillment and even offered to attend a future service at Trinity. It certainly appeared that their fledgling relationship was on sound footing.

Since the two were talking so openly, Libby took a moment to confess something to Baker: On the evening of their first date, she had gone to dinner with another fellow from Match. He was a local business owner who had posted a profoundly clever profile, which made Libby quite sanguine about the whole online dating thing. However, when they met, he admitted that his buddy had written the entire thing. He then ordered a bottle of Coors Light and shook off the glass the waitress offered. He seemed terribly disinterested in the date and, after finishing his beer, handed

Libby his phone number and lamely told her to call him if she wanted to go out again. She and Baker both had a good and grateful laugh about it.

They were on a roll. It was a Monday, and Libby had the day off from school. This would make three days in a row. Baker's idea was to do something spontaneous, such as getting in his car and letting the tailwinds of life take them somewhere.

That somewhere turned out to be Hagerman, Idaho, some one hundred miles to the south and east of Boise and home to the best sweet corn and watermelon in North America. But once they got there, they didn't eat, nor did they soak in the hot springs. They went to a modest general store, bought a six-pack of beer, hiked half a mile into a secluded meadow, and without further delay, started to make out.

It was an unforgettable spring afternoon of recaptured adolescence and sweet temptation. The late March sun warmed their skin as they spread a blanket over tall grass dotted with early wildflowers. The distant sound of the Snake River mingled with birdsong and the whisper of wind through the trees. The yellow meadow ants came up through the grass and were a great nuisance, but the two lay still and carried on without a care in the world. The taste of cold beer and each other's lips, the scent of sun-warmed skin and fresh grass—everything heightened their senses. They had no differences to resolve, and if the beer had lasted longer, they might have stayed there until dusk.

During the two-hour drive back to Boise that evening, they talked about when they could meet again. Their beginning together had been a whirlwind, one date after the other deepening their connection at a pace that surprised them both.

"I need to head out tomorrow," Baker explained, glancing briefly at Libby before returning his eyes to the road. "Just for three days. Some guys I met when I first moved here invited me up to northeast Oregon."

Libby nodded. "The timing works out. I've got a light schedule this week, but once you're back, end-of-quarter exams hit, and I'll be buried in paperwork."

Baker mentioned that the next time, whenever that might be, would be their fourth date. "And you know what that means," he added with a grin. "All bets are off as far as chastity."

Libby laughed softly, though her expression suggested she had no idea what he was talking about. She was not aware of the "three dates before sex" rule popularized on television by the *Sex and the City* character Carrie Bradshaw and her friends, but Baker was—in fact, he had made this rule long before the show was aired.

Even as he made the comment, Baker felt a twinge of guilt. The "rule" hadn't applied to Katherine—that had been pure impulse, back-seat fumbling born of loneliness and too much wine. But this felt different. This time he wanted to do things right, to build something that might last. Whether that made him principled or simply a hypocrite rewriting his own history, he wasn't entirely sure.

They drove in comfortable silence for a while, the highway stretching ahead of them, the last light fading from the western sky.

Out of the blue, he looked at her and asked, "Would you ever consider getting married?" The question had just tumbled out, bolder than he'd intended, and he felt exhilarated. It seemed to catch Libby off guard. He watched as she opened her mouth, then closed it again. The silence stretched on, each second feeling like an eternity. He could see her thinking, weighing something in her mind, and his stomach began to knot. Had he pushed too hard? Was she trying to find a gentle way to let him down?

"Yeah, maybe," Libby answered, hesitating slightly. The words seemed to surprise her as much as they did him.

"Why would that matter, though, as far as our fourth date?"

He kept his eyes on the road as he explained his philosophy about intimacy—how sex was meant to be shared with someone who saw it as a way to enhance a relationship, not destroy it. She listened without interrupting. As the two planned when that fourth date might be and dropping Libby at home, he realized he should call Karl. He was moving fast with someone who'd only just admitted the possibility of marriage.

Chapter Nine

HE MADE THE CALL, AND AFTER HE AND KARL EXCHANGED pleasantries, Baker jumped to this most pressing question: "Am I wasting my time pursuing someone my age who has never been married?"

At first, Karl was calm with his response. He asked Baker to back up a bit and describe where he was in his relationship with Libby.

"We have crossed the three-date threshold," Baker shared.

"Three dates and you're already dropping the *M*-word?" Karl practically shouted into the phone. "Baker, when I said you needed a partner, I didn't mean you should propose to the first woman who gives you the time of day. You're operating at break-neck speeds here."

Baker held the phone away from his ear. "It just came out."

"Things that 'just come out' are usually the most honest," Karl said, his voice softening. "But marriage? To someone who's been out of the game for a long time? That's like buying concert tickets before checking if the other person even likes music."

"So it's hopeless?"

"I'm saying you need a real conversation about expectations.

Not some vague 'yeah, maybe' exchange." Karl paused. "But I'd still like to meet her."

"Really? How about brunch next week?"

"Brunch works. Tuesday." Karl's tone turned sincere. "Look, I'm not saying pump the brakes because she's wrong for you. I'm saying slow down enough to make sure you're both heading in the same direction."

Baker sighed, watching the afternoon light cast shadows across his living room. "What if we're not?"

"Then you'll know before you've driven too far down a one-way street." Karl paused. "And if you are? Well, I haven't seen you this excited about anyone besides the coquette."

He just had to throw that in, didn't he? "Thanks, Karl."

"Don't thank me yet. I'm still planning to ask her all the embarrassing questions."

Baker groaned. "I'm starting to regret this."

"That's how you know it's going to be good." Karl laughed. "See you Tuesday."

Baker told Libby about the brunch date and apologized for not asking her first. She immediately seemed nervous—perhaps not expecting to need someone else's approval before their fourth date. Truth be told, Baker couldn't predict what questions Karl might ask, but since Baker's parents and sister were far away, he wanted a "family" member to meet his new lady. Karl was the closest thing to family he had in Boise.

In the end, Libby didn't need much convincing to meet Karl.

They met up at Le Café de Paris, a downtown bistro that served spectacular pastries and coffee without even a hint of pretension. It was a one-of-a-kind spot in Boise, and their chef raised the culinary bar with evening dishes such as pork tenderloin with zucchini, roasted apples, and garlic potatoes; rack of lamb with asparagus, red-wine-glazed potatoes, and tomato jam; and braised chicken with almond couscous.

The waitress stopped at their table with a knowing smile. "Bishop, the owner wanted me to let you know that we can make our crepes for you today—even though it's not technically brunch hours," she said. "They're really something special. We use a traditional French batter that we let rest overnight, which makes them impossibly tender and delicate. Then we cook them on our cast-iron griddle until they're just barely golden, so they stay soft in the center. Most places rush them, but ours are worth the wait."

Karl placed an order for crepes for the whole table straight away. Baker knew his friend didn't like disruptions when it came time for conversation. The espresso machine hissed in the background, releasing steam that carried hints of vanilla and caramel.

Once the waitress left, Karl asked Libby to introduce herself, and she politely obliged, covering various topics, some of which were new to Baker—particularly her involvement in the Boise Humanist Group, whose members attached prime importance to human rather than divine matters. Baker watched Karl notice the electricity between them and suppress a knowing smile.

Under the table, Baker's knee occasionally brushed against Libby's, and each time it happened, she'd give him a quick sideways glance, as if to say, *Yes, I feel you too.*

"Do you attend church?" Karl asked, taking a sip of his coffee.

"Honestly, I haven't been to a Sunday church service for a few years, but I did attend a wedding at Trinity last summer," she acknowledged. She looked at Baker with a smile, her fingers tracing the rim of her cup, because she hadn't shared that with him before.

"How did you enjoy that?" Karl inquired.

"I loved being inside that church, looking at all the glass and artwork. But something didn't sit well with me," she continued.

"What was that, if I may ask?"

"I didn't connect with the priest," she freely admitted. "He had a curious and, frankly, unnecessary air of superiority, particularly the way he spoke. I just thought to myself, 'Doesn't he realize that he's officiating in front of some average Joes from Idaho?'"

Karl didn't exactly burst out laughing, but he wore an impish look because he knew damn well that Libby's assessment was spot-on.

"This may sound odd, but as soon as my father became a Holy Roller and was constantly in my face about being with the Lord, I started to lose interest," she explained. "I am also passionately pro-choice, and I volunteer at Planned Parenthood when I can. That has created an even bigger wedge between me and my family."

"Well, Libby, I don't blame you. I wouldn't want to go to church either if people were beating me over the head to do so," Karl confessed.

Libby excused herself to use the facilities, and while she was away, Baker admitted he had a nagging question about his own suitability to court the vibrant, self-assured Libby, who was in the process of winning Karl over at a single brunch. He asked whether Karl believed he was worthy of being with Libby.

"What makes you think that Libby deserves you?" Karl shot back. His wisdom resonated with Baker well beyond their brunch meeting.

When Libby returned from the restroom, Karl leaned forward slightly. "Libby, I was wondering—would you be willing to attend the Palm Sunday service at Trinity with Baker? It's this coming Sunday."

Baker felt his pulse quicken. He hadn't expected Karl to extend a church invitation so soon.

Libby considered this for a moment, her fingers still wrapped around her coffee cup. "I think I'd like that."

"Wonderful." Karl smiled. "If you come, please be sure to find me after the service. I'd like to introduce you to my wife, Margaret."

She promised that she would.

Karl was delighted. Suffused now with both crepes and the Holy Spirit—that peculiar fullness that comes from feeding body and soul in tandem—he found himself witness to something rare: his protégé navigating what might prove the most consequential relationship of his adult life. As Baker and Libby departed Le Café de Paris, their hands clasped together in that tentative yet determined way of new lovers, her slender fingers woven through his larger ones, their shoulders meeting and parting in companionable rhythm as they moved toward the bright rectangle of the doorway. He felt something settle deep within him: a satisfaction, yes, but also the quiet triumph of a gardener who had planted seeds in fertile soil and now watched the first green shoots emerge.

He had long harbored the conviction that Trinity needed an infusion of vitality, more middle-aged couples to breathe life into its aging congregation, to fill the pews with something other than the faithful elderly counting down their Sundays. His new project crystallized before him with the clarity of stained glass catching morning light. The parish must come to see Baker—childless or not, unconventional or not—as a family man. A man worthy of the leadership roles he had been quietly, methodically preparing him for, laying groundwork as patient and deliberate as a mason setting stones. And if Libby could find her way to faith alongside Baker, threading her own path toward belief while walking beside him, well, that would constitute precisely the kind of miracle Karl had been praying for—the sort that arrived not in thunder and flame but in the quiet accumulation of ordinary graces.

THE FOLLOWING DAY BROUGHT a call from the church administrator, who asked him "pretty please" to fill in as an usher during the Palm Sunday service. Baker explained that he was bringing a new girlfriend to Trinity for her first visit and suggested that perhaps this Sunday would not be the best time to serve as an usher.

"Oh, Baker, don't you worry. We'll take good care of her while you are working," she assured him. Baker said he'd get back to her with an answer within the hour.

When Baker and Libby discussed the matter, they found themselves reluctant to decline the request, to disappoint the church in its moment of need. She insisted that he commit to the job, her generosity in this small sacrifice already marking her as someone who understood the delicate choreography of belonging.

When they arrived at church half an hour before the service was to begin, Baker guided Libby through a brief tour of the nave—his hand at the small of her back, his voice low and reverent as he pointed out the architectural details, the history embedded in wood and stone—and offered her a glimpse into the sacristy with its vestments hanging like the shed skins of holiness itself. She told Baker to go about his business, releasing him to his duties with an ease that suggested self-sufficiency rather than dismissal. She'd walk the two blocks down to Human Bean and have a quick cup of joe before returning.

Libby was by nature independent and possessed of a shyness that manifested not as weakness but as a kind of protective reserve, a careful guardedness born of experience. Upon her return, she instinctively sought anonymity, her eyes scanning for a seat in a pew toward the back of the nave where she might observe without being observed, where she could slip into the service like a shadow at evening. Though a hundred or so worshippers had already claimed their territories, their familiar seats worn smooth by years of the same bodies settling into the same spaces, plenty of spots remained available, scattered throughout the nave like unclaimed promises.

Baker had been standing at his usual post by the narthex, wearing his usher badge and holding a stack of service bulletins, when he noticed Libby pass by him to enter the nave. She had that somewhat bewildered expression of someone uncertain where to sit. He watched her walk past four pews, her footsteps amplified by hardwood, then turn right to sit on the outside— that liminal space between commitment and escape. There he saw an older lady pivot in her seat to address her.

"That's where Harriet Keller sits, dear. That's her seat!"

"Oh, I'm so sorry, I didn't realize—" Libby said, fumbling with her purse. The woman had already turned back around, dismissing her.

Libby scanned farther down for a seat. She paused near the sixth pew, then stepped back as an elderly woman in a burgundy hat gave her a polite but pointed look. Libby moved again, only to meet a family who outmaneuvered her with the confident stride of people who knew exactly where they belonged.

He could almost see the gears turning in her mind. She'd mentioned visiting Boston and the Old North Church, where a docent had told her about well-heeled worshippers who purchased and sat in their own pew boxes. But seeing this modern iteration, this unspoken hierarchy of longtime members claiming territorial rights over particular pews, must have seemed like a terrible blow to progress.

He stepped away from his post and walked down the central aisle, ostensibly to check that the pew cards were properly arranged but really to assist Libby. She was already headed his way, looking rather defeated, and finally settled into a spot in the very last pew. Baker caught her eye and offered what he hoped was an encouraging smile. He watched her straighten her shoulders and open her program, determined to navigate this unfamiliar social terrain with grace. The irony was priceless: Here was a woman from the Humanist Group, putting human dignity above divine doctrine, sitting in what was essentially Trinity's version of steerage.

Baker was still in the narthex greeting latecomers when the service began. He worried about leaving Libby to navigate the liturgy alone—he knew from experience how overwhelming Trinity could be for newcomers. The regulars recited prayers and creeds from memory at a breakneck pace that even he had struggled with during his first visits years ago.

From his position at the back of the nave, Baker could see that Libby had stopped trying to follow along in the prayer book. Instead, she was taking in the congregation during the opening hymn. Baker knew what she was seeing: Trinity on Palm Sunday was a showcase of Boise's upper crust—although that term wasn't commonly used in a "Mayflower-lite" state like Idaho. The fashion at this gathering, and particularly the following week's Easter Sunday celebration, was much smarter than at the first time Baker had attended years earlier. Women wore dresses in white, pastel shades, or floral patterns while men wore either decades-old Brooks Brothers Golden Fleece suits from the backs of their closets or a pair of nice slacks and a tie.

Baker noticed Libby's posture shift, her shoulders tensing slightly. Following her gaze, he spotted the source of her discomfort: a woman about Libby's age but much harder looking, with pouty lips that made her appear dejected rather than sexy. She was staring directly at Libby with a sullen, pouty expression.

Baker's stomach dropped.

He watched Libby's brow furrow, clearly trying to place where she'd seen this woman before. Baker could practically see the moment of recognition cross her face—the slight widening of her eyes, the way her hand pressed unconsciously against her breastbone. He knew what she was remembering: the Press, their evening before they'd gone back to his apartment together.

The woman—whose name Baker preferred not to think about—was wearing a lovely floral dress that seemed entirely at odds with how he remembered her appearance that night outside the bar. Baker had hoped she'd moved on, found someone else to fixate on. Apparently not.

He could see Libby glancing back toward where he stood, clearly desperate to catch his eye, to ask him what the hell was going on. Her confusion was palpable even from across the sanctuary. Baker could read the questions in her expression: *Am I supposed to speak to this woman? Why is she so damned interested in me?*

Baker kept his expression neutral, but inside he was calculating how quickly he could get to Libby's side if this situation escalated.

He sat with Libby during the sermon before leaving to assist with the collection plates during the offertory. He returned and stayed with Libby until Communion began, then left again. He wouldn't see Libby until the service was over and the last parishioner had said their goodbye to the rector.

Libby waited for Baker alongside dozens of other parishioners outside the church. She sensed several people approaching to welcome her to Trinity, but unexpectedly, the woman who had been staring made a beeline for her, introduced herself as Katherine, and initiated a conversation. She was unusually cordial at first, asking Libby numerous softball questions. However, the conversation took a sharp turn, and Libby began to feel as though she was being grilled about her relationship with Baker.

The woman walked half a block in lockstep with Libby, just inches from her face, delivering dire warnings about Baker's alleged sexual uncleanliness and promiscuous behavior. Departing worshippers couldn't help but observe this chaos. Although they wanted to be polite to Libby, they felt so uncomfortable with Katherine's rising voice and accusations that they sidestepped the scene.

When Baker finally finished his duty, he dashed down the block to rescue Libby and walked briskly with her to his house. Once inside, they sat on the sofa, the tension still hanging between them. Baker searched for the right words to explain what had just happened, to make sense of Katherine's behavior, to reassure Libby that this situation was under control, that it was all behind him.

"Did you stick your dick in crazy?" Libby interrupted.

"Yes and no," Baker answered.

"What does *that* mean?"

"It's complicated, so let me try to explain."

"Go ahead."

Baker ran his hand through his hair and avoided Libby's eyes. "Look, I need to tell you about Katherine. That woman who was staring at you today." He took a deep breath. "We had one fling. A bar thing. We both got completely wasted, and…well, we ended up having sex in the back seat of my car like a couple of teenagers." Baker's face reddened. "I'm not proud of it."

Libby waited, sensing there was more.

"She called me the next day, wanting to see me again. I tried to let her down easy, you know? I told her I had a nice time, but that it was just one of those things. One and done." Baker shook his head. "She heard me clearly enough, but she refused to believe I was making the right decision. She took my rejection about as well as Glenn Close took the boot from Michael Douglas in *Fatal Attraction.*"

"Baker—"

"She started harassing me. At home, at Trinity. She knew I worked in the volunteer office most days, so for weeks she'd show up to give me an earful about how I was making a mistake, how we were meant to be together." Baker's voice grew quieter. "Then when I started avoiding her at church, things got . . . stranger. My phone would ring at one, two in the morning, just hang ups. I'd come out to my car in the Trinity parking lot and find my seat adjusted, the rearview mirror tilted differently. Little things that let me know she'd been inside."

He paused, his jaw tightening. "There was this unfamiliar sedan—a gray Camry—that started showing up near my house. Different times of day, always parked just far enough away to seem coincidental. And then one morning I found footprints in the flower beds outside my bedroom window. Fresh ones, from the night before. "I asked Phil to step in and have a chat with her, but he wouldn't do it. I honestly think he enjoyed watching me squirm."

Libby's eyes widened. "This gets worse, doesn't it?"

Baker nodded grimly. "I need to tell you about Katherine. Not the version I've been telling myself, but what actually happened." He took a breath. "One night—it had to be three in the morning—she came to my house. I never lock my back door, and she just . . . walked in. Stood in my kitchen waiting for me to respond." His hands clenched into fists. "Libby, she was within arm's reach of my knife block. I just lay there pretending to be asleep, praying she wouldn't do anything stupid or come any closer."

"Jesus, Baker."

"The next morning, I called Karl and begged him to contact the rector. I told him someone needed to talk to Katherine—maybe the police—before she became truly violent." Baker finally looked at Libby. "Even if she couldn't have me, she sure as hell didn't want anyone else to either." Baker paused, remembering. "Karl asked me, 'Do you feel safe at the moment?' Like it was some intake interview at a domestic violence shelter." His voice took on a bitter edge. "I told him, 'Safe? Karl, she broke into my house in the middle of the night and stood next to my kitchen knives. How safe would you feel?'"

Karl had assured Baker he would speak with the rector and encourage him to act. Technically, Phil didn't report to him, but everybody at Trinity indeed acknowledged that Karl, not Phil, was the "head knocker."

When Karl finally heard back from Phil, the message was clear: Baker should keep his distance from Katherine. How in the hell was he supposed to do that? And why did Phil have such a hard-on for him?

Baker was still explaining Karl's reaction when the banging started.

Bang, bang, bang!

Both froze. The sound came from the front door, then moved around to the back.

Bang, bang, bang!

"Is that—?" Libby whispered.

"Katherine." Baker's face went pale. "She's here."

The banging stopped, but then they saw movement at the front window. A face pressed against the glass, hands cupped around eyes, trying to peer inside.

"That's it." Baker stood up abruptly. "I'm done with this shit." He walked to the window and yanked the curtains shut, then grabbed his phone. "I'm calling 911."

"Nine-one-one, what's your emergency?"

"This is Baker Vaughan at 1706 West Resseguie Street in North End Boise. A woman is harassing me, banging on my doors, and looking through my windows. I need someone here now."

The officer arrived within minutes, but Katherine's car was already gone.

"Can you tell me what happened here?" the officer asked, notebook ready.

"This woman—Katherine House—she's been stalking me for weeks," Baker began. "She broke into my house once, showed up at my church, and just now she was banging on my doors and peeping through my windows."

"And you are . . . ?" the officer asked Libby.

"Libby Bradshaw. I was here when it happened. I saw her at Trinity Episcopal this morning too—she was staring at me during the service."

The officer looked up from his notes. "Trinity? Were there other witnesses this morning?"

"Oh yes," Libby said eagerly. "Lots of parishioners were leaving when we saw her in the parking lot. I could research names if you need them."

Baker shook his head. "You know what's frustrating? I told Trinity's rector about this weeks ago. He told me he'd handle it, but he never did anything."

"Trinity Episcopal," the officer mused. "We have an ongoing relationship with them, mostly concerning the homeless population. I know the officer who liaises with your rector. I'll speak with him today. "In the meantime, I'd advise you both to stay away from this Katherine."

Baker stared at him. "Stay away from her? Officer, she's the one stalking *me*. She broke into *my* house. She shows up at *my* church. How exactly am I supposed to stay away from someone who won't stay away from me?"

"I understand your frustration, Mr. Vaughan. But if there's another encounter like this, we might have sufficient grounds to get you a restraining order."

After the officer left, Baker and Libby sat in heavy silence. He could see the weight of the afternoon settling over her—the hostile stares during the service, the confrontation in the parking lot, and now police at his front door because of a woman with whom he'd once had a quickie. Baker watched Libby's face as she processed what she'd gotten herself into by dating him. He could practically see her calculating whether this level of drama was worth it, whether she wanted to be part of whatever mess his life had become.

"Hey, look, Baker, this church thing is not working for me. I would just as soon let you continue what you've been doing alone," Libby confessed.

Baker was entirely empathetic and, at that moment, couldn't provide Libby with a valid reason to continue going to Trinity. However, he was undeniably heartbroken about what was happening to her. This wasn't the same feeling he had when Michelle chose to stay home while he attended Sunday worship. She hadn't been made to feel unwelcome. After the painful lesson of living with an atheist, Baker yearned to spend Sundays with someone from start to finish, holding hands while reciting the Lord's Prayer, ushering together, serving coffee after the service, and even selling Christmas wreaths from the back of their car. Many other couples at Trinity were doing this, so why not Baker and someone like Libby?

Baker called Karl on Sunday afternoon and explained that the situation with Katherine had not been resolved to his satisfaction. Karl was furious—not just at her, but at Phil.

"Let me make sure I understand this correctly," Karl said, his voice tight with controlled anger. "Katherine is a parishioner at Trinity. Phil is her rector. You went to him multiple times, asking him to intervene with her as her priest, and he refused?"

"He told me to keep my distance from her," Baker said bitterly. "Like I was the problem."

"That's a complete abdication of pastoral responsibility," Karl said. "When a parishioner is harassing another member of the congregation, it's the rector's fundamental duty to address it. Phil should have spoken with her immediately—counseled her, set boundaries, involved the bishop if necessary. Instead, he did nothing. He let this escalate from harassment to breaking and entering." Karl paused, and Baker could hear him breathing heavily on the other end of the line.

"This isn't just about Katherine's behavior anymore, Baker. This is about Phil's failure as a priest. He had a duty to protect you, to maintain order in his parish, and he completely failed. And now the Trinity name is being dragged through this mess—police reports, stalking, a woman terrorizing people in our parking lot. That's on Phil." His voice hardened. "I'm going to try to have him removed from the church."

Baker knew that Episcopal priests were rarely fired unless they were caught having sex with a parishioner on the main altar. They were either advised to retire or reassigned to another diocese. But Karl wasn't just worried about Baker—he was distraught by the way both Katherine and Phil were abusing the Trinity brand. In Karl's mind, that was blasphemy. He decided to take matters into his own hands.

The next day, he contacted Bishop Gallagher and suggested they meet with Phil to discuss a pressing issue. Of course, Gallagher asked why, and Karl responded that he wouldn't bother such an important person if the problem wasn't urgent. The bishop agreed to the meeting and assured him that he'd get Phil to attend.

ON TUESDAY MORNING, BAKER arrived at the volunteer office at nine a.m. In addition to brewing the requisite pot of ashy and overly charred church coffee for the staff, Baker also put the kettle on to make tea for Karl, who couldn't drink Trinity's coffee. If it were his call, he'd fire the supplier. He'd also put an end to the equipment workarounds and purchase a new, state-of-the-art coffee maker, stat.

The trio arrived soon after, stopped at the volunteer office to greet Baker, and then proceeded to a space that served as both a conference room and a library. They shut the door behind them, and Baker tried not to speculate about the outcome of the meeting. He went about his business, which that day involved answering the phones and affixing address labels to the latest church newsletter.

The men concluded their meeting quickly, and the two bishops exited the building through the front door, giving Baker a brief wave but not stopping to speak. Karl also winked at him, as if to convey *Mission accomplished.* Phil departed in the opposite direction, returning to his office and shutting the door behind him. Baker glanced at the switchboard, contemplating whether to dial Karl's cell phone. As he did so, he noticed a red light appear on Phil's telephone extension. Less than a minute later, it disappeared.

A bit later, Baker picked up an inbound call. It was Officer Evans from the Boise Police Department "returning the rector's call." Baker put the officer on hold and tried to reach Phil. After the phone rang five or six times, he returned to the officer and explained that Phil was unavailable.

"I know he's in the building, but he's escaped me at the moment," Baker explained. "Is there any message I can leave him?"

"Just let him know that I've spoken with his parishioner, and everything has been sorted out," the officer replied.

Baker hung up the phone and walked to Phil's office. The door was open, so he knocked lightly and stepped into the room. The rector wasn't anywhere to be found, so Baker moved on to check the men's room. Not there either. That left only one other possibility—the rector had gone through the day-care center door in the back of the building. That was the only way he could have exited without being seen.

A few minutes later, the rector reentered the building through the front door and hung a left into the volunteer office.

"Baker, may I see you in the office?" He didn't include the word *please.*

Baker obliged, asking the administrator to cover the phones for him.

"I hear that Katherine has been bothering you," the rector stated.

"Actually, she's been stalking me," Baker replied.

"Well, that's quite an accusation. Don't you still have a relationship with her?"

"Look, Phil, I've never had a *relationship* with Katherine. I went out with her one time. That's it. I fucked her, OK?"

"Well, I've had no one else at Trinity ever complain about Katherine, and I can't ask her to stop attending events here unless she poses a real threat to you."

"Do you consider her breaking into my house in the middle of the night a real threat? Do you consider her shouting at Libby within earshot of dozens of parishioners a real threat?"

"Well, as of now, you are the only one telling me that."

"What about the police coming to my house on Palm Sunday? Did you hear about that?"

"Well, you're getting confrontational, and I won't go there with you. I'd suggest that if you want my help, you and Libby both need to write a formal complaint and address all the issues you've had with Katherine. I'll then decide whether there's anything I should do."

"Phil, I know you've already spoken with the police."

"Excuse me? What did you say?"

"I said I know you and Officer Evans had a chat about Katherine."

"Well, what makes you so sure about that?"

"He called this morning and asked me to give you a message about speaking with your parishioner. I put two and two together and got five."

Baker watched the rector fall silent. He was left wondering whether Phil was impatient, surprised, nervous, or some combination of the three. He felt so betrayed at that moment that he was ready to leave Trinity, abandon the priesthood, and move to a remote island with Libby if she would join him. He turned around and stomped out of Phil's office. He stopped briefly at the volunteer office to pick up a few personal items, then left. He was calling it quits for the day, that was certain. He reached above the doorframe to retrieve a key to lock the panic bar and signal to new arrivals that the office was now closed.

The rector ambled out of his room, apparently unaware that the front door had already closed behind Baker. Assuming Baker was still within earshot in the courtyard, he yelled into the distance, "I shouldn't have to remind you that Karl doesn't run Trinity, should I?"

His impotent words fell on deaf ears.

Chapter Ten

An alpha rector. A deranged bunny killer. A police officer misusing his "professional discretion." A parishioner questioning Libby's right to a free seat. Baker decided it was time for a break from Trinity and Boise—a chance to introduce Libby to his family in Lynchburg and the Oaks. The Thompsons would be in Oregon for a month to manage early spring duties in their orchard, and since they had effectively become Baker's protectors, their absence made this the perfect opportunity. He hoped to resume an everyday life once he returned to Boise.

Libby had never visited the mid-Atlantic. When Baker invited her, her eyes widened. "Your family? The Oaks? Yes, absolutely." No hesitation, no nervousness about meeting his parents and sister. Instead, she peppered him with questions: What was Lynchburg like? Would they visit Monticello? Could they see the mountains? Although Baker had spent an evening doing anxious Google searches that led him down a rabbit hole of *Men's Health* and *GQ* articles with titles like "How to Prepare Your Girlfriend for Meeting Your Family" and "The Dos and Don'ts of Family Introductions"—research that proved completely unnecessary—Libby was still flattered by the gesture.

They flew through Chicago into Washington National—the name Baker preferred over the newer Reagan National. (It was not meant as a slight to the fortieth president, as he'd voted for Reagan twice.) He toed the Vaughan family line. From there, they hopped on the subway to the Metro Center station in downtown Washington, walked two blocks to the Willard Hotel and checked in, just like Charles Dickens, Buffalo Bill, David Lloyd George, P. T. Barnum, Walt Whitman, Mark Twain, and Emily Dickinson had done at one time or another.

Baker had scored opening-day tickets to watch the Washington Nationals play the Cincinnati Reds and beat them in ten innings, with Ryan Zimmerman scoring the winning run on a wild pitch. Zimmerman had played college ball at the University of Virginia, where Baker and his dad attended two of his games: one in Charlottesville against Duke and the other in Lynchburg against Liberty.

Baker was impressed that Libby not only enjoyed the Nats game but also drank two overpriced beers and didn't fidget at all during the slower innings. During the seventh-inning stretch, he took a picture of Libby with Screech, the Nationals' bald eagle mascot, and sent it to his dad. Unlike the day at Cadillac Ranch, he received an immediate response: Nice picture! How did Zim do?

I'll let Libby tell you when we get to your house. She kept the box score. Baker didn't even know until the game started that she had been recording every at-bat, base advancement, and special event in a book since her first game at Candlestick Park as a teenager. She even had autographs from some of the Giants' greats, like Mays, Marichal, and McCovey.

The successful afternoon put Baker in the perfect mood to reconnect with an old friend, Tim Cartwright. They had been inseparable since middle school in Lynchburg—the kind of life-long pals who could communicate with just a look and got into trouble together with equal enthusiasm. Tim's family lived just a few streets over from the Oaks, and the boys spent countless afternoons swimming in the James River and playing golf at the country club where their families held memberships. Unlike most teens, they often found themselves discussing questions of faith and meaning—the kind of earnest conversations that revealed their parents had made wise decisions in sending them to an Episcopal school. They even loved attending morning chapel and encouraged each other to participate fully; how bad could twenty minutes be?

Baker was eager to introduce him to Libby, especially now that Tim had become a canon priest at Washington National Cathedral—that magnificent Gothic structure that dominated the DC skyline. He was also curious to hear about the earthquake that had shaken it years earlier.

From news reports, Baker understood that millions of dollars had been raised by members and friends of the Episcopal cathedral in the months following the disaster. He'd read that hundreds of stone finials, crockets, and gargoyles had been twisted, shifted, knocked off the building, or beheaded. But he wanted to hear firsthand from Tim what the damage had really been like and how his congregation had weathered the crisis.

That evening, Baker, Libby, and Tim met for dinner at the Willard. Baker scanned the cocktail menu out of habit, though he already knew what he'd order. Legend credited the Willard as the first to serve Bloody Marys, though other bars in New York, Chicago, and New Orleans likely made the same claim. But it didn't matter to him; the Willard's version was exceptional, featuring premium vodka, perfectly seasoned tomato juice, and a dedicated customization bar where guests could add their own touches. They were so damned good that he insisted all three of them order one.

Once they'd placed their order for drinks and soft-shell crabs, the trio rose from their table to examine the bar's walls, which were adorned with pictures of many notable figures and places. The two men, as competitive individuals often do, attempted to outsmart each other regarding historical facts. During their little contest, while gazing at a picture of a woman "swimming" in the tidal basin in the 1970s, they tried to guess the name of the congressman—Wilbur Mills, they got that one—but stumbled over the real name of his stripper girlfriend, whose stage name was Fanne Foxe. Libby, who'd been quietly observing their attempts, offered with a slight smile, "Annabelle Battistella. The Argentine Firecracker." Both men turned to her, surprised, then laughed.

They returned to their table just as the first round of Bloody Marys arrived. After a few minutes, Libby excused herself to examine more of the historical photos and memorabilia on the walls. Tim glanced around to ensure she was out of earshot. The soft clatter of silverware and the gentle hum of conversation from nearby tables provided cover. He leaned forward and asked Baker, "Have you told her yet?"

"No," he replied. "I plan to tell her only if I propose to her."

"You think that might happen?"

"Well, let's see what Mom and Dad think. Emma, of course, will remain neutral. We're heading down to Lynchburg after stopping to visit Oscar overnight in Middleburg."

Tim was keen to speak with Libby and learn more about her. She returned to the table just as dinner arrived, accompanied by a second round of drinks. The rich aroma of the soft shells drifted across the table, and the trio agreed that the Bloody Marys paired better with them than an unoaked chardonnay would have.

"Libby, I don't know where to start, but there's so much I'd like to ask about you," Tim said.

"Likewise, Tim, but why don't you start?" Libby suggested.

"First of all, I hear you love baseball. I'm thrilled to hear that."

"Been a fan nearly all my life."

"Did you play sports in high school or college?"

"I played basketball and ran track in high school, and I also skied a lot during school breaks."

"How about in college?"

"Just some intramural squash and tennis at Bowdoin."

Tim wore a smirk. Baker knew precisely what his friend was thinking—how competitive Oscar had always been in life and in sports like squash. Baker tried to imagine a match between his uncle and Libby back in the day. Maybe she could have sweet-talked him into letting her win.

As unlikely as that seemed—Oscar never intentionally let anyone beat him at anything—Baker was confident that the two would hit it off, and he hoped for the same outcome in Lynchburg. His mom, however, could be challenging to read at times.

"Baker tells me you're a math teacher. What levels?" Tim asked.

"Algebra and geometry, mostly. My students are in grades seven through nine. I can also tutor older students in precalculus or calculus, which I do occasionally because I'm at a private school."

Tim leaned forward slightly, his fork pausing halfway to his mouth. "That's quite a range. You must enjoy the challenge of adapting to different learning styles."

"I do," Libby said. "Each age group brings something different to mathematics."

Baker noticed how Tim's questions were becoming more thoughtful, more engaged. And Libby hadn't even mentioned the orchestra yet.

"Aside from the earthquake damage, how do you like being at the cathedral?" Baker asked his friend.

"We're getting a new dean, who's a great man, and the rest of the clergy and staff are wonderful people. The past five years have been tumultuous, to say the least, but we've done a lot of soul searching and think the future is quite bright."

"Wouldn't it have been amazing if we could have worked here together?" Baker said.

"So you're back in the saddle?" Tim asked.

"Well, I'm giving it a go, provided I fulfill one more requirement."

"What's that?"

"Getting married."

Tim and Libby fell into silence, which stretched uncomfortably between them as they both processed Baker's unexpected revelation about marriage being a requirement. Before either could respond, Baker's phone rang, providing a reprieve from the conversation he wasn't ready to finish.

"Excuse me," Baker said, glancing at the caller ID. He stood and walked toward the bar's entrance, finding a quieter alcove near the historic photographs where the soft murmur of conversation from the dining room mixed with the gentle clink of crystal from the bar. The rich mahogany paneling seemed to absorb sound, and the warm glow from the brass wall sconces created just enough privacy for a serious conversation.

"Baker, so glad to catch you, and apologies for interrupting your time out East. But I have some serious news and a couple of questions for you," Karl said immediately upon Baker answering. "The rector was mugged last night in the stairwell by the choir room door."

"Is he in the hospital?" Baker asked with evident schadenfreude.

"No, he's just shaken up a bit. The police are looking for a suspect and a motive. "Where are you right now?" Karl asked, his voice catching.

"I'm in Washington, DC, heading to see my folks in Lynchburg."

"Wonderful news!"

"Why do you say wonderful?"

"Your name surfaced as a possible suspect, and the police wanted to ensure you had an alibi."

"*My* name? How in God's name did *my* name surface?"

"I reason Phil told Officer Evans that you had it out for him. Don't worry, and don't feel singled out; Evans had Katherine on the list too, and her alibi does not completely exonerate her."

"Why's that?"

"Apparently, she was out walking her dog pretty close to Trinity at the time."

"Meaning close to my house. Sounds like she was up to something."

"The police investigation should finally send her the message to stay away from you."

"Any witnesses to the mugging?"

"None have come forward."

"Is it OK for me to continue my trip to Lynchburg?"

"Of course, but you should reach out to Phil and offer your condolences. As hard as it may seem, you've got to keep trying to kill him with kindness."

"Yes, I will. I understand," Baker said, taking a deep, slow breath. "Also, Karl, since I have you on the line, I need another piece of advice. I accidentally let the cat out of the bag about you advising me to marry Libby. How do I get it back in the bag?"

"Just make sure to emphasize the word *advise*. Avoid *require*."

Baker hung up and returned to the table where Tim and Libby were deep in conversation about the historical photos on the wall. They looked up expectantly.

"Everything all right?" Tim asked.

Baker nodded. "Just church drama. I'll fill you in later." He glanced at the photo they'd been discussing earlier. "So did you two finish your little history contest while I was gone?"

Tim laughed. "Actually, Libby was just schooling me. She knew Fanne Foxe's real name."

"How in the heck did you know that, Libby?"

"My dad was asked to back Mills for his bid for the presidency in 1972 and then again when he was on the short list as a Supreme Court nominee. Remember, before the incident, Mills seemed like the model of stability: a married father and grandfather in the twilight of a distinguished career."

On and on they went, their conversation flowing with the easy rhythm of lifelong friendship. If Tim hadn't married Lisa, or if Baker took too long proposing to Libby, he could have imagined Tim stepping in. She was a catch. The evening wound down with promises to stay in touch and plans for Tim to visit Boise someday. As he and Libby rode the elevator back to their room, Baker found himself replaying Tim's pointed question about whether he'd "told her yet" about Wendy. The secret sat between them like a third passenger in the elevator car, taking up space, making the air feel thin.

THE NEXT MORNING, BAKER and Libby checked out of the Willard, still recalling the pleasant evening with Tim and the unusual phone call from Karl. As they picked up their rental car and headed toward Middleburg, Baker couldn't shake the thought of how he let the marriage requirement slip out.

Oscar had been a fixture in Baker's early life: the sophisticated New Yorker who'd taken his nephew to museums and introduced him to opera. But they hadn't seen each other in nearly a decade, not since that celebratory lunch at the peak of Baker's advertising career. Their relationship had always been complicated: Oscar admired Baker's success in the corporate world but had little patience for his nephew's spiritual searching. Now, at eightysomething, Oscar had retired to Virginia horse country, and Baker was curious what had drawn his perpetually urban uncle to rural life.

Thankfully, the forty-mile drive provided a nice distraction. By traveling against the lingering morning rush hour into DC, they completed the trip in under an hour, watching the urban landscape gradually give way to Virginia's lush countryside. They arrived at Oscar's driveway off Hibbs Bridge Road and noticed the property was quite upscale, though perhaps too large for a single man in his late eighties. Nevertheless, no one could deny this wealthy man the right to own a well-appointed home in the heart of horse country.

As they pulled up the drive, a man Baker didn't recognize came bounding out the front door to greet them.

"Hello, my name is Julian. You must be Libby and Baker?"

"That's correct. Are you a friend of Oscar's?"

Julian paused before stepping forward to say, "Yes, we're good friends. Oscar has told me so much about both of you."

Baker watched Julian handle Libby's suitcase with practiced grace—late sixties, impeccably dressed, with a slight accent that sounded French. The orange-framed eyeglasses and carefully curated wardrobe indicated someone at ease with his own aesthetic choices.

"That's very kind of you to help with our bags," Baker said.

"It is my distinct pleasure, and I hope you enjoy your stay," Julian replied with a warm smile.

"Ah, so you've met dear Julian," Oscar announced as he stepped forward to greet his guests, offering no further explanation about just who the heck Julian was.

Baker embraced his uncle, then introduced Libby with appropriate formality.

"Hello, my dear. Welcome to my humble abode," Oscar said in a hyperarticulated manner, quite different from how he had been for years. This was certainly no grouchy person before them now. He proudly gave them a tour of his home—private and quiet, with modern conveniences like flat-screen TVs discreetly mounted in each room and the whole house wired for Wi-Fi and sound, all seamlessly blended with rustic charm. Inside and out, there were great entertaining areas offering beautiful views of the surrounding countryside. The extensive stonework and hardwood floors were impressive, but the most notable features were the large, beautiful woodburning fireplace and the gorgeous tongue-and-groove ceiling in the three-season room.

As they moved through the kitchen, with its professional-grade stainless-steel appliances and built-in wine refrigerator, Libby admired the lovingly presented array of vintage copper pots and the artfully arranged herbs in terra-cotta planters. "Oscar, you have such an eye for design," she said.

"Well, I can't take all the credit," Oscar said with a slight smile.

"Did you make these improvements or buy the house as is?" Baker asked his uncle.

"That's a silly question, don't you think?"

The response was vintage Oscar, but the tone was all wrong. There was no edge to it, no challenge. Just amusement, as if he genuinely enjoyed the question rather than resenting it.

Baker caught Libby's eye and tilted his head slightly. When Oscar stepped ahead to show them the three-season room, Baker leaned closer to her. "I never knew Oscar cared about herb gardens and copper pots," he whispered.

Libby's brow furrowed slightly. "Is that . . . unusual?"

"For Oscar? Completely," Baker said quietly. "Ten years ago, he wouldn't have been caught dead fussing over plants. He was all business. All competition."

Libby nodded slowly, processing this. A moment later, as Oscar gestured animatedly toward the kitchen, she leaned back toward Baker. "Did you notice how he keeps saying 'we' when talking about the house?"

"Yeah," Baker whispered. "That's what I'm trying to figure out."

"You don't know if he's with someone?"

"Not a clue. Last I heard, he was still alone. Still angry about it too." Baker glanced toward the three-season room where Oscar was adjusting a curtain with surprising care. "This isn't just age, Lib. Something changed him."

The herb gardens, the copper pots, the way he said "we"—they all pointed somewhere, but Baker couldn't quite see where yet. All he knew was that the pieces didn't fit the uncle he remembered, and whatever had shifted in Oscar's life ran deeper than new hobbies or fresh paint.

The shift from Brahmin to Bohemian didn't happen to men like Oscar. And yet, if he'd turned into a guncle—someone who'd given himself permission to stop performing—then maybe that explained the lightness in his shoulders, the way he moved through his own home like he finally belonged there. Baker understood suddenly, with the clarity of looking at his own reflection, what it meant to carry a secret so long that you forgot what it felt like to set it down. He wondered how many years Oscar had spent locked away, and how many more years Baker might spend the same way if he didn't find the courage to tell Libby about Wendy.

If Oscar could reinvent himself at eightysomething and find happiness, what did that say about the rest of the family's unfinished business? Baker found himself thinking about his mother, about all the conversations they'd never had, all the forgiveness offered in words but never truly felt in his heart.

BECAUSE OF HIS MOTHER'S lifelong struggle with alcohol, the two had maintained a strained relationship since Baker was twelve. She'd been to Betty Ford, had been sober for years now, but he sensed she still believed he'd never truly forgiven her. He said he had, verbally, but deep down, he still struggled with it. He could see it in her eyes whenever they were together—that cautious uncertainty of a mother who knew her son still carried old wounds.

But here at Oscar's, watching his uncle's transformation and newfound openness, Baker felt something shifting inside. Maybe it was time to stop dwelling on it and start embracing the possibility of change and forgiveness—both in his family and in himself.

That afternoon, Oscar rented Vespa scooters so the four of them could ride the Middleburg-to-Plains loop together—almost thirty miles of Northern Virginia farmland and vineyards, along with a few sights of Civil War history, that felt like a different world from Boise.

The foursome enjoyed a lovely dinner at Oscar's home, prepared almost entirely by Julian, and discussed a range of general and personal topics. Since Libby was new to the family and Julian was new to Baker, the conversation naturally turned to questions about Oscar and Julian's relationship. The conversation started in safe territory—how long they'd known each other and what had brought Julian to the area. For Baker, though, a more pressing question loomed: whether Oscar would actually come out that evening. Oscar had long set his sights on Middleburg for reasons related to his desire for partial ownership of the Red Fox Inn. But Julian had only gotten his first glimpses of hunt country about ten years earlier. He'd come in the fall and used the visit as inspiration for a book he was writing—a compendium of design, artwork, and interior ideas—while considering a new avocation since retiring from academia, having spent most of his career at George Washington University in the district.

"I take it you met in New York?" Baker asked.

"No, I'm not from New York. We met in Washington at a dinner party," Julian said.

"And what is your take on Middleburg?"

"I love the vastness of the area, and how local it all is," Julian cooed. "I began spending more weekend time here, always antiquing and sourcing things. There were so many wonderful shops with knowledgeable people who were passionate about what they sold. And I started to get back into riding, something I'd done as a much younger man."

"Was Oscar living here then?"

"No, he was still in New York and stopping here on his trips to and from Lynchburg."

"So did you plan a trip to visit Middleburg together, or did you perhaps meet here by accident?"

"Totally by accident. We were both shopping at Federal and Black, a lovely antique and furnishings shop on Madison Street."

"Was Oscar trying to buy something so you couldn't?"

That question made Julian laugh out loud. "We were both admiring a French cast-iron shop scale with brass pans and a marble top. I encouraged him to buy it, told him they were far more fun to use than digital scales. But then I said to him, rather flirtatiously, 'If you do buy it, we'll never be able to move in together because it wouldn't be practical having two of these pricey scales in one house.'"

"What was Oscar's response?" Baker asked.

Julian grinned at the memory. "He couldn't let go of that scale fast enough."

The table erupted in laughter, and Oscar shook his head with good-natured embarrassment. When the moment settled, he reached over and placed his hand on Julian's arm.

"Well, I suppose there's no point in dancing around it any-more," Oscar said, looking at Baker and Libby with a slight smile. "Julian and I have been together for three years now. We've been living here for the past two." He paused, studying Baker's face. "I know this might come as a surprise, but at my age, I've learned that happiness is too precious to waste time worrying about what others might think."

Baker smiled as all the small observations from the day added up to what he and Libby had imagined to be true. "Uncle Oscar, I'm happy for you. Both of you."

The conversation continued late into the evening, flowing between family stories and gentle teasing. As the fire burned low in the three-season room, Baker found himself thinking about how much courage it must have taken Oscar to finally live openly and honestly—and wondering if he could find that same cour-age when it came to his own unfinished business with his mother.

Before the evening ended, Libby had her turn in the spotlight.

"So, Libby, Baker mentioned you had some exciting news to share with us?" Julian said.

Libby's face lit up. "I've been working on a music workshop in Boise focused on developing orchestral skills. We'll offer en-semble playing, musical interpretation, and guidance on how to audition successfully."

"That's marvelous!" Julian said. "It sounds like you have a real talent for bringing people together."

Baker watched Oscar's face light up. He could almost read his uncle's thoughts: His preachy little nephew from days gone by had found a new soulmate and perhaps a prospective new wife who was his intellectual equal and wouldn't need to resort to using her musical skills to conduct a church choir. As they continued talking, he found himself reflecting on his teenage trips to New York and New Haven with his uncle, making amends with any ill feelings he'd harbored. His next project would be his mother. *How can I become a priest and not forgive her?* he thought.

LIBBY AND BAKER SET off for Lynchburg the next morning, stopping briefly in Charlottesville to visit a place on Libby's bucket list: Monticello. Jefferson's home featured front doors powered by cannonball weights that drove the Great Clock—the chiming of which controlled the daily routine for both the enslaved and the free—in the entrance hall and opened simultaneously when either door was moved. One set of weights also marked the day of the week as they fell and the approximate hour as they descended past markers on the wall. Despite all the other architectural features and ingenious inventions around them, the front doors rocked Libby's world.

"I can't believe I found absolutely nothing on the internet regarding the front doors," she complained. "Why isn't it a bigger deal?"

"It just doesn't appeal to most people; for example, when I think of front doors, I envision big, hunky, ornate ones visible from a mile away, like the Holy Door of Saint Peter's Basilica," Baker said.

"OK, I certainly wouldn't describe them as extraordinary as an aurora or an eclipse, but they feel impossibly modern for something Jefferson designed centuries ago."

They spent another hour wandering Jefferson's gardens and grounds, Libby photographing architectural details while Baker reflected on the contradictions of a man who wrote about freedom while enslaving others. The irony wasn't lost on him, given his own family's complicated legacy that he was only beginning to understand.

The drive to Lynchburg started pleasantly enough. The transition from rolling horse country to the Blue Ridge foothills lifted their spirits, and they held hands through the countryside, talking about Jefferson's ingenious door mechanisms. Every VIRGINIA IS FOR LOVERS sign they passed prompted kisses and laughter. But as he turned into the familiar driveway of the Oaks, Baker immediately sensed something was off. The house looked different somehow, too quiet, and Emma was hurrying toward the car before they'd even stopped, her face tight with urgency.

"Get out of the car," she said breathlessly. "Dad's had another stroke. We need to get to the hospital now."

"Another stroke?" Baker's voice cracked.

They piled into Emma's car, Baker in the passenger seat, Libby in the back. "Can you drive faster?" Baker demanded as his sister pressed harder on the accelerator. His hands were shaking when they pulled into the hospital lot, and he fumbled opening the car door.

Inside the hospital, Baker fired questions at her. "When did this happen? How bad is it?"

"He collapsed in the garden around noon. Lost his speech immediately." Her voice was flat, even clinical. "Mom's been here for two hours. The doctors haven't said much."

Libby sat quietly, now aware she was witnessing a family crisis about which she knew nothing.

When they reached the emergency room, the fluorescent lights cast everything in harsh white. That typical hospital smell hung in the air. Other families clustered in plastic chairs, speaking in hushed tones. Anne sat in the waiting area with her head lowered, remaining still. She didn't seem to be grieving yet—to Baker, she was somewhere else entirely, her mind drifting to dark possibilities about what would happen to her if Edward didn't make it through this.

As Baker sat next to his mother, a doctor in green scrubs appeared, clipboard in hand. "Vaughan family?"

Baker stood. The doctor's expression was carefully neutral, the practiced look of someone who regularly delivered bad news.

"I'm Dr. Bolling. I've been treating your father." He paused, glancing between them and then toward Anne, who remained seated nearby. "Could we speak privately for a moment?" He gestured toward a quieter corner of the waiting area, away from other families.

Baker called for Emma, and they followed him, their hearts already sinking at the gravity in the provider's voice.

"I'm very sorry," Dr. Bolling said gently, his voice lowered. "Your father's condition deteriorated rapidly. Despite our best efforts, he passed away about twenty minutes ago. The stroke was massive. There was nothing more we could have done."

The words hung in the antiseptic air. Emma's face crumpled, but Baker felt strangely detached, as if watching the scene from above.

"Did he suffer?" Emma asked.

"He lost consciousness quickly. It was peaceful."

Baker looked at his mother, realizing her stillness hadn't been about knowing—it had been about fearing exactly this moment. Now that fear had become reality.

"Mom," Baker said gently, approaching her chair.

She didn't answer. After a moment, she reached out her right arm so he could hold her hand.

"Was he able to say anything?" Baker asked the doctor quietly.

The doctor shook his head. "I'm sorry. No."

Anne Vaughan had retreated somewhere unreachable, shut down by grief. This scene reminded Baker of the times when his mother had passed out drunk, unaware from one day to the next whether her mood would ever normalize. *Such a shame*, he thought. Although his dad couldn't be brought back to life, she could. Worse yet, what a misfortune that his father and Libby hadn't met and would never meet, and the relationship between them, bound for glory, never took off.

Emma had gone to get help for her mom, who sat pale and unresponsive, her hands trembling as she stared blankly at the wall. Anne's breathing was shallow and rapid, her pupils dilated—classic signs of acute psychological shock. The ER personnel quickly arrived to assess her condition, checking her blood pressure, which had spiked dangerously high, and screening for any signs she might have self-medicated with alcohol or pills in her distress. Given her history of addiction, they needed to rule out any substances that could complicate her grief response and determine if her catatonic state was purely psychological or had a medical component. The attending physician recommended administering mild sedatives to help stabilize her blood pressure and keeping her in the hospital overnight for observation.

Emma kept a vigil over her mother while Baker arranged for his dad's body to be collected by the family undertaker. Libby patiently waited for Baker to finish and then left with him back to the Oaks.

BAKER TRIED TO APOLOGIZE for the surge of stress that confronted Libby on her very first day in Lynchburg, but she asked him to think of himself, not of her. Not tonight. Baker thought about suggesting a drink, but given everything with his mother, he didn't want Libby to think he was following the same path. So they settled on a movie—*You've Got Mail*—accompanied by odd bits and pieces of food from the refrigerator.

Halfway through the movie, as Tom Hanks was explaining his theory about *The Godfather* to Meg Ryan, Libby reached for the remote and paused it. Baker realized how surreal it was—watching a romantic comedy about email and bookshops on the night his father died. Nothing felt right anymore. They could have sat in silence or talked about funeral arrangements, or called more relatives, but instead they'd chosen this oddly comforting ritual of familiar dialogue and predictable plot points. Maybe this was what grief looked like: seeking normalcy in the face of something that made everything else feel impossible.

"I keep thinking about your father," Libby said quietly, curling her legs under her on the couch. "The way Emma described him this morning—still working in the garden, still so vibrant. It doesn't seem real."

Baker stared at the frozen screen. "He always said he wanted to die with his boots on. I just never thought it would happen that way." He picked at a leftover casserole. "I keep replaying our last text exchange. It was about baseball, of all things. He wanted to know how Zimmerman did in the game."

"That's not a bad final conversation," Libby offered gently.

"No, but..." Baker trailed off, then looked at her. "I never told him about you. Not really. He knew you existed, but I never told him how I felt about you."

Libby was quiet for a moment. "How do you feel about me?"

The question hung in the air between them. Baker set down his plate and turned to face her fully.

"I love you," he said. "I've been trying to figure out how to say it, when to say it. And now he's gone, and he'll never know that I found someone like you."

Libby's eyes filled with tears. "He would have liked that you're happy."

"Yeah," Baker said, his voice thick. "He would have." He reached for her hand. "I'm sorry this is how you're meeting my family."

"Baker," she said, squeezing his fingers, "this is real life. This is what families do—they show up for each other when everything falls apart. I'm honored to be here with you."

The familiar scent of his mother's lavender sachets drifted from the linen closet down the hall, mixing with the faint scent of his father's pipe tobacco that still clung to the leather furniture. In the foyer, the old grandfather clock chimed ten o'clock with the same resonant tone that had marked Baker's childhood bedtimes. Even the taste of one of his mom's casseroles carried the comforting flavors of home: cream of mushroom soup and the sharp cheddar she always used.

They sat in comfortable silence for a moment before Baker reached for the remote. "Should we finish the movie?"

"Only if you promise to cry at the end like you did the first time we watched it."

"I did not cry."

"You absolutely did. Right when she's standing on the bridge in the park with Brinkley, and he says, 'Don't cry, shop girl.'"

Baker smiled—the first time since Emma had run toward

their car that afternoon. "Fine. But if I cry, then I really would like to talk seriously about marriage."

"Deal."

The next morning, Baker made two phone calls before heading to identify his father's body. One was to Karl, an early riser, to share the family news and check whether rumors about Phil's assailant were still circulating.

"Baker, I'm so sorry about your father," Karl said immediately. "How are you?"

"It's been rough. I keep catching myself wanting to call him about little things. Baker's voice grew quieter. Death makes you realize how much of your thinking involves other people, even when they're not there." He paused, dreading what he would see when he got to the morgue. Emma had described his father the day before as still sharp, agile, and humorous until the very moment he collapsed in the garden. Soon Baker would have to reconcile that vibrant man with whatever lay waiting for him.

"There's something else I need to tell you," Karl continued hesitantly. "Phil has been telling people at Trinity that you must have been behind the mugging, at least as an accomplice. I've already informed Bishop Gallagher about his attempt to implicate you." He hesitated, then added with a note of delight in his voice, "It seems to be backfiring on him, though. While some members are genuinely concerned about Phil and rallying around him, there's an equal number who seem far less sympathetic. Apparently, his decision to publicly accuse you hasn't endeared him to the majority."

"He's actually telling parishioners I was involved?" Baker asked.

"I'm afraid so. But the bishop is taking it seriously. Time will tell if Phil faces discipline, either civilly or ecclesiastically."

The other phone call was to Oscar, who was busy shopping for a gift for Julian at the local saddlery. Oscar expressed his genuine sadness about Edward's passing but seemed somewhat distracted, quickly turning the conversation to concerns about Anne's emotional state and her potential for relapse, and how she would need help handling the funeral arrangements. While his worries weren't unreasonable given Anne's history, Baker had hoped for a more sustained focus on grieving their loss rather than managing logistics. Sensing Oscar's divided attention, Baker offered no further encouragement for his uncle to come to Lynchburg. *Maybe this is just how he processes grief,* Baker thought. *He's learned to show care through action rather than words.*

Anne had been admitted to the hospital the previous afternoon, when the ER doctor recommended observation, and Emma had stayed with her through the night. By the next afternoon, Baker and Libby were back there. Anne had stabilized but remained withdrawn, staring at the wall with the same vacant expression she'd worn the day before. The grief counselor warned them that shock manifested differently in everyone. Still, Baker recognized something more profound in his mother's stillness— a lifetime of unspoken pain that his father's passing had somehow unlocked.

He sat beside her bed for several minutes, watching her breathe, remembering all the times throughout his childhood when she'd retreated into herself like this. The harsh fluorescent lights above cast everything in an unforgiving white glare; the antiseptic smell of disinfectant mixed with the faint medicinal scent from the IV drip. Somewhere down the hall, a heart monitor beeped steadily, and the soft squeak of nurses' shoes on linoleum provided a rhythmic backdrop to his mother's shallow breathing. Anne lay so still against the starched white sheets, her face pale and expressionless, that she seemed to disappear into the clinical sterility surrounding her. Back then, he'd attributed that withdrawal to her drinking. Now he wondered if there had always been something more.

"Anne Millington speaking," she said as Baker approached her bed, as if she were answering an imaginary phone.

Baker was startled by her words. *She must be hallucinating,* he thought.

"Mom, we need to talk," Baker said gently, taking her hand.

"Baker?"

"It's me, Mom. We need to talk."

"About?"

"It's time for us to talk about forgiveness."

There was a long silence. The ventilation system hummed overhead, and from somewhere beyond the closed door came the distant sound of a television playing a game show, its cheerful jingles a jarring contrast to the weight of the moment. The smell of hospital coffee drifted in from the hallway, mingling with the faint scent of hand sanitizer.

Baker could hear his own heartbeat in his ears as he watched his mother's face, waiting for her reaction. She was pinching herself, the first real sign of at least a partial recovery, as if trying to determine why this moment—not a year ago, not ten years ago—was the right time.

As Emma and Libby watched from the doorway, mother and son began the healing conversation that was at least thirty years overdue. The late-afternoon sun filtered through the hospital blinds, casting honey-colored stripes across the bed.

"I've been waiting for this moment for so long," she whispered, tears in her eyes. "I didn't think it would ever come."

Baker squeezed her hand tighter. "Dad would have wanted this. And I need it too."

Anne's fingers traced the hospital blanket as decades of buried shame surfaced. "The New Year's Eve party at the Crawfords'," she whispered, her voice barely audible. "You were only thirteen. You'd gone to that bonfire party with your friends, so excited to be old enough to stay out until midnight. I'd had too much to drink before your father and I even arrived at the party."

Baker remembered that night all too well—how she'd knocked over the champagne tower; how she'd loudly contradicted the hostess when the woman complimented Baker's grades, insisting that he was "just average, nothing special" in front of everyone; how she'd stumbled getting into the car. But what he'd never told her was how he'd handled the aftermath.

"The next week at school," Baker said quietly, "when people asked about the holidays, I told them you'd called Mrs. Crawford a bitch for hitting on Dad. I made you sound like a jealous wife defending her territory instead of…"

He paused, the shame of that long-ago deception still fresh. "But you never called her anything. You just…you knocked over the champagne, and you couldn't walk straight, and I was so embarrassed, I invented a completely different version of you."

Anne's eyes filled with tears. "You were just a child."

"I was old enough to know that lying was easier than explaining the truth," Baker said. "And from then on, I kept covering for you. Making up stories, excuses. 'Mom's not feeling well.' 'She had an emergency.' 'She's traveling.' I became an expert at protecting your reputation." He squeezed her hand. "But I was really protecting myself. I didn't want people to know, to pity me, to ask questions I couldn't answer."

OVER THE NEXT SEVERAL days, as Anne regained her strength and prepared to leave the hospital, their conversations deepened. Baker would arrive each morning with coffee for them both, and he and Anne would pick up where they'd left off the day before. Emma returned to her usual routine, and Libby spent her time exploring Lynchburg's historic districts and Baker's old haunts, giving mother and son the space they needed.

It was on Anne's last day in the hospital before returning to the Oaks that she revealed the most profound truth. She had been sitting up in the bedside chair, looking stronger than she had since Edward's death, when she set down her teacup and met Baker's eyes with a resolve he hadn't seen in years.

"There's more to the story, Baker. It started when I was eight," she began, her voice calm and slow as she traced the rim of her teacup with a manicured finger. The hospital room felt too sterile for such raw confessions, but perhaps that was fitting—clinical surroundings for clinical disclosures. "Uncle James would come to visit during the summers. He always brought presents."

"He abused you?" Baker's voice rose sharply.

She remained silent until she knew her son had fully digested the truth. Baker noticed her shoulders tense and her hybrid Yankee-Southern accent thicken with emotion as she revealed this horrible truth. Then she described the visits from Uncle James, which always seemed to coincide with her parents' social engagements. She recalled how her grandmother would shake her head and tell her to "stop making up stories" whenever she tried to speak up. The family trust and that parcel of land that once served as a summer camp and a springboard for a young couple in love had paid for her silence after she threatened to go public at eighteen.

"The women in our family have always been good at keeping secrets," Anne said with a bitter smile. "My mother knew. I'm certain of it. But acknowledging it would have meant facing my father with it, and heaven forbid we disturb the Millington name with such unpleasantness."

Anne had never even told her husband about the dark past, so when she started to hit bottom, it seemed to everyone that she was a random victim of the disease. She knew better, of course, and didn't say anything to anyone except the therapists at Betty Ford. She wanted to protect her children.

This revelation struck Baker like a fist. He felt the breath leave his body and gripped the edge of his mother's hospital bed, his knuckles white, trying to steady himself against the vertigo of his shifting reality. The family didn't want him to know—the elegant Sunday dinners, the carefully maintained social standing, the generational wealth that had afforded him every opportunity—because the so-called perfect family was built upon a foundation of secrets and suffering.

A bitter taste of shame filled his mouth as he recalled his years of resentment toward his mother's drinking, his sanctimonious judgment of her weakness. All the while, she had been silently carrying this burden. He found himself reevaluating every childhood memory through this new lens, wondering how she had maintained her composure through decades of silent pain. A tear slid down his cheek as he realized that in his quest to become a spiritual guide for others, he had failed to truly see the person who needed him most.

"Did Oscar know?" Baker asked, the question tumbling out before he could stop himself.

Anne's laugh held no humor. "Oscar knows everything about everyone, darling. It's how he's maintained his position. He never spoke of it directly, but he arranged for me to see the best therapist in Virginia after your father and I married. The one time I nearly told Edward everything, it was Oscar who convinced me not to." She paused, looking at Baker with eyes so spent that he wondered how anyone could keep so much bottled inside and still be functional. "He said some burdens aren't meant to be shared. I think he was wrong about that."

Baker would spend another week at his mother's side, their conversations reaching into the darkest corners of her past: the emotional and physical abuse she had suffered from her own uncle, the lack of empathy from the women in her family, and the money meant to silence her. It was during one of these quiet afternoons—Anne resting, Baker lost in thought by the window—that his phone buzzed with Karl's name.

The news from Boise felt like it belonged to another lifetime. The real culprit in Phil's attack had finally been caught: a homeless man who was probably just looking for cash. Phil's charges against Baker were quietly dropped, though no formal apology was ever offered. Baker thanked Karl, ended the call, and slipped the phone back into his pocket. Whatever relief he might have felt was muted by everything else he now carried.

Chapter Eleven

BAKER AND LIBBY LEFT FOR BOISE AFTER THREE CHALLENGING weeks in Lynchburg. Difficult, yet purifying. His mother had finally shared the times she'd been called to the principal's office, drunk at pickup, and the small spaces she'd found to hide her gin: behind winter coats, under bathroom sinks, in the garage behind paint cans. She described the aches of withdrawal, the way her hands would shake during morning coffee, and the menace and specter of wanting to escape family and work and the big, impossible truth of existence that felt too heavy to carry sober. His mother's past and the pain it had inflicted on everyone had finally been laid bare, forcing Baker into his own complicated reckoning with forgiveness.

He had still not revealed the truth about his own past to Libby—that life-changing moment his friend Tim had referred to when he asked Baker, "Have you told her yet?" He had been so preoccupied with justifying sharing this truth with Karl before telling Libby, worrying about how Libby would react not only to the story itself but also to the fact that he planned to tell Karl first. The reasoning made no sense. Now, on the flight home, he felt it was finally time to unburden himself of that secret he'd carried for so long, a truth that had shaped his career choices and relationships ever since that fateful day in New Haven.

They settled into their seats on the plane, and Baker took Libby's hand. He provided a brief introduction to what was about to happen, but right as he'd prepared the story and it was all ready to leave his lips, he was thrown a curveball.

"Please let me go first," Libby interrupted, her voice steady though her eyes betrayed a flicker of apprehension. Baker could see she had witnessed so much courage in Lynchburg that remaining silent would have felt fraudulent. He nodded and gently squeezed her hand.

Libby drew in a deep breath, her gaze fixed on a point beyond Baker's shoulder as she began. "Remember when I worked in Courchevel with my college friends?"

Baker nodded, recalling her mention of it on their first date.

"The last night there, we had this incredible après-ski event. Maybe thirty of us, plus some hotel guests our age. The kind of party where the drinks flow freely and everyone feels invincible." Her voice dropped slightly, and Baker could sense something darker approaching. "This Austrian guy—premed student from Innsbruck, all charm and perfect teeth—asked my girlfriend and me to join him for what he called 'a short stroll' to a nearby mountain hut. Said he had mushrooms stashed there and we could get high together."

She paused, her fingers tracing patterns on the armrest.

"Which we did. But we mistook him for being a nice guy." Libby's fingers tightened around Baker's hand. "That wasn't his plan at all. He lied about three other guys coming to meet up with us there later, to continue to party." She paused, and Baker could see her searching for the right words. "They weren't coming to party with us at all. They were coming to..." Her voice trailed off, and she looked out the airplane window. "Let's just say their intentions weren't what we thought they were. What they wanted to do to us—to my girlfriend and me—" She couldn't finish the sentence.

"Oh my God," Baker gasped. "What? Did they hurt you? Did they...rape you?"

"Yes. I was dazed, scared, and confused. I could feel I'd been penetrated and could see my friend lying half naked on the floor of that cold, cold room, unmoving. I was shivering. It felt like a morgue."

"Had the guys left? Did you go to the authorities?"

"There are no authorities, as we perceive them, at a European ski area—just ski patrollers. Someone at the medical center could have assisted, but it was closed that early in the morning, and Le Centre Hospitalier Albertville-Moûtiers, which had specialized facilities, was so far away that I would have missed my flight home if I had gone. No one would have intervened anyway because authorities regarded our lifestyle up there as one big orgy. Moreover, none of this could get back to my father. He would have jumped on a plane to come strangle all of them."

"So what did you do?" Baker asked, his voice barely audible above the jet engines. The flight attendant's footsteps echoed in the aisle behind them, and the overhead reading light cast a small circle of warmth between their seats while the rest of the cabin remained muted in afternoon shadow.

Libby crushed her plastic water cup until it crackled. "I managed to wake my friend. Had to shake her hard. She was . . . she couldn't even . . . ." Libby's voice caught. "We got dressed somehow and stumbled back through the snow. Dawn, maybe. I don't know."

"Did you tell anyone?"

"Our roommate took one look at us." Libby stared at her hands. "She knew. We all knew. But what were we supposed to do? Report it to whom? Austrian police, who'd probably blame us for drinking too much?" Her laugh was bitter. "She made us promise to get the morning-after pill. Get tested. As if that would fix everything."

Baker waited.

"You know what the worst part was? At breakfast, those bastards—all four of them—they came to our table, all tickety-boo. Asked if we'd had 'fun.' Like it was some joke they were in on." Her voice went flat. "My roommate dumped hot chocolate on them. 'Oops,' she said. 'So clumsy.' I wished I'd done more. Wished I'd screamed. Wished I'd—" She stopped.

Baker's thumb moved in slow circles over her knuckles. The silence stretched between them, filled only by the steady hum of the aircraft.

Finally, Libby spoke again. "I know you're wondering why I'm telling you this now." She turned to face him directly. "It's because you need to understand why I am the way I am. Why I've kept everyone at arm's length for so long." She swallowed hard. "After Courchevel, I couldn't . . . I didn't know how to let anyone close. Every time a guy showed interest, all I could see was that Austrian bastard's smile. All charm and perfect teeth, right up until it wasn't."

"Libby—"

"I'm not finished." Her voice was gentle but firm. "I went on dates. Had a couple of boyfriends—if you could call them that. Even got engaged. But the moment things got serious, the moment someone said the word *forever*, I'd find a reason to end it. Too controlling. Too distant. Too something." She laughed without humor. "The truth is, they were probably fine. I was the one who was broken."

"You're not broken," Baker said softly.

"Maybe not anymore," she said. "But I was for a long time. And that's why I've remained single, Baker. Not because I haven't met the right person. Because I couldn't let myself trust that any person was right." She looked down at their intertwined hands, then back up at him. "Until now. Until you made me want to try again."

They sat in silence for some time after that, the weight of her words settling between them. The plane banked slowly westward, and Baker watched the landscape below shift from green to brown as they crossed into different time zones. The flight attendants made their rounds with drinks and pretzels, their cheerful voices a strange contrast to the heaviness that had filled their small space. Libby accepted a ginger ale and sipped it quietly, staring out the window.

Baker brought her hand to his lips and held it there for a moment before speaking. "I can't undo what happened to you. I can't go back and stop those bastards or make any of it right." His voice was rough with emotion. "But I can promise you this—I will never, ever give you a reason to regret trusting me."

It wasn't until they were somewhere over Colorado, the Rockies spread out beneath them like crumpled paper, that she turned back to him. He'd asked to go first—to tell his story—and she'd agreed. But now, as he opened his mouth to begin, she held up a hand.

"Wait, I know you wanted to start, but I have to ask you something first. Just one thing, then it's all yours." She paused, gathering her words. "One night at the Oaks, I saw that photo—the one on the shelf in the living room. You and a young woman, and there was clearly something between you. More than just friends. Why would your parents keep that on display?"

Baker adjusted his seatbelt and took a slow breath. "That was someone very important to me. We met as juniors and spent a gap year together starting a summer camp for our prep school."

"A girlfriend?"

The plane hit a pocket of turbulence, causing their cups to rattle on the tray tables. Baker steadied his and looked directly at her. "My wife. The love of my life."

Libby's hand went still on her armrest. "What happened to her?"

"She was pregnant," Baker said quietly. "Then there were major complications. Preeclampsia. They did an emergency cesarian at Yale New Haven Hospital, but . . ." He shook his head. "I lost them both the same day. My wife and my son."

Libby reached for Baker's hand. "Oh my God, Baker. You never—I had no idea. I just assumed you were divorced, not widowed. And you lost your child, too."

She wept quietly beside him. The flight attendant discreetly brought them some tissues and gave them space.

Baker fought to hold back the tears that were glistening in his eyes. By the time they began their descent into Boise, he felt lighter. Sharing this history with Libby had lifted a weight he had been carrying for so long.

"I'm so glad you told me," Libby said softly. "I can't imagine your pain—even now."

Baker laced his fingers into hers as the plane lowered to the tarmac.

TWO DAYS LATER, KARL and Baker sat face-to-face on vinyl task chairs in Karl's "office," an old supply closet off the administrator's open space that Phil had converted into a cubbyhole to embarrass Karl and make him feel insignificant, or at least unwanted at Trinity. Baker started the conversation by thanking him for his invitation to unload more than thirty years of pent-up sadness, anger, depression, and denial. While he had previously told Father John and one or two others that he had had a first wife and had committed to Christ, he'd never told the complete story to anyone—not even his immediate family. Now that Karl had become a trusted confidant, Baker felt ready to share everything.

"I told Libby about this on our flight," Baker said, his voice steadier now than it had been then. "But she only got the condensed version. There's so much more to it—things I've barely let myself remember all these years."

Karl leaned forward, his weathered hands folded in his lap. "Baker, if any of this becomes too painful, you stop. You hear me? We can always pick this up another time."

"No, I need to do this," Baker said, sitting up straighter in the uncomfortable vinyl chair. "Karl, you've become like a father to me. If I can't tell you, I can't tell anyone." He took a deep breath. "And honestly, after thirty years, I'm ready to let it out.

"Her name was Wendy," he began, his gaze drifting to the window. "We actually met as juniors in high school, but we really fell for each other during a gap year—both of us working at a church camp. Nineteen years old and absolutely certain we'd found the person we were meant to spend our lives with. You know how it is at that age."

Karl nodded, a slight smile touching his lips.

"Oscar saw something in both of us. He orchestrated our paths to Yale—me right away, Wendy after a semester at UVA." Baker's expression softened at the memory. "I went to New York alone to find an engagement ring—ended up at this Orthodox jeweler in the Diamond District. I was so young, didn't have much money. But the jeweler looked at me and said, 'Love shouldn't wait for money.' I carried that ring for nine months before I finally proposed."

Karl smiled.

"She had no idea it was coming. We married right after graduation. I went to divinity school, and Wendy got a job teaching at the Foote School while I pursued my calling." His voice remained steady as he continued. "She got pregnant. Surprised us both, honestly. At the twenty-week ultrasound, we found out it was a boy. That's when we decided—Jack, after John Davenport. Wendy was obsessive about her prenatal care. Did everything right, everything by the book."

Baker's hands began to shake. He gripped the arms of the vinyl chair.

"Two weeks before her due date, she woke me at three in the morning. Severe headache, seeing spots. When we reached the hospital, the numbers on the monitor kept climbing. Then the seizures started." His voice dropped to barely above a whisper. "This gaunt doctor came out—I'll never forget his face. All hope surrendered. Neither of them survived the surgery. My wife or my son."

Karl leaned forward but didn't interrupt.

"I collapsed to my knees right there in Yale New Haven Hospital. Oscar caught me before I hit the floor." Baker's eyes had gone distant. "At the funeral—Saint Paul's in Lynchburg—I walked up to the closed coffin, and I just . . . I howled. Like a dying animal. This raw, primal sound echoing through the church. I couldn't stop it.

"Tim Cartwright was officiating," Baker said more quietly. "My best friend, Grayson, ran up to hold me. He was such a big man that he could envelop me completely. Tim stepped down from the pulpit mid-homily and knelt beside me. He said, 'There are no words for this, but you don't have to carry this alone.'"

Baker drew a shaky breath. "I withdrew from Berkeley. George Levering proposed building a labyrinth in Lynchburg—a path with no wrong turns for people entering a maze of grief. He thought it might help me find my way through the pain. Professor Muehl suggested I might become a leader in the corporate world instead, someone who openly and proudly leads through godliness." His voice faltered. "But every turn felt wrong to me. How could there be a path forward when the God who was supposed to guide me had gone silent?" He looked down at his hands.

"But Karl, the faith that had been my anchor felt like a cruel joke," he said. "How could God call me to serve, then strip away everything giving my life meaning? Every morning, I'd wake believing it had all been a nightmare, only to have reality crash down again. I couldn't stand before a congregation and speak of God's love when my own heart screamed with questions of divine abandonment."

The small office felt thick with silence. Outside, the sounds of Trinity's hallways continued—footsteps, distant laughter, a door closing—but in this cramped supply closet, time seemed suspended.

Karl sat perfectly still, his eyes glistening. Finally, he leaned forward and gripped Baker's forearm with surprising strength. "Now I understand," he said. "Truly understand." He didn't offer platitudes about God's mysterious ways or suggest that time heals all wounds. He just held Baker's arm and let the weight of the story settle between them. After a long moment, he spoke again. "Baker, I'm honored you trusted me with this. Carrying that alone for thirty years . . ." He shook his head. "That takes a kind of strength I'm not sure I possess."

"I don't know if it's strength or cowardice," Baker admitted. "Maybe I was just too afraid to let anyone see how broken I really was."

"It's neither," Karl said. "It's survival. And now—telling Libby, telling me—that's healing. It won't erase what happened, but it means you're not alone with it anymore."

Baker nodded, feeling something shift inside him. The story hadn't changed. Wendy and Jack were still gone. But somehow, in this cramped office that Phil had meant as an insult to Karl, Baker felt lighter than he had in decades.

"Thank you," he said.

Baker found himself calculating: nearly five years together in New Haven before he lost her, three and a half years of undergraduate life, then almost another year and a half at seminary. Thirty years later, he still couldn't decide if that relatively short time together made losing her easier or infinitely worse. Maybe that's what grace looked like: not the absence of wrong turns, but the possibility that even the longest detour could eventually lead you home.

Karl squeezed his arm once more before releasing it. His eyes shone with renewed intensity. "Baker," he said, his voice thick with emotion. "I won't pretend I can imagine what you've carried all these years. But I want you to know something." He waited until Baker met his eyes. "You didn't lose your calling that day. You didn't abandon God. You found a different way to serve."

Baker felt himself relax from the inside out.

"Every person you've helped, every student you've mentored, every act of integrity you've brought to your work—that's been your ministry. Wendy would be proud of the man you've become, even if the path looked different from what you both planned." He stood slowly, moved around the small desk, and pulled Baker into an embrace. Not a brief pastoral hug, but the kind a father gives a son who has finally come home. "Thank you for trusting me with this," he whispered. "It's an honor to know you, Baker Vaughan. All of you."

When they finally separated, Baker wiped his eyes and managed a small laugh. "Thirty years," he said. "Thirty years I've been carrying that alone."

"Not anymore," Karl said. "Not anymore."

Chapter Twelve

Now that Baker had found Libby—the woman he loved and the key to priesthood (or not), he just needed to ask the question.

A wedding with Libby could not unfold the way he and Wendy had gotten married—no haggling over the price of a ring in Manhattan, no surprise announcement to their families, no wedding ceremony in an old New England church that held significant meaning for George Levering, who had embraced Baker like a son. Those moments belonged to Wendy, to their mutual first loves, to a time when Baker believed wholeheartedly he would take holy orders and Wendy would become a priest's wife. To recreate any of it with Libby would betray what these two had shared and be unfair to whatever new story they might craft together.

Baker didn't plan his proposal. They were sitting on Libby's small couch after dinner, her head resting against his shoulder as they watched the evening news. The anchor was droning on about local politics when Baker felt the words rise inside him like an irresistible tide he couldn't hold back.

"Libby," he said quietly, his voice rougher than intended.

"Mmm?" She didn't lift her head.

Baker closed his eyes, feeling the weight of what he was about to say. They weren't young anymore. They'd both survived decades of disappointments and small victories. He hadn't married Michelle for a reason—to honor Wendy's memory—and now he was at a crossroads. His overwhelming certainty that Libby was more—much more—than just a way for Karl to check off Baker's last box made him spit it out.

"I want to marry you."

She was still for a moment, then tilted her face up to look at him. Her eyes searched his with an intensity that made his breath catch, and he saw no surprise, only a gentle certainty that seemed to reach right through him.

"I want to marry you too," she said.

They sat there for a long moment, holding each other's gaze while the television chattered on about things impossibly distant. No tears, no dramatic declarations, no falling to one knee. Just two people who had found each other late in life, speaking a truth they both already knew but had been afraid to voice—afraid that naming it might somehow make it disappear.

Baker reached up to touch her face, his thumb tracing the line of her cheekbone. "I thought I was done with this," he said. "That I'd had my chance."

Libby covered his hand with hers. "But here we are."

Baker leaned forward and pressed his forehead against hers, their breath mingling in the quiet room.

"Should we tell people?" Libby asked.

Baker felt giddy. "Of course we should. I want to call the bishop tonight," he said, thinking of his mentor. "I want Karl to know."

"But what if—?" Libby stopped herself, then shook her head. "Never mind."

"What if what?" Baker sat up straighter, studying her expression. "What are you worried about?"

Libby was quiet for a moment, her thumbs twiddling in her lap. "What if he thinks we're moving too fast? What if he thinks we're being foolish?"

"We don't need anyone's permission."

It was eleven o'clock, but Baker reached for his phone, unable to contain himself. He dialed Karl's number, his hands trembling with excitement.

"Baker?" Karl's voice was thick with sleep. "What's wrong?"

"Nothing's wrong," Baker said, grinning. "Everything's perfect. Libby and I just got engaged!"

There was a pause. Then Karl's voice came through, warmer now despite the grogginess. "Great! Now go to sleep."

Click. Dial tone. Baker stared at his phone for a moment, then started laughing.

"What did he say?" Libby asked.

"He told me to go to sleep," Baker said, still chuckling. "Even with it only being ten o'clock in Medford, I still woke the poor man up."

She smiled and settled back against his shoulder. On the television, the channel 7 meteorologist was pointing enthusiastically at a high-pressure system moving in from the west, promising three days of sunshine and temperatures in the mid-seventies. "Perfect weather for outdoor activities," she chirped, "so get those barbeque grills ready, Boise!" The five-day outlook showed nothing but blue skies and gentle breezes.

The next day, Baker went to see Phil. After telling him that he and Libby were to marry, he made a pro forma pitch to Phil to marry them at Trinity. It was undoubtedly good form to give him the option, even though Baker and Libby wanted Karl to marry them.

Phil offered Baker a token congratulatory remark and then made this blunt, unmistakable comment: "I will not marry you at Trinity, and I will not allow Karl to marry you here either." He casually turned and walked away. No further explanation was given.

Baker's mind struggled to catch up with what had just transpired—the casual cruelty of it, the finality. He wasn't surprised about Phil opting out, but he was dismayed by the ban imposed on Karl. Frankly, Baker hadn't asked Karl to marry them yet, but he certainly felt it was Karl's decision to make, not Phil's. This arbitrary exercise of power felt petty and vindictive, precisely the kind of institutional control that made Baker often question whether he belonged in the priesthood at all.

Phil's obstinance would prove more costly than he anticipated. Word traveled quickly through Trinity's congregation—not through Baker, who maintained his characteristic discretion, but through the inevitable network of parish gossip. When longtime parishioners learned that Baker had been denied the simple courtesy of marrying in the church where he'd grown into a bona fide postulant, the reaction was swift and pointed.

Baker watched from across the fellowship hall as Laura Whitmore approached Phil after Sunday service. He could see the deliberate way she carried herself, the quiet authority in her posture that came from years of generous donations. Her family had funded the church's new roof, after all. Even from a distance, Baker noticed how she pointedly avoided calling Phil

"Rector." Her voice carried just enough for Baker to catch fragments: "Phil Harbaugh…deeply troubled by your treatment of Baker Vaughan . . . served this parish with distinction . . ." A flush of pride warmed Baker's face as he realized she was defending him. Then came the words that made his heart stop: "If Trinity isn't good enough for his wedding, then perhaps Trinity isn't good enough for the Whitmore family's continued support."

Soon after, Baker got word of others following suit. The Hendersons, the Clarks, and the majority of the vestry suddenly developed concerns about Phil's leadership style. Phone calls were made to the diocese. Questions were raised about pastoral judgment and Christian charity. Even Bishop Gallagher, who had initially supported Phil's appointment, began receiving pointed inquiries about "the situation at Trinity."

Baker could see it now—Phil had calculated that pushing him out of Trinity would eliminate a threat to his authority. But the rector had miscalculated badly. By denying Baker the grace that any decent pastor would extend, Phil had revealed the very character flaws that made him unsuitable to lead a congregation in the first place. Baker witnessed these developments with grim satisfaction. Phil was finally facing accountability that had long been overdue—not through Baker's machinations, but through his own vindictive overreach. Sometimes, Baker reflected, the best way to defeat someone was to give them enough rope to hang themselves.

When Baker called Karl to inform him about Phil's refusal, Karl's response was immediate and characteristically warm. "Well, that settles it then," he said with a chuckle. "You and Libby will come to the farm. I'll marry you right here in Medford, under the sixty-foot big-leaf maple tree in the front yard. Margaret's been wanting to host a wedding for years. She'll be over the moon." Baker could hear the smile in Karl's voice. "And I'll bring Grace with us; she'll want to be part of this. Screw Phil. We'll have something better—a celebration among people who love you both and wouldn't even want Phil at the ceremony."

Baker understood the weight of what Karl was offering. The bishop was a man who had established his own rule about not performing marriages for older couples—yet here he was, willing to break his rule and actively reject the conventional church setting in favor of a venue far more personal. The tree in Karl's front yard wasn't just a tree; it was sacred to Karl and Margaret, a place where they'd built their life. And his words—"among people who love you both"—struck Baker as more than mere comfort. Karl saw an unfathomable peace in their love for one another, well worth celebrating in his own sanctuary.

What type of wedding would Libby want? Baker asked himself. He didn't need anything complicated, fancy, or even involving his own family; still, he certainly didn't want to deprive Libby of anything. After all, this was her first marriage, and she was approaching sixty. She had no siblings and never mentioned cousins or any other family members, but maybe she had special people in her life whom Baker had yet to meet. Her father, Buddy, was still alive, but it was doubtful he'd travel to southwest Oregon for a wedding.

As it turned out, Libby's vision matched Baker's perfectly: something simple, something real, something that felt like them. When he mentioned Karl's offer, her face lit up with the kind of relief that comes when someone else has already thought of the perfect solution. "Under his big-leaf maple tree?" she'd asked, and when Baker nodded, she'd taken his hand and said, "That sounds exactly right."

The wedding was held on a Saturday afternoon in late September when the Oregon air carried just enough crispness to make people grateful for the warmth of gathered bodies. Libby wore a dress she'd wear again—soft blue linen that moved with her rather than against her—paired with comfortable shoes that let her walk across the uneven ground without worry.

About thirty people attended; each one knew and loved them both. Baker's sister Emma had made an extraordinary effort, flying from Virginia to Boise, then driving to Challis to pick up his dear friend Oletta Robinson before the two women returned to Boise and flew together to Medford for the wedding. When Baker saw the rental car pull into Karl's driveway, he felt that flutter of anticipation that comes when an unexpectedly good moment is about to happen. Through the passenger window, he could make out Oletta's familiar profile—a little more fragile than he remembered, but unmistakably her. She was already looking toward the house, and Baker imagined her taking in the beauty of this place: the way the old farmhouse sat perfectly among the rolling hills, how Karl and Margaret had created such an Eden here. He hoped she could feel what he felt about this sanctuary they'd found.

As his sister helped her out, Oletta spotted Baker walking toward them. For a moment, they just looked at each other across the gravel—this woman who was a steadfast friend as he moved on from grief.

"Well," Oletta said, her voice carrying that same dry warmth he remembered, "I see you're still too handsome for your own good."

Baker laughed. "I'm trying to outgrow that particular character flaw," he said with a rueful smile as he bent over to hug her.

"I told you once that you'd make a fine priest," she said, pulling back to study his face with satisfaction. "Turns out what you really needed to learn was how to be a fine husband."

FOR LIBBY, MEETING OLETTA was like finally putting a face to the voice in so many of Baker's Challis stories. She'd heard about the woman who'd been such a good friend during Baker's first months in Idaho, the one who'd told him he should become a priest, but seeing her in person made those stories come alive. And when Grace Hamilton stepped out of Karl and Margaret's car—they had driven her from Boise for the wedding—Libby felt the wedding party was finally complete. Here were two women who, in their own way, had helped guide Baker through different chapters of his healing.

Baker loved watching these women he cared for so deeply finally come together: Libby introducing Grace to Emma and Oletta, all of them forming the kind of instant connection that happens when people discover they share someone precious in common.

Margaret had strung simple white lights between the tree branches, not for drama but because they'd still be twinkling when the sun set. Folding chairs formed a loose semicircle, but half the guests ended up standing anyway, naturally gravitating toward wherever felt right in the moment. As Baker took his place beside Karl, his eyes moved across the small gathering— and stopped when he spotted Grace, a fellow parishioner from Trinity, seated with careful dignity in one of the front chairs. The irony settled on him quietly. Not long ago, she had asked him to escort her to her great-nephew's wedding in Portland, and he'd had to decline, caught up in his own uncertainty about the future. Now their roles had reversed completely. She had traveled even farther to witness his wedding, a testament to the kind of loyalty that transcends ecclesiastical politics and institutional disappointments. Baker felt quiet gratitude wash over him. Grace represented an essential connection he'd feared he'd lose at Trinity: a genuine fellowship that had nothing to do with theology or church governance and everything to do with simply showing up for each other.

Karl's ceremony was brief and personal—no formal scripts about duties and obligations, just honest words about what he'd witnessed in Baker and Libby's relationship. When they exchanged rings, Baker leaned close and whispered, "I still can't believe Karl's letting us use his tree. Pretty sure this makes us officially more special than his begonias."

Libby's laugh bubbled up before she could stop it, and she whispered back, "Don't let it go to your head, Baker. Those begonias are his pride and joy." That laugh became part of the ceremony itself, rippling through the small gathering like the best kind of blessing.

Afterward, everyone moved to Margaret's back porch, where dinner was served on mismatched plates—her famous lasagna, Karl's grilled vegetables, contributions from friends who'd insisted on bringing hors d'oeuvres like bacon-wrapped water chestnuts and deviled eggs. The wedding cake was three different desserts because Libby couldn't choose, and Baker had said, "Why should you have to?"

It was during this reception that Grace and Oletta found

each other, settling into Margaret's porch swing with plates of lasagna and an inexhaustible supply of stories about Baker. The former shared tales of his theological wrestling matches, his earnest questions about calling and purpose, his gradual emergence from the fog of early grief. Oletta countered with memories of the broken man who'd first arrived in Challis, how he'd sit at her kitchen table, unable to imagine a future. How she'd watched him slowly remember that he was still alive.

"He asked me once if I thought God had a sense of humor," Grace said, watching Baker across the porch as he helped someone with a second serving. "I told him to look around. Of course, He does. But I don't think Baker believed me then."

"Oh, he does now." Oletta laughed, her eyes crinkling. "Look at him. A man his age, finding love like this, getting married under a tree because some petty pastor tried to punish him. If that's not divine comedy, I don't know what is." They talked until the music started, comparing notes on Baker's transformation like two gardeners discussing a particularly stubborn plant that had finally decided to bloom.

People stayed until the lights came on naturally, not because tradition demanded it. Stories got told, second helpings appeared without fanfare, and somewhere around sunset, someone started playing guitar. It was the type of celebration where the wedding felt like the beginning of the party, not the end of an elaborate performance.

Baker and Libby stayed in the large room above the barn, which Margaret had transformed into an impromptu bridal suite. She'd moved her best quilt up there, placed fresh wildflowers on the nightstand, and somehow managed to hang curtains that matched. "It's not the Ritz," Margaret had said apologetically.

Still, to Libby and Baker, it felt more special than any hotel—a place where people who loved them had taken care to make their wedding night perfect in all the ways that mattered.

THE NEXT MORNING, AFTER Margaret's famous blackberry French toast and too many cups of coffee, Baker and Libby drove down to Bandon for a two-night stay at the golf resort—not really a honeymoon, but enough alone time to properly explore what it meant to be husband and wife without Karl's roosters as their alarm clock. As they pulled through the entrance and caught their first glimpse of the Pacific beyond the dunes, Libby reached over and squeezed his hand.

Baker thought back to the Sunday afternoon in his Boise apartment when they'd discovered their shared passion for golf—the Masters on television, sunlight streaming through pines at Augusta, the hushed reverence of the commentators. Libby had paused mid-sentence, transfixed by the geometry of an approach shot, the ball's arc against Georgia sky. "It's almost like watching ballet," she'd said, and Baker had known then that she understood.

After that, golf had become their shared language. They played occasionally—Libby had taken lessons and could hold her own on forgiving public courses—but it was the game's contemplative beauty that truly drew them. They'd drive out to Warm Springs on summer evenings, sometimes taking a few clubs to play the back nine in the golden hour, other times just walking and observing, discussing the architecture of holes, the psychology of risk. Baker appreciated how Libby noticed things: the way rough framed a fairway like negative space in a painting, how a well-placed bunker could make your heart race from a hundred yards away.

"There's a spot on the Oregon coast," Baker had said one afternoon, as they watched the U.S. Open at Chambers Bay on television in her living room. "Bandon Dunes. I think you'd love it. A bit like this, but more demanding. Classic wild Irish links."

Libby had turned from the screen, already smiling. "When do we leave?"

Their coastal retreat proved ideal. Baker surprised Libby by making reservations to play the par-three courses—first Shorty's, then Bandon Preserve. Walking those oceanside holes together, with the Pacific stretching endlessly before them and the wind carrying salt air, felt utterly natural. Libby had never played on courses like these, where the ball bounced and rolled unpre-dictably, where the elements shaped every shot. But observing Baker's countenance as he demonstrated how to read the wind, seeing him so completely in his element at what felt like golf's spiritual home, she grasped why the game meant so much to him.

"This is what golf was meant to be," Baker said as they stood on the thirteenth tee at Bandon Preserve, the green perched dramatically above the beach below. "I can see why," Libby re-plied, and meant it.

Karl called while they were having dinner on their second night. He invited them to stop at the farm for one more night on their drive back to Boise, for what he called "a proper conversa-tion." When they arrived back in Medford the next afternoon, Karl was waiting on the porch as if he'd been watching for their car. He stood and descended the steps as they pulled into the gravel drive, embracing them both with the warmth of someone who had some-thing important to say but wasn't quite ready to articulate it yet.

"Tea?" he asked, and without waiting for an answer, he led them not to the kitchen but directly to his study. "Sit, both of you." He gestured to the worn leather chairs across from his desk. "I have something to propose."

Baker settled into his chair, immediately wary. Karl's proposals tended to upend his life in the most fortuitous ways. But they also tended to require significant leaps of faith.

"You know I think you should pursue ordination," Karl began, looking at Baker. "But Phil's pettiness has made it clear that remaining in Boise isn't viable. Not for your formation, and, frankly, not for your sanity."

Libby took Baker's hand. They'd discussed this possibility—that Baker's path to priesthood might require leaving Boise—but hadn't settled on specifics.

"I have a friend," Karl continued. "Amy Benson, a priest at an Episcopal parish in Dripping Springs, Texas. Brilliant woman who's spent years doing exactly what you've been doing: interrogating the institutional church while still believing in its essential mission." He leaned forward, elbows on his desk. "She's also someone who comprehends that people come to this calling at different stages of life, with different kinds of baggage."

"Texas?" Libby said. Baker couldn't read her tone.

Karl nodded. "Hill Country. Beautiful territory. The seminary in Austin is different from most others around the country. Less concerned with producing company pastors. More interested in forming clergy who can think independently."

Baker felt that familiar stirring—part exhilaration, part terror—that accompanied Karl's grander ideas. "What exactly are you suggesting?"

"Go visit. Meet Amy. See the place. Get a feel for whether it's somewhere you could complete three years of formation." Karl paused, looking between them. "Both of you. This isn't solely Baker's decision anymore."

"Three years is considerable time," Libby said quietly.

"It is," Karl agreed. "But it's also not forever. And Austin's not Mars—you'd return here every summer, holidays. Margaret and I aren't getting any younger. We'd appreciate the regular visits."

Baker watched Libby's face, attempting to read her. They'd been married three days, and he was already asking her to consider uprooting her life for his uncertain calling.

"What's she like?" Libby asked. "Amy?"

Karl's face brightened. "You'll like her. She's got Margaret's pragmatic streak and my theological curiosity, plus she knows how to repair things with her hands. Builds furniture as a hobby. The sort of person who can discuss Tillich over breakfast and rewire a lamp after lunch."

"When would we go?" Baker asked.

"Soon. Amy is expecting my call. I thought you might consider spending a long weekend there next month. See if the place feels right."

Karl sat back in his chair. "Look, I know this feels abrupt. You just got married. You're settling into a new rhythm. But sometimes the optimal time to make a significant change is when you've already made another significant change. Momentum, you know?"

Libby looked into Baker's eyes. "What do you think?"

Baker regarded his wife—still strange to think that word—and saw not reluctance but genuine curiosity. "I think," he said slowly, "that three days ago I married someone courageous enough to say yes to an uncertain future. Maybe she's courageous enough to say yes to this one too."

"Is that your way of asking me?" Libby smiled.

"That's my way of saying I want to discover the answer together."

Karl reached for his phone. "I'll call Amy tonight."

That evening, they discovered online that Dripping Springs promoted itself as both the wedding capital of Texas and gateway to the Hill Country—though, as Baker noted, Saint Louis proclaimed itself gateway to the West, so such claims were negotiable.

A WEEK LATER, AFTER flying into Austin and spending the night near the airport, they were guided by a navigation system down a serpentine road lined with cedar trees until they reached a modest Craftsman house that looked like it could have been transplanted from Boise's North End. A woman emerged from the front door before they'd even extinguished the engine—midforties, with auburn hair pulled back in a loose ponytail and a confident stride that suggested she was accustomed to authority.

Stepping out of their rental car into the humid Texas heat, Baker understood why locals joked about the town's name—in this climate, everything dripped.

"Baker! Libby!" Amy Benson called out, arms spread wide in welcome. "You made it! How was the drive from Austin?"

"Beautiful," Libby said, accepting Amy's enthusiastic embrace. "The Hill Country is gorgeous."

"Wait until you see it at sunset," Amy said, then turned to embrace Baker with equal warmth. "Karl has told me so much about both of you. I feel like we're already friends."

She gestured toward the small structure behind her house. "That's your home away from home for the next few days. I had it built as a guest house. My older parishioners use it for their monthly domino tournaments, but mostly it's for visitors like you."

Amy led them across the yard, chattering about the property. "I know it's not fancy, but it's private and comfortable. You can come and go as you please. Please don't feel any obligation to keep me informed of your movements. Think of this as your base camp while you explore the area."

She pushed open the door to reveal a cozy space with whitewashed walls and a Murphy bed folded against one wall. "I installed the bed myself," she said with evident pride. "Beats spending money on a motel, and this way we can really get to know each other."

"This is incredibly generous," Libby said, running her hand along the smooth wood of the Murphy bed frame. "We really can't thank you enough."

"My pleasure. Please stay for as long as necessary," she suggested. "Spend at least a week familiarizing yourself with the area, the congregation, and of course, me." Baker also intended to allocate time to visit the Seminary of the Southwest in Austin, an accredited institution where he was certain he could resume his theological studies.

After dinner at her house, Amy walked them out to the casita. Her hand lingered perhaps a moment too long on Libby's shoulder as she pointed out the light switches. "The Murphy bed is quite comfortable," she said, her eyes moving between them with an intensity that made Baker suddenly aware of how close the three of them were standing in the small space.

"You've thought of everything," Libby said.

"Oh, it's my pleasure," Amy said. Something in her tone made Baker glance up from unpacking their overnight bag. Amy was watching Libby smooth the bedsheets, her expression one of frank appreciation. When she noticed Baker looking, she didn't look away. Instead, she smiled with a boldness that caught him off guard.

"I should let you two get settled," Amy said, though she made no move toward the door. "Unless you'd like to join me for a nightcap? I make excellent margaritas."

An hour later, they were sitting around Amy's firepit. The Texas night was surprisingly cool against their skin. Amy had changed into a flowered sundress that seemed designed to catch the firelight. She'd positioned herself in a way that let her observe them both simultaneously.

"So tell me," she said, swirling her margarita, "how does it feel to be newlyweds embarking on such a major life change?"

There was something in the way she said *newlyweds*. Not mocking, but with a kind of curiosity that felt almost scientific. As if she were studying them.

"Terrifying and exhilarating," Libby answered. "Baker's calling feels so clear to him, and I want to support that. But I'd be lying if I said I wasn't nervous about starting over in a new place."

"And you, Baker?" Amy leaned forward slightly. Her wide-rimmed glass rattled as she set it down. Woodsmoke curled around them as she shifted closer, and he caught the ghost of her lavender perfume beneath it—the morning's richness reduced now to something barely there, like vanilla and cedar fading into memory. "How are you feeling about bringing your wife into this world? Seminary can be . . . intense. All those passionate young theologians. All that spiritual searching." She paused, her eyes shifting to Libby. "Though I imagine Libby can hold her own in any environment."

Baker noticed how Amy's attention kept returning to Libby, watching her laugh and cataloging each gesture and expression.

But when Amy looked at him, there was something equally intense there. An assessment that felt both professional and deeply personal.

"Oh, I can see that," Amy said after Baker mentioned their partnership. "You two have something special. Something . . . rare."

When they finally said good night, Amy embraced them both. First Libby, her hands resting on Libby's waist for what felt like a full ten seconds. Then Baker, her body pressed close enough that he could smell her perfume—warm and complex, like vanilla and cedar. For just a moment, he was back at Trinity, remembering the way Darcy Calhoun's presence had unsettled him in ways he'd never quite admitted to himself.

"Sleep well," she murmured, her lips close to his ear. "Tomorrow we'll really get to know each other."

Back in the casita, Libby was unusually quiet as they prepared for bed. "What are you thinking?" Baker asked.

Libby sat on the edge of the Murphy bed, running her hands through her hair. "I think," she said slowly, "that Amy Benson is either the most welcoming priest in Texas, or she's interested in more than just your potential as a seminarian."

Baker sat beside her. "Did I imagine that, or was she…?"

"A little too friendly?" Libby finished. "No, you didn't imagine it."

They looked at each other in the dim light of the casita, both processing the same realization. Amy's interest wasn't just pastoral, and it wasn't directed at just one of them.

"Shall we cut our losses and depart tomorrow?" Baker asked.

Libby was quiet for a long moment. "I don't know," she said finally. "Ask me again tomorrow."

The morning sun was casting long shadows across the rugged landscape of Dripping Springs when Baker and Libby awakened in the casita. The Hill Country stretched out before them, a patchwork of limestone outcroppings and scrubby cedar trees. It reminded Baker of home in some ways, though the limestone and cedar were distinctly Texan. He sat up, running his hands through his hair. After last night's encounter with Amy, the casita felt too proximate to her house. Too much like they were still in her orbit. "Let's go somewhere," he said. "Find some breakfast where we can actually think."

They drove slowly through town, passing the usual suspects. A McDonald's that looked painfully incongruous. A couple of cafés with names like Oak Tree and Tillie's. But La Zamba Coffee Shop caught their attention with its converted farmhouse charm and the rich smell of beans roasting somewhere in the back. Perfect. They needed excellent coffee and a place to sit quietly and determine their next move.

Their waitress, a local woman with a thick Texan drawl, approached their table empty handed. "Coffee's fresh, and we've got some nice kolaches if y'all are hungry," she said. "Everything else is on the chalkboard there."

Baker wasn't surprised about the kolaches. He knew Texas had a substantial Czech and German immigrant heritage. Any place in West Texas would offer them as naturally as they'd serve biscuits and gravy.

"How are y'all getting along with Reverend Amy?" the waitress said, pouring their coffee without waiting for an answer.

"How did you know we were staying with her?" Baker said.

"People who look like you only come here to meet the reverend, and word travels fast in a town this size."

Baker and Libby exchanged glances. What exactly did people like them look like?

"What do you think of her?" Libby said.

"She's quite a character. Really shook things up when she arrived three years ago." The waitress wiped down their already-clean table, clearly weighing her words.

"What kind of character? Good, bad . . . quirky?" Libby pressed, always attuned to the nuances in people's voices.

"Well, she's not your typical priest, that's for sure. Very… modern in her approach. But she's grown the congregation, so they must be doing something right over there."

The coffee wasn't just good; it was exceptional. It gave them a nice little boost and helped them forget about the awkwardness of the previous evening. They spent hours driving through the Hill Country and an afternoon window-shopping in the heavily German-influenced town of Fredericksburg, noted as the home of Texas German, a language spoken by early settlers who stubbornly refused to learn English. The city was full of art, fashion, home decor, food specialty shops, and plenty of local flair.

That evening, they experienced their first taste of the local Tex-Mex cuisine at a restaurant called Julio's. The salsa came in three levels of heat. The margaritas were served in glasses the size of small fishbowls.

"To new beginnings," Baker said, raising his glass to Libby's.

"To careful decisions," Libby countered with a smile that didn't quite reach her eyes. Baker understood that she had supported his midlife calling to the priesthood but was hesitant at the prospect of uprooting their comfortable life in Idaho for three years of seminary in Texas.

Their formal meeting with Amy at Saint Anthony's Church

was uneventful. The humble limestone building had a small bell tower and stained-glass windows that shone like jewels in the morning sunlight. She gave them a tour, speaking passionately about the outreach programs she had initiated and the renovations she had supervised. However, as they moved into her office for coffee, her tone shifted.

"Of course, all these programs mean I barely have time to breathe." She sighed, dropping into her chair. "The congregation means well, but they're so demanding. Mrs. Hargrove called me at midnight last week because her cat was sick. A cat! As if I'm a veterinarian as well as a spiritual advisor."

Baker and Libby exchanged glances.

"That must be challenging," Baker said diplomatically.

"Challenging?" Amy interrupted. "Baker, let me warn you. You'll make very little and work your ass off. I only make a hundred and twenty thousand dollars a year all-in, and I'm on call twenty-four seven. Do you know what my seminary classmates are earning in corporate chaplaincy? Double that, easily. Meanwhile, I'm stuck in rural Texas dealing with people's petty dramas for what amounts to a middle-management salary."

The rest of the meeting continued in this vein. Amy detailed the various impositions of her parishioners while Baker and Libby struggled to maintain polite interest. When they finally left, walking back to their casita in the Texas heat, they were quiet.

"Well," Libby said, "that was . . ."

"Maybe she was just having a difficult day?" Baker offered.

On their third day in Texas, they visited Austin. While Libby explored the local farmers market, Baker visited the Seminary of the Southwest. The campus occupied a single city block on the north edge of the University of Texas campus. It was shaded by large, iconic live oak trees characteristic of Austin. Unlike the imposing Gothic structures of Yale Divinity School, this seminary felt deliberately understated. More like a thoughtfully designed retreat center than an institution of higher learning.

Baker parked near the chapel, a modest structure with floor-to-ceiling windows that framed the Texas sky. Inside, the sanctuary was flooded with natural light. The altar was simple and unadorned. No elaborate stained glass or carved stone. Just clean lines and honest materials that said, "Here, we focus on essentials."

The admissions office was housed in a converted ranch house. Baker met with Dr. Elena Munson, the director of contextual education. She was younger than he'd expected, perhaps forty, with graying hair pulled back in a practical ponytail and the kind of direct gaze that suggested she'd heard every excuse and sob story in the book.

"So you're Karl Thompson's protégé," she said, reviewing his file. "A career in advertising before answering the call to ministry. That's exactly the kind of life experience we value here. "We get plenty of twenty-two-year-olds who think they've got God figured out. What we need are people who've spent years navigating the real world."

She guided him through the program structure—three years of intensive study with a strong focus on practical ministry. Students served in parishes from their first semester onward. Baker didn't mention the credit he anticipated for time served at Yale.

"We don't believe in theoretical priesthood," she explained as they toured the library. "If you can't connect Christology to a hospital bedside conversation, you haven't really learned much."

They visited a classroom where students debated immigration policy and Christian hospitality. The professor let the discussion flow before asking, "And how do we preach this? How do we help a congregation grapple with these questions without alienating half the room?"

"That's the real work," Dr. Munson whispered to Baker. "Learning how to invite others into the conversation."

The student body was remarkably diverse—varied ages, races, and life experiences. Baker noticed what appeared to be a former businessman, a teacher, and someone with a military demeanor. All were engaged in an intense discussion that reminded him of his Yale days.

"What about housing?" Baker asked as they concluded the tour.

"We have apartments on campus for married students. Nothing fancy, but functional. Your wife would be welcome to audit classes if she's interested—many spouses do. It helps build a stronger foundation for ministry families."

As they returned to the parking lot, Dr. Munson asked the question Baker had been dreading: "What's your sponsoring parish situation? Karl mentioned some complications in Boise."

Baker found himself explaining Phil's pettiness, the wedding "ban," and the rising tensions at Trinity. Dr. Munson listened without judgment.

"Ecclesiastical politics," she said finally. "The bane of anyone trying to answer God's call. But here's what I've learned in fifteen years of admissions: If your calling is genuine, God has a way of clearing the bureaucratic obstacles. Sometimes through people like Karl, sometimes despite people like your Phil. . . . So what makes you want to do this?"

Baker repeated the same comment he once made to the proprietor of the Guest House in Boise. "I spent twenty-five years selling things people didn't really need," he said. "I'd like to spend whatever time I have left offering something they do."

Dr. Munson handed him a packet of application materials. "Don't let one petty priest derail what God is calling you to do. There are other ways to get endorsed, other dioceses that would welcome someone with your background and formation."

As Baker drove back to Dripping Springs, he felt something he hadn't experienced since leaving Yale: genuine excitement about learning again. The seminary felt like a place where his questions would be welcomed and his unconventional path to the priesthood would be seen as an asset rather than a liability. It struck him that while the seminary felt like a perfect fit, the situation with Amy complicated everything. As for living in Texas— the sprawl, the unwalkable distances, the endless big box stores stretching for miles—that was a whole different challenge.

That evening, Amy had invited them for what she called "a proper theological discussion" on her back patio. For the first time since arriving in Texas, Baker found himself truly engaged with her. She was articulating a thoughtful perspective on the tension between progressive theology and traditional worship—precisely the kind of nuanced thinking he had hoped to find in a mentor.

"The challenge," Amy said, swirling the wine in her glass, "is helping a congregation grow spiritually without losing their sense of rootedness. You can't alter everything they hold sacred, like moving the eight a.m. service to nine a.m., and expect them to follow along."

Baker nodded, feeling a flicker of the excitement he had experienced at the seminary. "That's exactly what I've been

struggling with. How do you honor tradition while still address-
ing contemporary issues?"

"It's like tending a garden," Amy said. "You must know which
plants to prune and which ones to let flourish. Sometimes the
most conservative parishioner becomes your strongest ally once
they understand you're not trying to destroy their faith but help
it grow."

Libby leaned forward, engaged in the conversation and perhaps setting aside her earlier doubts. "That's beautiful. It sounds
like you really understand your congregation's needs."

Amy smiled, and for a moment, Baker saw why Karl had recommended her. This was the kind of pastoral wisdom he had
been searching for.

The phone rang inside the house, its long tone breaking the
quiet evening air. Amy glanced at her watch. It was just past ten
p.m.

"Excuse me," she said, standing. "I should probably take this."

Through the open patio door, they could hear her voice,
though not clearly enough to make out the words. The tone
started out professional, then shifted to something more clipped
and impatient. "I understand this is difficult," they heard her say,
"but there's really nothing I can do tonight that wouldn't be better handled in the morning. I'll come by first thing, I promise."

A pause. Then: "Mrs. Harrison, I know you're upset, but sitting with the body isn't going to change anything. The funeral
home will take good care of him until tomorrow." Another
pause, this time longer. "I'll come around in the morning. We
can make all the arrangements then." Her voice had taken on
the practiced patience of someone ending a conversation. "Try
to get some rest."

Amy returned to the patio, settling back into her chair with a heavy sigh. "Sorry about that. Couldn't get her off the phone—her husband just passed."

Baker and Libby exchanged glances. "I'm sorry to hear that," Libby said carefully. "Were you close to them?"

"Oh, he's been dying for months. Cancer. We all knew it was coming." Amy reached for her wineglass. "She wants me to rush over there tonight, but honestly, what's the point? The man's already gone, and I have an important tennis match at eight in the morning. I can't be up all night."

The words were harsh and selfish. Baker felt his entire future in the church fade away as he processed what he'd just heard.

"The woman is probably in shock," Libby said quietly, her voice carefully controlled. "Doesn't she need someone with her right now?"

Amy waved a dismissive hand. "Her sister's driving down from Dallas. And like I said, there's nothing I can do for him now." She took a sip of wine. "People get so emotional about death. They forget that the practical arrangements are what matter."

Baker stared at her, speechless. This went completely against everything he'd learned about pastoral care. The power of presence, the importance of being there with people in their darkest times, and the idea that grief didn't follow office hours—all that seemed to mean nothing to Amy.

"I think we should head back," Baker said, standing up. "It's been a long day."

Amy looked surprised. "But we were having such a good conversation. Stay for one more glass?"

"No, thank you," Libby said, also rising. "We really should go."

As they walked back to the casita in the dark, neither said a word until they were safely inside, the door shut.

"Please tell me that didn't just happen," Libby whispered.

Baker sat heavily on the edge of the Murphy bed. "What a fucking hypocrite! A woman's husband just died, and she had time for another drink with us, but no time to visit her parishioner!"

They looked at each other in the dim light of the casita, both realizing their trip to Texas had just taken a decisive turn.

"We can't do this, Baker," Libby said. "We can't tie your future to someone like that."

Baker nodded, troubled. "I know. But she's my ticket to the Austin seminary. Without her sponsorship…"

"There are other sponsors, Baker. Other dioceses."

"But no other opportunities currently. If I wait, that's another year delayed."

They fell asleep with the question unresolved, the ceiling fan spinning lazily above them in the Texas night.

Their morning in Dripping Springs dawned clear and hot. Amy suggested that the Vaughans come over for coffee before their afternoon flight back to Boise. They gathered in her kitchen, the same comfortable craftsman where they'd been staying, with morning light streaming through the windows.

"Come in, come in," she called from somewhere inside when they knocked. They entered to find a spacious living room with minimalist furniture and abstract art on the walls.

Amy emerged from a hallway in a thin cotton nightshirt that barely reached mid-thigh, her hair damp from a recent shower.

"Sorry for the casual attire," she said, settling into an armchair opposite them. "I had an early tennis match and just got back. Coffee's brewing."

As she crossed her legs, the already short garment rode up, and she made no effort to adjust it. Baker found himself studying a painting above her head, but his attention kept fracturing.

"So," Amy said, leaning forward in a way that seemed calculated, "have you two decided? Is Texas in your future?"

"We're still discussing it," Libby replied carefully. "It's a big decision."

"Of course, of course," Amy nodded, shifting in her chair. As she did, she smoothed the fabric across her thighs, but instead of pulling it down for modesty, her hands lingered, drawing attention to the exposed skin.

Baker studied the carpet pattern intently. "The seminary program looks excellent, and we've enjoyed getting to know the area."

"But?" Amy said, leaning forward so the neckline of her sleepwear gaped open.

"We need to consider all aspects," he said carefully, his voice tight. He thought this couldn't be happening. Not here, not with a priest they barely knew, not when their entire future hung in the balance.

The conversation continued in this increasingly uncomfortable vein, with Amy finding reasons to adjust her position, each movement seemingly calculated. She stretched languidly, claiming the room was warm, revealing glimpses of her body beneath the thin fabric. When she uncrossed and recrossed her legs, she did so slowly, making it impossible not to notice she wasn't wearing underwear.

Libby's face stiffened, her hands clenched in her lap. How were they supposed to respond? Walk out and offend someone whose recommendation they needed? Pretend this wasn't happening? Baker was sweating despite plenty of air-conditioning, caught between propriety and politeness. Neither could believe what was happening. Was this respected Episcopal priest really trying to seduce them? Together?

"You know," Amy said, her voice dropping, "seminary can be a pressure cooker. You need . . . support systems. Ways to cope with the pressure." Her hand rested on Baker's arm a moment too long, her fingers tracing a small circle on his wrist. "I've helped other students navigate the challenges. Found ways to make the experience more . . . fulfilling."

"I think we should go," Libby said, rising from her chair with quiet determination. "We need to finish packing for our flight."

Amy's expression flickered with something—disappointment? Anger? But she quickly composed herself. "Of course. I didn't realize the time."

At the door, she embraced them both—lingering perhaps a moment too long with each, her hand resting on Baker's lower back in a way that felt more intimate than pastoral.

"Think about what I said," she murmured, her voice carrying an undertone that felt like an invitation. "About support systems. I'm always available to help promising students...navigate the challenges."

Baker pulled back quickly, his face flushed, and hurried after Libby without glancing behind.

"Did that just happen?" he asked, pacing the casita. "Did an Episcopal priest just . . . I mean, was that what I think it was?"

"Hell yes!" Libby exploded. "The nightshirt, the way she was positioning herself, that lingering hug—this is beyond inappropriate, Baker."

"What do we do?" Baker sank onto the bed, his head in his hands. "If we report her, who will believe us? She could say she was being friendly, that we misinterpreted her hospitality. And even if they did believe us, my chances at seminary this year would be over."

Libby sat beside him, taking his hand. "This isn't just about your seminary plans anymore. What if she's done this to others? What if she does it again?"

They spent their remaining hours at the Austin airport in intense discussion. Should they report Amy to the diocesan bishop? Would such a report be taken seriously or dismissed as a misunderstanding? Should they involve the police, though no crime had technically been committed? And what would this mean for Baker's calling?

On the plane that evening, the Texas Hill Country receded beneath them, beautiful and alien, like the church community they'd briefly glimpsed—a place of genuine faith complicated by very human failings. They even began to question Karl's intentions. Surely, he had heard complaints about Reverend Amy, just as he had about Reverend Phil.

"Can you call someone at Yale for advice?"

The mention of Yale brought Baker's thoughts to Devin Wilson. If anyone would know how to handle this awkward situation with Amy—the professional complications, the personal boundaries—it would be his old professor. Baker could almost hear the man's Paul Harvey voice offering practical wisdom about navigating parish politics and pastoral relationships.

When word had spread at Berkeley about Wendy's death, he had offered crucial counsel: "Don't go back to Virginia, Baker. That would be unhealthy. You need to move forward, not backward into memories that will trap you in grief." Known for his engaging humor, strong emphasis on self-awareness, and theological depth, he exemplified pastoral sensitivity when it mattered most.

Baker felt torn between loyalty and doubt. He could call Karl and demand answers—"Why her? Why is she still a priest?"—but the thought of losing the guidance of someone who had believed in his calling from the very beginning felt like starting over completely. Yet he couldn't shake the feeling that Karl's judgment had been compromised, that maybe he'd been too trusting of his mentor. He needed counsel from someone outside this web of relationships and expectations.

Back in Boise the next morning, Baker phoned Dr. Wilson, who answered on the second ring.

"Dr. Wilson? It's Baker Vaughan."

Wilson's unmistakable voice was immediately warm with recognition. "Baker Vaughan! It's wonderful to hear from you. What's going on?"

"Dr. Wilson, I'm actually looking into seminary again, and I could use some advice..."

"That's tremendous news, Baker. But I hear something in your voice. This isn't just about applications and transcripts. What's happened?"

The question opened the floodgates, and Baker recounted the entire Texas experience: Amy's behavior, the uncomfortable proposition, and his dilemma about Karl's role.

After a long pause, Dr. Wilson spoke. "This is deeply troubling, Baker. But consider this: Karl may have genuinely thought he was helping, even if his judgment was compromised. The question isn't whether to maintain the relationship. It's how to transform it into something healthier."

"What do you mean?"

"Confront him directly but pastorally. Allow him to acknowledge his mistake and make amends. If he's truly committed to your calling, he'll listen. If not, you'll have your answer."

After hanging up with Wilson, Baker found Libby in the bedroom, unpacking from the flight. He told her about the conversation with his old professor and Wilson's advice about confronting Karl "directly but pastorally."

"So you want to call him?" Libby asked.

"I think so. Wilson's right; if we're going to move forward with this whole seminary plan, we need to know whether Karl's judgment can be trusted. And if he really cares about my calling, he'll want to know what happened."

Libby nodded. "I think you should call him right now. *We* should call him—I was there too."

When Baker called Karl and asked if he and Libby could fill him in on Dripping Springs, he asked if they could call him around five o'clock, which they did. Karl's voice boomed through the speaker, Margaret chiming in with warm greetings.

"So," Karl said, "how was Reverend Amy? Did she give you good insights into parish ministry?"

Baker exchanged a look with Libby. "Karl, we need to talk about what happened. Amy made us both extremely uncomfortable. She propositioned us. Together."

The silence stretched uncomfortably long.

"I . . ." Karl's voice had lost all its confidence. "I had no idea she would . . ."

"Did you know about previous complaints?" Libby interjected. "Because this felt practiced, Karl. Like something she'd done before."

When Karl spoke again, his voice was smaller. "There were rumors. Nothing concrete. I thought maybe they were exaggerated. I was wrong to send you there without investigating properly."

Margaret's voice came through clearly: "Karl, this is serious. Our friends could have been seriously harmed."

"What do we do now?" Baker asked, surprised by the gentleness in his own voice.

"We report this," Karl said. "To the bishop. Today. And Baker, I'll do everything in my power to ensure this doesn't affect your seminary applications. I'll write additional letters, make calls, whatever it takes."

"And Amy?" Libby pressed.

"I'll contact the diocese immediately. If there have been other incidents, they need to know about them. I should have done this sooner. There was a complaint from a visiting priest last year about Amy being inappropriately forward, but she said it was a misunderstanding. And the search committee chair mentioned feeling uncomfortable during their meetings, but I thought that was just parish politics."

After they hung up, Baker felt not just relief but also respect for Karl's willingness to admit his error and act.

"Think he'll follow through?" Libby asked.

"Yes, I think he will," Baker said. "And if he doesn't, at least we'll know where we stand."

That evening, Baker called Dr. Wilson back to report on the conversation.

"Sounds like Karl might have learned something important today," his old mentor observed. "Sometimes our greatest failures become the foundation for deeper wisdom. The question is whether you're prepared to walk alongside him as he grapples with this."

"I think I am," Baker said. "With clear boundaries, but yes."

"Then you're already thinking like a pastor," Dr. Wilson said with evident pride followed by his signature phrase: "Finally, it's all thanks—even the difficult lessons."

Chapter Thirteen

TWO WEEKS AFTER THE TEXAS DEBACLE, KARL CALLED WITH NEWS that surprised no one: The Episcopal Diocese of West Texas had quietly transferred Amy to an "administrative role" pending a full investigation. More importantly, he'd been working the phones.

"I've found something closer to home," he announced during their weekly check-in call. "The Tuttle School for Ministry in the Episcopal Diocese of Utah. They offer continuing education and formation programs specifically designed for second-career candidates and lay leaders transitioning to ordained ministry."

Baker felt that familiar flutter of possibility mixed with caution. "Utah? That's still a significant move."

"Actually, no," Karl said, and Baker could hear the smile in his voice. "That's the beauty of it. It's a weekend program: five weekends in the fall, five in the spring. You'd fly to Moab via Denver—about four hours total—do intensive work Friday through Sunday, then come home. No relocation required, and no worrying about driving nine hours through mountain passes in winter weather."

"That's . . . actually manageable." Baker felt his interest sharpening. "What are the requirements?"

"Your credits from Yale more than qualify you academically. They want pastoral recommendations, which we can get, and a statement of purpose. The next fall cohort starts on August eleventh through thirteenth. You could easily be enrolled and starting classes by then."

Baker was quiet for a moment, processing. This wasn't some distant possibility requiring major life upheaval—this was real and immediate.

"But," Karl continued, "I still think we should get you some actual preaching experience. Not because Tuttle requires it, but because you need to know you can do it."

Baker waited, already sensing Karl's wheels turning. "Phil's been taking heat from the congregation since your wedding situation. The vestry's been asking pointed questions about his leadership. Laura Whitmore specifically asked me when you might be preaching—apparently several members have been enthusiastic about your 'theological development,' as she put it." Karl paused meaningfully. "I think Phil might be willing to let you deliver a sermon as a gesture of reconciliation. Let him save face while giving you what you need."

"You really think I'd be allowed to preach at Trinity?" Baker laughed despite himself. "Karl, Phil would rather set the church on fire."

"Not necessarily. Think about it from his perspective. Letting you preach makes him look magnanimous, like he's supporting your calling despite your 'abandonment' of the parish. He gets to play the gracious mentor while reminding everyone that you're leaving. Plus, if he refuses after Margaret's not-so-veiled threat, it will look petty."

Libby, who'd been listening from the kitchen, called out,

"What about that sermon you wrote for the second Sunday in Lent? The Genesis one?"

Baker had nearly forgotten about it. During his second year as a Trinity volunteer, while debating whether to return to the seminary studies he had abandoned thirty years earlier at Berkeley Divinity School, he decided to test his skills by writing a complete sermon based on the lectionary. He chose the second Sunday in Lent—March 12, 2017—and crafted a sermon around an Old Testament reading from Genesis 15:1–12 and 17–18. He spent about a week on it, not because anyone asked him to but because he needed to see whether he still possessed the skills Dr. Wilson had taught him and whether the theological insights remained after three decades away from a classroom.

"That could work perfectly," Karl mused when Baker explained.

"Can you remember what you thought when I shared it with you?"

Karl had read the piece carefully—Baker could tell from the way he immediately zeroed in on the Abraham narrative. "The timing angle," Karl said. "That's what makes it work. You're not just explaining covenant theology; you're giving people permission to wait."

Karl was clearly getting excited. "Here's what I propose: I'll approach Phil about letting you deliver this sermon as a farewell gift to the congregation. Frame it as your way of saying goodbye and thanking the parish for nurturing your calling."

"And if he says no?"

"Then we find another church. But I think he'll say yes. His ego won't let him pass up the chance to look like the magnanimous priest who launched your career."

"But I don't want to leave Boise or Trinity."

"Let's cross that bridge when we have to."

That evening, Baker dug through his files until he found the sermon manuscript. Rereading it after all this time, he was surprised by how much it still resonated. The exegesis was solid, the language accessible, and the message—that God's promises often unfold in ways and timelines we don't expect—felt more relevant than ever after his recent experiences with Phil and Amy.

"It's good," Libby said after reading it over his shoulder. "Really good. Are you nervous about actually delivering it?"

"A bit nervous," Baker admitted. "I've been thinking about preaching for years, but doing it in front of Trinity, Phil watching . . ." He shook his head. "What if I don't enunciate the words properly? What if I inadvertently skip a line of text? What if I discover that thirty years away from Yale was too long?"

"What if you're exactly as good as Karl thinks you'll be?" Libby interrupted gently. "Baker, you've been preparing for this your whole adult life. Maybe not formally, but every conversation you've had about faith, every time you've helped someone work through a spiritual crisis, every moment you've wrestled with your own calling—it's all been preparation."

Karl called the next day with surprising news: Phil had agreed.

"Just like that?" Baker asked, suspicious.

"Well, not exactly 'just like that,'" Karl admitted. "I may have emphasized that Laura Whitmore specifically asked about your preaching timeline, and that declining her request might raise uncomfortable questions at the next vestry meeting. Phil's practical above all else. He knows Laura's pockets are deep and she has influence over Gallagher."

Baker groaned. "You used congregation pressure."

"I used available leverage," Karl corrected cheerfully. "The point is, you're scheduled for March twelfth, and you're going to hit a home run."

"And what about Tuttle?"

"Get enrolled. That's your focus. This sermon is your first priority."

After hanging up, Baker sat quietly for a long moment. In two months, he would stand in Trinity's pulpit and preach for the first time. Phil would be watching from the front pew, probably hoping he'd fail. The congregation would be evaluating every word. But underneath the anxiety, Baker felt something else: readiness. For the first time since leaving Yale Divinity School thirty years ago, he felt that his path forward was clear. Not easy, but clear.

THE THIRD WEEK OF January brought dramatic shifts in the political landscape. President Obama would leave office in just days, to be replaced by someone whose leadership style Baker and Libby couldn't support. The ceremony loomed over Friday, January 20, and they knew all eyes would be tuned to the television.

Libby couldn't stand the thought of watching. She joined two friends for a trip to Seattle's symphony festival honoring Russian composer Dmitri Shostakovich, leaving Baker to face the inauguration alone.

The conversation at Lucky Chuck's was more heated than usual, fueled by the day's events and the weight of what they'd all witnessed on television. Someone wondered aloud how the country had reached this point. Another voice questioned whether the church had failed in its prophetic role, whether they'd been too comfortable, too silent about the moral crises building around them. The discussion meandered through fears about democracy and the rise of Christian nationalism, which seemed so far from the gospel they preached. Baker found himself nodding along, contributing little, his attention turning to another matter entirely as the alcohol loosened thoughts he'd been trying to suppress.

The events of inauguration night—Lucifer, Russ, Darcy's unlocked door, the Ada County holding cell—would haunt Baker for weeks to come.

Libby returned from Seattle the following evening, glowing from the Shostakovich festival, and found Baker unusually quiet and subdued. He hadn't told her anything about that night. How could he? *Honey, while you were enjoying Russian symphonies, I broke into my ex-lover's house, vomited on her floor, and spent the night in jail.*

"How was Friday night?" she asked, unpacking her weekend bag. "Did you and the Trinity crew have your usual political therapy session?"

"Something like that," Baker managed, turning back to his laptop screen where his sermon notes blurred together. "How was Shostakovich?"

Baker threw himself into sermon preparation with manic intensity, using his laptop screen as a shield against Libby's questions and his own conscience.

"You've been obsessing over that sermon," Libby observed, finding him hunched over his laptop at eleven p.m. "I'm sure it's good, Baker. Stop second-guessing yourself."

If only she knew what he was really second-guessing.

A week later, his attorney called with news. "The complainant has agreed to drop the charges. Case dismissed."

Technically, he was free and clear. Practically, Baker felt the weight of every poor decision that had led him to that jail cell. Hanging up the phone, he wondered if a man who'd spent a night in county lockup had any business preaching about God's faithfulness.

The miracle—if he could call it that—was that no one from Trinity seemed to know. The arrest had happened peacefully; the charges dropped quickly enough that his name never made the paper. Either Boise was big enough for this to slip through the cracks, or God was giving him one last chance to come clean on his own terms. Baker suspected the latter, which only made the weight of his secret more crushing.

February arrived with its gray insistence, and Baker fell into the rhythm of compartmentalization. Mornings were for homiletic preparation—easy enough work for something already written. Afternoons belonged to Tuttle, to the dense theological reading that would anchor his first semester in August. He moved through these tasks with methodical precision, the kind of focus that left no room for distraction.

Libby suggested they invite friends over to hear him practice his sermon, but he deflected. When she offered to help him rehearse his delivery, he claimed he worked better alone. The isolation was crushing, but confession felt impossible.

Karl called regularly to check on his progress, each conversation a fresh exercise in deception.

"You sound different lately," Karl observed during one of their calls. "More introspective. I think this preparation process is really deepening your spiritual life."

Baker almost laughed at the irony. His spiritual life felt like a wasteland, but apparently, he was getting better at hiding it.

"March twelfth is going to be a watershed moment for you," Karl continued. "Standing in that pulpit, delivering God's Word—it's going to confirm everything we've been working toward."

"Right," Baker said, staring at the case dismissal papers his attorney had mailed him. "God's faithfulness."

As the big day approached, Baker realized he was facing more than just sermon nerves. He was about to stand before his congregation—people who trusted him, who saw him as a man called to spiritual leadership—while carrying a secret that could destroy everything. Two weeks before his Trinity debut, the weight of his deception finally broke him.

"Libby," he said one evening, closing his laptop and turning to face her on the couch. "I need to tell you something about inauguration night."

She looked up from her book, immediately sensing the gravity in his voice. "OK."

"I didn't just have drinks with the Trinity crew. After Lucky Chuck's, I . . . I made a terrible mistake." Baker's voice cracked. "I went to Darcy's house. My ex . . . from years ago. The one who—"

"I remember who Darcy is," Libby said.

"I was drunk, and I thought I needed to apologize to her. For things I'd said about her to Karl, about her sluttiness, about how she used me for sex while leading me to think it would become a relationship, which she never intended. The door was unlocked, and I went inside." The words tumbled out now, unstoppable. "She called the police. I spent the night in jail, Libby. I was arrested for unlawful entry. I vomited all over her living room floor."

Libby stared at him, processing. "What time?"

"Around nine p.m." Baker's voice was now barely above a whisper. "I left Lucky Chuck's around seven p.m. Then I went to

Lucifer and met this guy, Russ, who kept buying rounds. I got to her house sometime after eight-thirty p.m. The police showed up maybe twenty minutes later."

Libby closed her eyes briefly. "So you were drinking for hours?"

"Yeah. I was completely wasted. That's not an excuse, but . . . I wasn't thinking straight."

Libby was quiet for a moment. Baker broke the silence with his deepest fear: "I've been carrying this secret too long, far too long. I'm supposed to preach at Trinity in two weeks, and I don't know if I can. I don't know if I should."

Silence stretched between them. Baker braced himself for anger, for disappointment, for the revelation that she'd married a man capable of such spectacularly poor judgment.

Libby stood up, putting distance between them. "You broke into our neighbor's house?"

"I didn't break in—the door was unlocked—"

"Baker." She turned to face him, and he saw something in her expression he'd never seen before: not just hurt, but a kind of exhausted understanding. "How long have we been living here? Across from her?"

"Since before we got married. You knew she lived there."

"I knew she lived there, but I didn't know you were still . . ." She trailed off, searching for the word. "Still carrying this. All this time, you've been looking out our window at her house, thinking about what you needed to say to her?"

"It wasn't like that—"

"Then what *was* it like?" Libby's voice rose. "Because from where I'm standing, it looks like you married me while still completely hung up on the woman across the street."

The accusation hung between them, brutal in its accuracy.

"No," Baker said quietly. "I love you, Libby. I chose you."

"Did you? Or did you just keep living in the same place, waiting for the right moment to—what? Get closure? Win her back?"

"I needed to apologize. For what I'd said to Karl about her, about how she used me—"

"Why does it matter what you said to Karl years ago?" Libby sat back down but didn't move closer to him. "Baker, people break up. People say things. But most people don't spend years obsessing about it while living across the street from their ex."

"Maybe we should move," Baker said suddenly.

Libby laughed, but there was no humor in it. "*Now* you think of that? After you got arrested breaking into her house?"

She pulled a duffel bag out of the closet and started throwing clothes into it. "I love you Baker, I really do." Her hands were shaking as she grabbed items from the dresser. "But I don't trust you anymore."

"We can rebuild the trust. Just give me a chance."

"I can't." She zipped the bag closed and turned to face him, tears streaming down her face. "I can't look at you without wondering what else you're not telling me. I can't do it, Baker. I'm not strong enough."

"You don't have to be strong. We can figure this out together."

She shook her head, shouldering the bag. "God help me, but I have to leave."

THAT WAS THE WAY the conversation might have unfolded had Baker not been prudent enough to buy a new house—albeit in the same neighborhood—before moving in with Libby, months before their wedding.

Instead, she studied him, her eyes boring into his, suddenly unsure who she was looking at. "Thank you for telling me," she said, her voice cold and measured.

Baker held her gaze, forcing himself not to look away. "I broke into my ex-lover's house and got arrested. I've been hiding it from you for weeks. And then I tried to keep hiding it from you. I realize that now."

Libby pulled her hand back and stood up, creating space between them. "Baker, you made a mistake. A big one. But you're not the first person to do something stupid when drunk, and you won't be the last."

She paused, her arms crossed, her face a mixture of pain and resolve. "I need some time to process this because I'll be honest, Baker, I'm devastated, and I don't know how I can ever trust you again. You—me—we need to get professional help. But in the meantime—"

"What about the sermon?" Baker interrupted, his voice desperate. "What about my calling? How can I stand in that pulpit knowing what I've done?"

Libby looked at him for a long moment, her expression unreadable. "I can't help you with that. Not right now."

Baker felt the weight of her words settle over him. The sermon he'd been preparing for weeks—about Abraham's covenant with God, about faith despite impossible circumstances, about God keeping promises even when we can't see how—suddenly felt like a mockery of his own life.

"Perhaps," Libby said finally, her voice softer but still distant, "you need to figure out what *you* actually believe before you stand up there and tell other people what to believe."

She turned and walked toward their bedroom, pausing at the

doorway. "You can sleep in the guest room tonight. We'll talk more tomorrow."

Baker sat alone on the couch, the silence of the house pressing in around him. The sermon notes on his laptop seemed to mock him now—words about faithfulness written by a man who had just confessed to betraying his wife's trust in the most humiliating way possible.

He stared at the blank wall, wondering if this was what rock bottom felt like, or if there were still deeper depths waiting for him to discover.

"God, Baker," Libby's voice came from the hallway, quiet but cutting. "All this time I've been wondering what was eating at you, and it was this?"

She didn't wait for an answer before closing the bedroom door.

IN THE DAYS THAT followed, Libby's words stayed with him. As March 12 approached, he realized that his Trinity sermon had morphed into something entirely different from what he had initially written back in the volunteer office. He wouldn't be standing in that pulpit as a man who had figured out faith, but as someone still grappling with it—someone who had made mistakes and was still learning to trust in God's grace.

Maybe he was precisely the kind of priest the world needed.

Then the day came. It was showtime. As he walked toward Trinity, Baker felt something he hadn't expected: excitement. Not the nervous energy of someone hoping to succeed, but the anticipation of someone who finally had something worth saying.

Libby walked beside him, her hand tucked into the crook of his arm. The March morning was crisp, and their breath was visible in the clean, slightly cold Idaho air.

"You're different this morning," she said, after a block of comfortable silence.

"Different how?"

"Calmer. Surer of yourself." She squeezed his arm. "It's like you've stopped trying to prove something and started trying to say something."

Baker considered this. "Maybe that's exactly what happened."

"Are you nervous about . . . the personal part? About telling them?"

"Surprisingly, no." Baker paused. "I think I'm more nervous about not telling them. About standing up there and pretending I have it all figured out."

Libby smiled. "Well, we both know that would be the bigger lie."

They reached the church steps just as Karl emerged from the parish hall, adjusting his stole and checking his watch.

"Baker! There you are. I was starting to worry." Karl paused, taking in Baker's relaxed demeanor. "You look . . . ready."

"More than ready," Baker said.

Karl studied his face for a moment, then broke into a smile. "Good. I can see it in your eyes. You're not just delivering a sermon today; you're sharing your testimony."

"Exactly," Baker replied.

"Remember," Karl said, placing both hands on Baker's shoulders, "God called you to this moment long before you knew it yourself. Trust that calling, trust your voice, and trust that the people in those pews need to hear exactly what you have to say."

His expression radiated pride and confidence. "Well, then." He clapped Baker on the shoulder. "Let's go change some lives."

After the gospel reading, Phil nodded toward the pulpit. Baker climbed the steps, thinking that for a man who'd recently spent a night in jail, he felt remarkably at home in the house of God.

"Brothers and sisters in Christ," he began:

I don't like the early part of Lent. Forty days of prayer, penance, repentance, almsgiving, and self-denial are hard commitments—any time of the year. But to make such sacrifices during periods of inversion, snowstorms, howling wind, and record-low temperatures, at least here in Idaho, where we have no spring, feels downright Catholic to me.

But here we are—the second Sunday of Lent. We can't change the calendar. And as we grapple with to-day's texts, which are full of fear and lament, I find myself wondering whether that's exactly where we're supposed to be. Maybe the discomfort of Lent isn't something to endure but something to embrace.

In the first Genesis reading, we feel Abraham's fear, don't we?

Poor Abraham. He had an apparent abundance of wealth, but no land, and even worse, no children. He was definitely not fearless and cheerful. The only one sitting pretty, it appeared, was his chief steward, Eliezer, who stood to inherit Abraham's wealth if God did not fulfill his promise.

God challenged Abraham. "Look up at the sky and

count the stars, if you can." This did not make Abraham feel chosen in the slightest. Anyone around the world could have taken this challenge on any given night. Don't blame Abraham for thinking God was stalling. *All I get are promises*, Abraham must have thought to himself.

As if that wasn't daunting enough, this old man had to round up a heifer, a goat, and a ram and make sure that they were each three years of age. It would take a board-certified veterinarian in today's world to provide such authenticity. Thankfully, God was far less fussy about his specifications for the turtledove and pigeon.

We all know how the story of Abraham ends. God kept the promise of land and many descendants he made to Abraham.

But here's what strikes me about Abraham's story— it's not really about Abraham being perfect. It's about God being faithful despite Abraham's doubts, despite his fears, despite his very human failures.

And like Abraham, there have been times in our lives when our world really did crash down on us. How many times have we thought, *If anything can go wrong, it will?* When life seems to be going in a downward spiral, we are at the end of our rope, and we can't tie a knot to hold on. Fear often takes hold of us. Fear traps us in the belief that nothing will ever improve, that we are ensnared and will never escape. When life gets us down, fear fills the void left by hope.

Let me share a more contemporary story of a man who thought he had found his way back to God, and that he had figured out faith, calling, and purpose. This man had experienced what he believed was a divine encounter, had found love, and had started down the path toward ordination. He thought he had his story all worked out—a neat narrative of redemption and grace.

But recently, this man made a terrible mistake. In a moment of drunken poor judgment, he violated someone's trust, broke the law, and found himself sitting in a jail cell, wondering if everything he thought he knew about God's calling was just self-deception.

Sitting in that cell, he wondered: *Does God's grace really extend to someone who makes such spectacular mistakes? Can someone who has shown such poor judgment really be called to spiritual leadership? Is it possible that God's promises are meant even for those who seem determined to sabotage themselves?*

That man is standing before you now. Yes, I, Baker Vaughan, am that man.

I wish I could stand here today and tell you that faith makes us perfect, that answering God's call means we stop making mistakes. But that would be a lie. What I can tell you is that, sitting in that jail cell, I finally understood something about Abraham's story I'd never seen before.

God didn't choose Abraham because he was perfect. God chose Abraham despite his imperfections. The covenant wasn't dependent on Abraham getting everything right—it was dependent on God's faithfulness.

In Psalm 27, we read, "The Lord is my light and my salvation; whom then shall I fear? The Lord is the strength of my life; Of whom then shall I be afraid?"

But what if we're afraid of ourselves? What if we're so

scared of our own capacity for poor judgment, for hurting others, for falling short of who we think we should be?

The psalmist would say, "Even then, especially then, the Lord is our light."

Fear cannot be conquered by trying harder or being better. Fear is conquered by love, by the love of a God who sees all our failures and chooses us anyway.

We see this in Luke's gospel. Jesus becomes transfigured, revealing his divine nature to his disciples. But this moment of glory comes in the context of Jesus's journey toward Jerusalem, toward suffering, toward the cross. His transfiguration doesn't exempt him from human pain; it reveals God's presence within it.

Not even a full two weeks into Lent, and some of us may already feel discouraged in our observance. We may have already failed spectacularly in our commitments. I know I have. That may be the point. Maybe Lent isn't about proving we are worthy—it's about facing our unworthiness and realizing that God's love is bigger than our failures.

Yes, in our covenants with God, we strive to keep our side of the bargain. But they are not contracts between equals. The Lord is the one who can do all things. We, on our part, have to be patient, love God and ourselves, and maintain hope—especially when we don't deserve it.

I'm learning that God's promises aren't conditioned on our good behavior. They're grounded in God's character, not ours. And that might be the most terrifying and wonderful truth of all.

God always keeps His promise—even when we don't keep ours.

Amen.

As Baker stepped down from the pulpit, he felt something shift within him—not the dramatic transformation he had once expected from preaching his first sermon, but something quieter and more confident. The congregation's faces reflected a mixture of surprise, compassion, and respect. Laura Whitmore was wiping her eyes. Even a few individuals who had seemed skeptical of his calling were nodding thoughtfully.

Phil sat in the front pew, his expression neutral. Baker had expected anger, disappointment, or even an attempt at humiliation. Instead, he observed something that resembled recognition—as if Phil might finally be acknowledging that Baker had the juice.

As Baker walked home with Libby after the service, he found himself thinking about Abraham again. Not the sanitized Sunday school version, but the honest Abraham: flawed, fearful, sometimes faithless, yet somehow chosen by God regardless.

"You know what's strange?" he said as they turned onto their street. "I've spent years thinking I had to become worthy of God's calling. I was convinced that my drunken mistake showed God the truth—that I wasn't worthy of ordination, that my calling had been self-deception all along."

"And now?" Libby asked softly.

"Now I think maybe it's the opposite. Maybe God calls people because they are broken, not because they are flawless and keep all the commandments. Maybe the church needs priests who know what it feels like to fail spectacularly."

In the days that followed, as news of his sermon spread throughout the Episcopal Diocese of Idaho, Baker began to realize something he had never fully understood before. Phil's rejection—his insistence that Baker couldn't serve God and, indeed, couldn't be married at Trinity—hadn't been an obstacle at all. It had been liberation. Phil had unknowingly freed Baker from a narrow vision of his calling that would have required him to deny the greatest gift he had ever received. In trying his damnedest to force Baker out of Trinity, Phil had revealed his own theological limitations and his inability to see that God's grace might work through love rather than despite it. The rejection clarified Baker's calling and revealed to him a path forward that honored both his faith and his heart. This was God's promise being kept, not in the way Baker had once imagined—held back by poor choices and circuitous paths—but through the unexpected gift of a second chance at both human and divine love, along with the hard-won courage to choose both.

Perhaps this was his calling: as someone who deeply understood that God's grace wasn't earned but given, someone who could stand before a congregation, not as a man who had all the answers but as someone still learning to ask the right questions. That was enough, even more than enough. That was everything.

THE SUMMER FLEW BY through ongoing education and spiritual direction sessions with Karl. In August, Baker arrived in Moab for his first weekend of classes, and the first thing he noticed when entering the classroom at Tuttle wasn't the stained-glass windows or the theological texts lining the shelves—it was the horseshoe-shaped table that dominated the center of the room. He would soon see that this setup was no accident, but a physical reflection of the Episcopal approach to theological education.

As he took his seat along the curved edge of the table, he realized how different this was from the traditional classroom setups at Yale. At Tuttle, everyone faced one another. There was no back row to hide in, no corners to retreat to. This arrangement fostered a sense of community, a physical reminder that in Episcopal tradition, theology is not merely taught but discussed, debated, and lived in relationship with others.

His professor, Reverend Jane Reynolds, sat at the opening of the horseshoe, not elevated on a platform or standing at a lectern but at the same level as the rest of them. "In Episcopal formation," she began, "we don't believe any single person holds all theological truth. We seek it together, through scripture, tradition, and reason—our three-legged stool."

Around Baker sat twelve classmates, each on a different path toward ministry. Some had just graduated from undergraduate programs, while others were in their thirties and forties—even one besides Baker in his fifties—embarking on second careers. A former lawyer sat next to a social worker, who sat next to a retired teacher. This diversity of backgrounds was intentional in Episcopal formation. The Church believed that varied life experiences enriched theological discussion.

As the class dove into their discussion of liberation theology, the horseshoe arrangement proved its worth. When a former corporate executive expressed skepticism about applying economic justice principles in parish settings, he looked directly at a community organizer whose face conveyed respectful disagreement. There was no escaping this tension, no way to sidestep the challenging conversation that followed.

The liberal theological perspective of many of Baker's classmates became evident throughout the morning. When discussing biblical interpretation, most felt comfortable using historically critical methods that contextualized scripture within its cultural background rather than interpreting it literally in all cases. A strong commitment to social justice was palpable, with comments made not just in isolated instances but with deep conviction.

Then there was the Saturday afternoon when each member of the class was asked to share a moment of regret from their past, something that might have changed the outcome of their ministerial journey. Other classmates began sharing their carefully curated confessions—academic struggles, career missteps, moments of spiritual doubt—all valid regrets but sanitized for theological consumption.

Baker's turn came sooner than he expected. He found himself rethinking his approach, wavering between honesty and sugarcoating. When his name was finally called, he looked around the table at those earnest faces and made a spontaneous decision that would define his entire Tuttle experience.

"Seven months ago," he began, "I broke into my ex-lover's house while drunk and spent a long, bitter night in jail."

The silence that followed felt fathomless. Reverend Reynolds's eyebrows raised slightly, yet her expression remained pastoral rather than judgmental. Around the table, Baker could see his classmates processing—some with shock, others with what seemed to be relief that someone had finally told an unvarnished truth. "I stood in my home-parish pulpit two months later," Baker continued, "and told my congregation about it. Because I realized that if I couldn't be honest about my failures, I had no business preaching about God's grace."

The former corporate executive leaned forward slightly. "How did they respond?"

"Better than I deserved," Baker said. "But more importantly, it taught me that God's calling isn't contingent on our perfection. It's sustained by divine grace despite our imperfections."

Reverend Reynolds nodded slowly. "Thank you, Baker. That kind of vulnerability is exactly what formation requires—not just intellectual engagement with theology, but integration of our lived experience with our understanding of God's work in the world."

That moment became the foundation of Baker's Tuttle experience. Over the following semesters, his willingness to bring his whole self—failures included—into theological discussion earned him the respect of both faculty and classmates. His insights carried weight precisely because they were grounded in real struggle rather than abstract theory.

By his third semester, professors were regularly calling on him to bridge theological concepts with pastoral realities. A paper he wrote during the prior semester on "Grace and Accountability in Parish Leadership" became required reading for incoming students. When visiting priests came to lecture, they often sought him out afterward for deeper conversation.

But perhaps most importantly, Baker discovered his path through failure had prepared him for the kind of ministry the church needed. His classmates began coming to him with their own struggles—not because he had answers, but because he had proven that survival was possible even after spectacular mistakes.

As his final semester approached, Baker felt something he'd never experienced before: complete alignment between his calling and his capabilities. The man who had once worried that thirty years away from seminary had damaged his prospects now realized those thirty years had been precisely the preparation he needed. The broken places had become the foundation of his strength. God's promise to Abraham—that of land and descendants despite perceived impossibility—was being fulfilled in ways Baker could never have imagined when he first walked into Trinity Episcopal all those years ago.

He felt ready to be ordained—as prepared as someone can be who's learned that God's path rarely matches human expectations.

Chapter Fourteen

BY JANUARY 2019, BAKER WAS IN HIS FINAL SEMESTER AT TUTTLE, SO close to ordination he could almost taste it. But he'd learned by now that the final mile was often where the real test began.

For his last weekend intensive, Baker had decided to drive the nearly nine hours from Boise instead of flying through Denver. He'd convinced Libby to join him for a little getaway after all the stress of his studies. She'd been excited about finally seeing the place that had consumed so much of his time and energy. But at the last minute, the flu hit her hard. She was burning with fever Thursday night, barely able to lift her head from the pillow.

"Go without me," she whispered, her voice hoarse. "You can't miss this."

Baker hesitated. He didn't want to leave her alone, sick and miserable. But a woman from Trinity—one of many on the church's phone tree—called immediately and insisted that she come straightaway to be with Libby.

"I'll make sure she has everything she needs," she said. "This is too important, Baker. You're so close."

Baker was relieved.

Friday evening, after settling into his usual dorm room on

the Utah State University campus, Baker walked the short distance to the labyrinth at Saint Francis Episcopal Church. The stone path spiraled inward through the Peace Garden, each step a meditation on the journey that had brought him here. Close to three years of classes, papers, and theological reflection, all of it leading to the first weekend of his final semester. The Utah mountains rose around him in the fading light, and for the first time in many years, he felt something approaching peace.

Saturday's intensive sessions were held on campus. The Tuttle School's partnership with the Iona Collaborative had created something unique: a program that combined academic rigor with practical formation, turning out deacons and lay ministers who understood both theology and the real challenges of serving small communities. Baker appreciated the intimacy of the campus setting: a small cohort of students housed together, sharing meals and conversations that extended their classroom learning into daily life.

Baker's presentation went better than he'd dared hope. His paper on pastoral care in crises drew thoughtful questions from his professors, their nods of approval confirming what he'd sensed all semester—that despite everything he'd been through, despite the detours and setbacks, he had found his calling and learned to articulate it clearly.

"You've grown tremendously since that first semester," Dr. Reynolds told him afterward. "Not just intellectually, but spiritually. You understand now that the broken places in our lives often become the very places where we can minister to others."

Sunday morning's final session focused on the practical theology that would guide their ministry, whether as licensed lay preachers, worship leaders, or candidates for the diaconate. The program's core values echoed in every discussion: educational excellence, local adaptability, collaboration, visionary leadership, community, and transformation.

It was after the session, as Baker was loading his books into his car, that he saw them.

Dr. Hawley, the married professor who taught Christian ethics and moral theology, was walking across the parking lot with one of the second-year students. At first, Baker thought nothing of it. Faculty and students often continued conversations after class. But something about their body language made him pause. They were walking too close together, their heads bent in conversation that looked more intimate than academic.

Baker watched as they reached the student's car. Dr. Hawley looked around quickly—the way people did when they were checking to see if anyone was watching—then leaned in and kissed her. Not a brief, friendly kiss, but something lingering, passionate. She melted into him, her body pressing against his as her hands tangled in his hair. Baker stumbled back, his legs shaking. The stack of books he'd carefully packed tumbled from his arms, scattering across the asphalt. His mind reeled. This was impossible. Dr. Hawley, who lectured on professional boundaries and ethical conduct, engaged in the very behavior he'd condemned in countless lectures. Numb, Baker gathered his books, his movements mechanical.

He pulled out his phone, desperate to talk to someone who could make sense of this. Karl's number rang once, twice, three times before going to voicemail. He tried again. Nothing. The silence felt like complicity.

By the time Baker reached his dorm room, the shock had begun to calcify into something harder. Betrayal. Confusion. A creeping sense that everything he'd believed about integrity was dissolving before his eyes. He sank onto the narrow bed, phone still in hand, the unanswered calls a testament to his sudden, profound isolation.

Sunday night, Baker couldn't sleep. He lay on the narrow dorm bed, staring at the acoustic tiles on the ceiling, counting the same pattern of holes over and over. Down the hall, someone was watching television, laughter from a sitcom bleeding through the walls. The normalcy of it felt obscene. He kept seeing Dr. Hawley's hand on the small of that student's back. The way she'd leaned into him. The casual intimacy of people who'd done this before, many times. How long had it been going on? Did other faculty know? Did the administration?

Around midnight, Baker got up and pulled out his laptop. His fingers hovered over the keyboard. He could email Tuttle's dean. Right now. Attach a formal statement. Be the one person willing to speak up, to demand accountability, to insist that if the church was going to preach moral integrity, it had to practice it.

But even as he opened a new message, he heard Phil Harbaugh's voice in his head: *These things are complicated, Baker. We don't always know the whole story.* What if there were complexities he couldn't see? What if Dr. Hawley's marriage was already over, and this student was an adult making her own choices? What if his outrage was just self-righteousness dressed up as moral clarity?

He closed the laptop without writing anything.

The radiator clanked and hissed. Outside, wind rattled the window in its frame. Baker got up, walked to the small desk, and pulled out the evaluation form Dr. Reynolds had given him earlier. *You've grown tremendously since that first semester. Not just intellectually, but spiritually.* Had he? Or had he just gotten better at performing the role of seminarian, at saying the right things in the right tone while his faith remained as fragile as it had been the day Wendy died? He thought about calling Libby, but it was very late, and she was sick. What would he even say? *Hi, honey. I just watched a professor having an affair with a student, and now I'm having a crisis of faith. Again.*

Baker pulled on his jacket and stepped into the hallway. The building was quiet now, the television silent. He walked down the stairs and out into the cold night air. The campus was empty, streetlights casting orange pools on the sidewalk. He found himself walking toward Saint Francis Episcopal Church, toward the labyrinth where he'd felt such peace just two nights ago.

But when he reached the Peace Garden, he didn't enter the labyrinth. He stood at its entrance, looking at the stone path that spiraled inward toward the center and realized he didn't want to walk it. Didn't want the meditation, the symbolic journey, the sense of moving toward anything. He just wanted to go home.

Back in his room, Baker sat on the edge of the bed and tried Karl one more time. Still voicemail. Still a full inbox. The phone's clock read 1:47 a.m. In a few hours, he'd load his car and drive home. The weather forecast was calling for snow, but he'd driven in snow before. Boise wasn't far. Libby was waiting. Something real and uncomplicated.

Baker set his alarm for six o'clock and lay back down. Sleep came in fragments—twenty minutes here, fifteen minutes there, interrupted by images of Dr. Hawley and the student, by the faces of his professors praising his theological growth, by Wendy's voice asking him why he was so surprised that people failed to live up to their own ideals.

When the alarm finally went off, Baker felt more exhausted than when he'd gone to bed. Showered, packed mechanically, carried his bags to the car as the sun rose over the Utah mountains. Beautiful and indifferent, witnessing nothing. The belongings hit the trunk harder than necessary, the sound echoing across the parking lot. A few other students were loading their cars, saying goodbye to each other, and making plans for the next intensive. Baker avoided eye contact. Leaving was all that mattered now. The weather forecast had mentioned snow—a significant storm moving in—but good tires, a full tank, and eight-plus hours between Moab and Boise would give him time to give the meaning of priesthood one final mental edit.

Settling into the driver's seat, starting the engine, his phone buzzed with a text from Libby: Feeling a bit better this morning. Drive safely. Love you.

Baker stared at the message. Three simple sentences. No theology, no moral complexity, no institutional betrayal. Just his wife, sick with the flu, telling him she loved him.

The car eased into gear. Highway ahead. Morning sun bright and cold in his rearview mirror. With him came not the sense of completion he'd hoped for, but something much darker—the growing certainty that his calling had been a delusion, that the church he'd fought so hard to join was irredeemably corrupt, and that it was time to walk away, finally and forever.

The mountains rose around him in the early light, but now they felt like walls rather than witnesses to his journey. He was driving home not as a man approaching ordination, but as someone fleeing the wreckage of a dream that had sustained him for thirty years.

The approaching storm that had the whole campus on edge the night before was the least of his troubles. The first thirty miles out of Moab were deceptively calm. Clear skies, dry pavement, the kind of winter day that made you forget how quickly conditions could change in the mountains. Baker let his mind wander over the weekend's devastating revelations, already planning how he'd tell Libby that he was done with it all, that three years of seminary had been a waste, that the church was too corrupt for him to serve.

By the time he reached the approach to US Highway 6, the wind had picked up—nothing dramatic—just enough to rock the car slightly as gusts swept down from the canyon walls. The radio crackled with the first weather warnings: "Winter storm watch upgraded to orange for central Utah mountains. Travelers are advised to postpone nonessential trips."

Baker glanced at his phone. No signal in these canyons. *Reaching her isn't nonessential,* he thought. Libby was sick at home, probably worried. He ached to be with her, to tell her everything, to let her steady him the way she always did.

The snow started as he entered the canyon proper—light flakes that danced in his headlights like moths. Highway 6 stretched ahead, that notorious ribbon of asphalt connecting I-15 and I-70, narrow and unforgiving even in good weather. Baker had heard there'd been dozens of deaths on this highway over the years, but warnings felt abstract until he was on it. Now the shoulders were disappearing, swallowed by accumulated snow, and the lanes seemed to be narrowing with each mile.

Within thirty minutes, the gentle snowfall had become a curtain of white. Baker's wipers struggled against the accumulation, creating brief arcs of clarity before the snow reclaimed the glass.

His headlights penetrated maybe twenty feet into the storm—enough to see the yellow line when it wasn't buried, enough to catch glimpses of the canyon walls pressing in on both sides.

That's when he first noticed the eighteen-wheeler behind him.

Its headlights filled his rearview mirror like twin suns, the massive engine's rumble audible even over the wind. The truck was close—too close for these conditions—but there was nowhere for either of them to go. No shoulders to pull onto, no passing lanes, just this narrow corridor between rock walls with the storm growing more vicious by the minute.

Baker tried tapping his brakes to signal the trucker to back off, but the lights only seemed to get brighter, closer. The truck's engine roared as if the driver was actually accelerating, trying to push through the storm by sheer force. Baker's speedometer read forty-five, which felt reckless in the conditions, but if he slowed, the truck might rear-end him.

The wind hit them both like a living thing. Baker felt his car shudder and drift toward the center line before he corrected, his knuckles white on the steering wheel. Behind him, the truck's lights swayed as the driver fought the same invisible force. Then a big gust hit—a wall of wind that seemed to come from everywhere at once. Baker's car lurched left, then right, the steering wheel spinning in his hands, the car choosing its own direction. He overcorrected and felt the wheels lose their grip on the snow-slicked asphalt, and time slowed to the speed of nightmare.

The truck driver, blinded by the same white chaos, never saw Baker's car slide into his path. The impact came from behind and to the side—a collision that sent Baker's sedan spinning before launching off the roadway entirely. There should have been a shoulder. There should have been a barrier, a guardrail, something to stop the car's wild trajectory. Instead, there was only the snowbank that had been building—a deceptively soft-looking wall of white that swallowed his vehicle.

The car hit the snow doing forty and disappeared as if the earth had opened up and gulped it down. One moment Baker was fighting for control on the highway; the next, he was buried in a cocoon of white silence, his headlights emanating an eerie glow in the snow-packed cave around him. The engine died. The radio went silent. Outside, he could hear the storm continuing its assault, but it sounded muffled and distant. His left leg felt wrong—twisted at an angle that sent lightning bolts of pain up his spine when he tried to move. Something warm was running down his forehead, and when he touched it, his fingers came away dark with blood.

Above him, maybe twenty feet away, he could hear a truck's air brakes hissing. Car doors slamming. Voices shouting over the wind. The sounds seemed to multiply—more engines, more doors, more voices calling to each other. Baker couldn't see what was happening up there, but he could hear the highway filling with vehicles. People were stopping, though; whether to help or simply because they couldn't get through, he had no way of knowing.

For two hours, Baker listened to the symphony of chaos beyond his buried car. Engines idling. Radios crackling. People calling his name—though how they knew his name, he couldn't figure out through the fog of pain and shock. The cold seeped through the cracked windshield, through the floor of the car, through his jacket that had been plenty warm in Moab but was no match for this tomb of snow. He tried his cell phone over and over, holding it toward what he thought might be the surface, praying for even one bar of signal. Nothing. The canyon walls that made Highway 6 so dangerous also made it a dead zone for communication.

The worst part wasn't the cold or the pain or even the growing certainty that he might die here. It was hearing all that activity yards away—people looking for him, trying to help—and not having the strength left to call out. His voice came as barely a whisper now. He was invisible to them, buried so deep that he might as well have vanished from the earth.

His thoughts began to fragment as hypothermia set in. He found himself thinking about the labyrinth at Saint Francis, how peaceful it had been just twenty-four hours ago. About Libby at home with the flu, probably wondering why he hadn't called. About Dr. Hawley's hand on that student's back, the way they'd looked around before kissing—the casual paranoia of people who knew what they were doing was wrong but had stopped caring. Three kids at home. A wife who probably trusted him. And the institution that would protect him because scandal was worse than accountability.

The cold made thinking difficult. He kept trying to hold onto the thread—Hawley, the church's corruption, his decision to quit—but it kept slipping away, replaced by images of the labyrinth's stone path spiraling inward, then Libby's face when she'd told him to go without her, then Hawley again, then nothing but white silence and the distant sound of voices that couldn't find him.

Baker's left leg screamed with pain, but it felt distant, unimportant. What mattered was that he'd almost given his life to something fundamentally corrupt, nearly pledged himself to an institution that preached integrity while harboring deceit. Maybe this snow tomb was God's mercy saving him from becoming complicit in something rotten.

Or maybe he was dying, and his mind was looking for meaning in the cold.

FINALLY, HE HEARD SOMETHING different cutting through the traffic noise—sirens wailing in the distance, growing closer despite the storm. Someone had managed to call for help, and somehow the emergency responders were fighting their way through the backup. But it took them two more hours to reach the accident scene, and another thirty minutes to figure out where Baker's car had gone.

When they finally found him, the paramedic's first words were, "Jesus, how long has he been down here?" Baker tried to answer, but his voice came out as barely a whisper. He was conscious enough to feel them cutting away the car's roof, to sense the helicopter's rotors beating overhead like mechanical angels, to understand that the pilot was radioing for special clearance because the storm was still too dangerous for normal flight operations.

But as they loaded him into the rescue helicopter and it fought its way into the screaming wind, Baker's last coherent thought before the morphine took him. It was a cruel twist: after defending a thesis on pastoral care in crises, he was now trapped in the very thing he'd theorized about. All his theological training felt useless against the simple, brutal facts of charred wreckage and cold steel.

The medical transport aircraft delivered Baker first to Salt Lake City, where an emergency team worked to stabilize him.

They determined that transferring him to Saint Luke's Trauma Center in Boise via air ambulance would give him the best chance for recovery. By the time they reached Saint Luke's, news of Baker's hospitalization had already spread through the Episcopal community—well beyond Idaho. The woman from Trinity called to say that despite her fever, Libby was preparing to drive to the hospital immediately.

"I wouldn't advise that," the doctor told her over the phone. "We're running tests and monitoring him closely through the night. He's unconscious and stable, but there's nothing his wife can do here. Tell her to get some rest and come first thing in the morning."

When the call came to Medford about the accident, Karl was immediately on the phone with the airline trying to book the next flight. In his mind, this felt like the culmination of some cosmic test that had been grinding Baker down for thirty years. First Wendy, then the long exile in advertising, then the painful resurrection of faith, now this—just months before ordination. Karl had watched too many promising seminarians get derailed by far less than what Baker had endured. He'd be damned if he was going to let his friend face this latest crisis alone, not when they were this close to the finish line.

When Karl reached Salt Lake City, he learned that Baker was being transferred to Boise. But the same storm system that had caused the accident was now grounding flights across the region. Karl spent the night in the airport, catching what sleep he could in an uncomfortable chair, watching the departure board hopefully as flight after flight to Boise was delayed, then canceled. He finally made it to Saint Luke's the next afternoon, just as Baker was beginning to show signs of waking up.

He found Baker in the ICU, a maze of tubes and wires connecting him to machines that beeped and hummed their electronic hymns. Traumatic brain injury, the doctors said. Internal bleeding they were still trying to assess. Multiple fractures. Touch and go. Karl pulled a chair close to the bed and settled in for what he suspected would be a long vigil.

Baker floated somewhere between consciousness and void, the morphine pulling him into a languorous descent deeper than sleep, where voices became visions and stories took on the weight of dreams. Karl's voice drifted through the medical fog— something about bishops being good at talking, whether anyone was listening or not. The ventilator breathed for Baker with mechanical precision. The monitors traced his vital signs in green and yellow lines across dark screens.

"I've been thinking about your story," Karl was saying. "How you got knocked down and kept getting back up. Reminds me of my own path, though mine was a lot more twisted. You want to know how a farm boy from Oklahoma ended up as a bishop?"

The question seemed to pull Baker deeper into the morphine haze, where Karl's words transformed into something he could see and feel. He found himself standing in a bar that felt like decades past, all chrome and leather, cigarette smoke curling toward pressed tin ceilings, the air warm and close despite the whirring ceiling fan. A young man who could only be Karl wiped down glasses behind the bar, his movements careful and deliberate.

"Uncle Dan was something else," a voice said—Karl's voice, but older, wiser. "Picture this: 1960, the Continental bar in Berkeley . . ."

Baker watched the scene unfold like a movie where he was both audience and participant. The young Karl moved between tables, clearing empties and restocking ashtrays, but his eyes were always drawn to the conversations happening around him. These weren't farm people talking about weather and crops. These were intellectuals, seminary students, professors—people who lived in the world of ideas that Karl had only glimpsed in Sunday school.

Baker understood that longing immediately—the hunger for something beyond one's experience, that desperate reach toward a calling that seemed impossibly out of reach. His attention was drawn to a corner of the bar, where a man sat alone reading. He could see the book's cover: *The Picture of Dorian Gray*. The seminarian was thin and serious, wearing a clerical collar that looked too big for his neck.

"He became my teacher without either of us realizing it," Karl's voice continued, and Baker understood that this must be the man Karl was talking about. "Left me that book. First real literature I'd ever read that wasn't the Bible or a farming manual, and the kind of book that would fundamentally shift how I saw the world."

Baker found himself reading alongside the young Karl, feeling his confusion and fascination with Wilde's decadent characters. He could sense Karl's struggle with the book—this farm boy from Oklahoma encountering a world of moral ambiguity and aesthetic philosophy that challenged everything he'd been taught about right and wrong.

But then the scene fractured, the way dreams do when the mind can't hold a single thread. Suddenly, Baker was back in the Tuttle parking lot, watching Dr. Hawley check over his shoulder before pulling that student close. The kiss superimposed itself over Dorian Gray's portrait—both images of beautiful surfaces hiding moral decay. Baker tried to look away, to return to Karl's story, but the morphine wouldn't let him escape.

"I was so naïve." Karl's voice continued from somewhere, but now Baker wondered if his own naivete was the same. Had he really believed the church would be different? That an institution run by humans would somehow transcend human weakness?

The continental bar reformed around him, Karl wiping glasses with careful attention, but Baker kept seeing those two figures in the parking lot. How many people had seen and said nothing? How many had chosen institutional peace over moral accountability? Baker felt Karl's embarrassment, his earnest attempt to understand something utterly foreign to his experience. But there was something else too—a hunger for knowledge, for experience beyond the narrow confines of rural Oklahoma.

The scene shifted again. Now the seminarian had returned, and with him stood a figure of such presence that the entire bar seemed to quiet in respect. The bishop: tall, distinguished, carrying himself with the kind of authority that came not from position but from genuine wisdom.

"He said to me," Karl remembered, "'I'm told you're a kind man and a good reader.'"

Baker watched the young Karl's face flush with pride and terror. Here was everything he'd never dared to dream of—recognition, opportunity, a chance to become something more than he'd ever imagined possible.

"And I, with the brutal honesty that comes from never learning to lie well, told him I hadn't read much, that I'd spent most of my life using my finger to loosen soil rather than turn pages."

The honesty was breathtaking. In the dream, Baker could feel the moment's weight—how easy it would have been for Karl to pretend, to oversell himself, to claim knowledge he didn't possess. Instead, he chose truth, even when it might cost him everything.

"You know what he said? 'I appreciate your honesty, Karl.'"

The bishop and the seminarian stepped away for a private conversation, and Baker found himself somehow privy to it, the dream, as dreams do, granting impossible perspectives.

"What do you think?" the bishop asked.

Baker tried to respond, to signal that he'd heard, that he understood. But the morphine held him fast, leaving him suspended between worlds with only the truths of the story burning bright in the darkness behind his closed eyes. In that darkness, Baker floated in a space between unconsciousness and waking. He could sense people gathering around his bed, could feel the weight of something important about to happen, but he couldn't quite surface.

Dr. Hawley was there again in his mind—not the passionate kiss this time, but the man's face in Christian ethics class, lecturing about moral theology with such conviction. Baker had taken notes, had written papers drawing on Hawley's teaching about integrity and accountability. All of it felt like a joke now, a performance by someone who knew exactly which words to say while living an entirely different truth.

But then another image surfaced: Mrs. Henderson at Trinity, holding her husband's hand as he died, whispering the prayers Baker had taught her. She hadn't cared whether the institutional church was corrupt. She'd just needed someone to show her how to say goodbye.

Other images emerged too: the teenagers in the youth group wrestling with hard questions about faith and doubt. The couple whose marriage he'd helped repair. The man he'd sat with months earlier in a different hospital, when silence was all that remained because no words could make cancer fair. They hadn't needed a perfect church. They'd needed a pastor who would show up.

By Wednesday, things weren't looking good. The doctors started using words like *uncertain prognosis* and *prepare for the worst.* That's when Karl knew he had to make some calls. He started with the bishop of Utah, then Colorado, working his way through the network of relationships that held the Episcopal Church together. Each conversation was the same. A good man was dying, a man who'd completed nearly everything except the final formalities, and time was running out.

Libby sat in the chair beside Baker's bed, exhausted from her sleepless night and the treacherous drive to the hospital that morning. Karl caught her eye, then picked up the phone to place the call he'd been building toward—to the Most Reverend Matthew Curtin, presiding bishop of the Episcopal Church.

"Matthew," he said when the familiar voice answered, "I need a favor. Actually, I need a miracle."

There was a pause on the other end of the line. Karl could picture Bishop Curtin in his office, probably working late as usual, the weight of leading a fractured denomination never far from his thoughts.

"Karl, good to hear from you. You certainly don't mince words. What kind of miracle are we talking about?"

"I'm sitting in an ICU in Boise next to a man named Baker Vaughan. You don't know him, but you should. He's been fighting for ordination since he was confirmed, and he might not make it through the night."

Another pause. Karl heard papers rustling and could imagine Curtin leaning back in his chair, preparing to listen to what was likely to be an unusual request.

"Tell me about him," Curtin said.

"He's fifty-seven. Started seminary at Yale back in 1984—top of his class, brilliant mind, natural pastor. His young wife died in childbirth, along with their son. Lost his faith, lost his way, left seminary and started drinking a bit too much. Got arrested on a misdemeanor recently after breaking into—technically walking into, he didn't break a thing—an old paramour's house with whom he was trying to make amends."

"Karl—"

"Wait, let me finish. Most people would have given up right there. But not Baker. He took responsibility, straightened up, and enrolled at the Tuttle School in Utah. This was after he'd already planned to attend Seminary of the Southwest, but he and his new wife were, shall we say, treated poorly by the sponsoring priest in Dripping Springs."

Karl could hear Curtin listening, that particular quality of attention that good bishops develop.

"This past weekend, he successfully defended his thesis—on pastoral care crises, of all things. He was driving home in the worst storm Utah's seen in a decade when an eighteen-wheeler hit him. He'd been buried in a snowbank for two hours, airlifted twice, and now the doctors are saying he might not survive the traumatic brain injury."

"That's tragic, Karl, but I'm not sure what you're asking me to do."

Karl took a deep breath. This was the moment everything hinged on. "He's completed ninety-five percent of his coursework,

Matt, just about everything except the final canonical exams and the formal approval process. The only thing standing between him and ordination is paperwork and bureaucracy. If we wait for normal procedures, we're going to lose him."

"Karl, you know I can't just—"

"Hear me out. This man has been to hell and back. He's faced personal grief and institutional discrimination, and he's never given up on his calling. When his rector, Phil Harbaugh, was doing everything possible to sabotage him, Baker fought for himself the right way—he came to me, made his case, but he never let it poison his ministry. He just kept showing up, kept serving, kept proving himself through actions."

"How do you know all this?"

"I've been by his side for years. His theological reflection papers would make you weep—not because they're sentimental, but because they show a depth of understanding that only comes from real suffering transformed into wisdom. This is the kind of priest our church desperately needs."

Karl could hear Curtin thinking, could feel the weight of consideration through the phone.

"And you're asking me to authorize an emergency ordination?"

"I'm asking you to let us bring the church to him. If he's going to die, let him die as an ordained priest. If he lives, we'll have given him the one thing he's fought for longer than most of us have been in ministry."

The silence stretched for what felt like minutes. Finally, Curtin spoke: "Karl, in thirty years of ministry, I've never approved anything like this."

Karl's heart sank. But then Curtin continued, "But I've also never heard a more compelling case for why we should. Tell me what you need."

He had to sit down. Tears streamed down his face. "I need you to waive the canonical exams and approve his ordination based on his completed coursework. I need authorization to perform the ceremony in the ICU if necessary. And I need it fast, Matt. His vitals aren't stable."

"You'll need witnesses. Proper documentation. This has to be done right, even if it's being done quickly."

"I can get the bishop of Idaho here within an hour. We'll have everything properly recorded."

Another pause. Then Curtin's voice, warmer now: "Karl, I've known you for over twenty years, even before I became bishop of Massachusetts. You don't ask for much, and when you do, it's usually worth saying yes to. Send me everything you have on this Baker Vaughan—transcripts, recommendations, and any other documentation. If it checks out, you have my blessing."

"Matt, I—"

"And Karl? Call me after it's done. I want to know how this story ends."

Karl hung up and looked at Baker, his face peaceful despite the tubes and wires. Libby remained quiet in her chair, watching her husband's steady breathing.

"You hear that? The presiding bishop just threw out the rulebook for a man he's never met. Sometimes the Spirit moves faster than the church can keep up with."

Libby reached over and took Baker's hand, careful not to disturb the IV line. "He'd be amazed," she whispered. "After everything, all the doors that got slammed in his face . . . I wish he could hear this."

Karl started making the next round of calls. There was work to do, and time was running out.

By Thursday evening, the ICU had been transformed into something resembling a chapel.

Bishop Gallagher had arrived wearing vestments and carrying all the necessary documentation. Two priests from local parishes served as witnesses, along with Libby, who hadn't left Baker's side since the storm cleared.

Karl had spent the day on the phone, ensuring every canonical requirement was documented correctly. The presiding bishop's authorization had opened doors that usually took months to navigate, but the paperwork still had to be perfect. If Baker survived, his ordination needed to be beyond legal challenge.

The medical team had been briefed. Dr. Cooper, the attending physician, was skeptical but not unsympathetic. "His vitals have been stable for six hours, but we honestly don't know if he can hear you or understand what's happening."

"That's between him and God," Karl said quietly. "Our job is to be faithful to what we believe He's calling us to do."

Baker's mother had arrived from Virginia that afternoon, and with her came Uncle Oscar—though they hadn't traveled together. She'd taken the first flight she could book, while Oscar had chartered a jet from Middleburg. They'd met in the hospital lobby by coincidence, their first time seeing each other since before Baker and Libby's wedding.

Now Oscar stood awkwardly near the window while Baker's mother clutched Baker's hand, still not quite understanding how her son had gone from that joyful day two years earlier to lying here unconscious, not knowing he was about to be ordained.

Even in his morphine haze, Baker could appreciate how up-side down this was. Oscar had been too busy to attend the wed-ding—some prior commitment in the Hamptons that couldn't be changed. Baker and Libby had set aside a seat for him any-way, hoping he might surprise them. Instead, Oscar had sent an expensive crystal vase and his regrets. Now here he was, having wiped his schedule clean within hours of learning about the accident.

Oscar's discomfort was palpable. His aesthetic sensibilities recoiled from the medical equipment and the brutal functional-ity of the ICU. But there was something else Baker sensed—his uncle's growing awareness of his mother's unconscious devo-tion, the way she smoothed Baker's hair and spoke to him as if he might respond at any moment.

Anne pulled Libby aside. "Have you heard from Emma?" she whispered. "I've been calling since you first told us about the ac-cident. Strangely, she won't answer. I just saw her yesterday. It's not like her to not respond, especially…"

What none of them knew was that Baker's sister was at that very moment driving through the mountains from Challis to-ward Boise, her phone showing no signal for the past three hours. She'd left early that morning, before anyone could reach her about the accident, on a trip she'd been planning for weeks: bringing Oletta down to Boise to visit Baker. The generous woman had been like a grandmother to him during those dif-ficult years, and Emma thought seeing Oletta again might lift his spirits as he finished seminary.

Oscar watched this exchange from the window, his expen-sive overcoat draped over a plastic chair. In his floating aware-ness, Baker could sense his uncle's internal crisis—the vertigo of watching love without performance, devotion without audience. Oscar's life in Middleburg, refined as it was, operated within careful parameters. But here, watching these women pour themselves into an unconscious void, he was confronting something that couldn't be aestheticized or controlled.

When Bishop Gallagher stepped into the room, Oscar retreated farther toward the corner, uncertain of his place in what was clearly becoming a sacred moment. Baker felt his uncle's desire to reach out, but sensed his hands remained folded, unused to physical affection not choreographed by social expectation.

At six p.m., as the winter sun set behind the hospital windows, Gallagher spoke the ancient words: "Dearly beloved, we are gathered here in the presence of God to ordain Baker Michael Vaughan to the sacred order of priests in Christ's holy Catholic Church."

And then something shifted. Baker's eyelids fluttered. A soft groan escaped his lips.

Dr. Cooper immediately stepped forward, checking Baker's pupils with a penlight. "He's coming around," the doctor said quietly. "His brain activity is spiking."

Baker's eyes opened, unfocused at first, then slowly taking in the room—the faces gathered around his bed, white blooms in a vase, the solemn atmosphere.

"What . . .?" His voice, hoarse from the ventilator, was barely a whisper. "What's happening?"

Karl leaned close, his hand resting gently on the bed rail. "Baker. Hey. You're OK. You're in the hospital."

Baker's eyes tried to focus on Karl's face. "Hospital?"

"Saint Luke's. In Boise. Do you remember the drive? The storm?"

Baker blinked slowly, his mind clearly struggling through fog. "Storm. Yes. I was . . . driving." His brow furrowed. "There was a truck."

"An eighteen-wheeler jackknifed. Hit you from behind. You've been unconscious for three days."

Baker's eyes moved slowly across the room, taking in the faces—Libby, tears streaming down her cheeks, his mother clutching his other hand, Oscar standing awkwardly near the window. Then the others, unfamiliar faces in clerical collars.

"Three days?" His voice was weak, confused.

"You have a traumatic brain injury," Karl said gently. "The doctors weren't sure you'd wake up."

Baker was quiet for a moment, processing. "But I did."

"Yes. Thank God, you did."

"Libby . . ." Baker's eyes found his wife.

"I'm here," she whispered, squeezing his hand. "I'm right here."

Baker seemed to relax slightly at the sound of her voice. Then his eyes drifted back to the bishops, the vestments laid out on a nearby table, the formal, almost ceremonial atmosphere of the room.

"Karl," he said slowly, "why are there bishops here? Why does it look like..." He trailed off, too exhausted to finish.

Karl glanced at Bishop Gallagher, then back at Baker. "We were about to ordain you."

Baker's eyes widened slightly. "What?"

"The presiding bishop gave authorization," Karl explained gently. "When we thought we might lose you, I called Matthew Curtin. Told him your story. He waived the canonical exams and approved your ordination based on your completed coursework."

Karl's voice softened. "We wanted you to die as a priest, Baker, if that's what God was calling you to."

Baker stared at him, his expression shifting from confusion to something deeper—shock, disbelief, something close to awe.

"You were going to ordain me while I was unconscious?"

"We were about to begin the ceremony when you woke up," Karl said.

Baker was quiet for a long moment, his mind working through what he was hearing. Finally, he looked directly at Karl. "You said you were about to ordain me. Does that mean…it hasn't happened yet?"

"No," Karl said. "We were just beginning when you woke up."

Baker closed his eyes, and for a moment, everyone held their breath. When he opened them again, tears welled up. "Karl," he whispered, "I was driving home to quit. After what happened at Tuttle, I was done. I was going to tell Libby I was finished with all of it."

The room was silent except for the soft beeping of monitors.

"What happened at Tuttle?" Karl asked quietly.

Baker stiffened. "I saw Dr. Hawley. In the parking lot with one of his students. They were . . ." He closed his eyes. "He's married, Karl. Three kids. And he was kissing her like—" His voice broke.

Karl was quiet for a moment. When he spoke, his voice was steady. "You're right. Hawley failed to live up to the church's moral code."

"Then how can I—?" Baker stopped, trying to find the words. His voice was raw. "I spent a quarter century at McCann. You know what advertising taught me? Perfection. If a campaign wasn't perfect, we didn't run it. If the copy was off by a single word, we started over. Excellence or nothing." He looked at Karl, then at Gallagher. "That's what I was doing—driving home to quit. Because if the church can't hold its own faculty accountable, then the whole enterprise is corrupt. And I don't serve corrupt institutions."

Karl knew he was perilously close to admitting defeat—to telling Baker he was right, that he should walk away from all of it. "So church is just a business to you," he said.

Baker's laugh was harsh, stripped of everything but anger. "Yes, the protection of assets. The management of liabilities. Oh, and don't forget the pensions."

Karl was quiet for a long moment. "The institution operates like a business, yes. It has legal concerns, financial concerns, reputational concerns. It protects itself. Sometimes at the expense of the people it's supposed to serve." He looked through Baker's eyes into his soul. "But the work itself—the actual ministry—that's not business. Being there for those in need. That's not a transaction. That's not asset management. That's just . . . showing up. Telling the truth. Trying to do less harm than the person before you did."

"That's not enough," Baker said.

"No," Karl agreed. "It's not. But it's what we have."

Before Baker could respond, Libby spoke. Her voice was quiet but firm. "Do you think Wendy would have allowed you to quit?"

Baker turned his head toward her, confused. "What?"

"Wendy." Libby's eyes were clear, direct, without a trace of jealousy. "Do you honestly think she would have let you walk away from this calling because you found out human beings run the church?"

Baker opened his mouth, then closed it.

"She loved you," Libby continued, her hand still holding his. "I know her through you—through every story you've told me, every time you've mentioned her name." Libby leaned closer. "And the Wendy I know would have told you to stop being such a self-righteous idiot."

Despite the rebuke, Baker almost smiled.

"She would have said, 'So what? You found out a professor is a philanderer? Congratulations, you've discovered that people are flawed. Now what are you going to do about the people who actually need you?'" Libby's voice softened. "She wouldn't have let you use your impossible standards as an excuse to run away from the hardest thing you've ever tried to do."

Karl nodded slowly. "Libby's right. The difference between advertising and ministry, Baker, is that in advertising, you're selling perfection—an image, an ideal. But in ministry, you're serving broken people in a broken world through a broken institution. The brokenness isn't a bug. It's the entire point."

"That's not . . ." Baker struggled. "That can't be the point."

"Why not?" Karl's voice was gentle but insistent. "Why do you think Jesus chose the disciples he did? A tax collector whom everyone hated. A zealot with a violent past. Peter, who denied him three times. They were all flawed, all compromised. The church was built on imperfect people from day one."

Baker closed his eyes. "I wanted it to be better than this."

"I know," Karl said. "But the question isn't whether the church deserves your service. The question is whether the people do. Widows and widowers who have lost a spouse. Teenagers who need someone actually to listen. People in hospital beds who need someone who understands suffering." He paused. "They don't need perfection, Baker. They need presence."

Baker felt Libby's warm, genuine hand in his.

"Wendy would have kicked my ass," he whispered.

"Yes," Libby said. "She would have."

The monitors beeped steadily. Outside the room, a cart rattled past in the hallway.

Finally, Baker looked at Bishop Gallagher. "If the offer still stands," he said slowly, "if the authorization is still valid . . ." He paused, his eyes moving to each face in the room—Karl, Libby, Bishop Gallagher. "For Christ's sake. I want this. God help me, I accept—flawed church, flawed man, all of it. I'm saying yes."

Bishop Gallagher smiled, tears in his own eyes. "Then let's continue, shall we?"

Acknowledgments

WRITING *BAKER VAUGHAN* HAS BEEN ONE OF THE MOST unexpected pleasures of my life. As someone who briefly entertained the possibility of priesthood in my early sixties, I learned valuable lessons about the institution of church, the behavior of its clerical and lay leaders, and why it has lost so much momentum in recent decades.

I started writing the novel in the COVID-19 era and got stuck in a creative ghetto. I needed a resource to challenge me to continue.

When I first moved to Boise at the end of 2009, I met a man named Christian Winn bartending at my local bar, the Falcon Tavern. Once I got to know him better, I understood that this was not his bread and butter. He was a distinguished writer, a professor at Boise State with an MFA, and most importantly, Idaho's 2016–2019 Writer in Residence. He had been mentored by the likes of Anthony Doerr (*All the Light You Cannot See*) and was writing his own new material as well as paying it forward.

When I called him in early 2025, I told him about the novel and asked for his help. What ensued over the course of nine months was, as we golfers like to put it, a "playing lesson." To keep the analogy going, I could hit great shots off the practice tee, but once on the course, I had little skill when it came to club selection, the correct stance on the side of a hill, or how important it was to give up a shot in order to save two.

As the pen got cranking, I fell in love with writing. I have three additional novels in various stages of completion. Perhaps I will even revisit Baker and Libby—should Baker pull through the accident.

Thank you to *New York Times* and *USA Today* best-selling author Eva Lesko Natiello for strengthening my resolve to publish this book. Seven different beta readers saw *Baker Vaughan* in different stages of its evolution: Eric Hartvigsen, Isaiah B., Jamie Pilkington, Simona M., Jonathan D. Bourdeau, Nadene du Plooy, and Stacey K. Thank you for your critiques and helpful words. But no one was more eagle-eyed and encouraging than my wife, Lisa—my very own Libby. I cherish her.

Putting the book into print required the expertise and dedication of multiple publishing professionals. I'm grateful for the collaborative editing process that refined Baker Vaughan through several rounds of careful revision. Special thanks to Lisa Bannick at Kirkus for providing the final editorial polish that brought the manuscript to its finished form.

In the book, you learned that Libby was raped as a teenager and Baker's mother experienced sexual abuse as a girl. While I aimed to handle these topics with sensitivity rather than graphic detail, the reality is that violence against women is pervasive and demands acknowledgment.

If you or someone you know has experienced sexual abuse, help is available:

National Sexual Assault Hotline: 1-800-656-HOPE (4673)
Available 24/7, free and confidential www.rainn.org
Childhelp National Child Abuse Hotline: 1-800-422-4453
Available 24/7 www.childhelp.org

www.ingramcontent.com/pod-product-compliance
Lightning Source LLC
Chambersburg PA
CBHW051301130726

47987CB00004B/1620